A TENDER
POWER

DR. ALY KHORSHID

A Tender Power

www.atenderpower.com

ISBN 978 0 9571407 0 7

Typeset by The Fast Fingers Book Formatting Services
www.thefastfingers.com

Cover design by Moustafa Hassan
www.moustafahassan.co.uk

Photography by Mayfairimages.com
www.mayfairimages.com

Printed and bound in Great Britain by
York Publishing Services Ltd.,
64 Hallfield Road, Layerthorpe,
York, YO31 7ZQ
Tel: +44 (0)1904 431213

Published by Academy UK LTD
21 Weighhouse Street,
London W1K 5LY
United Kingdom
Tel: 02074990600
Fax: 02073553711

www.academyuk.org

Acknowledgements

The Idea of this novel is inspired by my son Yousef Khorshid, he suggested that the uniqueness of Islamic finance should be serialised to a simple format as story for the average person to comprehend and appreciates

Without the help of the following people this book would not have been materialised, my wife Dr. Noha Khorshid, my sons Adam Khorshid and Yousef Khorshid, my daughters Sarah Khorshid and Iman Khorshid, Mrs Amanda Thomas for her great help, Mr Charlie Hankers for his overall editing, Mr Mustafa Hassan Mustafa for designing the book cover.

Dr. Aly Khorshid
1D St Dunstans Avenue
London W3 6QD
United Kingdom
e:alykhorshid@mac.com

PART ONE

Chapter One

Although it was still some time before noon in Cairo, the temperature had already climbed to 95 degrees. In the August heat, Amir Ali smiled as he put the phone down after am exhilarating call from his old classmate Anwar, who had become a father for the first time. Amir knew that feeling. He had a son, just a year old, and his wife would soon have their second child. He said a prayer for his friend and his new daughter, asking Allah's blessings on them all. It was a Thursday morning and he was due in Alexandria the following week to give a lecture to a group of foreign bankers. Amir smiled wryly as he wondered who had convinced the delegates that Egypt in the middle of summer would be a good time and venue for a symposium. Alexandria was no South of France or Spanish Costa; the heat was fierce and the mosquitoes unrelenting, despite the fact that they would be staying at the sea-facing Palestine Hotel, built ostentatiously opposite the gardens of the Montaza Palace which had once been the home of King Farouk. Amir was not looking forward to the drive. The road was dangerous, the other drivers unpredictable. In Cairo itself the driving was just as chaotic, but at least it was not possible to reach too dangerous a speed.

Amir opened his apartment door to go down to buy a newspaper. The heat surged in, hitting him in the face like a clammy hand and immediately steaming up his glasses. He took them off and put them in his pocket as he made his way to the newspaper stand. The ful seller standing over his cart with its deep metal container immediately beckoned him with his large dipping ladle. "Ful ya Sheikh?" he called, but Amir waved him away. Delicious though this traditional breakfast was, it had a way of sitting heavy on his stomach, making him sluggish all morning. It might be the perfect fuel for a morning's hard manual labour but it had more of a soporific effect on those who spent most of their working lives sitting down.

Scanning the headlines of the paper, Amir frowned. He could not read the small print without his glasses so he quickened his pace as he returned to the comfort and cool of his air-conditioned apartment. At the corner of his street a heated argument was going on between two drivers whose vehicles had collided. Both cars were covered in dents and scratches, which were not so much testament to the lack of driving skill of their owners, but more to the fact that the cars were being driven in Cairo. A crowd was gathering, the male onlookers joining in on either side of the debate. It was a common enough sight in this ancient city, now bursting at the seams; the throng would disperse as quickly as it had formed and the city would rumble on amongst the heat and the dirt of the crowded streets.

Back in his apartment Amir made himself a cup of strong black Arabic coffee and settled down to read the newspaper. The apartment was too quiet without Marwa and Ramsay. Amir missed his son's baby noises and the low soft voice of his wife. They were in the UK with Marwa's sister, escaping the punishing African summer. He would join them after his lectures the following week, and he could hardly wait. The lush greenery of England,

2

in particular the quiet Berkshire village where Marwa's sister lived, was a tonic to them all and contrasted direct with the heat and frantic activity of the Egyptian capital.

Amir turned his attention to his newspaper. Like every morning of late, this morning's was full of alarming news about the world's economy. He frowned; shares had plummeted again in London, New York and Tokyo, suggesting that the banking system of the West was unravelling. Not drastically, yet; but it would do – Amir knew. He could see the future and it would affect the whole world: rich and poor, Christian, Moslem, Jew, Hindu, Sikh – everyone. The way of the financial world as they knew it was not sustainable. Amir glanced over at his lecture notes. He had worried that his message was too strong. His call for Islamic banking to be given a fair hearing too extreme a notion, but maybe, just maybe, there might be someone ready to listen. He began to rehearse the beginning of his speech again.

"Musharakah literally means sharing. In Musharakah, the return is based on the actual profit earned by the joint venture. Interest is prohibited in Islam, as the rate of interest is the main cause for imbalances in the system of distribution. Musharakah favours the common people, as the financier must declare if the loan is to assist the debtor or to share the profits. Nothing can be claimed if the financier is assisting, and if the profits are shared, the losses (if any) are also shared. If the profits shared are large, it cannot all be secured by the financier, but will be shared among the depositors of the bank (the common

people). Musharakah, however is considered somewhat outdated, and there is no prescribed procedure, only a broad set of principles. New procedures can be accepted as long as they do not violate any basic principles."

On Saturday morning, the beginning of the working week, Amir set off for Alexandra on the 220 km desert road. When he had begun to prepare it, he had been sure that his lecture would be received by a polite but uninterested – or possibly slightly hostile – attitude, but now he felt the first glimmer of hope. If there was ever a time for intervention, a change of direction, it was now. Surely others could see what he could see? There must be at least one delegate who could see the truth in what he was proposing: the promise for a better future with a better system?

On the opposite carriageway a truck carrying grain started to veer towards Amir. As he saw the truck approaching, he glanced in his rear-view mirror and reached into the glove compartment for a tape. In the lumbering truck, the driver's eyes began to close and for a while his vehicle held its course. Then very slowly it began to move to the left, and before the muscles in his foot could relax in sleep and slip off the accelerator, and while Amir glanced down to see why the tape machine was not working, the truck ploughed into his car, pushing the old Ford sedan in front of it and off the road before tipping it over crushing half of the vehicle and finally toppling over onto its side in the dust like a dying bull elephant, its giant wheels spinning in the desert heat.

It would turn out that the truck had arrived the night

before in Alexandra. The container ship he had been waiting to connect with had been late docking and the truck driver had gone out drinking. The combination of the lack of sleep, the heat of the cab and the belly full of the previous night's liquor had taken their toll, precipitating his deadly drift.

Chapter Two

Three months after Amir had been thrown face down into the desert dust, he was ready to leave hospital. The truck driver who had ploughed into him had left the same hospital twenty-four hours after the crash and was back at work. Amir felt the constant pangs of bones that had been pieced together with rods and metal plates as he walked to the hospital door with Marwa at his side.

"Slowly, habibi," she whispered, her face full of concern. Amir smiled painfully; there was not much chance of anything above slow at the moment. The last time he had been outside it had been hotter than hell, but now the heat was pleasant, the warm sun on his upturned face feeling good. Even the smell of the Cairo Streets was welcome. He was alive; it had been touch and go for a while and he did not really remember anything of the first month he was in hospital. Probably just as well, he thought, although the idea that Marwa would have been desolate without him to comfort her caused him pain. Little Adam was walking now, and trying to say a few words; the fact that he had missed those events caused Amir more pain than his injuries.

His new son, Yousef, was already eight weeks old and his doting father had held him only twice. But, Amir thought, at least he was alive and in the twilight of his suffering and the long slog of his recovery he had decided something, something he had seen in a recurring dream that he kept having until it was etched on his battered brain like a movie that he had seen a hundred times. When he closed his eyes he would see himself standing before an audience of worried looking men, slowly explaining over and over again, and alternating with that image were visions of his childhood, himself as a boy sitting cross legged on the floor of the mosque, listening to the iman, his voice powerful, low and commanding, teaching them, explaining to them. He always sat next to Farouk Ammar, a boy who could not sit still and did his best to distract Amir. Amir would frown at him but Farouk would pull a face, and flick pieces of paper at him until Amir put his hand out to stop him. But this was what Farouk wanted, attention, and he would carry on annoying Amir until finally the iman would spot his antics and move him. Then Amir would sit back, his eyes wide, his mind open and his spirit eager to learn everything he could. He loved the cool interior of the mosque and his mind seemed to come alive when he was there, open to everything. He could hear that voice again now, its message laced with a new urgency for him, compelling him to listen and to act. Softly, Amir mouthed the words that he had known for so long:

"There are differences between the capitalist economic system and the Islamic economic system, one of the most obvious being that capitalist economies are not governed by divine ruling, and this has allowed practices such as excessive interest and gambling; these practices concentrate the wealth in the hands of the few. Monopolies are created, and these paralyse market forces. In Islam, divine restrictions are put onto economic activities, and these have the effect

of maintaining balance, justice and equality.

The conventional concept of financing is that the banks and institutions deal in money only. Islam does not recognise money as a subject matter of trade, except in some cases. Financing in Islam is always based on liquid assets, which creates real assets and inventories. Financing based on musharakah, mudarabah, salam and istisna' creates real assets. These means of financing are criticised as having the same result as interest-based borrowing. However, assets back them, and they can be distinguished from interest-based borrowing on the following grounds. In conventional financing the financier has no concern about how the money is used by the client in an interest-bearing loan. In murabahah, the financier purchases the commodity required by the client; thus assets back the financing. In murabahah the purpose of the loan must be under Shari'ah, but in conventional financing there is no such ruling. In murabahah the financier who purchases the commodity holds the risk, and the profit is the reward for this risk. This risk is not assumed in an interest-based loan. In an interest-bearing loan, the amount to be repaid increases with time, but in murabahah the price is fixed once agreed. As the risk of a lease is placed on the financier, it is the financier who will suffer the loss if it is damaged. Assets always back Islamic financial transactions; there is no gap between the supply of money and the production of real assets, which is the case in conventional economies that suffer inflation."

"Are you alright, habibi?"

Amir loved the way his wife's soft voice uttered the term of endearment; he had missed her so much. Feeling her hand at his elbow, the warmth of her flesh on his, made him feel a deep joy, a deep thankfulness that he was able to be with her and his boys again. But this little fellow, Yousef, looked at him with trepidation in his baby eyes. He did not know him. Amir remembered the hours he had spent at Adam's crib, familiarising himself with every feature of the child's flawless skin, every eyelash and every hair on his head. He knew the shape of his son's ears and the colour of his eyes as if they were his own. But this new little man was a stranger – they were strangers to each other – and it hurt Amir deeply.

Back in the cool of the apartment Amir sat back in his favourite chair while Marwa fussed over him, bringing him sweet tea and biscuits. Her mother took charge of the boys so that Amir and Marwa could be alone together. Marwa had slipped her scarf off her head and Amir ran his fingers through her shining hair as she sat on his knee.

With tears in her eyes she told him she loved him and how afraid she had been of losing him and the two wept together, their arms around each other. "You must take plenty of rest," Marwa said to him; Amir closed his eyes.

"I have work to do, habibti, work that cannot wait, work that the world needs. I believe that this time that I have had away from you all has been a sort of initiation for the work that I have to do. My mind has been focused, despite its battering; the things I need to know are bright and clear to me. The useless and petty information has gone. Don't ask me to rest when I cannot and I promise that when I can, I will."

Something in her husband's face, in his tone, his very being, told Marwa that there was no point in protesting, no point at all; it was as though her husband had been visited by a greater power, had a greater purpose a calling. Despite her joy to be holding his hand in hers again, she felt fear creep into her heart, a cold shiver run up her spine and instinctively she knew that the path ahead was not going to be easy.

At the door to the sitting room, Marwa's mother stood holding Yousef. Marwa beckoned her in and gently the older woman laid the child in Amir's arms. Tears stood out in his eyes and Marwa took her mother's hand and left the room.

Alone with his son, Amir let his tears come as the child on his lap held his gaze. Now he did not look afraid, and Amir wanted to hug him to himself, promise him the world, protect him. He bowed his head to pray and as he did he felt his son's fingers close around his thumb. "Forgive me, Yousef, if I do not spend enough time with you, if I do not show you every day how much I love you," he whispered.

* * *

Half a world away, Edward looked down at his son lying wide-eyed in the crib. It was unusual to find the infant alone, without one of the nannies or Arabella fussing around him. But some drama in the linen cupboard had all three gathered in the large drying room examining crib sheets. Edward tentatively held out his finger to the infant. Eddie took it in his baby fist and Edward felt his eyes fill with tears. For the first time in the month since Eddie's birth he felt a connection with this flesh of his flesh, and he felt love for his son well up inside him.

"You'll have a good life, son; I promise you," he whispered to the child, and Eddie gurgled.

"Edward? What are you doing?" It was Arabella. "I've told you before about coming into the nursery in your street clothes; who knows what germs you might be carrying?" The nannies shot him disapproving looks and he retreated from his son's crib. Did he imagine it, or did Eddie's eyes follow him as he went?

He had a meeting that night and he could not settle to the mountain of paperwork in his study. This was not the normal type of meeting, accompanied by reams of paperwork and legions of lieutenants, this was a meeting that Edward would attend alone, in the darkened recesses of a tourist hang out on Times Square, somewhere that he would not be noticed, a place where "his people" would never go. For a man whose life was regulated, and had been since he himself had lain in a crib, it felt like a break out, an escape.

He thought about what to wear. Something casual, obviously; he didn't want to look like some Mafia boss on a night out. Edward tried to analyse why he had accepted the invitation to this particular meeting. At twenty-five he was a bit young to be having a mid-life crisis, trying to break out of his regimented life, but he wondered if that was it, a last attempt to do something reckless, synonymous with youth? One thing was for sure: his son, his Eddie, would have a very different life, a proper boy's life, the childhood that Edward had not had.

When he left for his meeting that evening, Arabella was with a gaggle of her girlfriends in the huge drawing room that overlooked Central Park. Equally spoilt, vacuous and totally lacking in passion, they were not even a blip on Edward's radar. He preferred the secretaries in the bank, and there were never any shortage of offers. The ones he liked best were the ones with thick New York accents; there was something earthy about the way they spoke and often about the way they made love – abandoned, firing a passion in Edward that filled the void in his life created by his wife. In separate bedrooms now (she complained that he snored), Edward regarded Arabella more of a room-mate than a wife. As he walked out onto the street, heading for Times Square, he thought about Lucy, his latest conquest at the bank. She made life tolerable. On the corner of 53rd Street and Broadway a homeless man sat near a metal grille his hand out, his eyes hollow. Edward took a twenty out of his pocket and put it into the man's dirty hand. The man smiled a toothless smile of surprise. Edward liked that; he loved giving his money away, seeing the look of happiness on another man's face at such unexpected generosity. Sol, his colleague and old school friend at the bank, was scathing of Edward's generosity.

"Hell, he's probably got more money than I do!" he would say in his clipped New England accent. "These guys go home in limos at night, counting out the money schmucks like you have given them!" Edward smiled. "Hell of a way to earn your money, Sol; you fancy it? Even if you did go home in a limo each night?"

The café Edward was heading for was the The Stardust. The waiters, as well as offering up traditional diner fare, frequently broke off from serving their customers to sing songs. Their skill and talent were admirable and the fact that most of the diners were either taking photos or videoing these versatile workers made an anonymous meeting eminently possible.

Edwards settled himself in a booth after slipping the waiter $10 to let him sit in a booth that was normally only available for a quartet of diners. While he kept one eye on the door, he listened to a young waiter singing a faultless version of *My Way*. He had only spoken on the phone to the man that he was to meet, but when the door opened and a tall man came in, Edward knew it would be his contact and made no effort to attract his attention as he scanned the interior of the diner. As their eyes met and the man started towards the booth, and Edward felt his heart begin to beat faster.

The meeting took one hour. Risk and danger crackled in the air between the two men as waiter and waitress took turns in belting out modern classics and chart toppers and tourists trooped in with cameras at the ready. For the first time since he had joined the bank, hell, for the first time in his life, Edward felt alive, vital, as though he could tackle anything. The man sat across from him in the booth, his coffee untouched, his dark eyes impenetrable. He spoke in a low voice, his words rich with a Middle Eastern accent, exotic sounding, almost hypnotic. He spoke fast, as though he only had a limited time to get his message across. He brought nothing with him, not even a scrap of paper that would leave a clue to the fact that the young man, the heir to the biggest banking dynasty in America, and this man of Middle Eastern origin had met. Instead he held Edward's eyes with his own, his expression bland, his voice showing no emotion. Edward listened, felt himself drawn into that gaze, unable to tear his eyes away. When the hour was done, a deal had been struck, a deal that would grow slowly like a cancer, unnoticed at first but that would eventually grow to be capable of delivering a devastating death sentence.

After the meeting Edward called Lucy and she came to the flat he kept near the bank. The cocktail of adrenalin and danger made the passion more intense than he had ever before felt.

Chapter Three

In the fifteen years since that first meeting in the Stardust Café, Edward had thirty more meetings with his "client". He applied the term loosely and indeed, apart from his client's first name, Sharif, he had not learned anything more about the man in their biannual meetings. He had got used the thrill of meeting Sharif at various venues and at different times and although his message was always slightly different, his impenetrable persona left Edward none the wiser. He always asked how Sharif's family were; he knew enough about Arabic etiquette to do that and the other man would always incline his head slightly and say "Thank you," no more and no less. His unwillingness to talk about anything other than the business at hand was obvious and he always opened the discussion before Edward could say any more.

In the department of the bank that dealt with philanthropic endeavour, Edward had slotted in Sharif and his charity "Aid for war orphans of the Middle East" without giving rise to any comment or enquiry from the team that dealt with the bank's considerable charitable donations. Lancaster bank's donations had started out as a relatively modest amount but this amount was growing every year, and each year as he sent through the notification to increase the amount, Edward braced himself for a visit from Eugene, the head of the charitable donation Department.

Eugene wore glasses that constantly slipped down on his nose, and whenever he had cause to meet with Edward, his nervousness would trigger profuse sweating that made his nose a veritable ski slope for his heavy eyewear. Edward pictured him sitting in front of him over the desk, pushing at his sliding glasses, swallowing hard, his hand shaking as he queried the size of the donation to the Middle East war orphans that was rising so disproportionately compared to the bank's other supported charities. But the visit never came, and Edward's instructions were carried out without question. Edward frowned as the light for his private line blinked.

"Yes, Arabella?" he said in a resigned voice; it was the third time she had phoned that morning. Apparently Eddie had gone missing, not turned up at school. Not unusual for a 15-year-old boy, Edward thought, especially not Eddie, but Arabella, as usual, was demanding that he drop everything. The interjection of his private life into his office always annoyed him. He liked to keep the two separate. His life in the bank was his chance to express himself, to *be* himself. He was respected here. Nothing happened unless he said it should. Everyone looked at him with respect, perhaps even with awe. At home, Arabella frequently looked at him with a disdain that only a British person was capable of. It annoyed him, but he said nothing. When he was at work he could forget her and the life that he tolerated at home, and enjoy the life he loved at work – except now. Arabella was on the phone, her strident tone grating on his ear.

"Edward; you have to come home. Deal with your son; I simply cannot bear it!"

"Cannot bear what?" Edward tried not to mimic his wife's clipped remnant of a British accent.

"It's Eddie; he has turned up, but not at school, at some sort of brothel." She half spat and half whispered the word "brothel" and Edward had to stop his smile transmitting itself in down the phone line. Not that he thought it was funny that his son had turned up in a brothel; it was just the fact that Arabella had had to use the word, possibly for the first time in her life. As he spoke, Linda, his newest and possibly most accommodating secretary so far, came into the office, quietly locking the door behind her. She had applied fresh lipstick and opened another button on her blouse to allow Edward a glimpse of her chest. She came around to his side of the desk, putting some papers down beside him; but with Arabella in full rant, Linda would have to wait.

"I'll be home shortly, Arabella; try not to worry!"

"Well, I'm glad to hear from your voice that you are taking this seriously." Edward had to smile to himself. How could Arabella be expected to recognise pent-up desire? Linda, on the other hand ... Edward sighed; he felt weary. He would have to go home but he didn't know how to deal with the wild child that his son had become.

As Edward walked up through the town to his Central Park apartment he realised how amazing it was that it was never the same walk two days running. Outside the Stock Exchange on Wall Street several traders in their distinctive garish jackets came and went. Edward loved the buzz of Wall Street, the frantic energy and activity. Further up the road he watched as one of the tourist buses inched its way down the busy street by Macy's Department store, the tourists on the top deck standing up to take photos back up towards Times Square. Edward joined the crowds of people who waited at the pedestrian stop signs at each intersection before surging forward en masse on the green light. Most were New Yorkers, their accents colouring the cool morning air, their clothing marking them out as clearly as if it were a uniform. The women in tight skirts and stilettos, some in fur coats that were a definitely more show than function, the men in smart suits. All had the studied bored expression of the New Yorker. Newspaper sellers passed out copies of the New York Times in exchange for a few cents. Steam issued from the subway entrances that punctuated the streets. Sometimes Edward took the subway, if the weather was really bad, otherwise he liked to feel part of the city above. The city that never sleeps never bores either, he thought to himself.

Thinking about boredom reminded him how bored he was with Arabella. Normally he could ignore her; she had her life and he had his. They kept up appearances at interminable parties and social functions, but their only area of common ground was Eddie. Now 15, the boy was a rebel. Arabella blamed Edward for being to lax on the boy, but she was just as bad and Edward had been determined not to subject the boy to the rigid upbringing he had endured. The fact that he and Arabella more and more frequently had to join forces to deal with their son had brought sharply into focus just how much they had grown apart. Not that they had really ever been together. Edward thought back to the steamy sessions he had shared with Linda. That Arabella would ever be capable of anything approaching the raw animal passion that he and Linda had shared was laughable. But Edward was a realist. He knew that divorce was out of the question; they were together for keeps, and as long as he had Linda, or Lucy or whoever, he supposed he should not complain.

By the time he got back to the apartment Eddie was there, slumped in one of the Queen Anne chairs in the hallway, one long leg hooked over an arm of the ornate piece of furniture. He had a Nintendo Gameboy in his hands, and little tinny noises, whirrs and buzzes came from it. As he played, Eddie moved his hands to the left and right and tipped it forwards and backwards as though moving the small machine would help the progress the little avatar within it. Arabella stood over him, tapping her foot, her immaculate skirt and blouse, undoubtedly several thousand dollars' worth, rippled slightly in time with her exertions. Other than that her hair remained still, Edward noticed, despite the angry outburst she now directed at him.

"This is all your fault! This boy will not listen to a word I say. Maybe you can get through to him; after all it seems obvious that he has your whoring ways! Oh yes, don't think I don't know!" Edward looked at her in astonishment while Eddie tapped the pause button on the Nintendo Gameboy, looked up and said, "Way to go, Dad!"

Edward was speechless; he felt the urge to run out of the apartment to avoid dealing with either of them. Instead he sat down opposite Eddie. "Where were you? We were worried."

Eddie shrugged. "Out."

Edward stood up, crossed to his son's chair, took the Gameboy out of the boy's hands and clicked it off. "Your mother says you were at a—" Edward glanced at Arabella but she was staring fixedly at Eddie. "—brothel."

Eddie threw his head back and laughed. "A brothel!" he mimicked, taking off his mother's British accent perfectly. Edward had to fight the urge to smile. "Hell, man; that weren't no brothel, that was a sister's house in Harlem." Now Eddie mimicked the accent of an African American.

"For God's sake." Arabella stamped her tiny foot and turned away, down the corridor.

"OK, Eddie." Edward spoke in a low voice, his face four inches from his son's. "I'm going to level with you, son. I don't need this shit." Eddie looked at his father, less sure of himself now. "I don't need this shit and I will not put up with you behaving like a spoilt brat." The boy's eyes were wide now and Edward felt a pang of guilt. Eddie was still a boy, after all. "If I ever have to be called out of the office again because of you, you will suffer the consequences; you won't like them, but you will suffer them, I promise you that. Do I make myself clear?" Eddie looked about twelve now, as he nodded. He had never seen his father like this, never heard him swear. "First you will apologise to your mother and then to your school. If they will have you back you sure as hell better toe the line, boy. Understood?" Eddie nodded again and stood up to go and find his mother.

Edward sat still for a moment. He felt tired, sad and disappointed. He had wanted a freer life for his son, but the boy had crossed just about every line there was to cross. He hated having to speak to him like that, but if it worked, well, maybe it would be worth it. Sighing, he rose from his chair and let himself quietly out of the apartment.

* * *

In the centre of the Kingdom of Saudi Arabia, Leila Mansour was excited as she hurried home from school. A world away from the boy Eddie, her approach to school could not be more different. Despite her 16 years, Leila was as innocent as a 10-year old girl in the West, her focus being to make her parents proud, do well at her studies and follow them into the world of academia. As she sat in her classes she could imagine no better life than to be imparting knowledge to others, filling young minds with knowledge and experience, opening up the world and its possibilities to them. She had watched many videos of her mother and father lecturing students, giving speeches at seminars and as her heart swelled with pride, she became more and more determined to fulfil her dreams.

The heat in the desert city of Riyadh had faded now and although the sun still shone, in the evenings they would sit in front of a fire of sweetly burning olive wood and by day they could walk freely in the garden or around the crowded streets of the souk without racing for the nearest air conditioned room. The walk from school was not a long one and for part of the way she walked with friends past the high walls and gates of the villas near her home. Here and there the top of a palm tree was visible but privacy was a major consideration for a Moslem family, and upper windows of villas were often made of one-way glass. Leila's villa was at the end of the street, and beyond it was the desert. The city was creeping out all the time but for now she and her family were on the edge of town and at night if you looked far into the desert you could see the most complete blackness, with no streetlights to cast their haze on the dark air. Leila looked out over the expanse of sand, hard and compacted near the villas but turning softer the further you went. A stray cat was chasing something across the surface, its movements erratic as it deftly changed direction in time with its prey. Leila smiled; she liked animals even the mangy stray cats that her mother would not allow near the house. Leila had hidden a mother cat and her three kittens in the little room at the back of the garage; maybe she would be able to show them off later because she knew that when she got home, her father's friend Amir Ali his wife and their four children would be waiting for her. Their visits were always a great time for Leila. Adam, the oldest of Uncle Amir's children, was older than she was and Yousef the same age. But it was the adorable younger girls, Sara and Iman, that Leila loved the most. She would sit them down in her bedroom and pretend to teach them. The little girls would look up at her with wide eyes, and Leila would feel her heart sing. She knew it was wicked to wish her life away but sometimes she just couldn't help it. She just couldn't wait to grow up and become a teacher.

She ran most of the way home, pausing at the gate of her villa to hastily tuck a stray tendril of her long black hair under her hijab. Her mother and auntie Marwa were in the kitchen and Marwa clasped her hands to her face as she ran in.

"My goodness, Leila! You are so tall, and so beautiful!" Leila smiled shyly embracing her auntie.

"Where are—" Leila started.

"The girls?" interjected Marwa, laughing. "They are upstairs taking a nap but now that you are here—" Leila was already flying up the marble stairs that led to the cool, spacious upstairs accommodation of the villa. She was an only child and the visits of her father's old schoolmate and his family were very precious to her. She did not want to waste a moment.

As she ran up the stairs, Leila had bumped into Adam coming down. She and Adam had played together when they were young, but he was now much taller than her and looked more like a man that a boy.

"Hi, Leila," he said, smiling at her; for the first time since she had known him Leila felt self-conscious, and felt her face flushing as the young man in front of her looked at her appreciatively. She knew that in Egypt and in England where her uncle was setting up home, young people were much freer, were able to mix, not like in Saudi where it was haram for men and women who were not related to each other to meet without a chaperone.

"I'm fine Adam; and you?"

"Good." Adam continued down the stairs and Leila cursed her tendency to blush; what must he think of her?

Downstairs she could hear the muffled voices of her father and Uncle Amir. Poor Uncle Amir. Her mother had told her that he was still not walking properly; maybe never would again after his horrible accident. She would be extra kind to him while he was staying with them, but for now she had two little girls to treat.

Amir Ali shifted painfully in his seat and his friend frowned in concern.

"Are you in a lot of pain?" He offered his friend a cigarette and Amir winced as he leaned forward to take it.

"It's OK; it reminds me I'm alive!" Amir said, smiling. "I start lecturing again next week."

Anwar Mansour frowned again. "Isn't that a bit soon? It's not long since your last operation?"

"I know; my last in both senses of the word I hope, now that this last operation has been done. I should not need any more, Inshallah. But never mind that for now, Anwar." Amir leaned forward in his chair, his eyes bright. "There is no time to waste, my friend; the message we have to give is an urgent one. I truly believe that we have the power to change the course of the world for the better, to halt this dreadful boom and bust financial climate that is so unsafe, so unstable and threatens us all."

Anwar raised his eyebrows. Amir had always been a keen student of Islamic finance, graduating top of his class at university, but this new, driven Amir was something different. He felt a thrill of fear run through him – fear for his poor battered and bruised friend, who had once been a bear of a man and now looked frail and haunted and seemed to be on some sort of divine mission. He was afraid it would be all too much for him. It might, he thought to himself, account for the lines of worry etched around Marwa's eyes.

"Don't you agree, Anwar? This is the time, or at least close to the time when we will have a chance to show a better way."

"Of course I agree with you, but you know how the Islamic way is viewed in the West. Do you really think it possible that the old world order could change?"

"Yes! Yes, I do!" Amir's passion was palpable. "Maybe not yet, but the time is coming closer and we have to be ready, be ready to show what we believe in, and to back it up with hard facts. It is not going to be easy, but with every lecture, every talk, every banker and financier we speak to at home and abroad, we have to keep putting the message forward, lay the foundations, so that when we are called on we will have laid those foundations and be ready."

"Do you really think that the day will ever come when what we believe will be accepted all over the world – even replace the familiar systems?" Anwar looked at his friend sceptically.

"Anwar, Anwar, look at you! My own friend, a fellow believer, student and scholar – don't you believe in what you teach? Your face tells me you do not! Shame on you!"

Anwar looked at his hands uncomfortably. "It is not a case of being unconvinced; of course I am convinced that our way is the right way. But can't you see how difficult it is to imagine that a diametrically opposed way of running the world's finances could succeed? It's like saying that all the world's Moslems would wake up tomorrow and eat a bacon sandwich for breakfast! Theoretically it could happen, but we know it won't!"

Amir closed his eyes and leaned back in his chair. "I am being very rude to you, my dear Anwar, in your own home, and I am sorry for that. We will not talk of this any more now. I am tired and I would like to sit in your courtyard, watch the fish in the pond there, feel the cool air on my skin. I love this time of year; don't you?"

Anwar led his friend through to the courtyard where the women were already sitting on the swinging chair, deep in conversation. Both looked up as the men approached and Anwar could read their expressions. He was apparently not the only one worried about his friend.

Chapter Four

Eddie Lancaster was a jock. There were no two ways about that; there was not a sport that he put his hand, bat or racquet to that he did not excel at. His father and mother were proud of his accomplishments in the sports arena; it was one area where there was no friction, unlike his lacklustre academic record. His greatest triumph came on the tennis court and there were those who said that if he had the right support and training he could go far. But Eddie knew that was not an option. His future lay in the boardroom, not on the tennis court, and with a maturity and resignation that belied his otherwise irresponsible and reckless character he was due to enrol at Harvard to study economics and start on the road that would lead to his seat at the head of the biggest banking dynasty in America. Harvard, for a boy of such mediocre academic ability would not have been presented as even the remotest of possibilities if his surname had not been Lancaster. Big compromises were being made in his further education and despite his dubious ability to complete the course, there was no doubt that he would do – and graduate with honours.

But for now it was summer and he was enjoying his last summer before college on the beaches and in the bars of Miami at his father's condo. His mother had enrolled for a week at the Pritikin Centre in Aventura on Turnberry Isle. It was a longevity centre and his mother enjoyed a week of enforced tailored exercise and a severely restricted diet there every summer. Normally his father and he would enjoy a week of sailing and fishing while she was away but this year his father had been called at the last minute to the Middle East. Eddie had asked to go with him; Edward was going to Dubai and Eddie wanted to go with him. He had been surprised at his father's immediate and stern refusal, but shrugged and instead began to plan parties in the condo.

His friend Harry Masters was staying with him, and as the boys walked onto the beach together he nudged Eddie, pointing to two girls lying face down on beach towels, the top parts of their bikinis undone. Eddie glanced over and then down at his friend's swimming shorts.

"Jeez, Harry, Christ; it's no wonder they call you hard-on Harry – you can't even look at a girl without getting a boner. Grow up, man!"

Harry clutched his hands to the front of his shorts to hide his excitement and the two boys ran for the water.

Harry was not blessed with the good looks and athletic flair of his friend. He was tall and skinny and extremely uncomfortable around girls. Unlike Eddie, who had already notched up a dozen or more sexual experiences, he was yet to score.

"It's alright for you; chicks dig you," Harry said as they stood in the warm water letting the swell lift their feet off the sand and then drop them gently back down on the sea floor.

"Well they might dig you more if you didn't poke their eye out with a fucking great hard-on every time you said hello!" Eddie teased. "Look I've invited Sandy and Suzy Jessen around this evening. They are the horniest twins on God's earth, if we can't get you off with one of them, hell, either of them – they're totally interchangeable – then we better give up!"

Harry adjusted his swimming shorts again at the talk of the evening to come.

That evening the Jessen twins arrived at the condo on time and eagerly accepted the free flowing booze that Eddie offered. Within the hour the two girls were naked in the Hot tub on the deck, two identical sets of chestnut coloured nipples on identical full creamy breasts bobbing just above the surface of the water. Underneath the water, Harry had just added to the fluid in the tub for the second time. His balls were aching and his cock, even after two ejaculations, was as hard as a rock. He watched his friend for cues. Eddie was sitting back, his arms hooked over the back of the tub behind him as the girls inched closer to him, their eyes straining to see through the water. Eventually one of them reached under the water and grabbed his cock.

"Climb on board!" Eddie laughed, but Harry noticed his friend's eyes were brighter, his breathing more rapid, as the young girl positioned herself over him, eventually lowering herself onto him. Harry put his head back and closed his eyes as she started to bounce up and down, and cupped her breasts with their engorged nipples, taking first one and then the other into his mouth. Harry stared open-mouthed, and at first did not notice the other twin at his side, her breast brushing his arm. Suddenly he felt a hand on his throbbing cock, which immediately exploded in its third ejaculation. In the turbulent water the girl did not seem to notice and his cock was hard again almost instantaneously. Taking his lead from Eddie, with shaking hands he moved the girl round to face him and licking her lips suggestively she eased herself down onto his cock. Harry stared wide-eyed at her nipples as she cupped her breast and held one to his mouth. Closing his lips around it, he felt he was going to faint. Perhaps because he had already come three times, the motion of the girl sliding her warm soft vagina over his cock did not produce an instant explosion. He saw the girl's eyes widen with pleasure as she appreciated the size and length of him and she began to pant as she moved up and down, her hands on the rim of the hot tub behind him, his mouth clamped to her breast. As the friction increased, Harry could not be sure how many times he shot his load, but he sprang back to life after each release, as strong and as hard as ever and by the time his companion began to cry out as her orgasm wracked her body, he felt an overwhelming sense of gratitude to this lovely girl, whose first name he could not be sure of, but who had shown him what his mission in life was. He caught Eddie's eye as Eddie looked over at Harry's orgasming partner and said, "Way to go Harry; way to go!"

Rites of passage are rarely forgotten and the two boys would never forget the night that they shared the twins in the hot tub. But somewhere in that expression of youthful abandon, that night that every teenager should experience, something had started that would affect the future of both boys and bring tragedy to all those involved.

* * *

In Dubai, Edward was just finishing a steamy session with Linda. It was not the first time he had taken one of his mistresses travelling with him, but it was the first time he had really enjoyed it. Apart form the sex, he usually found that he had little in common with them, but Linda was different. She was a hell-cat in bed but out of it she had a rare ability to blend into any situation adapt to any mood. Now as she padded naked to the bathroom be admired the perfect silhouette of her body, the sensual curve of her thighs, the wiry dark red triangle of hair, still damp, and her auburn curls tumbling down her back. He wondered if he could muster the strength for another session ... no, he had a meeting to get to.

Feeling relaxed and refreshed after his shower, Edward headed out to the manmade Islands shaped like a palm tree stretching out into the Arabian Gulf. A feat of modern engineering, the eighth wonder of the world, Lancaster Bank owned an apartment block there, the penthouse of which was reserved for Edward. He had not stayed there on this visit, choosing instead the "seven-star" Burj al Arab Hotel. He wanted to be anonymous on this visit, and had arranged to meet Sharif in a coffee shop at the bottom of one of the other apartment blocks on the promontory.

Sharif was already there when he arrived, and half rose in his chair in greeting. Edward took the chair opposite him and asked, "Your family?"

"Thank you." The half nod. Their shorthand greeting complete, Edward ordered a coffee and sat back. Sharif, sitting opposite him, held his gaze with those intense dark eyes and began to speak in low tones. Every now and again Edward would nod and apart from the occasional twitch of an eyebrow, Sharif made no gesture, his hands remaining folded in front of him on the table.

When he had finished speaking, Edward sighed. "Things are not so easy for me at the bank at the moment. It might be very difficult to get extra funding; we have even had to drop a couple of our causes this fiscal period. frankly I'm amazed that no one in the department that deals with our charitable donations has questioned the regular increases I have ordered to be paid to you."

Opposite him a smile played briefly at the corner of Sharif's lips and Edward felt a cold hand squeeze his intestines. In that instant he realised that Sharif had infiltrated the bank, the department that dealt with donations, and Eugene himself. It felt like a violation and for the first time in his long association with Sharif he felt danger lift the hairs on the back of his neck and trail an icy finger down his spine.

"I see you have managed that possibility?" Edward said, his voice tight.

"I manage what I need to manage," Sharif replied, his voice soft, even apologetic.

"Well, I am afraid that I can no longer do business with you if you go behind my back; this is an outrageous breach of trust, an undermining of my authority. Tell me – what the fuck did you say or do to Eugene to get him on side? He is one of the oldest, loyalest of our employees!"

His dark eyes remained fixed on Edward's, and Sharif opened his hands, holding them face-up on the table between them as if in supplication, but did not reply.

Instead he got up from the table, gave the traditional Arabic gesture of a half bow with his hand over his heart, turned his back, and left.

Edward drove back to his hotel feeling alternately sick with fear and wracked with guilt. His situation was impossible. To confront Eugene would be to acknowledge what he was doing, and had been doing for all these years, with Sharif. But, hell, he wasn't even sure what he was doing. The amount of money being channelled every year into the accounts of The Middle Eastern War Orphans Fund was enough to finance a small country. What hold did Sharif have over Eugene, over himself, over the bank? How the fuck had he let things get to this point? It was almost as though he had sleepwalked through the past eighteen years, at least where Sharif was concerned. He knew no more about Sharif's organisation now than he had done when he first met the man, but one thing he now felt sure of was that whatever he was up to, Sharif wouldn't know a war orphan if he fell over one. What the hell was he going to do?

Back at the hotel Linda was waiting for him. She seemed to sense his mood and sat quietly, leafing through a Dubai property magazine while he paced the floor and finally took out his laptop, even although he knew he would find nothing to help enlighten him there. Several times he looked at her. He needed to unburden himself, talk it through with someone, but all these years he had been careful never to share any information about his meetings or his business with Sharif with anyone. As if she felt his eyes on her, Linda tossed her hair back over her shoulders and got up from the seat. As she uncrossed her long legs,

Edward saw that under her sundress she was not wearing any panties. Without a word he held out one hand while he unfastened his belt with the other. Smiling, she let him lead her back to the bedroom.

In the quiet of the dining room of the Pritikin Longevity Centre, Arabella tried to read. She loved the quiet and calm and the faded elegance of the Pritikin Centre. She enjoyed being anonymous, being just Bella, as she introduced herself. The morning exercise sessions were over now and lunch would be served soon. The food, devoid of salt and fat, made a lot of the guest grumble, but Bella was not motivated by food; she ate to live – she did not live to eat. The clientele at Pritikin were mostly old and mostly overweight, looking for a magic cure, a divine inspiration that would give them the longevity they craved. All were wealthy and trying to buy what they could not achieve through will-power and were desperate to prolong their lives so that they could enjoy the fruits of their labours. On one of the big round tables that encouraged Pritikin guests to mingle, a tall guest, an Italian with a massive stomach who was a chef, would mix sauces for them at each mealtime using the condiments that Pritikin allowed. Arabella would have been happy to eat the food as it was but she took some of the dressing at each meal to be polite. She could tell from the way he looked at her that he fancied her but she did not fancy him; she didn't want any man slobbering and sweating over her. Luckily Edward had got that message early on and amused himself elsewhere. Good riddance, she thought to herself. She knew that Edward saw her as asexual, a cold fish, a frigid Brit. But she wasn't; she had sexual urges like anyone else – she was just good at controlling them.

Next week when Edward got back from Dubai, the three of them would be together in the Condo. Arabella was not looking forward to it. At home in the huge apartment in New York it was possible to keep herself to herself; but the condo, although still huge, forced them all together more. She would just have to spend more time on the beach, under the parasols she had had especially made with Edward's initials on them.

* * *

Eddie and Harry Masters were having a meal in a nearby diner; they were hungry after the previous night's exertions. Harry seemed almost shell-shocked and had made arrangements to meet Suzy (or was it Sandy?) again that evening at a nightclub.

"How the hell do you tell them apart?" he asked Eddie.

"Why do you need to?" Eddie said.

"Come on, man; she was a nice girl. I want to get to know her better."

"Woah! Don't get carried away! I know she's your first and all that, but hell, she's been lots of people's first, seconds, thirds, whatever!"

Harry frowned. "Don't be such a prick, man; I liked her; we connected."

Eddie nearly choked on his mouthful of food "Well no argument there! I saw you 'connecting', don't forget!"

"Well you won't next time." Harry was looking peeved and Eddie smiled at his friend.

"Look, Harry; if you've got a thing for her, go for it. I reckon she was pretty impressed with you lat night!"

"D'you think so?" Harry glared over at his friend eagerly.

"Hell yeah!" Eddie said, returning his attention to his burger.

* * *

In Dubai, Edward was getting ready for the flight back. His private jet was parked at the airport, the pilot and crew discreetly waiting to welcome him and Linda on board. In the pit of his stomach, Edward felt the nervousness that had started the day before during his meeting with Sharif was there again. Edward was a man used to summoning people to him at any time of the day or night and being confident that they would be there. The fact that it was he who answered Sharif's summons bothered him – a lot. He was not used to being the summoned. And he was especially not used to this feeling that something terrible was about to happen. He could not shake it; even the three sessions he had had with Linda since his meeting had not relieved his tension. The next time he saw the man he was going to terminate their association. It would cost him, of that he was sure, but he hated the feeling that he was not in control.

In the same coffee shop in which he had met Edward the day before, Sharif sat looking out of the window. In front of him was a mobile phone. It made no sound but as the light on the screen sparked into life Sharif picked it up and held it to his ear.

A voice spoke softly.

"We have done it; the aircraft is due to leave from the private terminal in one hour. Shall we arm the device?"

For a long moment Sharif did not reply. He stared ahead, his face passive, his expression blank. The caller did not speak either. Apparently aware of Sharif's reticent style he waited, his breath soft and regular in Sharif's ear. Finally Sharif looked down at the table and said in Arabic, "la," repeating in English: "no."

When Edward's private aircraft touched down at John F Kennedy airport in New York, his security team discovered the device strapped to the underside of a storage bin in the hold of the aircraft. Two weeks later Edward sat opposite his explosive expert, Dawson, in his office.

"So the device failed to go off because it was faulty?" Despite the fact that he had had two weeks to get used to his narrow escape, Edward found he still had to fight to control the quaver in his voice.

Dawson looked at him sympathetically, and Edward clenched his teeth. He did not relish being an object of pity.

"No, Mr Lancaster, the device was not faulty, it would appear that it did not explode because whoever planted it chose not to detonate it."

"Why would they do that?" Edward looked at the man across the desk, who shrugged.

"Maybe it was meant as a warning."

Edward looked down at his hands. A warning. Sharif. It had to be Sharif. Dawson cleared his throat.

"This incident should be reported to the security forces. This may not be a matter that affects only you, Mr Lancaster; it may have been aimed at the United States through targeting one of its most successful sons."

"It wasn't," Edward said. "And if you report this I will ruin you." The man looked surprised as Edward rose from his desk. "This matter is not to be mentioned again. I can rely on the discretion of your staff?" Dawson nodded. "Of course."

"Thank you; goodbye."

Dawson rose from his seat and offered his hand to Edward, but Edward ignored it and crossed the office to his private bathroom. As he heard the office door close behind Dawson he leaned over the toilet as his stomach churned, sending waves of vomit up his throat.

* * *

As the autumn began and the trees in Central Park began to turn every colour from crimson to deep russet, Eddie was packing for college. His course had been set since the day he was born, so there was no particular fanfare about his departure. In fact he thought that his father had looked a little preoccupied since he had come back to Miami from his trip to Dubai. His mother floated serenely around the apartment as usual, making sure to keep out of his father's way and for a boy to whom family ties were not that strong Eddie found himself feeling sorry for his father. The older man had deep black rings around his eyes and suddenly looked older still. Eddie knew that his dad had his faults but he knew as well that he was a kind man. It had usually been he who had picked Eddie up and dusted him off when he was a child. People liked his father; hell, *Eddie* liked his father, and he wished he could help. As he walked past the huge lounge that looked over the park, he found his father staring out of the window.

"Hey, dad, how's it hangin'?" Eddie threw himself down into a chair with his leg over the arm. His father turned and gave him the ghost of a smile.

"You packed?" Edward asked.

"Yup. Hey, dad, is everything OK? I know it's a blow me leaving like this but hey man, I'll be back for thanksgiving!" Edward smiled again at his son's attempt at humour.

"I'll cope, son," he said. "Everything's fine. Just a few problems at work; you know how it is."

"Not really, dad, but then, I soon will, once get this pesky studying out of the way."

"Yes. About that, Eddie, I know that study doesn't come easy to you, but do your best won't you? It's important."

"Yeah, I know, I know; the bank, the great Lancaster dynasty!" Edward looked down at his hands and Eddie raised his eyebrows. "What no pep-talk?" Eddie lowered his voice two octaves and mimicked his father's accent "Now son, remember the bank is the future; the Lancasters will rule the world!" Eddie looked at his father for a laugh but his father just looked defeated.

"Maybe the bank isn't everything, son," he said softly, and Eddie sat up straight in his chair. Whatever he had expected his father to say, this was definitely not it. For a moment he felt a coldness make him shiver.

"Hey, dad, we're OK aren't we? I mean the bank, the family? You're not gonna throw yourself out of a Wall Street window, become street jam?" Eddie laughed, but it was a weak reedy sound. It seemed to shake Edward out of his reverie.

"Hey, come on, that's a nice way to talk about your old man – street jam? Nice! Nah, I'm fine Eddie. Everything's fine, just a bit tired; now how about a jog round the park? Last one before you go?" Just before he left the apartment to make the trip to Massachusetts Eddie took a call from Harry Masters. Harry was due to meet him at Penn Station to catch the train.

"Hi Harry!" Eddie said cheerfully "You ready?" Edward smiled at his son. Harry Masters was a nice boy; they were lucky to have each other at Harvard. But as he looked at Eddie the boy's face suddenly fell. "What? Shit! No man!" Eddie's face had gone white. His eyes fixed on his father, who looked wild and frightened. Putting the phone down Eddie slumped back onto his chair.

"The stupid jerk; the stupid, stupid jerk!"

And there it was; before their adventure had even started it was over. Whichever of the Jessen sisters had had the pleasure of deflowering Harry was knocked up, and

Harry the poor deluded sap was giving up his education to drop out and make a nest for his little family. Despite the fact that it meant telling his father of his antics in the hot tub that night, Eddie unburdened himself to Edward. Edward listened quietly and then said. "What do Harry's parents say about it?"

"How should I know?" Eddie jumped up from his chair and threw the phone across the room. "His old man could afford to keep the kid and the Jessen tart in a mansion of their own while Harry was at school, but, no that's not good enough for Harry, oh no, he's got to be 'there for them'. Jesus! We had plans, big plans. Damn!"

Edward listened in silence to his son's rant. Thank God it was not Eddie facing the prospect of becoming a father at 18.

"Well son, all I can say is haven't you kids ever heard of a condom? You always use one don't you, Eddie?"

"Of course I do, I'm not that stupid." Only he *was* that stupid, and on the night in the hot tub with the Jessen twins he, like Harry, had not even given a condom a thought. And that would come back to haunt him.

Chapter Five

In her world Arabella had very little to worry about, very little to fill her day. The recent scandal though – Harry Masters having to get married to Suzy-or-was-it-Sandy Jessen – had kept her occupied. Marina Masters was a close friend of hers; they had known each other for years, Harry and Eddie had grown up together. Arabella shuddered at the thought that it could have been Eddie in this predicament; she was under no illusions where her son was concerned. "Like father, like son," she muttered to herself as she put the finishing touches to her mascara in her dressing room. Sanding up, she smoothed down her Chanel skirt, turning sideways to admire her profile in the long dressing-room mirror. She frowned as the light caught the little wrinkles at the corner of her mouth; she would have to get more botox. It hurt like hell, but it was worth it. She didn't look a day over 25 – okay, maybe thirty, but she was in good shape for her 38 years.

She called the driver to bring the car round from the underground garage to the front of the building. Arabella enjoyed driving through New York in the limousine with the blackened windows, watching the tourists trying to get a peek inside, hoping to see a movie star. Once, at a stop sign, one of them had pressed her face to the window and Arabella had recoiled in horror. Even with the glass between them she could see the rough texture of the woman's skin, the bad teeth, the blackheads on her nose. No doubt a Brit, she thought; it seemed that her fellow countrymen were not as concerned with dental health as they were here in America.

Now as the limo purred down Broadway Arabella looked out at the streets of the city that she now called home. Somewhere out there her husband was at his desk, commanding his empire. Arabella supposed that all in all she could have done worse. Edward was a good man, a kind man really, who did not ask much of her, especially not in the bedroom, for which she was eternally grateful. She knew that he had his philandering, but to be honest she really did not mind, although if the subject ever came up, she made out that she did – it was always good leverage. Lately though he had seemed distracted, almost depressed, and for the first time in their marriage she had felt a slight regret that their relationship was not one that would allow her to ask him what was wrong.

The club at which she was meeting Marina Masters was in sight now and Arabella got ready to get out, lifting the Louis Vuitton bag containing her towel off the back seat. After she had met with Marina, she would have a massage at the club. She felt a little thrill of excitement travel up her spine; she hoped her favourite masseuse would be on duty.

Inside the intimate coffee shop of the club Marina was wringing her handkerchief. Arabella sighed; that massage might be a long wait.

"I can't believe it, Bella." Arabella winced; she disliked any shortening of her name. But Marina was upset so she said nothing. "Throwing everything away – there's simply no need for it. Why does he have to do it? Why?"

Arabella patted her friend's arm. "Now look, Marina; it's still early days. They may change their mind. What do the Jessens say?"

"They are as against it as we are; truth to tell they want her to have an abortion, but neither the stupid girl nor Harry will budge."

"Which one is it? Which twin?" Arabella asked.

"Sandy." Marina spat the name out.

"Has Sol offered them money?"

"Of course, but they say they are 'in love'!" Marina jabbed two vicious quotation marks in the air.

"I know that Eddie is really disappointed that Harry won't be at Harvard with him," Arabella said to fill the silence that ensued. Marina burst into a fresh bout of tears.

"His education! Throwing away his education! I just can't believe this nightmare!" Marina wailed and for the next forty-five minutes Arabella tried her best to comfort her while she stole surreptitious glances at her watch. Eventually a red-eyed Marina looked at her own watch.

"I've got to go; got to meet Mary Jessen." The women air-kissed and Arabella made her way down to the massage rooms.

The receptionist greeted her warmly and handed her a soft fluffy dressing gown. As she took it Arabella asked, "Who's on today?"

The receptionist consulted her book. "Chris will be with you today, Mrs Lancaster." Arabella tried to stop herself smiling.

"Good."

In the massage room soft music played as she settled herself on the couch, pulling the modesty towels over her back. As she waited for Chris she felt her breathing quicken.

"Mrs Lancaster; how nice to see you!" Her voice hoarse, Arabella muttered a greeting, holding her breath as Chris turned down the lights. Expert hands kneaded her back and shoulders and Arabella moaned in pleasure as the hands travelled down her back. Chris smiled down at her. Arabella smiled back, noticing the brightness of the other woman's eyes. She wished she could give another woman the pleasure that she had just enjoyed; she longed to explore the secret places of another woman's body but she could not. Maybe one day, and if that day every came, it would be someone like Chris, beautiful and dark-haired with an Amazonian body. Yes, it would be someone like Chris.

* * *

As Leila Mansour said her goodbyes to her parents at Riyadh's King Khaled airport, she felt the lump in her throat threaten to choke her. She knew her mother was struggling too, neither of them trusting their voices, looking around the huge vaulted ceiling of the international terminal with feigned interest, determined no to be the first to break down. Leila tried hard to concentrate on the year ahead.

She was going to Harvard! It was the culmination of her and her parents' dreams and she was so excited. Now she wished she could just go through to the departure lounge – her throat was really hurting now from her unshed tears and she did not want the last glance her parents would have of her for the year to be a blotchy, swollen-eyed mess. As if reading her mind her father said, "Come on, habibti, it's time you went through now." Gratefully Leila jumped up and hugged him and then her mother. She could feel her mother's shoulders shaking as the tears came and it was almost a relief to join her in her sobs. But her father was not going to let the situation go on for long and firmly took Leila by the arm and led her to the security check at the entrance to the departure lounge.

On the flight Leila began to imagine the year ahead. Her aunt and uncle would meet her in America and take her to Harvard. She was both excited and nervous. It was the first time that she had been anywhere without her parents and while she felt ready for the freedom, she knew that she would be a long way behind the other students in terms of their behaviour. Despite themselves Leila's parents had felt it necessary to tell her of the ways of the West, ways that they had been so careful to protect her from all her life. As her face blushed crimson, she listened to her mother tell her of some of the things that her classmates would be likely to try and encourage her to do. Smoking was an easy one, she hated the smell; her father smoked and she had no desire to do anything of the sort. Drinking was something she had no experience of, and her mother's colourful description of what might happen to girls who were drunk caused her to bury her head in her hands. The idea of doing anything at all with a boy before she was married was so alien to her that she begged her mother to stop. Her mother drew Leila's head on to her shoulder and put her arms around her.

"We know what a good girl you are, we could not have wished for a better daughter, but you have to understand the way that things are. It would be wrong if we were to send you away unprepared." Leila nodded; she knew that her innocence could be her undoing. Now she thought about the things that her mother had told her. She had no interest in boys, and hardly any interest in befriending girls. She just wanted to study, to get her degree and to teach. One day she would be the head of a school or even a university. She took out the leaflets that she had received from Harvard, even though she knew most of it off by heart. She could almost imagine the smell of the 18th-century Union Dormitory where she had been allocated her quarters. The air hostess offered her a tray but Leila waved it away. Her stomach was churning. What would the other girls be like? More worldly than her, yes, but would they resent her innocence and naivety? She was worried too, about how she would react to the boys, having never been in the company of boys apart from her cousins and close family friends. She really hoped that they would not notice her, let her blend into the background. But what if they found her a curiosity, picked on her? Leila shuddered; she could not bear to think about it. She also could not bear to admit that there was a small part of her that hoped that she *would* be noticed, wondered what it would be like to have boys look at her in the way that Adam Ali had looked at her last time he had been to visit. She was glad that she as a Moslem; it made things clear, easy, it made what she could and could not do simple.

Leila read her leaflet again.

The first-year experience begins with freshmen week and a full "opening days" schedule complete with orientation and social activities. Freshman week has traditionally culminated in the President's BBQ hosted at Loeb House. Throughout the year students can experience an array of social events from the Freshman Formal to the Halloween Catwalk. First-year students can participate in the freshman musical and a wide variety of intramural sports competitions. In the fall, parents flock to campus to visit their newly matriculated sons and daughters during Freshman Parents Weekend. Students have the opportunity to invite their favorite faculty members to a Faculty Dinner at Annenberg twice a year. Students receive an upper class House assignment before leaving for spring break and have opportunities to familiarize themselves with their House during the remainder of the spring term through House events and traditions.

Eddie's and Leila's experience of Harvard could not have been more different. Eddie knew many of his classmates from his family's wide social circle and spent much of his first day high-fiving friends from school, Miami café society and the New York elite.

Leila was completely overwhelmed by the atmosphere on campus as girls dragged huge trunks into dormitories and she wondered how she was going to manage with her modest suitcase. She had read that the weather on the day that freshmen moved into Harvard Yard dormitory was always a gorgeous one. Well, Leila was too stunned by the newness and strangeness of it all to notice or to feel anything more than mild panic. Her dorm, Canaday, did not have the charm of the historic buildings around it, having been built in 1974. Some of the other dorms she had seen photos of had hardwood floors and fireplaces but in Canaday the walls were a white cinderblock and the carpet, such as it was, looked threadbare in places.

Leila was assigned to a dorm that had four single rooms leading off a large common room. Leila said a silent prayer of thanks to Allah that she had been allocated one of the rooms that did not require her to share with anyone. She was keen enough to make friends, but the girls she saw around her all looked so much more sophisticated and worldly than she did. Some had on skirts that barely covered their bottoms. Her dorm was three flights up and as such offered high ceilings and skylights, and was, Leila noticed, very close to the dining room and many of her classes. The other four girls had arrived gradually over the sunny autumn afternoon and as the sun began to dip they sat together in the common room, making their introductions.

"Hi, I'm Laurie Walsh." A plump, red haired girl with twinkling eyes introduced herself to Leila. She reminded Leila of an eager puppy and thought that she and Laurie would get on very well. One of the other girls was crying, dabbing at her eyes with her handkerchief and sniffing loudly while another girl sat on the arm of the settee beside her patting her arm occasionally.

"Hi; I'm Suzi Jessen," she said between sniffs. The fourth girl looked haughty and was wearing very expensive clothes.

Looking at Leila and Laurie she could not hide her contempt. "She's upset; her sister was supposed to be here but she got knocked up and, well—" Suzi Jessen sniffed again.

"And your name is?" Laurie asked.

"Helena Lowestein," the girl answered reluctantly, turning her face away from them to discourage any more interaction. The last roommate was a beautiful, tall black girl, who had been sitting quietly watching what was going on.

"I'm Princess Eme Assiak," she said eventually and Helena looked at her sharply, her dark glinting, eyes reminding Leila of those of a rat.

"Are you a real princess?" The girl nodded.

"From Nigeria," she said quietly. Eme looked at Leila. "Where are you from?"

Leila cleared her throat. "I'm Leila Mansour; I'm from Saudi Arabia," she said hesitantly.

"Don't they cut people's head's off where you live?" Helena asked, her tone accusatory.

"If it is necessary," Leila said, looking down at her hands.

"How barbaric," Helena said, looking at Leila with thinly veiled disgust.

"It is sometimes difficult for those who have lived a very sheltered life to appreciate the wide world around them," Eme said to Leila. Helena shot her a hostile look, and the battle lines were drawn. Helena and Suzy shared the biggest room and Leila, Laurie and Eme had rooms to themselves. Leila felt sorry that Helena and, she suspected, Suzy would be hostile towards her, but she felt comforted to have Eme on her side. The tall elegant African girl had smiled at her as they got up to go to their rooms, and as Laurie scampered along excitedly beside them, Leila felt happy that she had at least two friends already in this new and frightening environment.

Later as the three girls entered the dining room for their evening meal, Leila caught her breath. The dining hall was magnificent – Annenberg's tables, chairs, floors, walls and lofty ceilings are all made of a gorgeous dark wood that was so impeccably polished that it shone. Looking around her, Leila stared at the chandeliers that lined the hall, the vibrantly coloured stained glass windows and the statues and portraits of famous figures from Harvard's past.

In the same hall, Eddie was sitting with some of his friends. He was still sore that Harry Masters was not with him; they were almost like brothers, but there was a fair sprinkling of his classmates here and although they were not Harry, they would do.

Sitting together, the boys watched the girls coming in in twos and threes, making very colourful remarks as to what they would like to do with them. When Leila, Eme and Laurie came in, Eddie gave a low whistle.

"Wow, now that's one foxy lady; she looks like class," he said, admiring the statuesque Eme.

"She'd eat you for breakfast – look at those legs!" Eddie laughed at the teasing. His eyes passed briefly over Laurie and Leila but did not linger. In fact many eyes in the hall swivelled towards the handsome black woman as she made her way to her seat. This fact was not lost on Helena who followed the three girls into the dining room, a snivelling Suzy beside her. Helena Lowestein was used to being the centre of attention. With her perfect figure, alabaster skin and tumbling golden hair she was usually the one who drew the admiring glances. Although a few of the boys looked at her, people seemed mesmerised by Eme. But, Helena thought, if she's going to hang around with a decapitator in a headscarf and an obese idiot she wouldn't be much of a threat. It was going to be an interesting term.

Chapter Six

On the flight over from London, Amir looked through the notes of the lectures he was to give in the USA. His first port of call was Harvard. It was the first time he had been there and he was looking forward to it immensely. His friend's daughter, Leila Mansour, was at Harvard and he was looking forward to seeing her again. It was her freshman year and she and her fellow students would be attending his lectures. He thought again about the message he needed to get over. He had lectured students many times, but this was one of the most prestigious seats of learning in America. His message was hard for even an older professional to take in; young people, apart from Moslem young people, had no idea that the concept of Islamic Finance even existed. But somehow he was going to have to capture their interest.

As he arrived at Harvard Amir was impressed at the efficiency of the place. His name was noted down and a guide had been assigned to him. As he waited for the young man who was to show him around, Amir thought what a privilege it was for any student to come to Harvard – all the history, the famous names of former students, statesmen, the great and the good of every profession. Just the list of former presidents was impressive enough: John F Kennedy, Franklin Roosevelt, Theodore Roosevelt, George W Bush, the writer T.S. Elliot even the Fourth Agha Khan could claim Harvard as their alma mater.

Amir looked around him at the historic landmarks that filled the Old Yard at Harvard. He felt humbled in the face of such distinguished history. The student assigned to show him around pointed out the oldest standing Harvard building, Massachusetts Hall; the young man who had introduced himself as Marcus Drew explained that the Hall had been built in 1720 and that during the Revolutionary War it had sheltered soldiers of the Continental Army. "Today the President of the University, vice presidents, and other officers are housed on the first two floors."

As they passed, Amir looked in awe at the old building, its strength and constancy an inspiration to so many and in the history of the relatively few who had been lucky enough to be educated here.

Dean Grey, the Dean of Theology, had sent him an invitation and he was looking forward to the meeting at University Hall. As they passed the huge statue of John Harvard located in front of University Hall his student guide told him that the statue had been cast in 1884 by Daniel Chester French who had also sculpted the Lincoln Memorial. "The statue," the student said, "is known as The Statue of Three Lies."

Amir looked at him quizzically: "How so?"

The student smiled, obviously pleased that Amir did not know the story. "Well," he said in a conspiratorial tone, "although the inscription reads John Harvard, Founder, 1638, believe it or not, none of that is true. The figure is not really John Harvard – it couldn't possibly be as no pictures of Mr Harvard exist. Secondly, John Harvard was not the founder of Harvard College; and lastly the College was founded in 1636!" Amir looked at the young man amazed. "It's true" his guide said, "but despite all that, or maybe because of all that, this statue is a really popular draw for tourists, and thousands of visitors come every year to rub John Harvard's shoe for luck. Would you like to see Wadsworth House before we go in?"

Amir looked at his watch. "I would love to; we have time."

As they drew level with the antique wooden Wadsworth House, his guide told him that it had been built in 1726. "It served as temporary headquarters for General George Washington in 1775," he said.

"What happens in there today?" Amir asked, marvelling at the site of the building built so long ago, its wooden frame bowing with age but still standing after all this time. Amir wondered how many of the buildings we prize so dearly in this day and age would stand as long.

"Today it is home to the University Marshal's Office, the Office of the Director of the University Library, and the Alumni Office." Marcus said.

"Well, thank you very much, Marcus; it has been very interesting, but now I had better get to my meeting with Dean Grey."

"It's been a pleasure, Dr Ali," the young man said.

Back at University Hall Amir was shown into the office of Dean Grey. The two men had met several times over the years, and Amir was pleased to see Simon Grey again.

"Welcome to Harvard!" Simon Grey held out his hand.

"Thank you," Amir said, shaking it warmly. "I have had a very interesting look around the campus." He settled himself in an old leather armchair in front of the Dean's desk and accepted a cup of tea.

"I'm very interested in your lectures – linking religious doctrine so closely to finance is something new to me," Simon said. "What proportion of the tenets of Islamic finance are bound to religion?"

"One hundred per cent," Amir answered. "We have direct quotes from the Quran which show us the way. For instance: Allah will deprive usury of all blessing, but will give increase for deeds of charity."

"We have similar in the bible – the story of the moneylenders in the temple," Simon said.

"I know it," Amir said, "but the Quran goes further, gives far more comprehensive guidelines. On the subject of interest I can quote you another verse: 'Allah's Messenger cursed the accepter of interest and its payer, and one who records it, and the two witnesses; and he said: "They are all equal."' Abu Huraira related that the Prophet said: 'On the night of the Miraj I came upon a group of people whose bellies were like houses. They were full of snakes which could be seen from outside their bellies. I asked Gabriel who they were, and he told me that they were the people who had practiced Riba, or interest.' And another commentator, Abdullah ibn Hanjalah related that the Prophet said: 'A dirham of Riba, that is interest, knowingly taken by a man is a sin worse than committing fornication 36 times.'" Amir smiled at Simon. "So, as one example, you can see how strongly the Prophet feels about the payment of interest?"

Simon laughed "Well, there certainly is not much ambiguity there! But tell me, do you think that these ancient texts can still be relevant today?"

"Ah, my friend, you ask the question that is asked of you and of your bible every day – can any ancient text be relevant after all this time has passed? I believe that it can. In the same way as we learn our moral and ethical behaviour from study of the Quran and see it as relevant to the way we live our lives today, then the lessons we learn about how we should conduct our financial life remain as relevant – if they do not then none of the ancient teachings are relevant and if any of the ancient teachings is relevant still, then they all are!"

"Touché!" Simon Grey poured another cup of tea for them both.

"In fact," Amir continued, "the Prophet Mohammed foresaw this and in the Quran it is written: 'The time will come upon the people when one will not care how one gains one's money, legally or illegally.' It was reported that the Prophet said, 'The flesh and body that is raised on unlawful sustenance shall not enter Paradise. Hell is more deserving to the flesh that grows on one's body out of unlawful sustenance. The truthful and trustworthy businessman will be in the company of Prophets, saints and martyrs on the Day of Judgment.'" Amir looked at Simon, his gaze direct. "Tell me, my friend ..." Amir leaned forward. "Where does your religion stand in the face of a capitalist society that is out of control, where the weak man is trampled by the strong, the poor man thrown on the street in the name of capitalist venture?"

Simon Grey moved uncomfortably in his seat. "But you live in this society, Amir; we are all subject to the vagaries of the financial market. It is the system that has developed – no amount of posturing, pleading, begging or referring to scripture will change things."

"You are right, Simon, but mark my words: this system will bring the world to the edge of destruction, and when it does, we had all better hope that the world is prepared to listen to an alternative."

"Islamic finance?" Simon asked.

For a moment Amir did not answer. As they sat together Amir studied the tea cup in his hands, and Simon, smiling gently, waited for an answer. As an old grandfather clock ticked against the wall, Amir raised his head and looked into the eyes of his friend, and something in Amir's eyes made the hairs on the back of Simon Grey's neck stand on end. "Yes, Simon," Amir said softly but with a strength that seemed to come from the bedrock of the earth itself. "Islamic finance."

The first term of the freshman year was well under way at Harvard. Leila was doing well, enjoying the lectures and was hungry to learn everything that she could. Today was an especially exciting day and she hurried to take her seat in the lecture hall. Making her way to the back she took her customary seat and watched as her fellow students filed in. A group of boys laughed and dummy punched each other as they took their places, slumping in their seats in the customary nonchalant pose popular with freshmen. Leila thought how at home they looked in the surroundings of the great college, as though they had been resident here all their lives, unlike herself who had to struggle all the time not to feel like a fish out of water. She was so grateful to have Laurie as a friend and Eme too, although the amount of male attention the African woman attracted was a bit intimidating. Leila always felt like a spare wheel when she was out and about with Eme. But Leila knew that Eme was not as confident as she looked and had spent many nights comforting the girl, who was afflicted with the most awful homesickness. It made her more human to Leila and her heart went out to her. She missed her family too but her excitement at the opportunity that she had been given over-rode the homesickness she felt.

As their lecturer for the day arrived, Leila held her breath. How would he be received? She thought that the numbers present today were a slight increase on the normal turnout: curiosity, no doubt.

Amir Ali surveyed the sea of faces in front of him. Some of the students were doodling on their pads, others staring out of the window, but a few were looking at him with interest, hungry for what he had to say. Amir was aware that the message he had, the facts he was imparting, carried with them his responsibility to the message it was so vital that the world should hear. In front of him were the students of today who would become the bankers and the financiers, the statesmen and the politicians of the future. His message had to hit home. He challenged himself to win the interest, pique the curiosity, gain the trust of the students who sat in front of him now, until every one of them was concentrating on him and not one of them was looking out of the window or doodling on their note pads. In his head he could hear the voice of his teacher at the school, the Madrasa that had been the bedrock of his learning. *"When you teach, Amir, give it your passion, your love, one hundred per cent of yourself. If you do not feel worn out after you have finished, you have not given your all, and when 'your all' will contribute but 25 per cent to the knowledge of your students, can you afford to give less?"* Amir drew himself up. He cleared his throat and prayed silently for Allah's inspiration and guidance. Then in a voice that had every head in the hall swivel towards him he continued.

"Today we will continue with the tenets of Islamic Finance by looking at Shirkat-ul-milk. This is joint ownership of a property of two or more persons. This is used in two ways, firstly optionally, by the decision of the parties to purchase something jointly, and secondly compulsorily, such as after a death, in which property inherited will be jointly owned."

The students were all concentrating now and Amir continued, holding himself tall, catching the gaze of each student in turn. He continued, "Now we shall look at Shirkat-ul-'aqd." Amir pronounced the words carefully and the students repeated them. "This is a partnership affected by a mutual contract, or joint enterprise and is divided into three kinds." Amir held up three fingers. "Shirkat-ul-amwal: partners invest capital into a commercial enterprise. Shirkat-ul-A'mal: partners provide a service and according to an agreed ratio, fees are distributed among them. Shirkat-ul-wujooh: partnership in goodwill; they purchase commodities and sell them on the spot, and distribute the profit to an agreed ratio. Musharakah has been introduced recently by those who have written on the subject of Islamic modes of financing, and is restricted to this type of Shirkah: Shirkat-ul-amwal. However, in some cases it includes Shirkat-ul-a'mal."

Amir paused, looked over the sea of faces and with his eyes bright jabbed his pointer at first one student then another, asking for and receiving the three divisions of Shirkat-ul-'aqd. The pronunciation was a bit ragged but the students who had supplied the answers repeated the Arabic words again and Amir nodded, a thrill travelling up his spine. They were taking it in; the uninterested and bored expressions had gone. He pressed on with the lecture, his adrenaline fuelling his animated delivery. "Now for the Rules of Musharakah," he said, and the students bent over their writing pads, pens scribbling furiously. "I will break this down for you into four sections, and these are very important. Firstly, the contract must take place with free consent of the parties without fraud or misrepresentation. Secondly, the distribution of profit must be agreed at the time of the contract. In the third place, the distribution of profit is determined by the profit accrued, not the capital invested, i.e., an agreed percentage of the actual profit. Fourthly, the ratio of profit and loss has been debated among Moslem jurists. According to Imam Malik and Imam Shafi'i, each should get the profit in proportion to his investment, but according to Imam Ahmad, the ratio of profit may differ from the investment ratio if it is agreed between them. Imam Abu Hanifah argues that the ratio of profit may differ from the investment in normal conditions, but if the partner expresses in the agreement that he is a sleeping partner, then his share cannot be more than his investment. For the ratio of loss, there is a consensus that each partner shall suffer the loss according to the ratio of investment. The view of Imam Ahmad and Imam Abu Hanifah is a principle mentioned in the maxim 'Profit is based on the agreement of the parties, but loss is always subject to the ratio of investment.'

"If a partner wants to participate in a musharakah by contributing some commodities to it, he can do so according to Imam Malik without any restriction, and his share in the musharakah shall be determined on the basis of the current market value of the commodities at the time of contract. According to Imam al-Shafi'i, however, this can only be done if the commodity is from the category of Dhawat-ul-amthal, a commodity which can be compensated with similar commodities such as wheat or rice. According to Imam Abu Hanifah, if the commodities are dhawat-ul-amthal, mixing the commodities of each partner together can do this. And if the commodities are dhawat-ul-qeemah – commodities not able to be compensated with similar commodities such as cattle – they cannot form part of the share capital. The view of this Imam meets the needs of the modern business and is more reasonable.

"Every person has a right to manage the principal of musharakah, and an agreement can be made for one to carry out the management."

As he spoke, Amir watched the students, looking for any sign that they were becoming bored, their attention wandering, but there was none. He did not know how he had done it, and he was sure that his efforts alone would not have achieved this astounding result. He said a prayer of thanks, as his passion for his message infected his voice and his very demeanor, and he concluded his lecture.

"Finally we will talk about the termination of Musharakah. The Musharakah is deemed terminated only according to the following conditions: Every partner has a right to terminate the musharakah at any time after giving his partner notice. The assets, if in cash form, will be distributed between them. If they are not liquid, they may agree either to liquidate them or to distribute them as they are. If the assets are machinery, it will be sold and the profits shared. If one partner dies then his part is terminated, his heirs will have the option to withdraw the share or continue. If a partner becomes insane or incapable of effecting commercial transactions, the musharakah will be terminated. By mutual agreement, one of the partners can terminate the musharakah while the others continue, and may purchase the share of the terminating partner. The price of the share is also determined by mutual consent."

As he finished speaking, the hall fell silent. Amir felt exhausted, drained but elated at the response of the students. As he surveyed the faces turned to him, he said, "So who can tell me what they understand that Islamic finance is all about, what is the the ideal? What is at the heart of the concept?" Amir watched several hands go up and pointed to a tall boy, his long legs crammed uncomfortably underneath him.

"Fairness, sir; it seems to be about fairness," he said.

"Exactly!" Amir said, his eyes bright with passion, "Anyone else?" he pointed to a girl with short blonde hair and glasses.

"Is it about spreading risk? No one taking all the financial risk; instead, everyone is sharing the risk and the reward?"

"Absolutely hit the nail on the head! Well done." The girl blushed and slid down in her seat a little, but she looked pleased. As he looked around the students Amir saw on several faces evidence of the response he needed to see, a realisation, even an epiphany; the startling understanding of a different way, a new way, maybe even a *better* way of handling finance. A way that took account of human frailties and limitations and that dealt fairly with all involved. For several moments there was silence in the lecture hall as students came to terms with the fact that the only way they had ever considered dealing with money and finance might not be, indeed certainly was not, the only approach. This was as stunning a revelation to most of them as it would have been if they had been told that the world was in fact flat, and Amir let his message sink in for a few moments longer.

"Any questions?" he asked and as he sat down he was astonished to see a line forming of at least half a dozen students. Even the ones that were leaving the hall were nodding to him and speaking to each other in animated tones. For the first time in a long time Amir felt hope rising in him and a real optimism wash over him.

At the end of the line of students a young girl held back; she was wearing a hijab and Amir had noticed her at the back of the lecture hall, her head bent over her notes. When her turn came he suddenly recognised her.

"Leila! How are you? What a delight to see you here, but of course I should have realised you would be in this lecture. I was going to find you as soon as I had finished my programme for the day!" Leila smiled shyly and kissed Amir on both cheeks.

"Uncle Amir, your lecture was so inspiring." The young girl had tears in her eyes.

"It was so full of conviction, even the most lazy of the students were taking notice of you!"

"Yes, I felt it too!" Amir said. "I prayed for the strength to make a difference to what happened here today and Allah answered my prayers."

"Thanks be to God," Leila said in Arabic.

"So now, will you walk with me and tell me how you are settling in?"

"Very well' thank you," Leila said. "The girls that I share with are nice – well, mostly!"

"That is great, habibti; I have a meeting with the dean now, but we must meet later. Will you come out for a meal with me this evening? You are welcome to bring a friend."

"Thank you, Uncle – I will. Can we meet at the main gate at about 7.30 p.m.?"

"Yes – I'll see you later and give you all the news of the family!"

As Leila watched Amir walk away, his limp was still present though less pronounced and she prayed that he would not have to endure any more pain.

As she made her way back to the dorm, Leila frowned to herself. She would ask Laurie if she wanted to come to dinner with herself and Amir. But then that would leave Eme out. There was, of course, no question of asking Suzy or Helena – they had made it quite clear that the less they saw of her or Laurie the better they would like it. Still, the dorm was, by and large, a peaceful place punctuated only by the occasional dramas in the love lives of Helena and Suzy. Leila had been told by her mother that Western girls approached these things very differently to Moslem girls but Leila still had to hide her shock at the casual bed hopping that went on between the two girls and various jocks that they met on campus.

The evening before, three boys had been lounging on the sofas in the communal area when Leila and Laurie had come in from lectures. Leila recognised one of them from her course, Eddie Lancaster. Laurie said he was from a big banking family. He had been the only one to get to his feet as they came in and he had recognised Leila.

"Hi – Leila, isn't it?" He had put out his hand and she had let her hand meet his for a brief moment.

"I've seen you in lectures," Leila said with a nod. "But you weren't there today?"

"No" Eddie looked again at the girl. He was surprised she had noticed his absence and she obviously felt embarrassed that she had mentioned it, as her face flushed. She had beautiful eyes and an exquisite heart-shaped face. The tendril of hair that had escaped her hijab was dark and lustrous. If she was not wearing the scarf, Eddie thought, she would probably be one of the most beautiful girls he had ever seen. Hell, even with it she had a serenity, a goodness about her that almost took his breath away.

"How do you find the course?" he asked.

She said, "Very interesting; and you?" But before he could reply Suzy had taken him firmly by the arm and was propelling him out of the door with the others.

In the staff room Amir was talking with some of the other lecturers. One in particular, Leila's tutor, was very complimentary about her work.

"She could teach some of the others a thing or two in dedication," he said. "I was thinking of getting the students together in teams to undertake projects connected to the work we have been doing. How long are you here for? I have an idea that one or two of your lectures could be used to base their work on."

"I'm here for the rest of the week," Amir said; "I would be delighted to have the students involved. Which particular lecture were you thinking of?"

"I was thinking of the one that concerns women and Islamic finance. Obviously Leila will be involved in that one but I have to think about a partner for her, and I'm thinking of one of the young men who is showing scant interest in his studies at the moment. This change of direction and foray into the unknown is just what he needs.

Chapter Seven

Two days later Leila was assigned her new partner to prepare a paper concerning Women in Islamic finance. There was a lot of cat calling and whistling when Eddie was paired with Leila but the young man was surprisingly uncomplaining as he took his seat next to a blushing Leila.

"You will find Professor Ali's lecture very interesting," she said quietly.

"I am sure I will," Eddie said; and he would go on to be surprised to find he was.

They listened to their tutor as he announced the lectures they would have to attend and they parted. As Leila walked away Eddie watched her as his friends caught up with him. Following his gaze they started to tease him again. Leila heard them and cast a glance behind her. As she met Eddie's gaze she saw something that she had never seen before in the eyes of someone looking at her. She couldn't put a name to it, but she felt it and she welcomed it. She felt happy and sad, worried and elated, all at the same time. She put her head down and almost ran to her dormitory.

Amir started his lecture the next day to a full house. He saw Leila, this time sitting at the front with a young good-looking boy beside her. Their body language and her expression set alarm bells ringing in Amir's head. He pulled his thoughts back to the lecture, prayed silently, and began.

"An opinion that is often expressed from outside the world of Islam is that Moslem women are treated as second-class citizens, with few options or opportunities in life. Like most prejudices, this opinion is not based on much of a solid foundation. Whilst the equality gap certainly could – and should – be narrower, it would be wrong to assume that the problem is significantly worse than in Western society.

"I will explore the historical, Quranic and contemporary roles of women, particularly in Islamic finance, and point out some notable women who have made contributions that simply would not have been possible were the imagined restrictions based on truth. The resulting picture is of an encouraging level of involvement of women that points to women having a bright future in Islamic finance at all levels of management and ownership of business.

"To evaluate the effect of Islam on the status of women, we must discuss the status of women in pre-Islamic Arabia."

Amir glanced at Leila and her partner. She was making notes and he was staring at her. Amir frowned; he must not be put off his course. In his imagination he could see the face of his childhood teacher in that dusty Madrasa in Egypt, he closed his eyes and kept that beloved and learned face in his mind. He began to speak again, opened his eyes, and the image was gone, replaced by the faces of his students, and as the passion shone from his eyes, he continued.

"Some evidence shows that women before Islam were more liberated, particularly with respect to marriage and worship, although women's status was in general poor because they had been deprived of their inheritance by men."

Some of the boys sniggered, but a chorus of "Shhh" soon silenced them.

"Pre-Islam women were more or less the property of men, as is similar to the situation found in any other world religion, especially Hinduism, Christianity and Judaism.

"Islam changed the structure of Arab society and to a large degree unified the people, reforming and standardizing gender roles throughout the region; Islam improved the status of women by instituting rights of property ownership, inheritance, education and divorce.

"During the early reforms under Islam in the 7th century, reforms in women's rights affected marriage, divorce and inheritance. You will perhaps be surprised to know that women were not given such legal status in other cultures, including the West, until centuries later."

There were murmurs of surprise, and Amir felt a surge of energy; he was reaching them, they were taking in what he was saying.

"Under Islamic law, marriage was no longer viewed as a 'status' but rather as a 'contract', in which the woman's consent was imperative. Women were given inheritance rights in a patriarchal society that had previously restricted inheritance to male relatives; they were supposed to be the property of the man, and if the man died everything went to his sons. Muhammad, however, by instituting rights of property ownership, inheritance, education and divorce, gave women certain basic safeguards. Prophet Muhammad granted women rights and privileges in the sphere of family life, marriage, education and economic endeavours, rights that help improve women's status in society.

"In terms of women's rights, women generally had fewer legal restrictions under Islamic law than they did under certain Western legal systems until the 20th century. For example, a restriction on the legal capacity of married women under French law was not removed until 1965."

Amir was gratified to see that the students appeared interested in what he had to say. Split into their teams they were whispering comments and making notes together; even the young man sitting next to Leila appeared to be concentrating on what he had to say.

"The history of women in Islamic trade and finance is not adequately written," Amir continued. "At first sight, Moslem women's stories, and the general interest in them, seem to focus on family matters like marriage, divorce and children. Stories about the Prophet's wives focus, in most cases, on the Prophet and their relationship with him rather than their own activities, personalities and interests. Five examples are Khadija, Hind, Zaynab, Shifa' and Ijliyah. We will look at the story of Khadija for this lecture."

The students struggled with the unfamiliar names but repeated them and Amir continued.

"Khadija is often proudly pointed out as the first Moslem and one of the Prophet's greatest spiritual, emotional and material supporters. She is known as a businesswoman who employed young Muhammad and then married him. After that, details are scarce, except for the children she had, her reaction to the prophetic revelation and a number of beautiful stories about angels greeting her. Questions beyond that might not be compatible with habitual thought patterns:

"How did she become the rich businesswoman she was at a time when newborn girls were sometimes buried alive?

"What were her arrangements with Muhammad regarding the work he did for her and in respect to how she continued business after their marriage?

"Some of the answers can be found by drawing conclusions from various traditions. She inherited the import-export business from two previous husbands; as women in those days did not normally inherit, she probably kept charge on behalf of her children. Why did she not travel to Syria herself? Were business trips impossible or unacceptable for a woman, or were the children too young for her to get away? We do not know how many employees she had beforehand.

"The agreement with Muhammad was apparently based on profit sharing, with her investing capital and administration and him investing the work. We hear how impressed she was with his reliability, but would that be enough for marriage, even considering that, in principle, the idea of a marriage contract is not too far away from a business contract? Perhaps this was a key point. But there was also another similarity. Both of them were committed to the cause of the poor: she had contributed to projects like sponsoring and running a hospital during the plague epidemics, and he had been involved in the Hilf al-Fudul movement to stand up for the rights of the underprivileged. Except that the business continued to be successful, we have no information about their respective agreements, but considering both their personalities and later Islamic property rules, they cannot have been far away from a similar partnership that lasted though the years of persecution and boycott after Muhammad started teaching in public until Khadija died.

"In later societies where segregation of the sexes often limited women's access to the public sphere, especially among the ruling class, we repeatedly come across women who made profitable use of the rights guaranteed in Islamic law by managing and investing their property, either directly or through their agents. For example, going back to a class of slave soldiers with a high mortality rate among men, the Mamluks in Egypt used to leave the management of their property to their wives. Whatever the popular image, the harem system such as was practiced in the Ottoman Empire, was not necessarily an obstacle: comprising wives, daughters, indoor and outdoor servants and slaves as well as unmarried sisters and elderly relatives, it provided access to education and management skills. That is how many women became famous for sponsoring and managing awqaf, endowments for needy relatives or philanthropic endowments like hospitals, colleges, Sufi convents, libraries, mosques or orphanage projects – but also roads, bazaars and rest-houses that paid for the former."

As he surveyed the lecture hall Amir caught Leila's eye; her pride and passion for his teaching shone out and he smiled back at her as he continued.

"The average spectator from Western countries might consider women in the Moslem world as introverted and restricted to their homes by their male partners. In fact real life is different, particularly over the last few decades. Women in Islamic countries are now in charge of large corporations, are ministers and prime ministers and have reached top jobs and are imposing success on their own terms. As HE Queen Rania Al Abdullah of Jordan said on the subject, 'The landscape is starting to change.'

"Women are now business owners in Jordan, Bahrain, Lebanon, Tunisia and the UAE. They are finding their own place in the business and community worlds and creating opportunities for themselves. Their participation in business is on an upward trend. Making a significant contribution in the booming economies, women's business networks have grown rapidly across the region. And not just business – the advancement of Arab women in all occupations, particularly in this millennium, is certainly impressive.

"As HE Sheikha Lubna Al Qasimi, the UAE's Minister of Foreign Trade, says: 'The participation of women in business and investment has become a key economic booster for the region and has empowered many women.'

"Salma Hareb, CEO, Jebel Ali Free Zone and Economic Zones World, said, 'Women in the UAE are as much part of the corporate world as anywhere else on the globe. This signals a significant change in a society where women's roles used to be marked differently by our social customs earlier. Being an entrepreneur is about more than just starting a business or two – it is about having the attitude and the drive to succeed in business. Businesswomen in the Middle East are doing just that. We observe women as corporate heads occupying various decision-making positions in the public as well as the private sectors.'

"Arab first ladies are leading by example. These include, among others, women such as Princess Haya Bint Hussain, wife of His Highness Sheikh Mohammad Bin Rashid Al Maktoum, HE Queen Rania of Jordan, Mrs Suzan Mubarak, first lady of Egypt, HRH Princess Moza, wife of Sheikh Hamad bin Khalifa Al-thani, Qatar Ruler.

"Recent statistics show that women in the Gulf region represent 35 per cent of the total Arab workforce. The UAE alone is home to more than 11,000 women entrepreneurs managing investments worth more than four billion dollars. Women are increasingly becoming very proactive investors; women investors in the UAE now manage investment worth more than 38 billion dollars; and these numbers are growing at an extraordinary rate. Women have been involved in medicine, education, engineering, research, academics, sports, business, law or media; they are now judges and are involved with Moslem jurisprudence. Women's rights in the region have been progressively enhanced.

"Over 40 per cent of the workforce of UAE, Bahrain, Kuwait, Egypt, Jordan, Morocco, Tunisia and Algeria is composed of women. Women hold 30 per cent of management positions in finance, 32 per cent of the transactions of the financial and banking sector is done by women, and 20 per cent of management jobs in financial institutions are held by Women. The number of women heading businesses in the Middle East has grown significantly; there are a growing number of highly skilled Arab women in the Middle East region who are putting to good use their education, intelligence and creativity.

"Arab countries have invested significantly in human resource development and in providing equal opportunities for both men and women to have access to education and other opportunities. That has helped in providing women with a proper education and skills. With more open-minded leaders of Moslem countries, there are increasing opportunities for women to do extremely well in the workplace if they have the qualifications and drive.

"According to a report by the Hawkamah Institute for Corporate Governance based at the Dubai International Financial Centre, women's businesses in the MENA region are among the most sizeable entities. A larger share of women are principal owners in family-owned businesses. They own close to 40 per cent of the individual firms in the region, and there is a direct correlation between corporate performance and women's participation on boards. Based on a survey conducted last year, among the Fortune 500 companies, those having more women board directors have shown stronger financial performance, in terms of return on equity, return on sales and return on invested capital, than those having the fewest women as board directors. Women business owners surveyed in the MENA region are well ahead of their counterparts in Western Europe and North America with respect to the size of their firms and many report substantial levels of revenue. It also says that the majority of the women surveyed in Bahrain and Tunisia are sole owners of their firms, at 59 and 55 per cent, respectively. This compares with 48 per cent sole owners in Jordan and the UAE, and 41 per cent in Lebanon. Most survey participants own established businesses and many have extensive years of experience.

"On average, women in Lebanon have owned their businesses for 10.6 years, in Bahrain for 10.2, in Tunisia for 8.6, in Jordan for 6.1 and in the UAE for 5.9. Female-owned firms in the MENA region are as large, successful and tech-savvy as male-owned firms. Apart from being successful businesswomen, a number of Arab women have also excelled in the public sector. Even on a much smaller scale, micro-finance initiatives have helped scores of women across the region to gain access to financial services and enabled them to start up business ventures.

"According to the report based on a survey of more than 5,100 male- and female-owned firms in eight MENA countries, of the formal-sector female-owned firms surveyed, only 8 per cent are micro firms and more than 30 per cent are very large firms employing more than 250 workers. Furthermore, the average age of female-owned firms is slightly higher than that of male-owned firms – 21 years across the region, compared with 18 years for male-owned firms.

"The World Bank report adds that more women in the Middle East are individual owners than expected. It says: 'The share of women in the MENA region owning their firms individually instead of as part of a family is higher than expected. In Syria and Yemen, most women own their firms individually, at rates comparable with male individual ownership. In Egypt, Lebanon, and Saudi Arabia, however, the proportion of female-owned firms owned individually is significantly lower than that of male-owned firms.'

"Although women still do not have equal access to economic opportunity, they are in control of their own wealth according to Islamic principles. As a businesswoman or an entrepreneur, women in the Middle East have an amazing opportunity to step into their destiny and live out their full potential. However, in order to become more diversified and globally competitive, more needs to be done to empower women and address issues that inhibit female entrepreneurship.

"A significant contribution by women to Islamic finance and to financial institutions has been noticeable in Malaysia, as well as in global finance. Women in Islamic financing are much more able to follow the principals of Shariah than are men because their main concerns are to details and efficiency; they are less likely to engage in speculative or risk-taking behaviour and the sale of financial assets. Women have become a powerful force in the economy, and this success should be recognized. Although there are still obstacles to overcome, there are a number of women who have reached the highest positions in financial institutions, as is shows in this survey: American women constitute the largest economic force in the world, spending 4.9 trillion dollars a year.

"The estimated growth rate in the number of women-owned firms was twice that of all firms. Women own an estimated 10.6 million firms that generate $2.5 trillion in sales.

"Women are expected to acquire 94 per cent of the growth in US private wealth by 2010.

"Women in the 2005–2006 school year will earn 59 per cent of the Bachelor's degrees and 60 per cent of the Master's degrees. Women today face unique financial challenges, but with careful planning, these challenges can turn into opportunities. Financial advisors are dedicated to empowering women through education, support and knowledgeable advice.

"Women are researching, educating themselves and taking more control of their finances. When it comes to investing, women make fewer mistakes, are more risk averse and more consistent during volatile market times. These positive investment tendencies are necessary when it is considered that women face unique challenges and pressures that make it essential for them to be proactive with their investments.

"Some factors that are unique for women include the following: women live on average seven years longer than men; women earn 23 per cent less than men, creating a risk of outliving their retirement savings; women currently influence 80 per cent of financial decisions in the household."

There was a slight rustle around the hall as girls nudged boys. Amir smiled and paused; he was gratified to see that their attention was still focused on his message.

"On average, women take about 12 years off work to care for children or elderly parents compared with less than two years for men; and American women constitute the largest economic force in the world."

This time there was a more audible chuckle of delight from the girls and Amir laughed with them.

"It will help us to understand the differences between women and men in doing business, and their approach and style of business. By style, we mean the way people choose to do business. What are their priorities? How do they choose to communicate them? One of the biggest style differences is the relative importance individuals put on relationships and connection, as opposed to tasks. We have to ask few questions: and these are the questions I want you to use for your projects: Are there real differences in how the brains of men and women work? Do they have different styles of doing business, for example in their priorities or the way they communicate?

"A survey conducted by Prudential Financial in February 2006 found that women are capable of taking financial decisions wisely, for example only one in five women feel very well prepared to make wise financial decisions; the others admitted they need assistance; 43 per cent of women's top priority is getting out of their debt; 53 per cent of women are saving or investing their money; and the majority of women place a priority on health. There are now a host of women-focused products. Examples include conventional products that already exist to cater for women investors, e.g. women only insurance; hotels catering to women travellers; wealth consultation services specifically for women; products that cater for women's different investment needs. Women are more ethical investors. Women have an appetite for lower-risk, capital-protected products. Women have social restrictions in the access of ordinary products.Women-focused financial services. Et cetera.

"And now for a very interesting part of the lecture," Amir said. "Out of 497 billionaires in the world, 35, or 7 per cent, are women. In the US, there has been equal opportunity for women only in the past 20 years. It was not until relatively recently that women could be found as chief executives of blue-chip companies. Twenty years may not be enough time to build the kind of fortune that lands a person on Forbes' World's Richest People list. There are self-made billionaires such as Oprah Winfrey, Nina Wang, Abigail Johnson, Miuccia Prada, Maria Aramburuzabala, Marilyn Carlson Nelson and others.

"Now to conclude my lecture I will summarise," Amir said, gratified to see that his students were still as engaged with his message as they had been at the beginning of the lecture.

"Women in Islamic financing are much more able to follow the principals of Shariah than men because of their tunnel vision on details and efficiency; they are less likely to engage in speculative or risk-taking and the sale of financial assets; they have certain limitations but overall performance is encouraging, particularly in Malaysia. One of the main difficulties is that the men do not give them enough opportunity for training, education, top jobs and responsibilities. I believe that women are capable of playing a larger part in Islamic finance, but they are either frightened of making mistakes or they are leaving the men to make the mistakes and they learn from them before taking the responsibilities.

"I expect to see more women than before in top Islamic finance jobs, particularly in the fast growing businesses.

"Thank you, everybody; it has been a pleasure to talk to you today. If there are any questions I will remain for a few moments, and don't forget that the projects that you have been given will be marked by Professor Anderson who will let you know their submission date but don't think I will not follow up the work I have given you. With the miracle of the world wide web, there is a very good chance that I may have some input!"

The students laughed as they gathered their books together and Amir sat down wearily at his lectern smiling to himself. If his feeling of exhaustion was anything to go by his old teacher would be proud of him!

As the line of students at his desk grew, Amir saw Leila hovering in the background, the young man beside her. Something in the way he looked at her and she at him made Amir feel sad. He could see no good coming of their relationship. After the last student had gone and while Eddie waited outside for her, he took both her hands in his.

"Be careful, Leila; be careful." Leila blushed, and Amir felt a sense of foreboding that she did not even have to ask him of what she should be careful.

"Silly uncle; of course I will be careful. Have I not always been?"

"Yes, habibti, you have, may God go with you."

Chapter Eight

That night Leila slept badly. In the few hours that she did manage to sleep she had vivid dreams that she was being chased through a labyrinth, her hijab flying and her clothing coming loose. She ran fast to stop anyone seeing her but the faster she ran the more her clothing became loose. As she lay awake in the dark, her heart racing, she did not have to look too far to analyse her dream. Although he was not in her dream, she knew that the person chasing her was Eddie. She was unaccustomed to feelings like this and had even had trouble in concentrating in Uncle Amir's lecture because of Eddie's disquieting presence. If she could feel that this was a schoolgirl crush that would never be reciprocated she would feel less worried, but somehow, maybe from a look, a smile, something quite unconscious, she knew that Eddie liked her too. She thought of Suzy and Helena, the kind of girls that Eddie would normally be with, and shuddered. Her own moral code was a million miles away from theirs. Would Eddie expect her to behave like them? Would he try to ...? She closed her eyes in the dark and as she did the certain realisation that Eddie would always treat her well swept through her, making her smile. She tried to tell herself that speculating like this was ridiculous, that he had not even asked her out, not even talked to her about anything other than their studies; but she knew, somewhere deep inside, that he would ask her out, and would talk to her of many things, that this young man would be someone significant in her life.

Eme and Laurie noticed the difference in their friend that morning as they ate croissants and drank coffee for breakfast that morning.

"What's up, Leila?" Laurie asked, her face concerned as she looked at the dark circles under Leila's beautiful eyes.

"Nothing; I just didn't sleep very well." Leila looked down as colour flooded her cheeks as she remembered the dream that had kept her awake.

Eme and Laurie exchanged glances. "Uh huh!" Eme exclaimed. "In my experience there is only one thing that can give a girl like Leila sleepless nights. Who is he?"

"No one!" Leila felt herself blushing again. "I just had a disturbed night."

Her friends looked at each other again and smiled but said no more.

As Eddie chugged back a whole pint of milk for his breakfast he was thinking about Leila. He had never met anyone like her before and there was something about her that frightened him. It was almost as like standing in a boxing ring, allowing your opponent to hit you without raising a hand to defend yourself. It felt like something momentous, something that would be a marker in his life, but it also felt like something that could hurt him. Eddie was not keen on being hurt; in fact he never had been although he had left dozens of female hearts broken in his wake. He knew his worth, both as a good-looking, healthy, all-American male and as the heir to an almost unimaginable fortune. But he also knew that these things would mean nothing to Leila. She was different to other girls; her gentle dark eyes had a serenity that he had never seen in the eyes of anyone he knew. He was not used to deep analytical thought but, frowning, he tried to fathom what it was about Leila that was different, what made her eyes bright in a totally different way to the avaricious way that his customary girlfriends' eyes shone. That was it! It was a lack of greed or calculation, a depth of calm and an inner peace that he was seeing in Leila. He let out a low whistle. This was heavy stuff for him.

As he played a few baskets before lectures Eddie found himself struggling to concentrate. This feeling of mixed excitement and foreboding was new to him and he was not sure if he liked it. One thing he did know was as soon as he saw Leila he would feel nothing but joy. He was due to meet her in the library in the afternoon to go over the work they needed to do for their project. With only one lecture in the morning Eddie surprised himself by arriving at the library before lunch. Taking down a book written by Amir Ali that detailed Islamic Finance as it applied to women, he started to read, making notes on a pad beside the book. He wanted to be ready to contribute something useful to the project that he was doing with Leila; he wanted to show her that he would be pulling his own weight, that she would not have to carry him he would contribute as much as she would, despite the fact that she had an obvious advantage. He remembered the comments of his friends when the pairings for the projects were read out.

"Typical Eddie, man; trust you to land on your feet – you won't have to do a thing, it's like being teamed with a cow on a project about eating grass!" The group of boys laughed and Eddie only joined in for show. He felt his jaw tighten at the implied insult to Leila and immediately checked himself. Hell, he knew these boys, they could smell weakness, would rip him apart mercilessly if they got even a whiff of his feelings. So Eddie had forced himself to laugh with them, "Yeah, well, you know dudes, you either got it ..."

Now as he sat with the book in front of him he found himself immersed in the words. The fact that there should even be a distinction between men and women in relation to finance was something he had never thought of. The hard-bitten, angular women who worked with his father at the bank were every bit as capable and hard-headed as the men; in fact his father would sometimes say that they were more ruthless than men. Eddie supposed that was the major difference. He had always thought of money and moneymaking as a ruthless, cutthroat and highly competitive thing. One of Eddie's earliest memories was his father telling him about the great Wall Street Crash of 1929, painting a vivid picture of successful men, men like his father, throwing themselves out of the windows of their office blocks to a certain and violent death on the pavement below. Eddie had got the message – money was all-important, money was worth dying for, money was everything. Yet the message he was getting here was quite different. The words fair, equal, share, seemed to jump off the page at him and as he read he felt, for a time, like the first man on the moon. This was a revelation, something so different yet so human that he was amazed he had never heard anyone speak of it. What did it have that the Western system did not? Fairness, equity a lack of killer instinct? Did that mean that nobody made money in the Moslem world? Clearly it did not. Eddie thought about his father, the tense set of his mouth when he took calls from the bank on some matter of crisis or another. Of the funerals he had attended with his parents for his father friends and colleagues who had dropped dead on golf courses, squash courts or at their desks from heart attacks and strokes. A disturbance outside the library's full-length wall of glass made him look up. Dressed in tennis gear some of his friends were making their way to the courts. They had spotted him and were making gestures, Danny Savage even turned his back and pulled down his shorts exposing his white backside until one of the librarians tapped furiously on the glass and they ran off laughing. She shot Eddie a disapproving look and he bent his head over the book again, scribbling furiously on the pad.

Leila spent the morning studying in her room. She had also written home but unusually she had found it difficult. Her usual easy style of writing seemed to elude her – it was as though she had done something that her parents would disapprove of and she was trying to avoid mentioning it. She had not and she would not, but suddenly she felt tired. It was as though she had had a premonition of how much her relationship with Eddie would take out of her. She felt the weariness in all of her limbs, she felt as though her mind was closing down, as though it could not cope with the scale of what was to come. But the feeling passed and in its place came a sort of tingling anticipation of the meeting that she would have with Eddie later that day to work on their project. As well as actually seeing him again Leila felt the responsibility she had to guide him through this project, to bring him to the realisation that there was a different way to the way that he and his forefathers had conducted their lives in banking. Leila believed passionately in Islamic banking principles and wanted more than anything to share her knowledge with someone to whom this knowledge might actually make a difference.

Arriving at the tennis courts halfway through the first game, Eddie smiled good-naturedly as his friends cat-called and teased him about his studious interlude. But his game was off, and he took more ribbing about his fluffed serves and wide returns. He would not admit it to anyone, could hardly admit it to himself, but his stomach was in knots. It was only an hour now until he was to meet Leila and he had never felt like this before. He was not sure he liked it. He was used to being in control and this felt very far from that. He tightened his jaw and completely missed a ball served from a soft second serve.

"Give up, man," Joe Pecardi said. "You are worse than crap today." So Eddie did. As he showered he thought about the meeting ahead. It was going to be so awkward if he felt like this – he had to pull himself together.

As Leila brushed her hair and put on her hijab, straightening the blouse she was wearing with the pale blue cardigan on top she looked at her face in the mirror. Her cheeks were pink, as though she had been running, and her breath was coming a little too fast from between her parted lips. She slapped herself gently on the face. This served only to make her right cheek pinker. She slapped the other side of her face a little harder and tears sprang to her eyes. Suddenly she found herself sobbing, her head in her hands in front of her mirror. She felt excited and at the same time afraid and alone. She wanted her mother for guidance for the loving way she would help her through this. She wanted not to feel like this about a boy she hardly knew. Wiping her eyes, she saw how the tears had made her eyes brighter. She felt the butterflies in her stomach begin to flutter in earnest as she dabbed at her long lashed eyes and took a deep breath. She had to pull herself together.

If you had been a bird perched on the top of a lamp post on Massachusetts Avenue outside the Widener Library which housed the Gibbs Islamic Seminar Library you would have seen approaching from the west a girl, her steps hesitant, her hands clutched tight around her folders while from the east a boy, his stride long and nonchalant, hands in pockets, a folder tucked under his arm, watched with a keenness that gave the lie to his studied casual stride, for the first glimpse of the girl he was to meet.

When they did meet, their hands touched in a brief greeting, while their eyes locked in a recognition that would last a life time.

Chapter Nine

While her son was suffering the first pangs of love, in New York Arabella was shopping. The actual process of shopping was not the exciting affair that most people enjoyed. It was more a matter of making sure that she was clad and shod in the latest that New York's 7th Avenue designer shops had to offer, so that, at the many fund-raisers and social events that she attended both with and without her husband, she was always at the cutting edge of fashion. She was lucky to have a near perfect figure that she guarded well with an almost superhuman abstinence. As she looked at a rail of newly arrived shrugs from Paris a couple of young girls giggled their way in from the sidewalk and started to pull out various items from the sparsely populated clothing rails, uttering loud wows and parading up and down holding the clothes in front of them. One of them was slightly plump and with her lip curling disdainfully Arabella thought that there was nothing in this store that would even remotely cover the girl's podgy flesh that wobbled as she laughed. Arabella hated fat; she saw it as a self-inflicted injury, a hideous admission of weakness, and lack of self-control. By the confident way that the girls were looking at the clothes Arabella guessed they had the money to pay for them and by the way that the haughty shop assistant was ignoring them she guessed they had shopped here before.

She was about to leave when something stopped her. Normally she would ignore silly young girls like the two now tottering around in a couple of pairs of shoes from the boutique, but something about their happiness, their youth, the fact that they were full of life gave her a feeling like heartburn, a feeling that was a mixture of resentment and jealousy. Had she ever been that carefree? The girls noticed Arabella staring at them as she stood with her hand on the handle of the shop door. They looked at her, their faces open and friendly, not very far from the chubby faced pre-adolescent children they had so recently been, their expressions curious but trusting. They knew that this elegant woman wanted to speak to them and they waited obediently as Arabella fixed her best emotionless smile on her smooth botoxed face.

"In order to wear these clothes, both of you need to loose weight – especially you." Arabella curled her lip as she looked the chubbier of the girls up and down. "What are your mothers thinking of, allowing you to get so, so fat?! I think they do a plus size range at Macy's; why don't you do us all a favour and shop there? Nothing at all in this shop will fit you, and even if it does it will look awful." Arabella watched in satisfaction as the girls' faces crumpled, the enjoyment of the day, the joy of being young and carefree snatched from them. They looked as though they had been slapped, so shocked were they that this stranger had spoken to them so cruelly.

"Bye, girls!" Arabella smiled her tight smile, noticing with satisfaction the smirk on the boutique sales assistant's face. Behind her she heard the door of the boutique open again and looked over her shoulder to see the girls walking in the other direction, the chubby one being comforted by her friend. "Sometimes the truth hurts," she said, smiling to herself.

After her encounter in the shop Arabella visited another three boutiques, her enthusiasm for shopping rekindled by her run-in with the girls. Each time she tried on a tight skirt that showed off her hip bones or a jacket that hugged her figure she thought how lucky she was that she could wear these lovely clothes, the fact that the girls would not look nice in them somehow making the experience all the more enjoyable for her. If she had thought about it Arabella would have realised that her attitude was unhealthy at best and downright dangerous at worst, but Arabella was not used to criticising herself or recognising any of her own shortcomings. No, as long as Arabella was happy then all was right with the world. She had arranged to meet a friend for lunch at the Rockefeller Centre. Another thing that Arabella never was was on time for anything. She thought it made one look needy and she liked people to wait for her. Looking at her Tiffany watch she sighed. She would have to wait for 10 minutes at the foot of the building – she was only twenty minutes late.

Taking a careful seat on a stone bench in the warm autumn sunshine, Arabella closed her eyes for a moment, tilting her head back to allow a few of the sun rays to kiss her face. She would never do this in summer, but now there was not much heat left in the sun and it did feel good. A shout made her open her eyes with a start in time to see a young hooded lad making off with the bags she had put down beside her. A man in a very expensive looking suit was giving chase and a few hundred yards further on the boy dropped the bags, running on empty-handed. The man in the suit gathered up the bags and came back to where Arabella was standing.

"Here we are, Ma'am." He returned the bags with a little bow. Arabella spotted a platinum Rolex on his tan skin with an expensive shirt held together at the cuff by platinum cuff link with a small diamond embedded in it. Taking off her dark glasses she looked at his face. He was obviously an Arab but a very handsome one who smelt of Abercrombie and Fitch Fierce, an aftershave she often bought Edward. Normally she would have nothing to do with anyone of colour by choice but as she looked into his eyes, she felt as though she was drowning in their liquid depths. The darkest of brown with occasional gold flecks framed by luxurious eyelashes, he seemed to see into her soul. Arabella felt as though she had been caught naked, so intimate was his gaze, and words escaped her. But this unusual man took her by the arm and led her to the terrace coffee bar at the foot of the towering Rockefeller Centre. Snapping his fingers he helped her into a chair while a waiter appeared at the table, pen in hand.

"You've had a shock – some coffee?" he said, and Arabella nodded. His voice was soft and strong at the same time, commanding yet concerned and gentle.

Finding her voice at last Arabella said, "I'm fine, really; thank you so much for helping me – not many people would trouble themselves these days."

"It was no trouble at all, for such a beautiful lady." Far from sounding corny, Arabella thought his words, which spoken by anyone else would have had her lip curling in derision, sounded as sincere, genuine and unique as he was himself. Arabella felt herself blushing. When had she last blushed? She felt like one of those silly girls she had met in the boutique earlier. Why was she blushing? Hadn't she decided that she preferred girls to boys? The tremor she felt in the pit of her stomach gave the lie to that. Arabella was confused and felt more vulnerable than she had ever felt. Her rescuer was still holding her gaze with his unblinking stare. She could not seem to pull her eyes away from his and it seemed as though unspoken messages were passing between them. He smiled gently, taking one of her gloved hands in his, perfectly manicured, strong and the lightest of browns, Arabella could not pull her hand away.

For some time they sat together, while several stories above them Marjorie Hillman looked at her watch for the fifteenth time. Arabella was late; even for her, the stuck-up bitch, she was late. When Marjorie gave up waiting a few minutes later and took the elevator down to the street she walked past her friend, sitting hand in hand with a man on the terrace at the foot of the Centre; in fact Marjorie glanced at the bags that were beside Arabella, even cast a cursory glance at her friend but she did not recognise her. In those moments outside the Rockefeller Centre as Arabella sat hand in hand with a man that she did not know, even her mother would have had trouble identifying her. The woman who gazed into the eyes of the dusky skinned man had an expression on her face that no one that knew her would have recognised. Managing even to defy the botox, the soft and vulnerable, even girlish smile on Arabella's face was a million miles away from her usual set sneering expression, and it changed her completely.

Walking back up the street towards Arabella and her rescuer, the boy in a hood counted out fifty dollars, smiling to himself. Easy money. He saw the woman that he had taken the bags from and the man who had paid him to do it sitting outside the Rockefeller Centre. They were staring at each other like a couple of shmucks from a movie and neither noticed him. Stuffing the money into his pocket, the boy smiled to himself.

As they sipped the coffee that arrived steaming at their table, Arabella felt she wanted to speak, to ask him who he was, anything, everything; but somehow the words would not come. The silence between them was full of charged energy yet neither of them felt the need to break it. It was almost as though breaking the silence would kill the magic. People came and went around them. The sun moved across the sky and shadows became longer as they sat.

Finally in a low and compelling voice he began to speak. He spoke of many things, none of them personal yet all of them so intimate that Arabella began to feel breathless. Nothing of what he said needed an answer from her and all of what he said made perfect sense to her. As she drank in every nuance of his expression and his face, explored the depths of his eyes and watched the fluid movement of his lips Arabella wondered if somehow he was putting her under some sort of a trance. She had never felt so exposed, although apart from the light pressure on her hand by his he had made no move towards her physically and she felt completely safe with him, safe, protected and treasured, as though they were the only two people in the world. She wondered if he had put something in her coffee until she looked down at her cup and found that apart from one or two sips her cup was almost full and now cold.

"My name is Arabella." The man put his fingers to her lips to stop her before she could say her surname.

"Arabella is enough, no more," he said. She felt that she was telling him something he already knew but he did not offer his name. As the sun dipped behind the towering New York skyline Arabella shivered and a waiter leapt forward to light a patio heater. As the warmth spread over them she had the first realisation that this time would have to end. Until that realisation she had not really thought about how or when their time would end and it did not seem necessary to ask when they would see each other again, or where that meeting would be. It was almost as though they were two components of a larger entity like and arm and a leg. Barring serious calamity, they would always be moving in the same sphere, always be working together for the greater good of their entity, always be united by tissue, bone and blood.

As they stood and he hailed a cab she said nothing. But as she got into the cab she looked over her shoulder.

"Your name. I must know your name."

He smiled a small smile. "Sharif."

* * *

As Arabella made her way home in New York, her son was lying on his bed, his hands behind his head. If he shut his eyes he could still see Leila's face, and the dark tendril of hair that kept escaping each time she tucked it back into her hijab. It was an unconscious gesture, and one that she had doubtless done many times before, but to Eddie it was mesmerising. They had shaken hands very briefly as they arrived at the library that day and the softness of her palm had etched itself on his memory. Maybe it was because, he thought, that was as much of her smooth coffee-coloured skin as he was ever likely to touch. He frowned. What was wrong with him? He never normally had difficulty in speculating about the flesh of any girl he fancied, but somehow this was different. He drew in his breath sharply, there it was again – the feeling, not entirely pleasant, a feeling that he was at the edge of something momentous, but something that had the potential to wound him deeply. He shook his head slightly. In the room beyond his closed door he could hear his friends laughing and talking and he put his iPod's earphones in; he didn't want them disturbing his reverie.

He thought back to the time that they had had in the library. If truth be told Leila had already worked out pretty comprehensively what they would do with the project. But despite the fact that normally anyone doing his work for him would have been thanked and the project promptly forgotten about, Eddie found himself interested in the outline she had put together for the project. They went over it together and he found himself listening intently as her soft voice, filled with passion for the subject, seemed to imprint her words on his brain. He found himself asking questions, and taking heed of the answers, until he felt an urgency to keep learning. Once they had exhausted the still rudimentary outline of the project, he found himself asking more questions. Leila looked pleased but slightly confused at his enthusiasm and closing the folder with the project in she began to talk to him directly. Her hands folded in her lap, only moving to tuck in that stray lock of hair from time to time, she began to talk to him about the subject of one of Amir Ali's lectures.

"Mudarabah," she said, and Eddie attempted to repeat the word. When she was satisfied with his pronunciation she moved on. "Mudarabah is a partnership where the investment comes from the first partner, 'rabb-ul-mal', and the management and work is the responsibility of the second, 'mudarib'." She looked at him with raised eyebrows and he nodded, signifying that he had understood. He repeated the words and she went on. "We can summarize the points like this." Leila held up one hand, and bent over one finger. "In musharakah, investment comes from all partners, but in Mudarabah, investment is the responsibility of the rabb-ul-mal." Pushing the second finger into her palm she said. "In musharakah, all partners participate in the management, but in Mudarabah, the mudarib alone conducts the management." A third finger. "All partners in musharakah share the loss to the extent of their ratio of investment, but in mudarabah the loss is suffered by the rabb-ul-mal only as he is the sole investor. However, if the mudarib has been negligent, he will suffer the loss." Eddie nodded and she pushed down a fourth finger. "The partners' liability in musharakah is unlimited. In mudarabah the liability of the rabb-ul-mal is limited to his investment, unless he has permitted the mudarib to incur debts on his behalf." Eddie found himself taking notes as she pushed her thumb in to hr palm. "In musharakah, the assets, once mixed in a joint pool, become jointly owned by them according to the proportion of investment. In mudarabah all goods purchased by the mudarib are solely owned by the rabb-ul-mal. The mudarib can earn his share in the profit should he sell the goods profitably. He is not entitled to claim his share of the assets." She paused and Eddie, stumbling sometimes over the unfamiliar words, repeated the gist of what she had told him. Leila clapped her hands together softly. "Yes, yes, that's right! I am so pleased that you find it so interesting!" Eddie might have said it was her that he found interesting, and it was true he did, but something in the message in the unfamiliar words and in the concept was captivating him and he asked her to go on.

"Restricted Mudarabah, known as al-mudarabah al-muqayyadah, is when the rabb-ul-mal specifies a particular business for the mudarib to invest the money in. Unrestricted mudarabah, or al-mudarabah al-mutlaqah, is when it is open for the mudarib to undertake whichever business he wishes."

Eddie wrote a few notes, but he found that his mind was opening to the message and to the unfamiliar language; he felt almost as though he was a blind man suddenly able to see. Leila could see the enthusiasm in his face and continued, her voice tinged with excitement, the excitement of imparting a dearly loved message to a willing audience.

"In cases where the rabb-ul-mal contracts mudarabah with more than one person through a single transaction, the mudarib shall run the business as if they were partners. The distribution of profit must be agreed upon at the beginning of the contract. The mudarib cannot claim any periodical salary, fee or remuneration for the work done by him for the mudarabah. This is agreed by most schools of Islamic Fiqh, however Imam Ahmad has allowed for the mudarib to withdraw his daily expenses of food from the mudarabah account. The Hanafi jurists restrict this right of the mudarib only to a situation when he is on a business trip outside his city. Any profit will first be used to offset any loss, and the rest will be distributed according to the ratio."

Eddie was nodding slowly, such was his immersion in this new and fascinating information that he felt almost as though he already knew what Leila was saying, that he was merely being refreshed in a long understood principle. Without encouragement this time, Leila continued. "Next, let me tell you about combining musharakah and Mudarabah. The two systems may be combined in order for the mudarib to contribute some money into the business. In this, the mudarib may allocate for himself a certain percentage of profit on account of his investment as a sharik, and allocate another percentage for his management and work as a mudarib. The normal basis for allocation of the profit in the above example would be that B shall secure one third of the actual profit on account of his investment, and the remaining two thirds of the profit shall be distributed among them equally. However, the parties may agree on any other proportion. The one condition is that the sleeping partner should not get a larger percentage than the proportion of his investment. Do you understand?"

To his amazement Eddie found he did. He nodded. "Go on, please," he said.

"Okay." Leila smiled shyly. "In the Islamic Fiqh it

is not seen that the partners may leave and join the enterprise and not affect the continuity of the business. However, these were written before the modern age of large-scale commercial enterprises. This does not mean however that musharakah and mudarabah cannot be used for a running business. If the basic principles are followed their application may be varied as follows." Up came the hand with the fingers extended again, "One," Leila said; "Financing through musharakah and mudarabah participation in the business, and in musharakah sharing in the assets of the business to the extent of the ratio of financing. Two." Leila bent another finger into her palm. "An investor must share the loss incurred by the business to the extent of his financing. Three, The partners determine the ratio of profit; and four, the loss suffered by each partner must be exactly in proportion to his investment." This time hr thumb was not needed and she used it to tuck her stray lock of hair back into her hijab.

For a while they talked about what Leila had been saying and she was pleased and surprised to find how much Eddie had taken in; he even seemed to be getting the hang of the Arabic words. Leila felt her heart beat faster. Firstly, the part of her that wanted to be a teacher was exhilarated that her message was being so well received by her pupil and secondly, well she did not want to think to much about the other reason for her excitement, the nearness of this young man with his earnest blue eyes and open mind made her feel things that she had never felt before, that she should not feel until she was married. She carried on hastily.

"Okay, Eddie." Eddie smiled; he loved the way she

said his name. "Musharakah securitization. So, in the case of big projects where huge amounts are required, every subscriber is given a musharakah certificate, which represents his proportionate ownership of the assets. After the project has started, these certificates can be bought and sold in the secondary market, but not when all the assets are liquid. When there is a combination of liquid and non-liquid assets, it cannot be sold unless the non-liquid part of the business is separated and is sold independently. However, the Hanafi school asserts that whenever there is a combination of liquid and non-liquid assets it can be sold and purchased for an amount greater than the amount of liquid assets. For example, a Musharakah project contains 40 per cent non-liquid assets i.e. machinery, fixtures etc. and 60 per cent liquid assets, i.e. cash and receivables. Each musharakah certificate having the face value of 100 riyals represents 60 riyals-worth of liquid assets and 40 riyals-worth of non-liquid assets. This certificate may be sold at any price more than 60 riyals. If it is sold at 110 riyals it will mean that 60 riyals of the price is against 60 riyals contained in the certificate and 50 riyals is against the proportionate share in the non-liquid assets. But it will never be allowed to sell the certificate for a price of 60 riyals or less, because in the case of 60 riyals it will not set off the amount of 60 riyals."

Eddie was making notes again and Leila paused to let him catch up. "So lastly we will talk about single transaction financing." Eddie nodded, and caught her eyes before she quickly lowered them. "Musharakah and mudarabah can be employed for financing imports and exports. For exporting, musharakah will be easier to use. Since the price of the goods to be exported is known beforehand, the financier can calculate his profit. There may be a condition to secure the financier from any exporter negligence. The condition would be that it is the responsibility of the exporter to export the goods in conformity with the conditions of the letter of credit, and the exporter would be liable for any discrepancies. On the basis of musharakah or mudarabah, an importer can approach a financier. If the letter of credit has been opened without any margin the form of mudarabah is used, and if the letter of credit is opened with some margin, the form of musharakah is used, or a combination of both. The importer and financier, according to a pre-agreed ratio, might share the sale proceeds. The musharakah can be restricted to an agreed term, and the importer may purchase the financier's share if the goods are not sold in the market before expiry. However, this price would be at the current market value, and not at a pre-agreed price."

Eddie looked at her, his eyebrow raised in expectation and Leila laughed. "I think that is enough for one day – my throat is dry and I think your brain might explode with any more information!" Eddie laughed at her little joke and went to get her some water in a little plastic cup from the water cooler. As she sipped it he watched her; her lovely face was flushed from the effort of talking to him for so long and from delivering her message with such passion and conviction. But there was something more to this lovely girl than the usual standards that he used to measure female suitability. There was something precious and fragile that made him want to protect her and keep her safe from everyone and anything that might hurt her. Now as he lay on his bed thinking about their afternoon together he realized that the biggest threat to her might well be him. The feeling of unease that seemed to be haunting him made him close his eyes tight, as though he was trying to blot the world out.

In her room Leila awoke from a nap that, exhausted, she had, fallen into as soon as she had returned from the library to the same feeling of unease. Her problems were more clearly recognizable, like her moral parameters, but her heart was warning her that trouble lay ahead. But the smile that played on her lips as she thought of her afternoon with Eddie shooed away any such negative thoughts, for the time being.

Chapter Ten

In New York, while his son and his wife were suffering in varying degrees from the emotional hand grenades that had been thrown into their lives, Edward was waiting in the Stardust café for his meeting. He hated to admit it but his stomach was churning. The episode with the explosive on his private jet was still fresh in his mind and he had no doubt that his mysterious acquaintance was behind it.

He almost did not recognise Sharif as he came into the Stardust. Edward had tied the belt of his raincoat tight around his waist to disguise the suit that he wore underneath it, a suit that looked out of place here amongst the tourists and less elite of New York's population. Sharif however had on a suit that would rival any Edward had in his wardrobe, with a coat that Edward knew was from Hermes draped around his shoulders. He looked totally different, taller some how, more tailored, his hair short and tidy, his hands manicured with an expensive looking platinum ring on his finger and a Rolex on his wrist. A waft of aftershave, the same as one that Edward wore, wafted ahead of him as he came to the table. It was all Edward could do to stop his mouth dropping open in surprise. He felt his heartburn bubble up in his throat. His money was paying for this, his money! He hated Sharif more than he could say, but he feared him as well.

Sharif gave a little bow, holding his right hand over his heart for an instant as he sat down, and Edward clenched his teeth. He was afraid of this man, the only time in his life that he could remember being afraid of someone. He knew how much damage Sharif could do to him and he hated being so vulnerable.

"Your family?" Edward said stiffly and Sharif nodded muttering under his breath Al ham d'Allah, God be praised.

He fixed Edward with his intense and fathomless dark eyes and said "Yours?" Edward was about to reply when he noticed the smallest twitch at the corner of Sharif's mouth, and for the second time in this man's company he felt a cold hand squeeze his intestines. His first thought was for Eddie; he knew immediately that Sharif would be aware of every member of his family, who they were and where they were. The thought terrified him. But Sharif said nothing and looked at him with an eyebrow raised, waiting for an answer.

"Fine; they are fine." Edward hated the strained sound of his own voice. Hell, he had held his own in some of the most important meetings in world finance, facing other multi-billion-dollar bankers, usually emerging victorious with Lancaster a few million dollars the richer.

"Now look," Edward hissed through clenched teeth. "I know about the plane; I don't appreciate being intimidated – I am a very powerful man, and right now I am a very angry man!" Sharif was looking at his manicured hands placed face down on the table between them.

"And yet," Sharif said softly, "powerful or not, you seem to be very frightened, almost like a young boy."

Sharif placed an emphasis on the last word of the sentence and Edward knew immediately that he was referring to Eddie, and his stomach clenched again.

"How dare you?" he hissed again, his own hands shaking, itching to hit the man in front of him to wipe the smirk off his self-satisfied face.

"What have I said?" Sharif was playing with him now, feigning surprise and raising his hands palms up, in a gesture that showed him to be innocent. Edward could take it no more. He got up from the booth and left, slamming the door of the diner behind him.

Alone in the booth, Sharif smiled.

In the noisy departure lounge of Heathrow airport, Amir Ali sat opposite his friend, Anwar Al Mansour before they caught their respective flights.

"Tell me, old friend, how was Leila? Did you manage to spend much time with her?" Amir smiled to himself; he was a father too and knew how much it meant to have news of a child that was separated from you.

"She was fine – better than fine – doing very well with her studies and very well thought of within the faculty."

"How about her friends – has she made many friends?" Amir hesitated for a moment and his friend picked up on his reticence.

"What, Amir? Tell me, I know there is something – please do not torture me."

Amir patted his friend's hand.

"Calm down, Anwar. It is nothing really, she has been paired with a young lad from a very good family to do a project and I just, well, I just warned her to be careful."

"Why did you warn her? What has happened? What do you know? Is she in danger?"

Amir laughed now. "Anwar, have you not raised your daughter to be a good Moslem girl? Do you have any doubt that she would be true to herself and to you and Maysoon?"

"No, of course not, but ..."

"But nothing. I just warned her to be wary, but she was ahead of me as she is in most things; I have no worries about her, and neither should you. I should never have brought it up – I am sorry, Anwar."

"No; you did right and thank you so much for being so caring of our child."

On his flight to Egypt, Amir sat by the window. He had reassured his friend about Leila but somehow the thought of her and Eddie Lancaster still preyed on his mind. It was something in his look or her glance, some unconscious body language, something that maybe no one else would notice, and most certainly no one else would be concerned about, but it was something, nevertheless, something that did not sit easy with him. Amir thought about his own children, how dear to him they were, how they were his heart, his life, and he knew that he had somehow to look out for this most precious child of his friend. He, like her father, trusted Leila implicitly but it was true that she did not have the experience of Western girls, and it was true that she faced many challenges as she tried to fit in and to study against all the distractions that she now faced in her life at Harvard.

His own sons Yousef and Adam would finish university soon and make their own way in the world. His girls still had some time to go, but he knew that the day would come when he had the same worries as Anwar. He smiled and moved gingerly in his seat, his old injuries were playing up, but the thoughts of his lovely daughters kept the smile playing around his lips.

* * *

The first thing that popped into Eddie's mind the next morning was Leila. He felt at once exhilarated and then hot on the heels of his unbridled joy came that inexplicable sense of impending doom, not something that he had experienced before in his dealings with women. He tried to shake it off and a cold shower and vigorous run before breakfast almost did the trick. But the strangest thing was that he could not get the thought of what they had studied out of his mind either. His mind was working overtime, trying to understand the concepts, or at least what their flaw was and to compare them to the system that he had be born into. The word "fair" kept occurring to him and there was no doubt that the Islamic system was fair, it was equitable and it was, it seemed, confined to Islamic countries in the main. His knowledge of the Western banking system was not comprehensive by any means but he could not help seeing that it favoured the brave or the fortunate who, like him, were born into it. He picked up his speed for the last half-mile of his run, hoping to clear his fevered mind of the jumble of thoughts that invaded it.

He had just stepped out of the shower for the second time that day when his phone rang.

"Hey, Dad!" Eddie was pleased to hear his father's voice.

"Good morning, Eddie; how are things going?" Eddie thought his father's voice sounded tense.

"Great, but Dad, I wanted to ask you something. I'm doing a project here at school on Islamic finance—" Was that a sharp intake of breath from his father? Eddie continued. "D'you know anything about it, dad?"

There was a long pause, and then his father's voice, sounding tense, said, "Why, who has put you up to this?"

Eddie laughed "Woah, dad; I said I was studying Islamic finance, not the devil – chill!" Edward laughed a short strained noise that was completely unconvincing.

"Sorry son, I've been under a lot of pressure; yes I know something about it, but it's not really relevant to what we do here in the West – what the hell are they teaching you at Harvard? Studying Islamic finance seems like a waste of time to me!"

"No, it's really interesting, there's this girl that I'm doing the project with, she explains it really well." Edward's shoulders relaxed and he smiled with relief. He knew his playboy son of old, if there was a girl involved even studying a house brick would be fascinating.

"Yes, well, keep your mind on your work. See you soon, son." And he was gone.

But as he took his seat in his office that cold autumn morning Edward thought again about his meeting with Sharif the night before. Could he possibly have infiltrated Harvard? Could he have planted someone there to get at Eddie. Of course he could; the man had strapped a bomb to his private jet! He had a meeting with Eugene this morning, the first one since he had come to realise that Sharif had "got to him". He sighed; he felt uneasy, even a bit frightened and it was taking its toll. His blood pressure was up and he wasn't sleeping and he had almost constant heartburn. As he took two more Maalox, there was a tap on the door. It was Eugene, armed with several files that represented Lancaster's charitable causes.

"Good morning, Mr Lancaster." Eugene sat down at the opposite side of Edward's desk, spreading his files out in front of him.

"Good morning, Eugene." Edward studied the man's face for signs of discomfort but the older man's face was placid and apart from occasionally pushing his glasses up the bridge of his nose, he gave no sign of nervousness.

They started the discussion with a couple of the usual suspects. This was an area of the bank's finances that Edward handled alone, free of meetings and consultations with other bank staff. The amounts for the donations were meant to be reasonably small in relation to the bank's overall holdings and profits and as the two men studied the first two medical research charities they agreed that their overall funding for the next quarter would increase by only half of one per cent. The next charity, an environmental charity, had recently been in the news for misleading the public on climate change research findings.

Edward sighed; he was finding it difficult to concentrate with the elephant in the room. "Half of one per cent," he said, perfunctorily. Eugene cleared his throat and pushed his glasses up on the bridge of his nose. He had a clipping for the New York Times outlining the criticisms that had been levelled at the charity. Edward looked at it half-heartedly but Eugene argued forcibly that no increase should be made this quarter until more was known about the irregularities with the charity. "Fine, no increase," Edward said.

The ten charities that at any one time benefited from Lancaster Bank funding enjoyed roughly the same amount of donation, around half a million dollars a year. The rest of the increases were decided upon and Eugene scribbled Edward's instructions on the notepad he had brought with him to the meeting. Finally the Middle East War Orphans Fund folder reached the top of the pile. The file was thin. No letters from grateful charity commissions, no brochures showing the work that was being done, no hand-written letters from grateful orphans enjoying a better life because of Lancaster's Bank. Just the charity donation forms and tax notations made by Eugene over the years that the "charity" had been with the bank.

For a long time the men were silent, Eugene fingering the flimsy sheets in the Middle East War Orphans Fund file and Edward drawing recurring interlinked figures of eight on his jotter. Eventually Eugene cleared his throat, pulling Edward out of his daydream.

"How much is the annual donation at the moment, Eugene?" Edward did not look up as he spoke, continuing his doodle, the pencil marks making deep grooves in the paper of the jotter pad.

"Five million," Eugene said.

"Double it," Edward said as the pencil he had been using to make his interlinked eights snapped.

Eugene nodded, his face impassive and wrote × 2 on the corner of the uppermost paper in the file.

* * *

At the first lecture of the day in Harvard, Eddie sat with his friend and tried to concentrate on the subject: hedge funds. To his right and nearer the back of the lecture hall Leila sat, the lock of hair that she was always tucking back into her hijab enjoying a brief moment of freedom before her had came up to tuck it away again. Eddie felt an overwhelming tenderness towards this vulnerable girl, this girl who was so clever yet so modest, so gentle, so determined, and so beautiful that it literally made his stomach flip. Following his gaze his friend dug him in the ribs and whispered: "Any luck with Miss Frigid? Jeez, Ed, God knows how many willing bits of skirt there are here, and you pick on the one with iron clad knickers!" Eddie tried to smile, aware of how important it was that he maintain his jock image. He thanked God they were in a lecture so his shrug was response enough. Inside though the insult to Leila cut him to the quick. He tried to control the feeling of anger, of hostility even that he felt towards his friend with whom he would have had a good laugh over this just 48 hours previously. God, what had happened to him? It was simple. Leila had happened.

* * *

In his office, in the silence, Edward swivelled his chair towards the picture window from which he could survey the skyline of New York. The Maalox he had taken was not working; he felt a rage like none that he had ever felt well up inside him. He felt sick, helpless, and afraid. And he felt the deepest sense of foreboding he had ever felt. He knew that there was nothing he could do. He had no idea where or when he would see Sharif again, how or when this nightmare would end. His mind went over the conversation he had had with his son that morning. The nagging cold fingers that squeezed his intestines with a grim regularity squeezed again as he tried to imagine how and when Sharif had infiltrated his life to this extent. Had he planted the girl? Even the most cursory private eye would have been able to point out to Sharif the Lancaster men's weakness for tail. Had he used that knowledge? Had he used a private eye? What did he know about Eddie, about himself, even about Arabella? Edward dismissed this last thought. The cold fish that was his wife hated foreigners, was wildly prejudiced and as cold as ice. Sharif would get no purchase there. Despite his misery, Edward smiled thinly as he imagined his wife's reaction to the very obviously Middle Eastern Sharif. She would try her best to keep that stiff upper lip that the British were famous for from curling. She might even succeed! No, thankfully, he was not worried in that quarter.

As he turned his thoughts again to Sharif and anything that he might be able to remember from their meetings that would give him a lead to who he was and what his plan was, Sharif himself was bringing Arabella to orgasm; the first she had experienced in her life.

Chapter Eleven

Lying in his bed in the early morning at home in New York, Eddie was counting the weeks, days and hours till he would return to Harvard. Usually he enjoyed the holidays – Christmas was his favourite time of year, but not this year. His first term at Harvard had gone by in a flash, and leaving Leila to spend the festive season with his parents had seemed like a torture. He and Leila were close now, even with their project complete and forwarded to Amir Ali, the pair met often, and each time he asked to meet again Eddie would find himself holding his breath, afraid that this time she would look at him quizzically with those lovely dark eyes and that shy smile that she had and ask why. Why did they need to meet again with their work complete? So far she never had but Eddie found himself tortured day and night with the thought that over the holidays, that she was spending with her family in Saudi Arabia, she would forget all about him, about their friendship, because however much it was killing him, that is all that it could be called, a friendship; they had never even held hands!

Eddie pulled his pillow over his face and screamed into it. The frustration was torturing him, the need to take this relationship to the next step, hell, just to be able to call it a relationship was giving him sleepless nights and restless days. Of course he would love a physical relationship with Leila – he wasn't dead – but somehow that seemed less important to him now. What was important was that in some way she should be his forever. If it was only as a friend then he would accept that, but he wanted so much more. He wanted to be the one she turned to for comfort, for inspiration and for love, he wanted to make her proud and to provide for everything she needed. He wanted to protect her, to share everything that life had in store, with her. To be there on her high days and her low ones.

Eddie was in love.

The realisation had hit him hard. It had taken its toll on his social life at Harvard, although his grades had improved as a result, so that was something, and he couldn't really say that he missed horsing around with the guys. It was as though someone had hit him with a sensible stick and overnight he had turned into someone who was aiming for more in life than drinking, womanising and playing the fool. He was even finding his studies interesting. But the thing that interested him most was the time he and Leila spent talking about Islamic finance. As he understood more, Eddie found himself questioning more, he wanted to find time with his father to discuss what he had learned, although he knew he would have to tread carefully, his father seemed surprisingly hostile to any mention of anything Islamic. In fact both his parents had appeared to be preoccupied since he had come back. His mother was like a cat on hot bricks, jumping each time he came into a room and distracted to the point of being totally absent most of the time. She looked flushed a lot of the time, and had a strange hard brightness to her eyes, whenever she met his, which wasn't often.

Eddie felt sorry for his parents. He knew what love felt like now and could imagine what a life of bliss he could have with Leila. That his parents were denied that, living in their sterile, loveless marriage saddened him. His father was tense but that was not unusual and Eddie was aware that the world seemed to be teetering on the brink of some sort of global financial disaster that his father would be in the thick of. Leila and he had talked about it, the sub-prime lending problems that were beginning to give rise to concern, a subject they had recently covered in lectures. It looked like if this problem was not tackled, the ripples from the boulder thrown into that particular pond might spread far and wide and affect almost every country in the world. Their assignment had been to suggest ways in which this problem could be dealt with.

Eddie remembered their last meeting, when they had sat together in the library, the light fading outside, and he had looked at her and said, "This couldn't happen within Islamic financing, could it?"

"No," she had said quietly, "it couldn't." Not for the first time Eddie wondered why more attention had not been paid to a system that seemed to have all the answers. The problem was, he thought, no one was asking the question.

It was the last time that they met before the term ended and Eddie found himself eager to know more, to make notes that he could look back over when he was at home. He was aware that at the beginning of their friendship she had thought he was only showing an interest in Islamic finance to be close to her, but as his interest had grown, so had her confidence until now she shared the knowledge she had with an unconfined passion, confident in her student's genuine interest.

"You could take musharakah financing and objections to this as an example of what is going on in America at the moment," Leila said. This is how musharakah deals with the risk of loss." Eddie sat poised with his pen hovering over the paper. "In fact," Leila continued, "the arrangement of musharakah is sometimes seen as more likely to pass on losses of the business to the financier bank or institution, and to the depositors. In this case, investors will not want to deposit their money, and savings will remain idle. However, this misgiving is not entirely justified. The banks study the potential of the business and if they form the view that the business is not profitable, they refuse to advance a loan." Leila paused.

"Not like the sub-prime sector that lends against, well, nothing!" Eddie said and Leila nodded.

"No bank can restrict itself to a single musharakah. The profitable musharakah are expected to give more return than interest-based loans because the actual profit is supposed to be distributed between the client and the bank, and so the musharakah is not expected to make a loss. The theoretical loss is much less than the possibility of loss in a joint stock company whose business is restricted to a limited sector or commercial activities. Also, any possible loss in one musharakah will be compensated by the profits earned in other musharakah." Leila paused so that Eddie could keep up with her. When he had she continued. "Of course, it is always possible that dishonest clients may exploit musharakah by not paying any return to the financiers. To overcome this, a well-designed system of auditing should be implemented whereby accounts of all clients are maintained and controlled. If profits were calculated on gross profits, the possibility of disputes would be minimized. If misconduct is established, the client will be deprived of using any facility in any bank in the country. This will serve as a deterrent. The banks also cannot afford to show artificial losses. Another perceived failure is that Islamic banks work in isolation of conventional banks, and thus do not receive much support from central governments." Leila smiled at Eddie, his face a study in concentration. "Another possibility is that the financier who is made a partner in the business of the client may disclose the secrets of the business to the traders. To solve this, the client may put a condition in the musharakah that the financier will not interfere with the management affairs, and will not disclose any information about the business."

Eddie nodded for her to continue. "As with all affairs that concern money," Leila said, "clients are often not willing to share with the banks the actual profits of their business. This may be for two reasons: they might think that the bank has no right to share in the actual profit, because the bank has nothing to do with the management or running of the business, and they question why they should share the fruit of their labour with the bank that provides funds. The client might also argue that conventional banks are content with a meagre rate of interest and so should be the Islamic Banks." Leila looked up as Eddie smiled at her, urging her on. "Another reason may be that the client is afraid to reveal their true profits to the banks. In case the information is passed on to the tax authorities and clients' tax liability increases."

Eddie nodded. This was familiar territory – dodging tax

liability was a whole industry in America. Leila continued. "This is another form of musharakah, in which a financier and client participate in a joint commercial enterprise, shirkat-al-milk. The purpose of diminishing musharakah is for the financier to get his money back in a specified period. The financier's share is divided into units, to be purchased by the client until he is the sole owner. This has mostly been used in house financing. In this example, the financier acquires rent according to the proportion of his ownership in the property, and as the client periodically purchases each portion, the rent goes down.

"The following conditions are composed for the house financing arrangement: The agreement of joint purchase, leasing and selling different units of the share of the financier should not be tied up together in one single contract. However, the joint purchase and the contract of lease may be joined in one document whereby the financier agrees to lease his share, after joint purchase to the client. This is allowed through ijarah.

"At the time of purchase of each unit, sale must be affected by the exchange of offer and acceptance at that particular date. The purchase of different units by the client is affected based on the market value of the house as prevalent on the date of purchase of that unit. It is also permissible that a particular price is agreed in the promise of purchase signed by the client. Diminishing musharakah can also be used for a service business and trade."

Eddie could almost hear the last words that she had said in their last session on Islamic finance, delivered in her clear quite tone, somehow making even the most dry of subjects come alive with her passion for it. Now that she was on the other side of the world he would give anything to hear her voice again, to be able to talk to her, as had been their habit for every day of the term since their first meeting in the Islamic library. He had thought of and rejected a hundred reasons for calling her. He could not; he knew that it would cause a lot of speculation by her family and he knew she was not ready for that. He knew that she loved her religion and was a devoted Moslem. He had even gone so far as to look up on the Internet what the form was for a Moslem marrying outside the faith. There was provision for it but somehow he knew that Leila would not be availing herself of it.

Talking of marriage he thought about the wedding he was attending that afternoon. Harry Masters was marrying the twin that he had knocked up in the hot-tub that night in Miami that seemed a lifetime ago. Poor sod; it was a high price to pay for your first night of passion. He had seen Harry and 'the twin' – he never could remember which one it was – when he had got back from college. She looked like she had swallowed a basketball, she had thick ankles and puffy arms and his heart had gone out to his friend. He thought about the experiences he had had at Harvard, the fun with the guys, admittedly not so much recently, but still, Harry would have loved it. Why the hell he had had to drop out Eddie had no idea. Old man Masters could have bankrolled the whole thing, but Harry had been tight lipped as to why he had not come to Harvard and Eddie was too preoccupied with Leila to press him. He wanted to talk to someone and had thought that might be Harry but Harry was busy fawning over the beached whale that was soon to be his wife and Eddie kept his thoughts to himself.

a tender power

*** *

At the wedding the Masters family were pretty boot faced, the Jessens' less so. Sandy-or-was-it-Suzi looked a bit better with her legs and arms covered by an expansive gown that puffed out like one of those old fashions toilet roll holders that your grandmother had in her restroom, and Harry looked nervous, his Adam's apple bobbing up and down in his scrawny neck. Eddie felt a pang of sorrow for his friend. He looked so young – he *was* so young – and to be saddled with a wife and a baby at his age. He sighed to himself; who was he kidding? He would take that deal in a heartbeat if he could marry Leila. Beside him his mother was sitting staring into space, that faraway look in her eyes that had become so common this holiday.

Arabella's mind was a whirl. She smoothed her dress down compulsively. She could not stop thinking about Sharif. The man was in her mind from the moment she woke up until she went to sleep. He had coaxed her body to experience things that she had never thought herself capable of and now like a junkie that can't get hold of a fix she was twitchy. How could she ever have thought that she could prefer the softness and yielding of a woman's body to the hard strength of a man's? Casting a sideways look at her husband, Arabella supposed that it very much depended on the man. It had been 48 hours since she had last been with Sharif and her spine tingled with the memory of it, the smell of him, the gentle power in his hands, the depths of his eyes.

She let out a little moan and Eddie said, "You alright, Ma?" Normally Arabella would have chastised Eddie for using the hated diminutive Ma. How many times had she asked him to call her Mother? Much more becoming; they weren't hillbillies, after all.

Embarrassed that she had let the sound escape her, Arabella nodded. "Just a bit of a headache." On her other side Edward looked at his wife quizzically; he had been watching her, deep in thought, and he had recognised the sound that had escaped her lips, not that he had ever heard it from her lips before, but he had had a couple of afternoon sessions with Linda recently to try and relax him and that noise had been a feature of both. Could it be that Arabella was seeing someone? Edward doubted it. A cold fish like her? But still, that noise, he knew he wasn't mistaken.

As the organ started up Edward, Arabella and Eddie got to their feet as the newly married couple swept past them. Eddie looked towards the seat that his friend had occupied so nervously before the ceremony started. A boy he didn't even know had been Harry's best man and that had hurt Eddie, even though he had made no secret of the fact that he disapproved of his friend's decision to marry.

Eddie got more or less blitzed at the reception and so did his father. That is probably why neither of them noticed Arabella slipping out of the Waldorf Astoria's banqueting lounge and into an elevator, a crumpled piece of paper in her hand. As she walked down the deep carpeting of the 7th floor looking for the room number that was on the paper, her breathing came fast and her mouth was dry. She was so nervous, she could barely walk; every pore and every overstimulated nerve in her body was screaming out for the only touch that could quiet them. As she finally identified the door that she needed she raised a trembling hand to knock, only to find that the door was ajar. Barely able to stand she held onto the door as it opened. On the opulent bed inside Sharif lay, completely naked, a smile playing around his lips and his readiness to pleasure her evident. Kicking the door shut behind her, Arabella ran to the bed and collapsed beside him, her mouth seeking his for that first longed-for kiss that would lead on to pleasure that she could only ever have dreamed of. As he helped her out of her clothes, Sharif smiled to himself. He liked the thought of making love to Arabella while a few stories below them Edward sat unaware that his old adversary was succeeding where he had so obviously failed. As he held her trembling body to him Sharif smiled again. Yes, his plan was coming together very well – very well indeed.

In the same hotel a few floors higher, Harry and Sandy Masters were spending their first night together as man and wife, he on the large chaise longue in the bridal suite and she on the bed, complaining bitterly of how much her back was aching. Harry felt sorry that he not had more time to talk to Eddie that day but his friend had that pitying look in his eye and Harry knew that whatever it was that had once made them close was now lost forever. He would be happy with Sandy, they would have a lovely baby and maybe more babies in the future, although Sandy was having such a tough time with this pregnancy that Harry doubted he would ever get to make love to her again. As he pulled the counterpane that Sandy had allowed him from the bed around him, Harry closed his eyes and a single tear rolled down his youthful face onto the brocade cushion he was using for a pillow.

* * *

In Riyadh, Leila sat in the courtyard of her home, her face lifted towards the sun. The weather was lovely at this time of the year, warm sun by day and by night there were cold cosy nights in front of the big open fire her father had put in to their villa. It was a rarity, as was the chimney that rose from the roof of their villa. It was really quiet seldom needed but nights in December could be cold and the sight of the flames dancing in the grate cheered them all.

Her parents had been delighted to see her and the endless visits from relatives all wanting to know how she was doing had all but worn her out. Now, however, she had satisfied the curiosity of all her aunts, uncles, cousins and grandparents and was looking forward to spending time with her friends who had also returned to Riyadh from far-flung seats of learning all over the globe. But there was a problem. However involved she got with the visits, with the telling over and over again, of what it was like at Harvard, of the people she had met the sights she had seen, there was one person that she did not mention and that person occupied her every waking moment, and even peeped through the most involved descriptions she was giving, his face popping into her mind and making her falter in the tale she was telling.

"Listen to her," he aunt had said; "she is so excited by all she has seen and done she is stumbling over her words. It's marvellous, Maysoon; you have a wonderful daughter, she is doing so well." Leila had to smile to herself; if only they knew that her lack of concentration was not to do with her excitement, or at least not in the way that they thought, but she could not share her thoughts, not with anyone. Although she had done nothing wrong, she knew how easily she could, if she weakened, and it frightened her.

Now sitting in the courtyard with the sun on her upturned face and her hair cascading over her shoulders, she could indulge in her daydreaming, going over the times she had spent with Eddie, the gentle way he treated her, and the fact that she now felt that she could relax with him. He had proved that he would respect her and her boundaries. This man, who had the most lively of reputations on campus, showed no sign of it in his dealings with her. She had wondered what it meant, but really she knew. He was in love with her. And more than that, she was in love with him. A small and solitary cloud obscured the sun for a moment and Leila opened her eyes. It was rare for there to be a cloud in the sky and the momentary shadow that it cast made her feel cold, and something else that she had so far denied. She felt a sense of foreboding. This could not end well, or at least it could not end to everyone's satisfaction – she knew that. As much as she loved him and he her, they would never be together. She thought that deep down he knew that, as she did, and that that was why there had been no talk of how they felt, no hand holding, no attempts to kiss her, not even an arm around her shoulder. His future as the heir to a huge Western banking dynasty could not, would not, accommodate its WASP leader converting to Islam. Leila knew that.

As snow fell in New York Eddie found himself struggling with the season. Christmas was nearly upon them and he had bought no gifts, in fact apart from imagining what he would get for Leila if he had the chance, he had not acknowledged the season at all. His parents were still distracted, his mother wound even more tightly than usual and his father, it appeared, in a deep slump. His father had asked Eddie if he wanted to go ice skating in Central Park, a ritual they had observed since Eddie was a small boy. When Eddie said no, Edward did not protest, so half-hearted had the invitation been. Eddie was miserable. He felt even further apart emotionally from his parents than he had been before and he was physically thousands of miles away from the only person he wanted to be with.

On New Year's Day Eddie could wait no longer to hear Leila's voice. She had given him her number reluctantly and the message was there, unspoken but there. By the 1st of January however, Eddie had convinced himself that wishing Leila a Happy New Year was a good enough reason to call. Her father answered and Eddie swore at himself. What was he doing? What kind of pressure would this put Leila under? Her father sounded like a nice man, a kind and gentle man. But still, there was no doubting the reluctance, the suspicion, and the unease that his call was causing. Eddie asked to speak to Leila. There was a pause. Anwar asked for and got Eddie's name. The wait for Leila to come to the phone seemed endless. When she came she was breathless and sounded worried.

"Happy New Year." Eddie said, but it sounded lame.

"Yes – Happy New Year," Leila said, but her voice was not so clear, as though she was looking away from the phone, looking over her shoulder, maybe.

"Is everything alright, Eddie?" she asked.

"Yes, I just wanted—" Eddie hesitated. He was going to say "To wish you Happy New Year" but he didn't. He cleared his throat. "Look, Leila, I had to ring; I miss you so much. The truth is, I'm in love with you." There it was – he had said it. There was a long silence and the sound of a door closing. Now Leila's voice was clear.

"I am very fond of you too."

"No, Leila, no, you love me too. I know that you do. Say it!"

There was a long pause and Eddie thought that he heard her sob. Then in a small voice she said, "I do love you, Eddie, but—"

"No, don't say but, just let me have this moment," Eddie said, and now he was sure that she was crying softly at her end of the line. He sighed. "I can't talk to you now, Leila; God, every piece of me wants to be with you now, but I don't want to hear the reasons why we can't be together. Do you understand me?"

"Yes, Eddie, I understand."

"Well goodbye then, Leila."

"Goodbye, Eddie," she said, and she was gone and for the first time since he was a child, Eddie cried.

* * *

It was going to be a difficult meeting; Eddie knew that. He had kicked himself every day since the New Year. Why had he called her? All his instincts and everything he understood about her had told him that he should not be in touch, but he had still gone ahead and made the call. And now he had forced them to acknowledge what was going on between them, and maybe even frightened her off for good. He felt sick as he threw things into the drawers in his room, barely passing the time of day with his room-mates. They were beginning to tire of him, he knew that, but he was powerless to stop them drifting away. He had noticed over the holidays that he had been invited out less, called seldom and approached for conversation almost never when he was in social gatherings. The part of him that could still think straight knew that he was making a big mistake. What was it he and his buddies had always vowed?

"Never let a piece of tail see a brother's friendship fail."

It was a stupid piece of nonsense made up by one of the group who fancied himself as a poet. They had laughed at him and the ditty at the time, but it had stuck and never was it more appropriate than now, Eddie thought. Good buddies would always be there as skirt came and went, he knew that, and he hated himself for blanking his friends but he could not help it. He felt at once miserable and elated, euphoric and depressed, and he could not really say that being in love was suiting him at all. But then this was not a normal situation.

The guys were back as well, causing havoc in the dormitory block. A few of them came up to him, testing the water, seeing what his mood was. But he could see in their eyes that they had given up on him, hell he had given up on himself. He thought about Harry Masters, wondered how his friend was doing. That was another link in his past that was broken. He knew that they would never get the closeness back that they had had in their carefree youth. Could it really only have been a few months ago that they were in Miami, having the time of their lives. And look where that had got Harry, he thought.

In her room Leila was also unpacking. She had kept in touch with Eme and Laurie over the holidays and the three girls were delighted to see each other again. Leila had said nothing about Eddie's call to them and like Eddie she had butterflies in her stomach at the thought of their meeting. Their two roommates arrived in customary form, looking down their noses at Leila and Laurie and when they thought no one was looking, casting envious looks at the African beauty Eme.

"What did you do for Christmas, Leila? Watch someone having their head cut off?" Suzy Jessen said, and she and Helena laughed uproariously.

"And what did you do, Suzi?" Eme said. "Go to your knocked up sister's wedding?" Leila held her breath as Suzy's face darkened. "Don't rise to it, Leila," Eme whispered to the crestfallen Saudi girl, "she's not worth it."

And so the new term had begun and Leila knew that she was facing some of the toughest times of her life so far. Her mother had already called her, aware of what her daughter had ahead of her.

There had been an inquest at home following Eddie's call. Her parents had asked her gently for details about this young man who was calling her from so far away. Anwar remembered his friend Amir's words and was immediately wary. Leila reassured them that nothing improper was going on and they could tell that what she said was true. Not that they ever really doubted their daughter. They had raised her well and they knew that she would never do anything to dishonour herself or her family.

When she had finished speaking to her parents, Leila had gone to her room. Later that day she found her mother and asked to talk to her. She told her mother how she felt about Eddie and that she was afraid that things could only get more difficult for her. Maysoon listened to her daughter, proud of her maturity and at the same time afraid for her. It had always been a possibility that she would meet someone while she was studying abroad, and it was obvious that her daughter had deep feelings for this boy. They talked for many hours, and they both cried and laughed and hugged each other and by the time that Leila returned to Harvard, a decision had been made.

Chapter Twelve

In their accommodation block, Eme had found a note pinned to the door before any of them had got there that afternoon. It was for Leila from Eddie and it asked her to meet him at the library in their customary spot at 6 p.m. As the time approached Leila felt the butterflies she had become a swarm and her legs would hardly carry her to the meeting.

He was already there, and Leila felt her heart melt as he jumped to his feet, his face breaking into the widest smile she had ever seen. His eyes lit up as he looked at her and she offered him her hand. For a moment he looked at it and then, unable to help himself, gathered her into his arms for a momentary hug. He let her go as quickly as he had grabbed her to him and Leila, despite herself, felt her body arch towards his for that brief moment. Her face flushed and she took a seat opposite him and he held the tips of her fingers on his for a moment. They were alone in their corner but despite that Eddie kept his voice to a whisper.

"I missed you, Leila, and I am sorry that I called you. Did it make things difficult for you?"

"No; my parents are loving and fair, and they trust me."

"Good, I'm so glad; how have you been?"

"I've been very well, Eddie, and you?"

"To hell with it, Leila, what are we doing? What are we talking like this for? I told you that I loved you, and I know that you feel the same. We have to make plans, we have to talk the future, we have to—" Leila put her finger to her lips and he stopped talking.

"Eddie, I'm sorry, there will be no future; there can't be. I do love you but I will not marry a man who is not a Moslem. And before you offer to convert think about your future, Lancaster bank; it just could not happen." She looked down at her hands.

"This will be my last term at Harvard. Next semester I'm going to a different university."

To Leila, the silence that followed seemed never to end, and from the look on Eddie's face anyone watching could well have thought that she had slapped him or spat at him. Leila had never seen an expression of such raw pain. Her heart broke and she closed her eyes, thinking back to the conversation she had had with her mother. Her mother had not pressured her, quite the contrary in fact – she had said she would support her daughter whatever her decision was. But the sad thing was that Leila really had no choice. She knew what she had to do. Making the decision to move college had been a natural progression. Leila had had an offer from Yale as well as Harvard and a few calls from her uncle Amir had smoothed the way for her to start the next semester. She would have wished to start this semester but she knew that she had to see Eddie, to have the courage of her convictions and speak to him face to face, maybe ease her departure over the time she had left at Harvard. Looking at his face, all that now seemed a vain hope. His heartbreak was etched all over his handsome face.

And then to her surprise he got up, quietly and without anger and left the library. This was not what she had expected, she expected him to plead, to beg to promise, to ... something, but not this silent exit. There was no element of temper or annoyance in his exit, just a feeling that he knew when he was defeated. Leila cried silently.

Back in his room Eddie felt bile rising to his throat and ran to the toilet. He vomited for what seemed like the longest time. Part of his brain was frightened; he never would have believed that love could make you physically sick. He was out of control, feeling as though he was desperately ill and helpless to help himself. He thought about giving up his inheritance – it meant nothing to him compared to this girl – but he knew that she would not let him and somewhere deep in his mind he knew that he had an important part to play in the future of Lancasters. He had read more about Islamic finance over the holidays. It made him feel closer to Leila, Leila who had now broken his heart just as surely as if she had driven a knife into it. And despite all the thoughts that crowded his brain, underneath it all he knew that what had happened was irreversible that there was no point in trying to persuade Leila. Part of the reason he loved Leila was for her strength, her unwavering obedience and love for her faith, something very rare in the West in his experience. He knew that she would not change her mind, could not change her mind, and in the meantime he was going out of his.

Unbelievably, Eddie did not see Leila again for three weeks apart from in the distance at lectures. He avoided her, tried to forget her, tried to throw himself into his work, into sport, back into the crowd he used to hang with. But he was not the Eddie that his old crowd knew. This morose, gaunt and haunted guy was not someone they felt comfortable with.

The return of their project with excellent grades from Amir Ali brought them together briefly to receive their tutor's accolade, and Eddie noticed that Leila had lost weight. Leila noticed that Eddie had too and as their eyes met, pain recognised pain as they held their gaze for a moment. As their tutor left the room Leila said, "Would you like to review any more Islamic finance before I go?"

To anyone looking in it would have been laughable, pathetic, even ridiculous, but Islamic finance was the currency they had traded in, their mutual interest, hers greater than his, admittedly, but he had found in the subject something that really did strike a chord with him.

"That would be good," Eddie said, and found to his huge surprise that he had missed the subject as well as Leila.

The next day they met in their usual spot in the library and once again Eddie listened to her gentle voice, full of enthusiasm for her subject, her eyes bright with intelligence, with passion.

"Murabahah is an Islamic mode of financing. In its original Islamic sense it is a sale, and it is distinguished from other forms of sale by the seller's telling the purchaser how much cost he has incurred and how much profit he is going to charge in addition. It is a mode of sale to escape interest." Eddie's eyebrows shot up. This was something hard to reconcile with the world he and his father lived in. Leila continued. "Musawamah, bargaining, is a sale without any reference to cost, ratio or profit. The profit is agreed upon by an agreed ratio. The cost price will include all expenses such as freight and custom duty. Costs such as salaries of staff and rent cannot be included in this cost. If the exact cost cannot be ascertained, the commodity cannot be sold on a Murabahah basis, but under Musawamah. The rules governing the transactions of Murabahah in financial institutions are as follows: The subject of sale must be existent at the time of sale. The sale is void under Shari'ah if a non-existent thing is sold, for example an unborn calf. The subject of sale must be in the ownership of the seller at the time of sale. The subject of sale must be in the physical or constructive possession of the seller at the time of sale. The sale must be instant and absolute. A sale contingent on a later date is void. The subject of sale must be a property of value. The subject of sale should not be something which is not used except for a haram purpose, like pork, wine, et cetera. The subject of sale must be specifically known and identified to the buyer. The delivery of the sold commodity to the buyer must be certain and should not depend on a contingency. The certainty of price is a necessary condition for the validity of sale. If the price is uncertain, the sale is void. The sale must be unconditional, unless a condition is recognized as a part of the transaction according to the usage of trade. If the seller does not abide by his promise to sell, it may be enforceable in court."

Leila smiled as Eddie frowned in concentration, trying to take in the foreign sounding words. She helped him with the spelling and their hands touched briefly as she passed the paper back to him. Eddie felt as though electricity passed between them and he heard her catch her breath before going on. "Bai' Mu'ajjal. This is a sale on a deferred payment basis; the rules governing this sale are as follows: This type of sale is valid if the due date of payment is fixed in an unambiguous manner. The date must be fixed, and cannot rest on an event with an unknown date. If a time period is decided upon for payment, it is effected from the date of delivery, unless agreed otherwise by the parties. The price must be fixed at the time of sale, and this cannot be changed. There may be a promise for the buyer to donate a specified amount to a charity in case of default. In payment of installments, any failure to pay on its due date will require the full amount immediately. To secure the payment there may be a security, such as a mortgage or charge on existing assets. Another possibility is to sign a promissory note. Murabahah as a form of financing. The ideal modes of financing, according to Shari'ah, are mudarabah and musharakah. Due to practical difficulties in using these, murabahah has been allowed as a mode of financing, subject to certain conditions. As it is not an ideal financing instrument, it should be used as a transitory step in the process of Islamisation of the economy, and its use restricted to cases where musharakah and mudarabah cannot be used. Some rules govern the use of murabahah as a mode of financing: It is not a loan, and so can only be used for the purchase of actual commodities, and not for paying for goods already purchased or electricity bills."

Eddie nodded his understanding. Leila smiled briefly

and continued. "Now make these points as a list: The financier must have owned the commodity before he sells it to the client.In cases where the financier cannot directly purchase the commodity from the supplier, it is permissible for him to make the customer his agent to buy the commodity on his behalf. The customer then purchases the commodity from the financier for a deferred price.The commodity must be purchased from a third party. The financial institution, when using murabahah as a mode of finance, adopts the following procedure: The client and the institution sign an agreement whereby the institution promises to sell and the client promises to buy the commodities on an agreed profit ratio added to the cost. When a specific commodity is required by the customer, the institution appoints the client as his agent for purchasing the commodity on its behalf and both parties sign an agreement of agency. The commodity remains the risk of the institution until the next stage. This is the only feature that distinguishes murabahah from an interest-based transaction. The institution accepts the offer and the sale is concluded whereby the ownership as well as the risk of the commodity is transferred to the client. At this stage a promissory note may be signed to ensure payment to the institution.

"As for the use of interest rates as a benchmark ..." Leila looked at Eddie, his head bent over his writing pad, and she felt so proud of him. He was really interested. Even in his heartbreak, he was giving the subject his full attention. "... many institutions financing by way of murabahah determine their profit on the basis of the current interest rate, mostly using LIBOR as the criterion. This is often criticized on the grounds that profit based on a rate of interest should be as prohibited as interest itself. However, a murabahah transaction is not rendered invalid if all the conditions are met and the rate of interest has been used only as a benchmark. Using this benchmark, however, is not ideal, as it takes the rate of interest as an ideal for a halal business, which is not desirable. Also, it does not advance the basic philosophy of the Islamic economy having no impact on the system of distribution. Islamic banks should strive to develop their own benchmark by creating their own inter-bank market based on Islamic principles. In this, a common pool can be created which invests in asset-backed instruments such as musharakah and ijarah. The next heading would be Murabahah promise to purchase. At the stage at which the financier has yet to acquire the commodity required by the client, the financier is at risk if the client is not bound to purchase the commodity once the financier purchases it. The client signing a promise to purchase solves this; this is distinguished from the bilateral forward contract by being a unilateral promise. This is however debated, as this promise is a moral obligation and cannot be enforced in Shari'ah. Many scholars such as Imam Abu Hanifah, Imam al-Shafi'i, Imam Ahmad and some Maliki jurists are of the view that fulfilling a promise is a noble quality and it is advisable for the promissor to observe it, and its violation is reproachable, but it is neither mandatory, nor enforceable through courts."

"What about security? How is it all policed, so that things are done on time and according to promise?" Eddie asked. Leila nodded.

"In order to ensure that the price will be paid on time,

the following conditions must be met: The security can be claimed where the transaction has created a liability or debt. The security is established after the commodity is sold to the client and the price has become due to the financier. However, there may be a security earlier to ensure the financier's liability while in possession of the commodity. It is also permissible that the sold commodity is given to the seller as security. According to Hanafi jurists the seller will have to bear the loss of the commodity to the extent of its market price or agreed sale price, whichever is the smaller. The Shafi'i and Hanbali jurists hold that if the commodity is destroyed by the negligence of the mortgagee, he will have to bear the loss according to its market price. In this scenario it is necessary that the point of time on which the commodity held by the mortgagee should be defined. The financier can ask for a guarantor in the event that the client cannot make payment. The classical fiqh literature is unanimous that the guarantee is voluntary and no fee can be charged on a guarantee, although secretarial expenses may be incurred, otherwise it would be riba. However, in the modern age, in transactions such as international ones it has become difficult to find guarantors who are free of charge. Contemporary scholars argue that the prohibition of guarantee fee is not based on any specific injunction of the Holy Qur'an or Sunnah, only deduced from the prohibition of riba." Leila paused. "This is interesting, Eddie. The price cannot be increased if the client defaults. This is sometimes exploited by someone who deliberately avoids paying the price at its due date, as they know they will not have to pay any additional amount on account of default."

"So what if someone uses that to their advantage?" Eddie asked. Leila smiled.

"This should not create a problem in a country with banks run on Islamic principles because the government can create a system whereby defaulters are penalized. However, in countries where Islamic banks are working in isolation, even if the client is deprived of using an Islamic bank thereafter he can approach conventional institutions. Some contemporary scholars have proposed that they should be made liable to pay compensation to the Islamic bank for the loss. This amount may be equal to the profit given by the bank to its depositors during the period of default. Those who allow this base it on the following conditions: The defaulter should be given a grace period of at least one month after the maturity date during which he must be given weekly notices warning him. It must be proven beyond doubt that the client is defaulting without valid excuse. If it is due to poverty, no compensation can be claimed. This is expressed in the Holy Qur'an, "And if the debtor is short of funds, then he must be given respite until he is well off. The compensation is allowed only if the investment account of the Islamic bank has earned some profit to be distributed to the depositors. There can be an extension of deferred payment but this is not allowed under Shari'ah but has, however, been implemented in some Islamic banks that have misunderstood murabahah. Extending the due date for another term is analogous to interest-based financing."

Eddie raised his eyebrows and nodded. "Is there any advantage if a client repays his debt early?"

Leila leafed forward in her book. "With early payment

rebate, if the client pays earlier than the specified date, some jurists allow a discount on the price and some do not. The four recognized schools of Islamic jurisprudence do not allow this. Those who do allow this base their argument on a hadith in which Abdullah ibn 'Abbas is reported to have said that when the Jews belonging to the tribe of Banu Nadir were banished from Madinah because of their conspiracies, some people came to the Holy Prophet and said, 'You have ordered them to be expelled, but some people owe them some debts which have not yet matured.' Thereupon the Holy Prophet said to the Jews who were the creditors, 'Give discount and receive your debts soon.' The majority of Moslem jurists do not accept this hadith as authentic. Even if it is, the exile of Banu Nadir was in the second year after hijrah, before riba was prohibited. However, if the creditor gives a rebate voluntarily it is permissible."

Leila paused for Eddie to catch up. "Now I will tell you about cost calculation in murabahah. The murabahah must be based on the same currency as that in which the seller has purchased the commodity from the original supplier. This may be difficult in international trade, but it can be solved in a number of ways. If the laws of the country allow and the purchaser agrees, the price of the second sale may be determined in dollars. The cost price can include the cost in converting them into dollars and the profit added thereon. However, this is not valid because it leads to the price being uncertain at the time of sale. There are some options open to the bank in this issue: The bank should purchase that commodity on the basis of letter of condition at sight and should pay the price to the supplier before effecting sale with the customer. The bank determines the murabahah price in US dollars rather than in Pak rupees, so that the deferred murabahah price is paid by the customer in dollars. The bank will be entitled to receive dollars from the customer and the risk of the price fluctuation in the dollar will be borne by the purchaser. Instead of murabahah, the deal may be on the basis of musawamah and the price may be fixed, to cover the anticipated fluctuation in the currency rates. If installments are rescheduled in murabahah, no additional amount can be charged as in conventional banks. Some Islamic banks proposed to reschedule the murabahah price in a hard currency different from the one of the original sale. However, rescheduling must always be on the basis of the same amount in the same currency. Murabahah cannot be securitized for creating a negotiable instrument to be sold and purchased in secondary market. A paper of evidence of indebtedness towards the seller cannot be exchanged for money at a lower or higher price. However, if there is a mixed portfolio consisting of a number of transactions like musharakah, leasing and murabahah, then this portfolio may issue negotiable certificates subject to certain conditions."

As her last words hung in the air between them, Eddie savoured them. Somehow being with her, even though their talk had been of Islamic finance, calmed him and made his feel the first glimmer of happiness he had felt since she had told him she was leaving. Something in the message that she was giving him transcended whatever they had, or rather might have had together. Eddie could hardly believe what he was thinking. He was not in the habit of complex analysis of his feelings and at times the way that Leila had altered his thinking on all sorts of things frightened him. No wonder the attempts he had made to fit in with the guys again had failed – he was no longer like them.

But unknown to him, as the weeks counted down before Leila left Harvard, events elsewhere were conspiring to derail Eddie even more.

Chapter Thirteen

As Sandy Masters approached the eighth month of her pregnancy, things began to go wrong. She had had difficulties almost from the beginning, but now, in a midnight dash to hospital, she was about to deliver Harry's child early. Harry carried his wife's bag, his face white and his Adam's apple bobbing precariously in his thin neck. Even although he had been woken from sleep he looked clean-shaven; in fact he looked like a boy of maybe fifteen. And he felt it.

From nowhere, Eddie came into his head. He had thought about his friend a lot recently, about how differently their lives had turned out. Nowadays Harry was surrounded by female members of the Jessen family fussing around Sandy, who now bore no resemblance at all to the girl that had given him his first sexual experience eight months earlier. He loved her, of course he did, but then again did he? Did he really know what love was? Her constant whining and asking him if he loved her always solicited the same response: "of course I do, Sandy Pandy." But was he really 'in love'? Too late now anyway, he thought, feeling disloyal at having such thoughts as Sandy and their baby were being rushed into hospital. God, he wished he had Eddie with him now; Eddie was always such a rock, although he had seemed a bit preoccupied at the wedding in the holidays. Where had those carefree days gone?

As his mother had said, more than once in all of this, "You've made your bed, now lie in it." And by and large that is what Harry was doing. His father had fixed him up with a clerical position at Lancaster's bank, without any qualifications, what else could he do?

Now standing in the corridor of the private hospital that old man Jessen was paying for he could hear the low voice of the doctor and Mrs Jessen who were talking over Sandy's bed. He felt as though he should be in the room too. He was the father after all, but he was not invited and stood outside, almost as though he was standing outside the headmaster's office at school.

Eventually the doctor came out and Harry stepped forward, expecting to speak to him. But the doctor swept down the corridor and Harry looked back into the room. Mrs Jessen saw him and almost as an afterthought said "Oh hello, Harry" before looking back at her daughter.

"How is she?" Harry asked.

"Not good; the doctor is going to operate. I've signed the consent."

"But I'm her husband," Harry said and she gave him a withering look as one might an annoying fly that had flown into the room.

"Yes, and I'm her mother." And that was the end of it.

Three hours later Harry was a father. But his infant son was in trouble – underweight and very small, he was in an incubator while Sandy, who looked every bit as bloated now as she had before the baby was delivered, sniffled in her bed, her mother patting her hand.

Eventually someone came to take Harry to see his son in the neonatal ICU. The child looked weak and was a strange colour. The little mite was attached to tubes and machines which beeped menacingly, and Harry felt his mouth go dry. He stared at the crumpled scrap that was his child and his heart went out to him. He dared not touch the infant; there was hardly a spot on him that was not attached to some monitor or another. The doctor was telling him that his child's condition was critical, that he would be transfused for anaemia and severe jaundice. Harry nodded, unable to speak. He did not want to ask if his child would die, but he wanted the doctor to tell him. He did not really know what to do. Should he wait by the baby's incubator? Should he go back to Sandy? He thought that he should stay with his son as his wife was being attended by her mother and they had made it clear that he was not wanted, or welcome. Old man Jessen had now arrived. Harry could hear his voice booming down the corridors, and he knew that his son's illness, his wife and her mother's unhappiness in fact everything would be blamed on him. He sighed. The baby in the incubator moved slightly, screwing his tiny yellow face into a scowl as though he was going to cry, before he relaxed again. Harry felt tears come to his eyes; poor little guy didn't even have enough strength to cry.

He wondered what they would call the little fella. At the moment the label on the incubator said 'Baby Masters'. He had not really bothered to think of any names for his son as he knew that the decision would be made by his wife and her family.

It was dawn now, although the sun was reluctant to rise in the cold February sky. Harry wanted to ring someone, to tell them that he had a son. He thought about ringing his mother but he knew what she would say: "You've made your bed, now lie in it." He felt his parents' disappointment in him and it hurt. He would have liked to think that the arrival of his baby would make everything right between them, but he knew it wouldn't.

The blood transfusion was being done. He and Sandy had been tested before they were married and Harry knew they were both type 'O'. As the nurse carried the bag in that held the blood for his son, Harry saw a big 'B' on it. His grasp of blood typing was rudimentary but even he knew that two type 'O's could not produce a baby with blood type 'B'.

"Hold on a minute," Harry said, his voice cracking. The nurse looked at him with raised eyebrows.

"He can't be group 'B'. His mother and I are both 'O'. If you give him the wrong blood it could kill him, right?" Harry's voice tailed off. It had been a feeble attempt to save his son's life, more like a plea rather than the command it should have been.

"Right," the nurse confirmed, putting the bag of blood down and picking up the notes, which already looked substantial, considering that his son was only hours old.

"He is blood type 'B'. It says it right here," she said, flashing a complicated chart under his nose for the moment. But his eyes seemed to home in on the value he wanted, no needed, to see. Under blood typing, there it was, a typed 'B'. "There's no mistake." The nurse looked at him as if seeing him for the first time. "Your baby is definitely type 'B'." Harry felt his face drain of blood and she seemed to hungrily drink in his discomfort. "Maybe you are mistaken about his mother's blood group, or yours," she said, but the faint smile that played around her lips told him that she didn't really believe that. Her look said it all – she was thinking, "God, I would cheat on you too, you puny wimp."

But Harry had lost interest in her, and wasn't even aware enough of her disdain to feel embarrassed. His mind was back at the night in the hot tub, and then further back to the trip he and Eddie had taken from school, the one where their medical notes had got in the wrong envelope when they had been given back to them at the end of the trip. They had laughed about it, Eddie had teased him about the un-descended testicle operation he had had that was listed on his notes, and Harry had got his own back by teasing his friend about the 'unspecified rash' he had had on his behind at the last camp. But he had noticed something else on his friend's notes.

Eddie was roused from sleep to answer the phone on that cold February morning. The last person he expected to hear was Harry but he mumbled sleepily, "Hey man; how ya doing?"

"I'm fine, Eddie; oh, and congratulations, man – you're a father."

PART TWO

Chapter Fourteen

Eddie Lancaster smiled thinly and took a piece of cake. He hated these occasions, when he and Harry and the entire ranks of the Jessen family assembled for Byron's birthday. And he hated his son's name too. Pretentious and definitely Jessen inspired.

Eddie looked at his watch surreptitiously. Byron was sitting in a chair, his asthma inhaler in hand. He was a weak boy; he had never really thrived following his premature birth. He bore no resemblance at all to the son that Eddie had always thought he would have, a little clone of himself, born with a baseball bat in his hand. This sickly pale child was small for his age and delicate. The secret of his parentage had been maintained. He and Harry had made a bond that they would tell no one and so far their secret had been safe and Harry and Sandy had produced a bouncing baby girl two years later. But Eddie felt that he had to be involved somehow, and since he had been made Vice Chairman at Lancaster's he had made sure that he supplemented his friend's clerk wages. He might feel no affinity or bond to his son, but he knew his responsibilities. Certainly no one would guess that Byron was anything to do with him.

As he sat on the settee looking out at the snow-covered lawn of his friend's Long Island house, paid for by old man Jessen, Eddie reflected on how much people change. When he looked at the Jessen girls that he and Harry had

had so much fun with in the hot tub that long ago summer night, he shuddered. They both looked matronly now and totally unappealing to Eddie. He sighed. There had only been one woman that had truly appealed to him and although there had been many women since, none had even come close to his lovely Leila. When she had moved to Oxford University in England he had kept in touch with her for a while, but her letters in reply to his passionate entreaties were always polite, perfunctory, almost like a letter from an unmarried aunt and in the end they broke his heart more than not having contact with her at all.

So despite pressure from his mother and father, he remained single. He sometimes thought that he should settle down, consign the past to the past and get on with his life, but he could not bear to have a marriage like his parents', a 'going through the motions' life. He knew what it as to be in love and that was what he was going to hold out for.

The party over, Eddie returned to his apartment in the same block as his parents still lived in, over looking the park. He knew that his father was looking to leave the bank as soon as he knew that it was safe in Eddie's hands and the enormous amount of work that that involved kept his mind focused. He picked up a pile of buff coloured folders. He frowned; there was something he had to raise with his father. It was about the charitable donations that Lancaster's made to various concerns. He had tried to tie his father down to a discussion about them but Edward always came up with an excuse. It was the only part of the bank's dealings that Eddie still had no knowledge of and something was bugging him about it, something wasn't right. He felt almost as though there was something that his father did not want him to know.

Two stories above his son's flat, Edward sat looking at a single folder on his leather-topped desk in his wood-panelled study. He flipped it open and read the entries in blue ink from a traditional fountain pen made in Eugene's distinctive neat handwriting. As he turned the loose-leaf pages, his face darkened and his lips thinned. Eventually he slammed the file shut. Eddie must never know, but how was he going to stop him? It had been more than a year since Sharif had contacted him. It had always bothered him that Sharif was completely in control; he knew no more about the man now than he had done more than thirty years ago.

Arabella, however, thought she knew Sharif very well. She had been a slave of Sharif's touch, his magic, for more than ten years now. In that time she had become hungrier and hungrier for him as she explored the sex life that she had never had. But she too was at the beck and call of this mysterious man. She had no way of contacting him, and he always seemed to know the exact amount of time that he should leave it to make her ravenous for him and his body. He made her scream with ecstasy for hours and then melted away again until every nerve in her body was craving his touch. Then he would materialise again, inflame and then calm her starving body. It had been longer than usual since she had seen him and she was as jumpy. She was snapping at everyone and clutched her mobile phone to her as though it was a life-support machine. Every time the little machine buzzed with a text message she almost dropped it as she fumbled to see the message that she wanted, always with the sending number withheld.

As he settled into his room at the Waldorf Astoria, Sharif sighed. It was getting harder and harder to rise to the occasion for Arabella. Over recent years she had taken to having botox and plastic surgery and she now resembled a startled elderly Barbie doll. He smiled to himself; it was nearly time. If he could just keep the insatiable Arabella under his spell for a little longer ...

He thought that perhaps on this trip to New York he might contact Arabella's husband too. It had been over a year and no doubt the old man was getting twitchy, for a different reason than his wife, but twitchy none the less. Sharif smiled to himself. It made him happy to think that he had held this man in his hands for all these years, he knew more about him than maybe anyone else, through what he had found out from his wife and other sources and yet Edward Lancaster still knew nothing about him.

* * *

In London Leila was saying goodbye to her children. She had the opportunity to attend one of Uncle Amir's lectures at Oxford University and was looking forward to it. She had seen Amir several times over the years but these days everyone seemed so busy and settled, as she was with her husband in London, that she did not see either of her parents or Amir and his family so much. Her husband, Nasser was from a prominent Saudi business family and he took care of things in the UK. Now he kissed her warmly on the cheek, holding their twins, Hiba and Hannah, who were holding each of his hands.

"Enjoy yourself at the lecture, Leila, and come back soon; we'll miss you." Leila smiled as she got into her car. It was nice to be loved and nice to be wished home soon. She was only going for the week, but it already seemed too long before she would see her babies again. Their nanny was a good girl and the twins adored her but she as going to miss them. She had not been back to Oxford University since her graduation and she was looking forward to seeing some old friends at the 'World Banking and Economy' week of lectures.

She turned on the car radio and listened to the news bulletin.

"The announcement by Dubai that it would defer repaying 35 billion dollars of its debts for six months caused chaos in the markets, with almost 44 billion pounds being wiped off the UK's top companies as the FTSE fell by more than 170 points and in Europe, France and Germany's indices fell while the price of crude oil dropped by two dollars a barrel."

Is a country that has become synonymous with excess now on the brink of a spectacular fall?

Leila frowned to herself. She was suddenly back in the library all those years ago with Eddie Lancaster, talking about Islamic finance and how with that system the financial crisis facing the world could not happen. There had been many near misses since she had graduated and started lecturing in Islamic finance but something told her that they were now on the brink of something momentous.

As he prepared for that morning's lecture Amir Ali was

also listening to the bulletin. He decided to skip breakfast and make a few changes to his notes to accommodate the day's news. As Leila had, he felt a strange feeling in his stomach, nervousness, or was it anticipation? Amir prayed before he went to his desk, prayed for the strength to get his message across at this time when it was most needed, that it could be of most help, but mostly he prayed that minds would be open to what he had to say.

The conference was an important one. There would be representatives from many of the world's banks and they would all have heard the news, as he had. It was too late to change his whole lecture content but he decided that he would open with a statement on Islamic banks, just to lay the groundwork, get those that were there and watching their own banking system collapse to see that there was an alternative.

The hall was full and polite applause greeted Amir's walk to the podium after the opening addresses by the University hosts and conference organisers.

He cleared his throat and bid the audience welcome. He heard papers rustling as the delegates found the place in their guide that related to his talk.

"Islamic banks have made great breakthroughs in the present banking system by establishing Islamic financial institutions following Shari'ah. They present a living and practical example for the theoretical concept where it was claimed that no financial institution can work without interest. The Holy Qur'an and the Holy Sunnah of the Prophet have laid down broad principles in the light of which scholars have deduced specific answers to the new situation arising in their age. This exercise is called Istinbat or Ijtihad. However, during the past few centuries the political decline of Moslems stopped this process to a considerable extent. Another major contribution of the Islamic banks is that they have now asserted themselves in the international market, an international market that, as we have heard this morning, ladies and gentlemen, sorely needs a solution to its current ills."

As he spoke he saw several delegates frown and leaf back and forth between the sheets. He had departed from the order, but he thought the situation warranted it. There were murmurs around the hall, and as he flicked his eyes over the rows of seated delegates, Amir picked out several world bank leaders. His eyes rested for a moment on a face that was smiling up at him. Leila! He knew she was coming but picking her out of the crowd spurred him on.

"After that brief statement, ladies and gentleman, I will return to the programme for my talk and begin with the subject of Ijarah. This means to give something on rent. In Islamic jurisprudence it means 'to employ the services of a person on wages given to him as a consideration for his hired services'. The employer is 'musta'jur' and the employee 'ajir'. Ijarah in the second sense is to transfer the usufruct of a particular property to another person in exchange for a rent claimed from him. This is analogous to leasing. The lessor is 'mu'jir', the lessee 'musta'jir' and the rent 'ujrah'. This is the most relevant as it is used as a form of investment and a mode of financing. The rules are very similar to the rules of sale. However, the ownership of the property remains in the possession of the transferor, and the lessee has only the right to use it.

Taking his electronic pointer in his hand Amir began to show the slides he had prepared for the talk.

"Some stipulations of Ijarah are: The subject of lease must have a usufruct otherwise it cannot be leased. The leased property remains under the ownership of the seller. The liabilities of the ownership are borne by the lessor, but the liabilities of the use are borne by the lessee. The period of lease must be determined in clear terms. The leased asset cannot be used for any other purpose not specified in the lease agreement. The lessee is liable to compensate the lessor for harm to the leased asset caused by misuse or negligence. Any harm or loss beyond the control of the lessee shall be borne by the lessor. A property jointly owned can be leased out, and the rental distributed according to the proportion of each of their share. A joint owner of a property can lease his proportionate share to his co-sharer only and not to any other person. The leased asset must be fully identifiable by the parties. The rental must be determined at the time of contract for the whole period of lease. The lease is not valid if the rent for a phase of lease period has not been determined or left at the option of the lessor. The lessor cannot increase the rent unilaterally and any agreement to this effect is void. The rent may be paid in advance of delivery of the asset to lessee, but the amount will remain as 'on account' payment and adjusted towards the rent when it is due. The lease period shall commence from the date on which the leased asset has been delivered to the lessee, regardless of whether the lessee has started using it. The lease will terminate if the asset has lost its function for which it was leased and no repair is possible. If this loss is caused by misuse by the lessee he will be liable to compensate the lessor for the depreciated value of the loss."

He looked over the sea of faces. Some had already tuned out, he could tell; they were fiddling with their mobile phones, probably checking the market reports. But others were looking at him intently and some were taking notes.

Amir looked back at his papers. "I want now to talk about Financial Leasing," he said, and some more heads looked his way. "This type of ijarah was not intended as a mode of financing, but certain financial institutions use it instead of long-term lending on the basis of interest. Leasing is a lawful transaction according to Shari'ah and can be used as an interest-free mode of financing. However, there must be substantial difference between leasing and an interest-bearing loan. Some basic differences between contemporary financial leasing and actual leasing allowed by Shari'ah are indicated on these slides" Amir picked up his pointer again. "The agreement can be effected for a future date on the condition that the rent will be payable after the leased asset is delivered to the lessee. There are two separate relationships between the institution and the client. In the first, the client is an agent of the institution to purchase the asset on the latter's behalf. The second begins from the date when the client takes delivery from the supplier, and the relationship of lessor and lessee comes into play. In the first stage the client cannot be held liable for the obligations of a lessee. The lessor is liable to bear all expenses as the owner of the asset in the process of the purchase and import, such as freight and customs duty. A loss caused by factors beyond the lessee's control is not liable to the lessee; this factor is not differentiated between the losses caused by negligence of the lessee in traditional 'financial lease' agreements. In long-term leases it is not to the benefit of the lessor to fix one amount of rent for the whole period of the lease, as market conditions change from time to time. If payment is late, the same solution comes into effect as in murabahah. The lessee will pay a certain amount to a charity. The lease may be terminated if the lessee contravenes the terms. In other cases it can be terminated by mutual consent. In the 'financial lease' the lessor has unrestricted power to terminate the lease unilaterally according to his judgment; this is against the principles of Shari'ah. The lessor is responsible for paying the insurance under the Islamic mode of takaful, not the lessee as is the case in financial leases. Contemporary scholars have suggested that the lessor may enter into a unilateral promise to sell the leased asset to the lessee at the end of the leased period. The lessee cannot sub-lease the leased asset except with permission from the lessor. The schools of Islamic jurisprudence differ in opinion about the rent charged from the sub-lessee. The lessor can sell the leased property to a third party whereby the relation of lessor and lessee shall be established between the new owner and the lessee."

A hand went up in the audience and Amir smiled to himself; this was a good sign. But he had to carry on, so he said, "I will be taking questions after the lecture, if that is alright, Sir?"

As the man nodded, Amir recognized him; it was Eddie Lancaster from Lancaster's bank. He looked at Leila at the other side of the auditorium. From where she was sitting she would not be able to see Eddie. A thousand questions went around in Amir's brain. Had they arranged to meet here? Did Leila know Eddie was coming or did he know she was? Amir chastised himself. It was a banking conference; Eddie was a banker and Leila lectured on Islamic finance. Why would they not be here? There was a restless shuffling in the auditorium, rustling of paper and clearing of throats. Amir had lost his thread as he tried to guess the implications of Eddie Lancaster and Leila being at the same conference. He looked down at his notes.

"Next I will tackle the subject of murabahah and ijarah leasing. The differences between murabahah and leasing are subtle but significant. Murabahah cannot have a sale attributed to a future date, but leasing can. In murabahah the seller cannot claim a profit over a property that never remained under his risk. In leasing the asset remains under the risk of the lessor, and so does not violate the principle of Shari'ah of not claiming a profit or fee for a property the risk of which was never borne by him. Going on to securitization of ijarah, we see that the lessor can sell the asset, in whole or part, to a third party. Some jurists are of the opinion that this sale will not take effect until the lease period is over. However, Imam Abu Yusuf and others argue that the sale is valid, the purchaser will replace the seller and ijarah may continue. The sale of a portion of the asset may be evidenced by an ijarah certificate, and assume the obligations of the lessor to the extent of his ownership. These certificates can be traded in the market and serve as an instrument easily convertible into cash. These may help solve the problems of liquidity management faced by Islamic banks. It is not allowed in Shari'ah for ijarah certificates to represent the holder's right to claim a certain amount of rental only without assigning to him any kind of ownership in the asset." The auditorium was quiet, and Amir felt optimism rise in him like a wave. Were they listening? Would they at last realize there might be another way?

"Carrying on now to head leasing. Head leasing is an arrangement in the modern leasing business where the lessee sub-leases the property to a number of sub-lessees. Then, others are invited to share the rentals received by his sub-lessees and charges them a specified amount for this. This is not in accordance with Shari'ah, because the lessee does not own the property and only benefits from its usufruct. Trading in rent is a form of riba, which is prohibited."

There was a murmur around the room, as the delegates digested the message. Amir continued. "Salam and istisna'. As mentioned earlier, these are the exceptions to the commodity having to be in the physical or constructive possession of the seller. They are two types of sale. In salam, the seller undertakes to supply some specific goods to the buyer at a future date in exchange of an advanced price fully paid at spot. The original purpose of this sale was to meet the needs of small farmers who needed money to grow their crops and to feed their family up to the time of harvest." Amir paused to drink some water.

"I want to turn my attention now to agriculture financing methods and introduce to you salam as a form of financing. Modern banks and financial institutions can use this mode of financing, particularly to finance the agricultural sector. The only problem with salam is that the banks will receive certain commodities from their clients and not receive money."

There was stifled laughter around the hall and Amir heard several chicken imitations. "Yes, gentleman, you may laugh but in a world fast running out of oil, and in financial melt down, bartering may be what we are left with."

The auditorium quieted.

"However, if banks want to earn a halal profit they have to deal in commodities. There are a few ways of benefiting from the contract of Salam: firstly, after purchasing a commodity by way of Salam the financial institutions may sell it through a parallel contract of Salam for the same date of delivery. Secondly, if a parallel contract of Salam is not feasible, they can obtain a promise to purchase from a third party. This should be unilateral from the expected buyer. Their buyers will not have to pay the price in advance. Thirdly, at the date of delivery the commodity is sold back to the seller at a higher price. But this is not in line with Shari'ah."

Taking up his pointer again, Amir loaded more slides with the heading "Rules of Parallel Salam."

"The rules of parallel Salam are as follows: the bank enters into two different contracts. In one, the bank is the buyer and in the other, the bank is the seller. Each must be independent of the other, and its performance not contingent on the other. It is allowed with a third party only. Otherwise it will amount to a buy-back arrangement, which is not permissible in Shari'ah. Istisna' means a commodity is transacted before it comes into existence, such as ordering a manufacturer to manufacture a specific commodity for the purchaser. The price must be fixed with the two parties and that there is a specification of the commodity. The contract is a moral obligation on the manufacturer, but before he starts work any of the parties may cancel the contract by giving notice. The contract cannot be cancelled unilaterally after the manufacturer has started his work. Now to clarify the difference between salam can be effected on anything, but for Istisna' something must be manufactured. The price must be paid in advance in Salam but not in istisna'. The Salam contract cannot be cancelled unilaterally once effected, but in Istisna' it can be cancelled before the manufacturer starts work. The time of delivery is essential in Salam but in Istisna' it does not need to be fixed. And also now the differences between Istisna' and Ijarah The transaction is not Istisna' if the material used is provided by the customer and the manufacturer uses his labors and skill only. In this case it is an ijarah transaction whereby the services of a person are hired for a fee. Imam Abu Hanifah is of the view that the purchaser can exercise his option of seeing the goods once manufactured, and if somebody purchases a thing, which is not seen by him, he has the option to cancel the sale after seeing it. However, Imam Abu Yousuf says that if the commodity conforms to the specifications agreed upon, the purchaser is bound to accept the goods and cannot exercise the option of seeing."

The auditorium was quiet now, and something in what he was saying was capturing the attention of the delegates. Amir felt his heart quicken as he pressed on: "Now to the time frame for Delivery in Istisna' The time of delivery is not fixed in istisna', but there can be a maximum time for delivery, and if this is exceeded the purchaser is not bound to accept the goods.[1] If agreed by both parties in the case of late delivery, the price shall be reduced by a specified amount each day. Itisna' as a Form of Financing is especially used in the house finance sector. It is not necessary that the financier constructs the house, as he can enter into a parallel contract of Istisna' with a third party or hire the services of a contractor. He can calculate the cost and fix the price of Istisna' with his client. For security, the financier may keep the title deeds of the house or land until the client pays the last installment. In this case the financier will be responsible for the construction of the house in conformity with the specifications in the agreement. If there is any discrepancy the financier must correct it at his own cost.Istisna' can also be used as a mode of financing for large projects such as building a bridge or highway. It can also be used for modern BOT – buy, operate and transfer – agreements whereby a government wants to construct a highway and the cost of istisna' gives the right to the builder to operate the highway and collect tolls for a specified period.

Amir took another drink of water. He had finished the material he had prepared for the day but felt that he could go on. The organizer however was tapping his watch, although he looked pleased with the response to the lecture.

"Any questions?" Amir said. A few hands went up and he noticed Eddie Lancaster again, but did not point to him. Somehow he felt it was important that he not draw Leila's attention to Eddie, vitally important. Eventually Eddie's hand went down. Whether because Amir had answered his question in a reply to someone else or whether it was because he had got tired of waiting Amir could not tell. Lancaster was leaving the auditorium now and Leila was making her way to the podium. Amir breathed a sigh of relief.

As Eddie Lancaster stood in the door of the auditorium speaking to an investment banker from HSBC he glanced back at the podium where Amir was greeting a woman wearing a hijab on her head. There had been several Moslem women at the conference and Eddie had looked up as each one had passed, hoping to see Leila. He did not kid himself. He knew that he wanted to see her, knew that it was more than possible that she could be here at the lecture and his stomach had been in knots since he arrived the day before. The prospect of meeting her, bumping into her by chance in one of the hallowed halls of her alma mater had his stomach churning and his mind going twenty to the dozen. He had doubted that he would be able to concentrate at the lecture, but he had found that he could, was hungry even for more of the subject that he had been introduced to by Leila. The news from the city was alarming and his Blackberry had been red-hot all day with bulletins from Wall Street, his office and his father. Thing were going into meltdown and no one seemed able to stop it.

Like Amir he had noticed that during the lecture the usual restlessness of the largely banker audience had been stilled. It seemed that people were paying close attention to what Amir was saying. But would any of them act on it? It seemed that the gulf between what was accepted practice and Islamic finance was one that could not be crossed in such a short timespan, but if it may be the answer to the world's financial woes, wasn't it worth trying – could they afford not to try? He frowned to himself; he could not imagine where the current financial crisis would end. The markets were jittery and the movement of funds had virtually dried up as banks and financial institutions played their cards close to their chest. There had already been rumours of banks collapsing, giants in the banking world that Eddie could never have imagined failing faced that very real possibility.

A buffet had been put on for lunch and Eddie crossed to a large smoked salmon displayed beautifully on a silver salver, surrounded by delicate baby vegetables. As he reached out for the tongs to take a piece of the fish his hand knocked that of another diner.

"I'm sorry – after you," Eddie said, looking up from the table.

The eyes that met his were as familiar as his own, as longed-for as summer after a harsh winter, and as loved as his life.

"Hello, Eddie" Leila said.

Chapter Fifteen

For a long moment there was silence. The spot on the back of Eddie's hand where Leila's hand had brushed his felt as though a bolt of electricity had passed through it. For the longest time Eddie held his breath before finally gulping in a ragged breath. In a voice that sounded hoarse and tired he said, "Hello, Leila." He felt like crying and laughing at the same time; a hundred questions were buzzing around in his head. As their gaze held he wished he could drown in the depths of those rich brown eyes. His eyes wanted to look down, needed to look down, at the fourth finger of her left hand. Was she married? He kept his eyes on her face, not wanting to end this perfect moment. But she was the one to look away and his eyes, released from hers, darted down to look at her hand. There was a ring there, and somehow he had known that there would be. His heart had broken so many times over this woman he thought by now there would be no more of it to break. He was wrong – the pain of seeing that neat gold ring on her long elegant finger cut him like a knife.

Leila was surreptitiously looking at his wedding finger. No ring.

Eddie stood, empty plate in hand, while Leila helped herself to some of the salmon. He watched her every move and noticed that her hand was shaking slightly. As she leaned forward the wayward strand of hair that had always escaped her hijab came loose and rested on the side of her face. Eddie felt a tenderness for her well up in him. How he longed to lean forward and tuck that stray lock back into her head-dress. But he could not, especially now that she was married.

Eddie followed her to a table, where they sat, her food untouched , his plate empty.

"So how have you been, Eddie?" she said in that soft melodic voice that had captivated him all those years ago. As he drank in every detail of her face he could see that her girlishness had gone and in its place was the face of a truly beautiful woman. She almost took his breath away and he had to concentrate hard to get the words out.

"Fine, very well; and you, Leila?"

"Yes, very well thank you, Eddie. I have two daughters – twins." She fumbled in her bag and brought out a little leather wallet, showing him the faces of two lovely girls who were the image of their mother.

"They are lovely." Eddie heard his voice break. "How old are they?"

"They are six," Leila said, smiling proudly at the photos.

"Is your husband at the conference?"

"No; he is a businessman; this is not really his field."

"I see."

"And you, Eddie – are you married?"

Eddie dropped his gaze. "No, never married," he said.

The unspoken words hung between them but neither would acknowledge them, Eddie because he did not want her to know how badly he had missed her and she because her life was settled and had no place for him.

In the doorway, freed from the clamour of bankers waiting to speak to him at the podium, Amir scanned the dining room for Leila. At first he did not see her as Eddie's broad shoulders in his expensive suit obscured her. As he walked forward, however he saw her, looking intently into Eddie Lancaster's face. Amir felt his stomach lurch and then immediately chided himself for his thoughts. Leila was a grown, married woman who could handle the situation herself. She had two daughter, she was happy and she was a good Moslem. What was he worried about? He decided not to interrupt them; after all, if Eddie Lancaster held Leila in such high regard, it could do no harm for the message that Amir was trying to get across.

So instead Amir sat with some of the other speakers, only to be bombarded with questions. He felt that little flicker of hope again. Could it be that the message was getting through? He was to speak the next day as well; it would be interesting to see the response to that talk and to see who turned up.

Long after the delegates had left the dining room, Eddie and Leila sat, her food still untouched before her and his plate still empty. They talked about all that had happened in their lives, of the times they had had at Harvard. Leila made Eddie laugh as she told him that Eme was now married to a multi-millionaire record producer, and ruling the roost with her four children, and he smiled as he heard how Laura was working with children in war-torn Afghanistan. And Eddie made Leila laugh as he described the Jessen sisters, Sandy married with two children and Suzi, unmarried and "holding out for the biggest wallet" as he put it. He did not mention that one of the children that Harry and Sandy had was his son, Byron.

The lectures had started again as they spoke and the waiters were clearing up around them. Eddie found that he could not begrudge Leila her happiness; her contentment and fulfillment shone from her like a beacon and her confidence in herself and in her life humbled him. When they finally finished talking, darkness was falling and the dining room was filling up again for the evening meal. This time they ate together, in companionable silence. After they had said goodnight Eddie had the best night's sleep he had had for years.

* * *

The second day of the conference dawned bright and clear and Eddie got to the auditorium early. He wanted to sit near Leila and so feeling a bit like a stalker he busied himself looking at the literature that Amir had left on the table outside the hall until she arrived. She did not see him and walked into the auditorium slightly ahead of him. He caught up in a few strides.

"Good morning, Leila!" he said.

"Eddie! I'm glad to see that you are attending Amir's second lecture."

"I wouldn't miss it, Leila; it reminds me of the days we

spent in the library all those years ago."

Leila smiled. "I am very glad that the things we talked about made such an impression on you."

"They did," Eddie said, taking a seat next to her near the front of the auditorium.

"Maybe you would like me to show you around the college after the lecture?"

"That would be great," Eddie whispered as the auditorium fell silent.

As Amir took the podium he scanned the room until his eyes settled on Eddie and Leila sitting near the front. He must not start thinking the worst again; he had to concentrate on the lecture. He lined up his slides and cleared his throat.

"Good morning, ladies and gentlemen, and welcome of this second lecture on Islamic finance. I will start with Islamic investment funds." The delegates turned to their programmes and many sat poised with their pens hovering over their jotter pads.

"Islamic investment funds are joint pools where the investors contribute their surplus money for the purpose of its investment to earn halal profits in conformity with the precepts of Shari'ah. Their subscription may be certified, entitling them to pro rata profits earned by the fund. These can be called certificates, units or shares. Their validity in terms of Shari'ah is subject to two conditions." Amir started his slide show.

"The subscribers must enter the fund with a clear understanding that the return on their subscription is tied up with the actual profit earned or loss suffered from the fund. If the loss is due to negligence or mismanagement, the management will be liable to compensate it.

"The amounts pooled together must be invested in a business acceptable to Shari'ah. For example, the company neither borrows money on interest nor keeps it surplus in an interest-bearing account and its shares can be purchased, held and sold.

"A variety of modes of investment may be accommodated keeping within these basic requisites," Amir said. "I will start with Equity Funds. In this the amounts are invested in the shares of joint stock companies. The profits derive through capital gains by purchasing the shares and selling them when their prices have increased, as well as from dividends. The following conditions must be met in dealing with equity shares for it to be acceptable in Shari'ah: the main business is not volatile of Shari'ah; if the main business is halal, but they deposit their surplus amounts in an interest-bearing account or borrow money on interest, the shareholder must express his disapproval; if some income from interest-bearing accounts is included in the income of the company, the proportion of such income in the dividend paid to the shareholder must be given in charity."

There were murmurs around the hall and Amir saw several of the delegates shaking their heads. One, the leading light of a particular aggressive hedge fund group was laughing openly. Amir smiled to himself. He only hoped they would still be able to laugh in a couple of years' time.

"Continuing," Amir said; "the shares of a company are negotiable only if the company owns some liquid assets. If they are liquid it cannot be purchased or sold except at par value, as money cannot be traded. Some scholars are of the view that illiquid assets must be at least 51 per cent. They argue that if such assets are less than 50 per cent then most of the assets are in liquid form on the basis of the juristic principle that 'The majority deserves to be treated as the whole of a thing.' Other scholars argue that if the illiquid assets are 33 per cent, its shares can be treated as negotiable."

Looking around the room, Amir said, "I will now continue with purification. This is the process whereby the profits earned through dividends must be given to charity. The Shari'ah scholars have different views about whether the purification is necessary where the profits are made through capital gain, i.e. by purchasing the shares at a lower price and selling them at a higher price. Other scholars are of the opinion that even in this case purification is necessary, because the market price of the share may reflect an element of interest included in the assets of the company."

The head of the hedge fund who had laughed earlier now openly snorted in derision, although gratifyingly Amir saw that others were shushing him.

"Moving on to the management of funds, the management of the fund may be carried out in two ways. First, they may act as mudaribs for the subscribers, in which case a certain percentage of the annual profit accrued to the fund may be determined as the reward for the management. The second option is for the management to act as an agent for the subscribers. They may be given a pre-agreed fee for their services. This may be fixed in a lump sum or as a monthly or annual remuneration. Contemporary Shari'ah scholars also argue that the fee can be based on a percentage of the net asset value of the fund. For example, it may be agreed that the management will get 2 per cent or 3 per cent of the net asset value of the fund at the end of every financial year. This way may be justified by the analogy of a simsar, a broker, for whom the fee based on percentage is allowed. Which method is to be chosen must be determined before the launch of the fund and agreed upon by all subscribers."

Amir paused for some water. "Now, ladies and gentlemen, I would like to talk about ijarah funds. Ijarah is leasing the detailed rules. In this fund the subscription amounts are used to purchase assets such as real estate, motor vehicles or other equipment for the purpose of leasing them out to their ultimate users. The ownership of these remains with the fund and the rentals are charged from the users. These rents are distributed among the subscribers. Certificates called Sukuk are issued to evidence each subscriber's share. These can be bought and sold in the secondary market, and whoever has one replaces the subscriber in the ownership of the relevant assets. The price of these are determined on the basis of market forces and normally based on profitability. These must conform to the principles of Shari'ah, as explained earlier under 'Leasing'. In this type of fund the management should act as an agent of the subscribers and should be paid a fee for its services. Most Moslem jurists are of the view that such a fund cannot be created on the basis of Mudarabah, because this is restricted to the sale of commodities and not to leases or services. However, according to the Hanbali School, Mudarabah can be affected in services and leases also. Contemporary scholars prefer this view."

Amir paused. "Now on to commodity funds. The subscription amounts in this type of fund are used in purchasing different commodities for the purpose of their resale. The profits generated from these are the income of the fund and are distributed accordingly. All the rules governing the transactions of sale must be complied with to make this fund acceptable to Shari'ah. These are outlined previously in transactions of sale rules. It is evident that the transactions in the contemporary commodity markets, especially in futures, do not comply with these conditions. Therefore, an Islamic commodity fund cannot enter into such transactions.

"Next I would like to draw your attention to mixed Islamic funds. This is where the subscription amounts are employed in different types of investments, such as equities, leasing, commodities and so on. If the proportion of liquidity and debts exceeds 50 per cent its units cannot be traded according to the majority of the contemporary scholars. In this case the fund must be a closed-end fund."

Amir looked around the auditorium. Many more delegates than yesterday had attended and many more were making notes.

"Now, to explain the next item, the murabahah fund, I can tell you that if a fund is created to undertake this kind of sale it should be a closed-end fund and its units cannot be negotiable in a secondary market. This is because the portfolio of Murabahah does not own any tangible assets.

"If you look at the next heading bai'-al-dain which means a person has a debt receivable from a person and he wants to sell it at a discount. The traditional Moslem jurists, fuqaha, and many contemporary Moslem scholars agree that this discount is not allowed in Shari'ah. The prohibition is a logical consequence of the prohibition of riba. However, some scholars of Malaysia have allowed this kind of sale. They normally refer to the ruling of Shafi'ite school wherein it is held that the sale of debt is allowed, but they did not pay attention to the fact that the Shafi'ite jurists have allowed it only in a case where a debt is sold at its par value. Once a commodity is sold, its ownership is passed on to the purchaser and the seller no longer owns it. What the seller owns is money; therefore if he sells the debt it is the sale of money, and this is prohibited. Limited Liability is an ingredient in large-scale enterprises of trade and industry in the modern world. It is a condition under which a partner or shareholder of a business secures himself from bearing a loss greater than the amount he has invested in a company with limited liability. This came about with the emergence of the corporate bodies and joint stock companies. The purpose was to attract the maximum number of investors to large-scale joint ventures and to assure them that their personal fortunes would not be at stake if they invested.

"If the liabilities of a limited company exceed its assets, the company becomes insolvent and is liquidated. The creditors may lose a considerable amount of their claims because they can only receive the liquidated value of the assets and have no recourse to its shareholders for the rest of their claims."

Amir took another gulp of water and glanced at Eddie and Leila. Eddie was writing on his pad and Leila sat, her face serene, looking up at him. No; he had no need to worry about her.

"Lastly, I would like to talk about juridical personality. In this concept a joint stock company enjoys the status of a separate entity as distinguished from the individual entities of its shareholders. The separate entity as an effective person has legal personality and may sue and be sued, make contracts and hold property in its name, and has the legal status of a natural person in all its transactions entered into in the capacity of a juridical person. Whether a juridical person is acceptable in Shari'ah is questionable. Once the judicial person is accepted and it is admitted that despite its fictive nature it can be treated as a natural person in respect of the legal consequences of the transactions made in its name, we will have to accept the concept of limited liability. If the creditors of a real person can suffer when he dies insolvent, the creditors of a juridical person may suffer too, when its legal life comes to an end by its liquidation. This has not been envisaged by the modern economic and legal systems and is not dealt with in the Islamic Fiqh, yet there are certain precedents from where the basic concept of a juridical person may be derived."

Amir started his last sequence of slides. "Waqf. This is a legal and religious institution where a person dedicates some of his properties for a religious or charitable purpose.

After declared as waqf, these properties are owned by Allah and not the donor. The beneficiaries can benefit from the proceeds of the dedicated property. Moslem jurists have treated the waqf as a separate legal entity and ascribed to it characteristics similar to those of a natural person. This is clear from two rulings given by the fuqaha', or Moslem jurists: Firstly, if a property is purchased with the income of a waqf, it cannot become a part of the waqf automatically. The property is owned by the waqf.

"Baitul-mal. This is another example of a juridical person in the classical literature of Fiqh. This is the exchequer of an Islamic state. Being public property, all the citizens of an Islamic state have some beneficial right over the Baitul-mal, yet nobody can claim to be its owner. Imam Al-Sarakhsi in his work Al-Mabsut says: 'The Baitul-mal has some rights and obligations which may possibly be undetermined.'

"Inheritance under debt. This is the property left by a deceased person whose liabilities exceed the value of all the property left by him.

"Master of a slave limited liability. This is the closest example to the limited liability of a joint stock company.

"The concept of limited liability can be justified from the Shari'ah viewpoint in the public joint stock companies and those corporate bodies who issue their shares to general public."

Amir let his shoulders drop. He always got tense at these lectures but today he felt that there was something more, an excitement, the thought that he was witnessing the stirring of something new in the psyche of these men who controlled the world's finances. He prayed he was right.

Leila had intended to speak to Amir after the lecture but the jostling crowd around him made her think again. She could catch up with him later.

"How about we take a look around?" she said to Eddie.

"As you know, I studied here; I am familiar with Oxford," Leila said.

"Yes I know; you were lucky. I've read a lot about it. Which college were you in?" Eddie asked.

"Exeter College. Come on; we can walk up there now if you like." Leila had prepared herself for a sense of anticlimax on her return so many years later to her alma mater. She had built up such exalted memories of the place, and now at last in Turl Street, she was about to enter, again, the quadrangle of Exeter College. She could hardly wait to see the Victorian Gothic chapel again whose spire they could see towering above them from the road. History seemed to seep from every brick of the magnificent old buildings. She imagined the feet that had trodden these floors before her, not least J.R.R. Tolkien, whose classic *Lord of the Rings* she had read over and over again. Just as she had remembered them, a tangle of students' bicycles leaned up against the old walls, where years of scuffs from handlebars had left permanent grooves in the old stone.

Leila was enjoying showing Eddie around the Oxford campus. They had not been inside any of the other colleges but she wanted to show him the famous Botanical Gardens.

Approaching winter had rendered the gardens largely dormant, but they were still a wonderful sight. Occupying four and a half acres in the centre of Oxford, this unexpected oasis was a vibrant splash of green in the middle of a city. As they wandered through the gardens, which were protected from the chill wind on all sides by the tall buildings, she felt the sun begin to warm her face.

Eddie smiled at Leila's obvious delight in showing him around. "Wow! You would never have guessed these gardens were here, would you?" he said.

"No, you wouldn't, but aren't they beautiful?" Leila said, her eyes dancing with delight. "They were opened in 1621. This was a great place to study in the warm weather or sometimes I just used to come here to get away from it all!"

"I can see it would be great for that," Eddie said.

"One of the alumni of Exeter College was JRR Tolkien and I read that he liked to relax in the gardens, under a certain tree," Leila said shyly.

"If you look you'll see it is surrounded by the original seventeenth-century stonework. The garden's oldest tree is in there."

"What type of tree is it – an Oak?" Eddie asked.

"No; it's actually an English yew," Leila said. "Over that way are the glasshouses for the plants that can't stand the British weather." They stopped under an enormous Austrian pine.

"Pinus nigra," Leila announced. "People think that it might have been the inspiration for the Ents of the *Lord of the Rings*, the walking, talking tree people of Middle-earth."

Eddie stood under the tree looking up. "Of course," he said, "I can see that."

"You know *Lord of the Rings*?" Leila asked.

"Almost by heart, I've read it so many times," Eddie said.

Leila threw back her head and laughed. "Me too." They sat down together on the bench, Leila staying silent to give Eddie a few moments to imagine the great Tolkien looking out over the same view that they now enjoyed, from this very spot. While she did Eddie observed her beautiful face, her cheeks flushed now with the cold of the day, her eyes bright and alive with her thoughts.

Eddie imagined what it must have been like for Leila, coming from Harvard to Oxford, two of the greatest seats of learning in the world. But she had obviously enjoyed her time; she was a woman who made the most of any situation she was in, and he admired her for that. He wondered what it must be like to be so sure of your religion and your beliefs that you would sacrifice anything for them, even your happiness. But maybe he was kidding himself – certainly his happiness had depended on her for a long time, and after this meeting she would no doubt haunt him and populate his dreams again. She, however, seemed very happy with her life, her twins and her husband. So why then was she spending so much time with him? Because, he answered to his own question, he was an old friend, no more or less than that. There had been not one word or gesture that spoke of anything other than a fondness for an old college friend. Sadness invaded his heart as he realised that he would have to make the most of this infinitesimal opportunity in the span of his life to be with the only woman that had ever touched his heart. He must no waste time feeling sadness for their inevitable parting – he must enjoy and store in his memory every moment they had together.

"Did you watch the boat race while you were at university here?" Eddie asked, as they strolled on towards the river.

"Oh yes; I found it thrilling!"

"I've often seen it on TV and it is a very historic event," Eddie said, watching the thin boats with their oarsmen moving in perfect synchronicity. In the cold air the breath of the cox at the front of the boat stood out as she shouted her commands and the men in the boat responded in unison. The river was glassy, still and cold looking, its surface only broken slightly by the narrow hull of the craft resting on it. Small ripples emanated from the points in the water where the oars dipped in and out; so precise were the movements that the blades made no splash.

"I'd love to have a go at that," Eddie said.

"And you would have been just the kind of man they were looking for, if you had been at Oxford," Leila said.

They had turned back now towards the college and the historic buildings rose to each side of them.

"The conference ends tomorrow," Eddie said.

"Yes; have you enjoyed it?" Leila turned to him, and he felt his heart melt as her lovely eyes sought approval in his, wanting him to have enjoyed it, especially the Islamic finance element. But that was all she was worried about; her heart was not breaking as his was at the thought of saying goodbye again.

"I have; it was good to hear Amir speak again."

"Oh yes, he is inspiring isn't he? Leila clapped her hands together in a girlish gesture. Impulsively Eddie captured them in both of his.

"Oh Leila; it has been so wonderful to see you again." She looked up at him, startled, and immediately he felt her pulling her hands from his.

"I'm sorry, Leila, I didn't mean ..."

"That's fine, Eddie. I have enjoyed seeing you again too." Leila tucked that stray tendril of hair into her hijab again.

Leila's mobile phone went off and she fished it out of her bag. Her face lit up and Eddie felt a dagger in his heart. He was pretty sure that it was her husband and any vain hope that he might have had that Leila had married him out of duty was dispelled as her lovely face became animated with happiness as she spoke to him.

"That was Nasser, my husband. He leaves for America

tomorrow night; he has just confirmed his flight with TransAtlantic Airlines. It leaves tomorrow at 8 p.m. so I think I will leave the conference a little early to have some time with him before he goes."

"Hey, I'm booked on the same flight! Although I think I might change it. I haven't been in London for some years; it might be nice to have a couple of nights there."

"That would be great for you – you might even find time to come over and meet the twins!"

"I'd love to," Eddie said, his sprits soaring at the thought of seeing Leila for a few more days before their lives tore them apart again. He knew that she could not invite him to stay at her home. He would not expect her to, but the chance to get a peek into the life she had was too tempting to turn down. He made a mental note to remind himself that he must cancel and re-book his flight. He was pleased at the thought that he would not be on that flight in first-class travelling with half a dozen of his colleagues from various banks in New York. He hated shop talk and given the state of finances in the world at the moment, the economy was likely to be the only topic of conversation.

In the event, Eddie forgot to cancel his seat on the otherwise full flight that took off over the Atlantic the next night. First class had one empty seat next to a garrulous trader from Wall Street who was spouting doom to anyone who cared to listen, oiled by several glasses of scotch that he had had in the first-class lounge at Heathrow airport.

Almost precisely below the empty seat, in the lower deck of the jumbo jet, far down in the hold of the huge aircraft a small light flickered on. If Eddie's father Edward had been there he would have recognized it as the same type of device that had been removed from his private jet all those years previously. Only that device had not been armed. This one, taped with duct tape to the inside of the wheel arch, was armed. It was ticking – it was counting down the minutes. Far above in the first-class cabin, Leila's husband Nasser was putting his earplugs in, choosing some soothing classical music to drown out the loud conversation that was going on around him amongst the delegates who had obviously been to the same conference as Leila.

Ironically, the loud Wall Street trader was saying, "You mark my words – it'll blow up in our faces!" when with a deafening white hot explosion, it did. In the silence that followed, human remains and thousands of fragments of belongings, seats and plane fell silently through the night into the Atlantic.

Chapter Sixteen

The news of the attack on flight 602 TransAtlantic Air ricocheted around the world like a hail of bullets. There had been no incident that put more fear into the hearts of people since the attack on the Twin Towers in New York in 2001. The fact that the first-class section of the plane had been largely comprised of America's most senior bankers on their way back from a conference in the UK made it appear as though the motive was obvious. It was another deadly attack on the already wounded and lumbering western economic system.

In New York as news got round, banks convened emergency meetings and families gathered at JFK to hear the worst. In London, Leila was asleep with her earplugs in. She felt tired after the conference and did not want to be woken by the traffic that trundled by on Park Lane. So she slept, blissfully unaware of the ringing phone and the messages building up on her answering machine.

In his hotel, The Cumberland, at the top of Oxford Street, Eddie saw the news as he flipped on the TV in his room. He did not hear the beginning of the news bulletin as he went into the bathroom, but when he came out he saw the familiar face of Doug Stratten, the head of Global Bank. Eddie thought he was probably talking about the conference, but there was something about the grey tinge to his face that made him reach for the remote and turn the sound up.

"Of course, it is a terrible loss to the bank. We had five of our finest men on that flight." As Doug started to read the names, Eddie felt a drumming in his ears. The flight, the one he had forgotten to cancel, had gone down somehow, and he should have been on it. Eddie ran back into the bathroom and threw up his evening meal. He kneeled by the toilet, the colour drained from his face. He should have been on that flight.

He rushed back into the bedroom and started to click between channels. Eventually he found what he wanted, CNN, the rolling 24-hour news channel. Along the bottom of the screen was the headline "Flight 602 TransAtlantic Air brought down over the Atlantic, terrorist attack suspected."

In New York Edward and Arabella sat, their faces ashen, listening to the policeman who had come from the district station to tell them what had happened.

"I'm sorry, sir, ma'am; we believe that your son, Edward Lancaster Junior, was booked on that flight."

"Yes." Edward confirmed the fact. "Yes, he was coming back from London from a conference."

The young officer nodded gravely. "There were a lot of people from the banks in New York on the flight, sir."

"Yes, there would be." Hearing the conversational tone of his own voice Edward could not believe that he was making small talk when his son had been blown into a thousand pieces in the dark of the night over the cold Atlantic. He felt sick but at the same time unable to move. Arabella had not spoken at all; she sat her pale face almost translucent, her hands calmly folded in her lap, her eyes fixed on a point somewhere over the young policeman's shoulder.

Edward put his hand on hers and almost immediately withdrew it. Arabella's hand was as cold as ice, and white as though she had no blood in her veins. She seemed not to notice his touch and kept staring into the distance. Behind her white expressionless face however, she was in turmoil. She was replaying the conversation she had had the day before with Sharif.

"How is your son?" he had asked while his fingers played a concerto on her taut flesh.

"He's fine," she had said in a breathy gasp. Sharif had immediately stopped his ministrations and instead stroked her corrugated hair away from her face. It was so full of hair spray and setting lotion that it did not move as strands of hair, rather as a massive quiff rising up above her pointed face.

"He's away," she had said while every nerve of her body screamed for his touch.

"Oh; you must miss him," Sharif had said.

Arabella had frowned, or what approximated a frown in her heavily botoxed face. Why was he so interested? Still, those fingers were hovering tantalisingly close to her neck now, above the spot that sent her into raptures of delight, and she knew that they would come no closer unless ...

"He's home in a few days ... Thursday," she had added as his eyebrow rose.

"Ah yes, the conference in the UK; I nearly went myself." For a moment Arabella forgot his hand tantalisingly close to her neck. It was the first thing he had ever said that gave any indication as to what he did, where he went, who he was. "I was going to come back on Thursday too, that TransAtlantic Air overnighter from Heathrow is a pretty good flight."

Concentrating on her screaming nerves again, Arabella had muttered, "Yes; he and his father always travel on that flight."

Now as she sat transfixed by a spot on the window Arabella's internal organs felt as though they were frozen in ice. She saw herself from above, a desperate ageing woman begging for sexual favours, giving out information about her family to a man about whom she knew nothing. And now Eddie was dead, and she had killed him, just as surely as if she had stuck a knife in his heart. It was not a matter of speculation; she knew that Sharif was behind it. Why he had done it or for whom he had done it she did not know but he was behind it, of that there was no doubt. She felt sick. But that feeling was not because of the death of her son, it was because of the knowledge that even now, if he were to call her, she would meet Sharif and her treacherous body would betray her the instant he laid his hands on her.

Louisa, their maid, was at the door of the drawing room, trying to catch their attention. She had been fielding calls in her broken English while the young policeman had been with them.

"Not now, Louisa," Edward said, but she did not move

from the doorway. Arabella moved her gaze to the girl and so did the young policeman.

"Missy Arabella, it's Master Eddie; he on the line!" She waved the cordless phone triumphantly.

Arabella and Edward both dived for the phone. Edward got there first.

"Eddie? Is that you? Is it really you, son?" Arabella held her breath; could this be a cruel mistake, an answerphone message or something like that?

"Yes, dad, it's me; look sorry I didn't call earlier. I only just heard. I missed the flight, forgot to cancel it, hell, whatever, I wasn't on it, but dad—" his voice broke "—I should have been."

"It's OK son, it's OK." Edward felt tears begin to stream down his cheeks. Next to him straining to hear what was being said Arabella leant against him. She was crying too.

As he stood, his arm around his wife, comforting his son on the phone, Edward thought how ironic it was that one of the only moments in their lives that they had truly come together as a family had only been possible because they believed that Eddie was dead.

After he had put the phone down, and let the slightly confused NYPD officer out, Edward locked himself in his study. Like Arabella, intuition told him that Sharif had a hand in this. Edward had met him earlier in the week, been called out of a meeting to see him, the first time that had happened, and he had caught a cab the short distance to the Stardust Café from his office off Wall Street.

As usual, Sharif said very little. Edward asked him why he had called him out of a meeting to see him. Why he had not made the usual call with the usual code for the time they were to meet?

Sharif had given a ghost of a smile. His expression said it all. He had called Edward out of a meeting because he could – no other reason – just because he could. The old expression came to Edward's mind; Sharif would say jump and Edward could do nothing but ask how high.

Edward's jaw had tightened. He could not believe that this situation was going on so long after he had first met Sharif. Well, he could not put up with it any longer.

"This is the last time I will meet with you, Sharif."

Sharif raised his eyebrows

"Yes, this is it, the end of the road. Soon my son will take over the bank and before that happens, the money that we are paying to the Middle East War Orphans Fund will have to stop. He will ask questions and I am sure you do not want that. He is unlikely to be as accommodating as I have been; in fact, he will not be, times are changing, my friend; we can't bury this any longer. Questions will be asked."

A brief expression had flickered over Sharif's face, which Edward tried to read. Had he got him worried? Maybe he had. He felt the first glimmer of hope that he could rid himself of this thorn in his side.

For a moment Sharif studied his hands. Then he rose from his seat, smiled briefly at Edward and left.

Now as he sat alone in his study looking over Central Park Edward let the tears run down his face for the second time that day. He had signed his son's death warrant. Sharif had obviously known that Eddie was booked on that flight. It wouldn't take much to find that out, and the flight was crammed with bankers. Edward put his head in his hands. He had signed the death warrant of every person on that flight. His son was safe, but his soul would have to carry the weight of every life lost, every career cut short, every parentless child and every friend lost on that flight. He had crossed Sharif and the message he was sending was crystal clear.

It was eight o'clock in the morning before Leila heard that she was a widow. Amir Ali had arrived early in the morning, coming straight from Oxford. The maid asked if she should wake madam.

"No; let her sleep. This news will not improve for its early telling." Amir said. He was left alone in the salon and began to pray. He prayed for the strength to tell this lovely woman that her husband was dead, killed in the most grotesque and horrific way, that she and her two daughters were left alone. Amir prayed for the wisdom to give her strength until her family could be with her.

Tying her dressing gown, her hair still messed from sleep, Leila ran into the salon to see him. Her maid had told her he was here and she knew that he would never come at this hour unless it was important. One look at his face and she knew that something awful had happened.

"What is it, Uncle Amir?" She sat down beside him.

He took both her hands in his. "My dear Leila, you will have to be very brave."

An hour later, Eddie arrived at Leila's front door. She had given him the address and asked him to call the following afternoon to meet the girls. Now he stood awkwardly on the door step, his eyes heavy from lack of sleep, wondering what on earth he was going to say.

Amir was startled to see him. Eddie could tell that. Amir held Leila closer to him as he comforted her. But when she realised that Eddie was there she ran to him, burying her head in his shoulder. Eddie knew that the gesture was no more than she would have done to anyone of her girl friends at this time, but God it felt good to have her in his arms.

He looked over Leila's shoulder at Amir. He could read the expression on the man's face. It was grief for Leila, who was like a daughter to him. Eddie had been aware in the past that Amir was cautious around him. Amir had seemed wary, suspicious of his motives and in a way that had been a comfort to Eddie. That Amir thought that there was anything to worry about was a glimmer of hope in his hopelessness. Now, however, when he should have been concentrating on the devastation of this vulnerable woman he was noting that Amir showed no sign of concern at all that Eddie was holding Leila in his arms. He pulled his thoughts back to Leila and the pain that she must be feeling. One of her twins appeared in the doorway, touseled from sleep and sucking her thumb. Leila flew to her and gathered her up in her arms. She hurried out of the room and Eddie heard them going up stairs.

Left alone together, the two men sat down.

"I can't believe this has happened," Amir said, shaking his head. "Did you ever meet Nasser?"

"No. I was hoping to, but no, I had never met him," Eddie said. His stomach was still churning when he thought about the narrow escape he had had. "I was booked on that flight," he said quietly, and Amir looked up sharply

"You were?"

"Yes; I forgot to change my booking."

"Do you think—" Amir did not finish the sentence; he did not have to.

"That I was the target?" Eddie said; he shrugged.

"There were a lot of very powerful men on that flight; I don't think that I was a target in particular, but certainly in general." his stomach turned over as he spoke. The fact that he had not slept was not helping. He felt weak, vulnerable and out of control.

In New York Edward's helplessness had been replaced by a murderous rage. He knew who was at the bottom of this, and the fact that Eddie had forgotten to cancel his seat on the flight confirmed it. Sharif had thought Eddie was going to be on it – how, he did not know. But if this man could get a device onto Edward's private plane then he was more than capable of sabotaging a passenger jet and more than capable of finding out who was on the passenger list. Besides which, the conference was well publicised; the delegates, including Eddie, interviewed on CNN. It was an important conference; some said that the fate of the world's finances rested on it. The city was in chaos, his phone had not stopped ringing and as Wall Street prepared to open the world braced itself for the inevitable drop. Usually Edward would have been in his office by now, waiting with everyone else to see how the market would react. But somehow it all felt trivial compared to what he had been through; believing his son dead, even only for a few hours, had brought sharply into focus what was important in life.

Now all he could focus on was finding Sharif. He had put a call in to the office and left a message for Eugene to come round to the apartment. Now Louisa was at his study door. Eugene had arrived.

Edward did not get up as the older man walked in. Instead he pointed to a chair in front of his desk without meeting his eye or taking his outstretched hand.

When he did look at Eugene's face it was drawn, dark shadows under his pale watery eyes.

"I'm so sorry, Mr Lancaster. Mr Lancaster Junior will be a sad loss of us all."

Edward looked at the man. "Did you come from the office, Eugene?"

"No; I picked up my message from home and came straight here." The older man was obviously confused, and obviously did not know that Eddie was OK. Had he been the one to tell Sharif Eddie's travel plans? Edward felt the murderous rage bubble up inside him again.

"The payment to the Middle East War Orphans fund – when is it due?"

Impossibly, Eugene went paler than ever.

"Next week."

"Cancel it. There will be no more payment to the fund." For a moment Edward thought Eugene was going to faint.

"Did you hear me? No more payments," Edward said through gritted teeth.

Eugene nodded.

"Now get out – you're fired."

The next visitor summoned by phone call to the apartment overlooking the park was a man in a long trench coat who limped on his right leg. He offered his left hand and as it met Edwards's right hand they formed, for a moment, a bizarre tableau, looking like they were holding rather than shaking hands.

"Hesham," the man said.

"Edward Lancaster," Edward said, offering a seat. As he sat down opposite Edward, Edward saw that half of his face was horribly scarred and his right eye was missing.

"Not going to win any beauty contests, am I?" the man said laconically.

"I'm sorry; I didn't mean to stare'" Edward said.

The man shrugged. "People do; it's part of what keeps me committed to do what I do."

"What happened?" Edward asked, wondering if he was pushing it a bit far. But the man smiled at him, or at least the left half of his face that still had working lips smiled at him.

"I was recruited as a suicide bomber, and for a while I was set on that path. But the problem was that underneath that I am a good Moslem and I knew that what I was doing, or planning to do was wrong, very wrong. When I got up the courage to break away from the lunatics who bring disgrace to the name of Islam they gave me a little going away present. Shrugging off his coat he showed Edward a withered arm and hand, the skin burnt and then scarred.

"They set fire to me," he said starkly. "By the grace of God, the fire burnt itself out before it engulfed my whole body. I was found by good people who brought me in from the desert and I spent over a year in hospital. I was very near to death many times but when I recovered I knew what I had to do. Which brings us to your dilemma. Tell me about it."

Edward began the story that had started so long ago, and was embarrassed by how little information he could give on Sharif. But as he spoke the man in front of him began to nod slowly, the taut burned skin on the right side of his neck pulling his head over to one side.

"The man you refer to as Sharif is called Ali al-Sharif. He is a dangerous man, a deadly man and I am surprised that you have survived this long with him at your elbow."

"I have been paying handsomely for the privilege of having his particular brand of threat hanging over me for many years."

Hesham nodded. "And now you think he has something to do with the flight that came down?"

"I know he did."

Hesham looked at him for a moment from his left eye, an intelligent and knowing eye that said a lot about who Hesham had been before his horrendous burns.

"You are right. It has all his hallmarks. I will know by the end of this day."

"So if you know him and what he is capable of, am I to assume it is also near to impossible to stop him?"

Hesham sighed. "He is a very intelligent man, who hates the West and what it stands for. He is dangerous because of his intelligence and his protection."

"His protection?"

"That is enough for now. I will find out what I can for you, and I will come back to see you one week from today, here, at the same time. Oh, and Mr Lancaster, do not do anything that will arouse his suspicion or his anger."

Edward thought about Eugene and his meeting with him. He had calls to make.

In the event, Edward was too late for Eugene. Eugene knew that he was between a rock and a hard place. The same thorn that had been in Edward's side for almost his whole life had been in his as well. Sharif had collared him first when he was a young man, a timid young man very unsure of himself, and of his sexuality. Eugene had been bought up by strict parents and he lived with them in a cramped apartment on the East Side. The young man who had befriended him was beautiful, a free spirit, as liberated as Eugene was restricted. It had taken time to win Eugene's confidence, to get him to admit to himself that this young man with his hard muscled body was what he wanted. That he did not, as he should have, lust after the soft yielding flesh of a woman. His mother nagged him incessantly about it. She wanted grandchildren, although they also wanted him right under their noses; they never even contemplated his moving out of the cramped flat, so how they thought that Eugene was going to find a woman prepared to join him, in his cramped room in the run-down brownstone that was freezing in winter and baking in summer and bring up a family there, was beyond him. One thing he did know though was that if they even thought for one moment that he was a homosexual, they would kill him.

So Eugene had taken his guilty pleasure where he could, far away from them in seedy hotels or in the summer down by the river, or Long Island. Joe had been an awakening to him, a chance for him to realise who and what he was, and Eugene loved him completely. His whole life changed and he could barely concentrate at work. But he was diligent, hard working and responsible so he did his job to the best of his ability, living for 6 p.m. when he could leave the office and go and meet Joe. His parents thought he was courting a girl; they even became quite animated from the filthy worn armchairs that they occupied from morning till night, an overflowing ashtray between them. And Eugene basked in their renewed admiration for him, let them think that he had a "young lady". He answered all their questions about her, omitting only the fact that she was a he called Joe and that he was totally in love.

And then one day Joe did not turn up to meet him in Times Square as they had arranged. Instead a tall man with dark eyes and a menacing presence introduced himself as Sharif and, taking Eugene by the arm, guided him into the Stardust Café.

In a soft, gentle voice and with a look of polite regret on his handsome face Sharif listed the times and the places that Eugene had met Joe and, in precise detail, what had occurred between them. He also described Eugene's flat and his mother and father, the chairs they sat in, the number of cigarettes they smoked every day, even describing the yellowed windows of the brownstone, coated in many years of nicotine. As Eugene's face drained of colour and the bile rose in his throat Sharif began to outline what Eugene would do for him.

As Eugene walked away from Edward's flat on that cold winter day, when his genuine desire to offer condolences had been thrown in his face along with his job, hopelessness overwhelmed him. As he walked to the subway tears streamed down his face. It seemed that his whole life had been spent at the mercy of other people's whims. His parents, now dead, had ruled most of it, Sharif and Edward the rest of it. He had had no other relationship since Joe; he could not face it, could not bear to have his heart broken again. He felt cheap and stupid, that he could have thought that a young man as handsome as a Greek god would have liked him, with his pale pimply face and sunken chest. "How love can make fools of us all," he said out loud as he descended the stairs to the subway. He thought of all the empty years after Joe when he did as he was told by his parents, and by Sharif, in case his secret was told, and endured meetings with Edward in which the obvious was never stated and the deception carried on. Now he had lost his job. The only human contact he had out of the brownstone were the people he worked with. He knew that they only tolerated him; he saw their glances at his dated clothes, frayed cuffs, greasy hair and acne. He was not popular, hell, he was hardly even noticed. He was tolerated. He could bear it no longer. As he reached the platform for the downtown train, this quiet man who had spent his whole life in the bank and even worked on beyond retirement age for Edward stepped off the platform in front of the subway train for Brooklyn.

By the time that Edward heard the news of his death, Eugene's mutilated body had been in the city morgue for the best part of the day. In the shock that had swept the financial sector of New York after flight 602 had been brought down, no one really noticed that Eugene had not come to work, although the woman who sat next to him in the open plan office, Marlene, who always complained bitterly about his stale body odour, was enjoying a day free of his pungent smell. It was unusual for Eugene to be absent, he almost never was, but Marlene was not complaining.

When it finally did break, the news of Eugene's death was almost pushed to one side. The deaths of many of the city's most eminent bankers far outweighed the death of an insignificant bank clerk, and as had been the case for all the time he was alive, in death, Eugene was largely overlooked.

Sharif heard the news of Eugene's death shortly after he heard that Eddie had not died on flight 602. For a man who never lost control and who was never caught on the wrong foot, Sharif experienced an alarming moment of light-headedness. He wondered what had tipped Eddie Lancaster off and what had tipped Eugene over the edge. He tried to tie the two occurrences together in his mind, to find a connection; there was one, he knew, but he felt disconnected, out of control. For the first time in his adult life he was foundering. His last meeting with Edward Lancaster had annoyed him and having it in his power to exact his revenge he had done so, or so he thought. Edward's only son and heir was, by now, supposed to be in a thousand different pieces in the Atlantic. The device he had had planted on the aircraft was even directly below his seat. Someone in London must have got sloppy, not to have realised that Eddie Lancaster had not even boarded flight 602.

Sharif rubbed his temples. He had a headache coming on. Still, he comforted himself. His work was being hailed as a triumph, the bonus of so many bankers being on the flight, a fact that had meant to divert attention away from Eddie Lancaster had, in his circles, been warmly received. But Eugene, the sad little man that Sharif had watched deteriorate over the years – what had happened to him? In all the excitement of the day Eugene had not been followed as he usually was. In fact he must have gone to Edward's apartment straight from home. What had been said there? What had happened to make him jump in front of a subway train? Had he jumped? Maybe he had tripped. Or could he have been pushed? Sharif did not like unanswered questions; he was used to being in control, used to having the answers to everyone else's questions. This was uncharted territory and he did not like it. He did not like it at all.

In her room at the far end of the apartment Arabella stared at her little phone. Would Sharif ever call her again? He must know that she had her suspicions about him. Would he dare to call her again? Would he imagine that she would never want to see him again, that she would never want to lie in his arms and feel his hands on her willing flesh, his fingertips playing concertos on her skin. At the thought of it a small moan escaped Arabella's lips. She hated herself for being in his thrall; she hated herself for being so weak, needing him so much. She recognised that she was eager and willing to forget the fact that he had planned to kill her only son, just for another afternoon of the ecstasy he and he alone could bring her. What kind of a person was she? As she wiped tears from her eyes, the little phone rang. She answered it. On the other end of the line Sharif was waiting for her reaction.

"Is that you? Is that really you? Please say something!"

The tone of her voice, the naked longing for him in her desperate plea told him all he needed to know. She may have some answers – he would have to meet with her.

"The Novotel, 4 p.m. Will that be alright, my love?" he said in honeyed tones.

"Yes. Oh yes!" She was crying now, with relief.

Chapter Seventeen

A month had passed since flight 602 had been brought down over the Atlantic, and as it always does, life soon returned to normal in the financial institutions of the world. Positions left vacant after the catastrophic events of that cold February night had been filled and desks that had been occupied by experienced and senior men now bore no trace of their ever having been there.

The financial climate was still uncertain; any little blip had markets going into freefall and currencies bobbing up and down like apples in a barrel. Banks chased major projects ferociously and the mood amongst the world's biggest banks was jittery.

When his father had first told him about the Lewa project, Eddie had been interested immediately. Sheikh Lewa of the UAE was a well-respected financier who usually held fast to his Islamic banking principles. However he had become involved in a multinational project that, alongside Islamic finance tenets, had elements of Western finance for which Lancaster Bank were to be responsible. The project, to build a multi-billion chain of high-profile hotels with golf courses across the Middle East, was an ambitious one. Eddie had met the sheikh, a charming and gracious man, and had put in place a team that included Bill Turner, an experienced bank negotiator, and Sam Mendez, one of their leading project loan officers and an expert in risk management. But while he had been in the

UK things had started to unravel and he had had several worrying phone calls from Bill Turner in Dubai.

Eddie looked at the file in front of him on his desk. It was the latest report on the Lewa project. It was the first really big project that his father had entrusted to him. He really wanted it to go well. There was a lot at stake.

Natasha, his secretary, buzzed him through and told him Sam Mendez was in her office.

"Tell him to come through," Eddie said through gritted teeth. He watched as the older man came in and took a seat.

Eddie stared at Sam Mendez. He had had a hard time even getting the man into his office. And no surprise – it looked like he was a total screw-up, and was jeopardising the bank's biggest project with Sheikh Lewa in the UAE.

"Look, Sam; as a project finance loan officer you are supposed to take end to end responsibility for the identification, structuring, negotiation and execution of project financing opportunities, in line with the bank's objectives. What the hell is happening with Sheikh Al Lewa's project? You know the problems we've had; this has been a very delicate negotiation. He is usually one hundred per cent Islamic finance." Mendez looked down at his hands. "I had a call from Bill Turner in Dubai last night. He seems to think you've taken your eye off the ball."

Mendez ran his finger around the inside of his collar nervously. "You know that you are supposed to be managing relationships with key clients, day by day and be following up on proposals and development in the market. We gave this to you because you were supposed to have in-depth knowledge of the local UAE markets and the relevant language skills. Specialist transactional history is required for this and you told me you had it! What I hear from the Sheikh's office is not encouraging. Fluent in Arabic? They beg to differ. Let me make it clear to you: as a credit risk officer in project and structured finance your primary responsibilities are to provide specialist structuring to support to the bank's loan origination teams, and the provision of credit opinions on a wide variety of non-recourse project asset finance and high yield lending operations, across a variety of sectors usually, but specifically at the moment, to the Sheikh's project. You are also supposed to be advising on the formulation and approval of these loan agreements and associated legal documentation, from draft term sheets through to final contracts. We are looking to you to bring solutions to complex, and quite often unique, deal structures. As a transaction management officer in project finance monitoring, you are supposed to be proactively following the EIB project finance loan book, post-signature, enabling this bank to act on post-signature events, to maintain the credit quality of its operations, and to protect its financial interests and reputation. When I gave you responsibility for a defined portfolio of project finance operations, you said that you would have no trouble in preparing regular financial reviews, and maintaining relationships with project finance borrowers, agent banks and our co-lenders. So far we seem to have been sailing by the seat of our pants. I'm asking you, Sam: are you up to the job? It doesn't look like it from where I'm sitting."

Eddie shook his head. "Look, Sam, we are at the stage now when you should be negotiating any necessary amendments and contractual waivers, and frankly I have no confidence in you at all."

Mendez was still looking at his hands. "I'm sorry," he mumbled.

"Sorry?" Eddie said. "Look, Sam, I need more than that! What's the problem? What's gone wrong? You have always been one of our best men."

"I'm sorry," Mendez muttered again, his head down. As he looked at his hands he saw the face of a handsome, softly-spoken Arabic man, someone who had made it clear to him that if he did not do as he said he would make it public knowledge that Sam had a penchant for young Asian girls, very young Asian girls. How would his family react to that? How would his colleagues? How would the police?

So Sam had sat on his hands while his phone rang off the hook, looked the other way when the fax machine spat out its daily offerings, and lost files and facts and figures on command. He felt sick about it, he felt trapped and vulnerable. He knew it was only a matter of time before he was hauled into the office. He could feel Eddie Lancaster's frustration and annoyance – it was almost palpable – and he could say nothing. He had to promise to do better, he had to keep his job. Sharif had been very clear about that; he needed him in the organisation, but he also needed him to make sure that the bank's project failed.

"I've had some bad news," Sam lied.

"Oh?" Eddie asked.

"Yes; my wife, Maria. She has cancer."

"God, Sam; I'm sorry to hear that. Why didn't you say? We could have let you have leave."

"No, no; I don't want any leave." Sam looked up, wild-eyed.

Eddie looked at him, puzzled, then shrugged. "OK. But let me move you onto something here so that you don't have to do the travelling, give you something a bit easier for the time being."

Sam was on his feet. "No. Please, no!" There was real terror in the man's eyes and Eddie felt strangely disturbed by it.

"I just thought—" Eddie started.

"Yes and I appreciate it," Mendez said, his face flushed. "But I want to stay on the project – please, please let me. I promise that I will do better, much better."

Eddie was confused. All his instincts told him that he should not have a man in such an obviously disturbed state in a key role on the project, but Mendez was so, well, desperate to stay on it.

"OK, Sam, I'll see you in a month. But listen, buddy, if I get any more reports—"

"You won't – I swear it." Mendez was pumping Eddie's hand, the sweat standing out on his brow. As the older man left the room, Eddie sat down, swivelling his chair around to the Manhattan skyline view. He felt sorry for Mendez. He doubted his father would have shown so much mercy, but he could see the man was desperate. Eddie frowned; perhaps he should have taken him off the project. Did he really want someone as obviously stressed heading such an important venture for the bank? He would have to go out himself, see what was going on. Eddie looked at his watch. He would put in a call to Leila in London.

"Hello?" Eddie could hear the pain in Leila's voice, still raw. He winced.

"Hi," he said, tentatively. "I just thought I would call you ..." What could he say, to see if you were OK? She would not be OK for a very long time. Luckily she saved him the chore of finishing his sentence.

"I'm getting there, thanks, Eddie."

"Oh, well .I just wanted to let you know I'm going out to Dubai; it's to do with a bank project."

"Oh really? Uncle Amir is at a conference out there next week. Maybe you could go to a couple of his lectures?" Eddie's heart beat a little faster.

"Are you going?"

"I was, but—"

"Yes, of course"

Eddie wanted with all his heart to plead with her to go and he hated himself for being so selfish. God, the woman had just lost her husband – how could he be so uncaring? But it wasn't that. He loved her so much he felt her pain and longed to comfort her, take her burdens on himself. But she was out of reach. Not just geographically. He knew that, widow or not, she would never consider him as a husband, and it broke his heart.

Eddie hung up. Normally speaking to Leila would make him feel better but today he just felt wretched. He looked amongst his papers for the paper about risk management by C.J. Williams that he was gong to distribute to some banking interns later. He thought ruefully that it would be a good idea to send a copy to Mendez.

He started reading underlining sections as he went. There were a couple of very bright interns in the intake and he had high hopes for them.

In many projects, risks are identified and analysed in a random, brainstorming, fashion. This is often fatal to the success of the project, as unexpected risks arise, which have not been assessed or planned for and have to be dealt with on an emergency basis, rather than be prepared for and defended against in a planned, measured, manner. Very early in the preparation and planning stage, it is essential that potential risks are identified, categorized and evaluated. Rather than look at each risk independently and randomly, it is much more effective to identify risks and then group them into categories, or, to draw up a list of categories and then to identify potential risks within each category. This way, common influences, factors, causes, potential impacts and potential preventative and or corrective actions, can be discussed and agreed on.

Categorising risks is a way to systematically identify

the risks and provide a foundation for awareness, understanding and action. Each project will have its own structure and differences, but here are some categories that are common to most projects (to which you can add your own local, sector, or project specific, categories). I have not given deep detail here, but your project team and sponsors should be able to relate to these categories and use them in the risk assessment process. For example, with "operational resources" your team can discuss issues such as, availability, delivery timing, cost, capability, necessary conditions for operation (eg. ground, weather, light); with "stakeholder resources" your team can identify all stakeholders and list potential risks that these stakeholders may generate, such as bad publicity from the media, delays caused by community or environmental groups, delays caused by utility companies, problems with trade unions. Related risks and potential actions, must then be documented in the risk management plan and discussed at all the key stages as the project progresses. All the details and the actual action taken and the outcomes, must then be recorded and reviewed during the closure and review stage, for lessons to be learned and applied to future projects.

Here the question that most project managers ask: "how do we know if we can manage the risk, if it arises?" Often, sadly, no evaluation is carried out to determine the expertise, experience, capabilities of the team, individuals, organisations that would be required to deal with, manage that risk, if it occurred. As a result, if it did, the team may not be able to deal with it effectively, even though the initial forecast was that the risk could be managed. This happens frequently when the planning team is not the project team that manages the project and/or when key individuals in the original project team leave the team during the project and are replaced by individuals with different skills, experience and capabilities. The clear message here is that setting a risk tolerance level is a dangerous business. Each potential risk needs to be carefully, rigorously, analysed and the project team, the supporting teams and individuals, the organisation(s) involved in managing the project, all need to be evaluated to determine whether there is the capability to manage that risk successfully, should it arise. Where gaps in capability are identified, then appropriate corrective action must be taken. During the project itself, this capability must be constantly monitored and, where necessary, action taken to return the level of capability to the required level.

Conflict over resources often arise during the middle to later stages of a project, because, often unexpected other, newer demands arise which are seen as being of higher priority. This can lead to resources that were originally allocated to the project being taken away, or reduced in quantity or quality, almost certainly to the detriment of the project. The answer to this dilemma is not easy, but in essence, the project management team must include "conflict over resources during the life of the project" as a major potential risk and plan for it accordingly by securing agreements and then monitoring the situation continuously. If a dispute does arise, there is a role here for the project champion and or the client to ensure that the allocated resources are not taken away.

Fundamental to many of the issues that we discuss

here is the question of who should be responsible for risk assessment and management. Too often the responsibility for risk identification, assessment and management, are left to the project team, especially once the project has started. But there are other individuals and groups, including some external stakeholders, who should be continuously monitoring particular activity and feeding back regularly to the project team leader. Some are easy to identify. They include of course, the client, the sponsor, key specialists in the project team's organisation, or organisations, the major external participants, such as emergency services, local authorities and contractors.

The easy way to identify other individuals and groups is to look at your list of stakeholders. Each one has a responsibility, to a greater or lesser degree, to help identify potential risk and give information on this to the project team. Again, the answer to managing the question of risk responsibility is to build discussion, planning and action, on this into the project planning and operational activity.

His private phone rang as he finished reading. It was Harry. His voice sounded high and sort of tight.

"Hey, Harry, how you doing, buddy?"

"Eddie, it's Byron, he ... he's been taken! Harry's voice broke now and the rest of what he had to say was indecipherable.

"Woa, Harry; what do you mean, taken?"

"Kidnapped, abducted, stolen, I don't know what the hell I mean. Hell, Eddie, what are we going to do?"

Eddie felt a little thrill of irritation run through him. He was automatically being included in the solution to Harry's problem. The fact was he felt nothing for the child, nothing at all, in fact if anything he really rather disliked him. He was every kind of sickly weak geek that Eddie despised and Byron's mother was so far removed from his ideal as epitomised by Leila that he shuddered every time he thought about the congress that had given rise to Byron. Still, he did care about Harry and it was a child, for God's sake.

"Have they asked for a ransom?" Eddie asked.

"No yet." Harry was crying softly now.

"Well let me know when they do. I have to go to the Middle East in a couple of days but I can be back in hours if you need me."

"You're going away?" Harry hissed as though Eddie had said he was going to boil Byron alive.

"Yes, I have to. Look, Harry, you gotta get a hold of yourself. We can't risk anyone finding out that Byron is my... son." Eddie found it difficult to get the words out.

"No one will find out – why should they?" Harry's voice was whining now, desperate. "But Eddie, I need you here – I can't cope with this alone."

"You've got the Jessens and your folks haven't you?"

Harry snorted. "Can you imagine the level of hysteria here now – can you? Hell, Eddie, the Jessens are acting like I personally handed Byron over."

Eddie tried to hide his irritation.

"Look, like I said, I can be back in a few hours but I can't cancel. I'm really sorry Harry, I just can't."

Eddie found himself listening to the dialling tone. Harry had hung up on him.

In London Leila sat looking at the phone. There was no doubt that it would be nice to fly out to Dubai, leaving her troubles behind her, to lose herself in a subject she loved for a few days, to try and numb the pain that she felt so keenly every waking minute of every day. Every time she looked into the face of one of the twins and saw their father's eyes staring back at her, every time a letter came for him from some organisation that did not know he was dead, every time she had to speak to his mother, her heart broke again.

Somehow hearing Eddie's voice was a big comfort to her. He was someone who had not known Nasser, someone who did not think of her only as Nasser's widow. But even in her grief she knew that to give him any encouragement would be cruel. She knew how he felt about her, and she could not bear to give him false hope.

As Eddie walked out of the airport from his private jet flight, he lifted his face slightly to the sun. It was a lovely time of year in the Middle East, warm but not too hot, perfect for barbeques and visits to the desert. Eddie had been invited to join Sheikh Lewa in the desert for a traditional camp and he was looking forward to it. It was a male-only affair and Eddie thought a few nights under canvas, albeit most luxurious canvas with mounds of soft pillows and blankets, would do a lot of good in clearing his head. Eight hours later, as the limousine that the Sheikh had sent for him silently transported him out of the city and into the desert, he started to list the things that he would try to forget for the next few days. Top of the list was flight 602 that he should have been on. He had woken up many nights sweating in terror, as his dreams seemed determined to make him aware of what would have happened if he were on the doomed flight. Second was Leila. She had made it clear that she would not be coming to Dubai and he must not be distracted by daydreaming about things that he wished would happen that never would. There was something else. Eddie frowned and then immediately felt guilty. Byron. How could he have forgotten the child created by him who was now God knows where and suffering God knows what at the hands of his kidnappers. He had heard nothing from Harry but he felt sure that he would do, after all, whatever the ransom was if it was over $100 Harry would need help to pay it. On the other hand, old man Jessen was probably masterminding some way of bypassing the police and finding the kidnappers himself. He had the money, but he did not like Harry at all. Still, Byron was his grandson. Eddie hesitated before switching his Blackberry off. He could check it in a few hours – for now he had to concentrate on getting the Lewa project back on track.

The Sheikh and his staff were warm and welcoming and Eddie changed quickly in his tent into shorts and a loose shirt before joining the men reclining on opulent cushions, passing round the hubble bubble pipe. Eddie had acquired a taste for thee aromatic shisha over the years that he had been coming to the Middle East and his first taste always seemed to him to complete his transition from his world to the more exotic world of the desert.

The sheikh spoke perfect English and after the pleasantries had been exchanged and he had been offered sweet black tea and pastries they began to talk business.

"Some aspects of the project are not sitting well with me, Eddie," the sheikh said. "You know, I think of my strong adherence to Islamic finance and Shari'ah law in respect to these things. I am aware that for this project to succeed we cannot do without the input both in cash and in ideas of our Western partners, but still I feel I may be in danger of being asked to compromise too much over this."

"I do know how you feel about this and it is our aim to make it work so that you will not feel any element of compromise. That is why I have come myself to see you," Eddie said.

The sheikh bowed his head slightly. "And I do appreciate it, Eddie."

"In New York we are aware that we have let you down somewhat and the agent concerned has been spoken to."

"Ah yes, the elusive Mr Mendez. I was assured that he was one of your best men."

"He is," Eddie said, "but his wife is ill with cancer and it has affected his performance. However, I think that the problems he has had have been resolved to a certain extent and he has assured me of his best attention to the project from now on."

The sheikh bowed his head again slightly. "I have a

friend visiting at the moment; he is an expert in Islamic finance. It would please me greatly if you would go and listen to a couple of his lectures so that you get more of an idea of what Islamic finance is all about. His name is Amir Ali."

"I know Amir!" Eddie said. "I have listened to him talk many times. I first heard him when I was studying in Harvard."

"Good; he will be joining us for a meal tonight and then tomorrow you can accompany me to the conference centre to hear his talk."

"I would be delighted to," Eddie said, and found that he meant it. As he sat back on his cushions he thought about those days, so long ago now, when he and Leila would sit together in the library and she had opened up the whole world of Islamic finance to him.

Towards nightfall, Eddie walked out to the edge of the camp and looked out over the sand dunes of the desert. In the distance he could hear the whine of the buggies that the local youths and tourists loved to drive up and down the shifting sands. Eddie had tried it himself and loved it. Like a lot of what he saw and experienced in the Middle East, he found himself very much at home.

As the sun set he thought of Leila, deep in her grief in London. He wished he could be with her, to comfort her, to hold her, to make her pain go away. But the distance between them could be measured in much more than miles. Their cultures had them separated by a fathomless gulf. For a while Eddie thought about his religion, about the fact that he used it only for weddings, christenings and funerals. Why was it that every Moslem that he knew seemed so devoted to their faith? What did Islam have that kept its followers so devout and its extremists, however misguided, so extreme, prepared to die, without hesitation, for their cause? He thought about the impact that learning about Islamic finance had had on him, how somehow he always wanted to know more. Maybe it was a sign, a sign that he should look further into this way of life for millions of people all over the world.

Now he could hear the plaintive call to prayer and in a corner of the camp, facing to the East, the Sheikh led his party in prayer. WEST of Dubai?

The sound of the call to prayer, on the air turning cold as the night fell, haunted Eddie's dreams that night.

His sleep was deep and studded with stars and a feeling of peace and happiness that he had not had in years. As he lay in the first morning light he tried to hold on the feeling. It had been a long time since he had felt so ... what? Comforted? Safe? Untroubled? All of these things, probably. It was how he had felt in the early days when he had known Leila when everything had been new and nothing had been excluded. Her love for Islam and her passion for Islamic finance shone from her eyes. Eddie dreamt that her eyes would shine with love for him one day.

Now as he waited for the Sheikh so that they could drive back into the city to hear Amir speak, he began again to think of the religion that ruled this wonderful place, that was present in every grain of sand under his feet and in the very air he breathed.

The Sheikh's horsemen were going out hunting now, their hooded birds of prey held by jesses to their fists as they rode bareback and one-handed into the morning. Their robes flew behind them as they rode beautiful horses, Arab thoroughbreds, their birds ready to kill, kept hungry to preserve their hunting spirit. They were eager to fly now, their powerful wings tensed above the fists of the horsemen.

It was as haunting a sight as Eddie had ever seen. The power and the gentleness combined to give the tableau a hear-aching beauty, one of those scenes that would always be in the photo album of his mind waiting for an opportunity for an airing. For now, though, he watched them as they cantered over the sand, their fleet hooves hardly disturbing a grain as they went.

"It is a splendid sight, isn't it?" The sheikh stood beside Eddie.

"It is; breathtaking."

"I think there are a lot of things in my world that take your breath away," he said with a smile. Eddie smiled back.

As they drove from the desert to the city, Eddie sat back and listened as Sheikh Lewa spoke on the phone. He had learned a few words of Arabic from Leila and found that every now and then he could pick one up. He liked the sound of the language and the way in which, not unlike the Italians and some other Latin languages, it could sound as though there was a huge argument going on when in fact all that was being said was mundane.

As the Sheikh closed the mobile phone he was using he looked at Eddie gravely. Eddie knew immediately that something was wrong.

"It's your Mr Mendez."

"Sam? Has he arrived back in Dubai? He was supposed to arrive yesterday."

"He did and, it seems, worked through the night to put things back on track. He has put right all that we have asked and in fact done more than we could have hoped for. The vital files for the project that were missing?" Eddie nodded "Well he found them. All the castings for the operation in Abu Dhabi – he found them as well. For a man preoccupied with his wife's health worries he really has done more than could have been expected of anyone."

"Good," Eddie said, but the Sheikh still looked sombre. Before he could speak, though, his phone went again. This time the conversation was a long one and as Eddie stared out of the limousine window at the desert passing by he felt pleased with himself. His talk with Mendez had obviously done the trick. He looked back at the Sheikh. There was obviously something wrong but from what he had told Eddie about Mendez's turnaround it could not be connected to him or the project. Oh well; he was going to have to wait until the Sheikh had finished his call. On the skyline he saw a bird, one of the ones from the hunting party maybe, soaring above the sand dunes its jesses dangling beneath its outspread talons. As he watched, it swooped down to the ground as its wings brought it into a perfect glide above its prey. Eddie lost sight of the bird for a moment but once it was air-born again he could see a small bundle held in its powerful talons.

The perfect killing machine. He had to wonder at the majesty of the bird, which in its own element was a peerless hunter. Only the trailing jesses hinted at the fact that even this majestic creature could be subjugated.

The Sheikh had finished his call now. He looked at Eddie with an emotion that he could not read.

"You were saying about Sam Mendez – things are back on track now?" Eddie said.

"With the project, yes. But Eddie, Sam Mendez is dead, murdered. His body was found this morning floating in the creek. He had been stabbed through the heart."

Chapter Eighteen

In the silence that followed, the limousine drew up at the conference centre.

Eddie's mind was reeling. There was no doubt that the death of Sam Mendez was in some way connected to the project but in his shock his mind jumped wildly from one random thought to another and although he knew that Sheikh Lewa was speaking to him, he couldn't even take in what he was saying.

The Sheikh took him by the arm and led him to the lifts of the hotel that was hosting the conference.

"I have booked a suite for you, Eddie. Take your time; make all the phone calls that you need. I am so sorry that this has happened in my country. You can be sure that there will be a full investigation. Unfortunately, recently there have been a spate of robbings and killing mostly carried out by an Eastern European contingent that have come here looking for work. Finding none they have taken to crime. It seems your Mr Mendez has been a victim of this. Again I am so sorry."

Eddie looked at the Sheikh hopefully. If the killing of Sam Mendez was a random act of a lawless faction of the cosmopolitan society in Dubai, then he could rest easy. He immediately felt guilty. A man was dead, a man whose wife had cancer. He held his head in his hands.

a tender power

As the lift rose silently to the thirtieth floor the Sheikh rested his hand on Eddie's shoulder.

The luxurious suite had panoramic views over the gulf the aquamarine waters sparkling in the sunshine, small dots representing boats on the water and further out the derricks of the off-shore rigs could be seen on the horizon.

The magnificent man-made Palm Island spread out below them, but Eddie could pay all of it nothing but a cursory glance.

As the Sheikh ordered strong Arabic coffee to be made in the kitchen of the suite, Eddie put in a call home. He did not consider the time difference and his father's voice when he answered the phone was heavy with sleep.

Eddie told him what had happened and felt relief flood over him as his father said, "OK, Eddie, leave it all to me – you just get on with what you went there for."

The Sheikh had noticed the change in Eddie and smiled slightly. He was pleased that the day seemed as though it could get back on track.

For a while the two men sat without speaking. Eddie was taking in the view now. The weight seemed to be lifted from him and the Sheikh spoke again, tentatively broaching the subject that would be the topic of Amir's lecture, a lecture that the Sheikh had had postponed until they were ready to attend.

"The reason I wanted you to hear the lecture today, Eddie, was because I wanted you to know more about Sukuk and Securitization."

Eddie nodded. The Sheikh looked at him carefully, wondering if he was just being polite, but there was an interest in his eyes, an alertness. The Sheikh continued. "Throughout the Moslem world, the twentieth century has witnessed the revival of Islamic finance as an alternative mode of financing that complies with Shari'ah. The Islamic finance industry today offers a broad variety of products and services as well as corporate finance, project finance, equity funds, personal and wealth management, venture capital investment, real estate investment and private equity – all from its very ordinary beginnings when Islamic financiers were chiefly providing Islamic trade financing solutions. Structured in accordance with Shari'ah principles are all these products and services, as interpreted in their respective jurisdictions. The range of products available are often priced according to the market needs and provide Moslems with a practical option to Islamically manage their finance."

The Sheikh broke off to look at Eddie, to check he was still listening. He was, and his eyes had the enquiring gaze that had drawn the Sheikh to him initially, and intelligence that shone is his blue eyes. The Sheikh continued. "With the dawn of the twenty-first century the Islamic finance industry is continuing to venture into new and exciting areas of finance. The development of Islamic debt securities, commonly known as Sukuk, is one of the most important recent accomplishments. Many Islamic financiers have ended up with high levels of liquidity through various reasons such as increased oil prices, petrochemical manufacturing output, increase in trade activities, new product innovations and above all the increased output of goods and from China and India, particularly in the last five years, which has created a large surplus instead of deficit in the world trade market."

Eddie nodded, taking in what the Sheikh was saying.

"A huge amount of liquid cash has been generated within the GCC area and the Middle East and North African region. The Islamic finance industry also lacks Shari'ah compatible derivative products that could mitigate any asset-liability mismatch risks. The high levels of liquidity often led to inefficiency in the market and the industry leaders actively have to find solutions. The Sukuk, which is a tradable liquid investment, was seen as a possible avenue for Islamic financiers to invest their surplus liquidity, but at a time of increased liquidity all over the world, that is not enough. It is estimated that the overall size of the Sukuk market worldwide is worth nearly 70 billion US dollars, the bulk of which are over-the-counter instruments. Listed Sukuk account for only 20 to 25 per cent of outstanding Sukuk issued worldwide, that is 10 to 15 billion dollars so far. There are more Sukuk listed in Dubai than anywhere else, but the secondary market is virtually non-existent. Second is London, where the secondary market for Sukuk totalled less than five billion US dollars in March 2007."

Eddie raised his eyebrows; this was information he did not know.

"Among listed Sukuk, Standard & Poor's Ratings Services rates close to six billion dollars, or roughly 50 per cent of globally listed outstanding Sukuk. According to conservative forecasts, new Sukuk issuance is expected to accelerate, and could reach 20 to 25 billion dollars in the next five years. The largest Sukuk to date were those issued by Dubai-based Nakheel Group for 3.52 billion early in the first quarter of 2007. These notes were listed in both London and Dubai."

"So what effect will this positive showing in London have on the world markets?" Eddie asked.

The Sheikh nodded and sat forward in his chair. "Globally, the Islamic financial industry will benefit from the UK's development as an attractive marketplace for Shari'ah-compliant financing and investment instruments on both the wholesale and retail side. Up to 300,000 retail customers in the UK are potentially customers for Shari'ah-compliant banking services. The establishment of these services in the UK would extend the reach of an Islamic financial model, which is so far still concentrated in a few countries in the Middle East and Moslem parts of Asia. As for wholesale banking, London has the capacity to become a hub for Shari'ah-compliant financial flows that seek recycling in Europe. For example, Islamic investment banks such as Bahrain's Arcapita Bank BSC and Gulf Finance House both have offices in London where vast amounts of liquidity from the Gulf meet attractive Shari'ah-compliant asset classes packaged in private equity, real estate and infrastructure funds domiciled in the more mature and stable European economies. London has a wide approach to Islamic finance, encompassing a broad range of financial instruments and asset classes. The UK's Financial Services Authority has recently licensed the European Islamic Investment Bank, a wholesale financial institution created expressly to recycle the massive amounts of institutional and private liquidity in the Gulf into Shari'a-compliant asset classes originated in mature, stable, and transparent western markets. UK tax law, which is Sukuk-friendly, could make London more attractive for issuing and trading Sukuk, although Dubai has so far been the most active trading centre for Sukuk notes. The UK intends to become a key player in market intermediation for Sukuk."

"I hadn't realised, "Eddie said.

"Yes," Sheikh Lewa continued. "Competition from Western financial centres is low, as limited appetite for Islamic finance is coming from New York, where facilitating the trading of Shari'ah-compliant stocks, especially through the Dow Jones Islamic Index and through the family of Standard & Poor's Shari'ah indices takes precedence. Once issued, debt securities are traded in the secondary market. This process contributes to efficient pricing for upcoming issues. Unlike the stock markets, or futures and options markets, secondary trading in debt securities remains decentralized in most countries, although some securities regulators have sought to promote trading by requiring that the debt be listed on stock exchanges. Liquidity of an issue is predicated on the breadth and depth of the buying base. It is measured with the help of the difference between bid and ask prices, generally called bid-ask spread, and is determined by the trading volume. For sovereigns or sub-sovereigns, high volumes lead to efficient pricing and lower bid-ask spread, while debts issued by lesser-known borrowers suffer from lack of liquidity, which leads to a higher bid-ask spread. The size of the international bond market is estimated at 45 trillion dollars and the size of outstanding US dollar bond market is estimated at 25.2 trillion."

Eddie nodded.

"And it is because of the excellent work that Amir Ali has done that I wanted you to come to the lecture. "Have we missed it?" Eddie asked standing up.

The Sheikh smiled and extended his hand palm down.

"Sit down, Eddie. I have asked them to rearrange the schedule; it will not start until you are quite ready. The conference is over three days so there is plenty of time to re-schedule."

"I see; I am grateful to you for this. I very much want to hear the lectures, and I do appreciate your changing things on my account. I think if you can just give me half an hour to make a few more phone calls I will be ready to attend."

"Excellent. Shall we say after lunch then? Will you join me at the conference lunch or shall we eat up here?" the Sheikh said.

"It would be nice to attend the conference lunch, I think," Eddie said. "I would like to see Amir before his lecture."

The Sheikh smiled. He rose and left the suite with his entourage, returning momentarily to say, "If he is downstairs I will have him come up and say hello."

Eddie called his father back. Edward had started the ball rolling.

"How did his wife take it? It must have been tough with her suffering from cancer and all," Eddie said.

"You must have got the wrong end of the stick, Eddie. Maria Mendez is fine. Your mother and I played tennis with her and her tennis partner last week. She's no more suffering from cancer than I am. What's going on, Eddie?"

But Eddie's stomach was churning again, like it had when he first heard the news that Sam had been stabbed. Why had Sam lied? Surely he would not say such an awful thing just to get off the hook for his poor performance at work? For the second time that day Eddie felt his world spinning out of control. He knew that there was more to this than a simple case of being in the wrong place at the wrong time – Sam had been murdered because of his involvement with the bank and the Lewa project.

"Eddie?" His father's voice was sharp, enquiring.

"Sorry, dad, it's been quite a shock. I must have got hold of the wrong idea. It has been quite a day."

"Right," his father said, but he didn't sound convinced.

"Call me later."

"OK, Dad."

As Eddie hung up, the door opened. It was the Sheikh with Amir.

"Eddie, I've got someone to see you," the Sheikh said. Eddie stood up, smoothing his suit trousers ready to greet Amir.

As the entourage entered the suite Eddie spotted Amir and walked towards him. Because he was smiling at the lecturer he failed to notice that among the rest of the entourage was a woman in a hijab. It was not until he had greeted Amir with the customary three kisses on the cheek that he saw her face over his shoulder smiling at him. It was Leila.

Eddie felt as though he could burst into tears. The tension of the morning and the sight of such a beloved face almost tipped him over the edge. As he had come to expect, Eddie saw Amir looking at him closely and managed to pull himself together.

"Leila! I thought you were not coming."

"Uncle Amir persuaded me and I had been looking forward to the lectures a lot." Her face suddenly changed and a frown creased her brow.

"I am so sorry to hear about your friend Mr Mendez. It must have been a horrible shock for you."

"It was, and I am very happy to see you, Leila. I feel so much better having an old friend here."

"Less of the 'old' if you don't mind, Eddie!" she said, smiling her shy smile. "Are you looking forward to the lecture?"

"I am." Eddie guided Leila to one of the sumptuous white leather settees in the suite and they sat down next to each other. In the corner Amir and Sheikh Lewa talked animatedly. Eddie ran his hands over his head. It had been a surreal day, the beginning of it so beautiful in the splendour of the desert then the shocking news about Sam and now seeing Leila so unexpectedly.

"Where are you staying?" Leila asked, accepting the fruit juice offered to her by one of the suite's butlers.

"I was staying in the desert in the Sheikh's tented camp. And you?"

"Uncle Amir has booked a room next to his for me on the executive floor. We have almost the identical view," she said, turning her lovely face to the view of the sea and Palm Island. "It really is a magical place, isn't it?"

"It is." Eddie was amazed to discover that the tension that seemed to have been rising in him all day had now completely gone. That was the effect this lovely woman had on him.

"Shall we?" The Sheikh was at his elbow now, and the party were leaving the suite for the conference lunch.

"Eddie, I will quite understand if you would like to stay on the suite rather than return to the camp. I can have your things sent to you."

Just half an hour ago, Eddie thought, he would have begged to go back to the camp if he had to. But things were different now – Leila was here and only three floors below him.

"I will stay in the suite if you don't mind. There will be a lot to do following Mr Mendez's death," he said.

"Of course. I quite understand," the Sheikh said, and Eddie followed him to the penthouse's private lift.

Later in the conference hall Amir had taken his place on the stage. Eddie and Leila sat beside the Sheikh and his wife, who was herself a senior banker.

Eddie studied the diagrams that were projected onto the big screen of the auditorium entitled conventional bonds vs Islamic Sukuk

"So, to start with, conventional bonds," Amir said. "Primary level – this is loan contract to create indebtedness. The return to investors is the extra amount charged on the loan amount minus interest charges. The loan indebtedness is securitized with zero coupon. At the secondary level – trading of the bonds amounts to trading of debts, normally with discount bonds represent pure debt obligations due from issuer. The core relationship is a loan of money, which implies a contract whose subject is purely earning money on money. Bonds can be issued to finance almost any purpose which is legal in its jurisdiction Bond holders are not concerned with asset-related expenses. Bonds depend solely on the creditworthiness of the issuer; in case of issue failure unsecured bond holders join the pool of general creditors seeking the assets of a bankrupt company. The sale of bonds is basically the sale of a debt; if the debt is not receivable, there will be no value to the bonds. And now for Sukuk versus Asset backed securities." Amir pointed to his chart. "Asset-backed securities usually refer to securities or Sukuk backed by assets sold or transferred, usually and SPV which is described as "asset backed the main source of payment for which is revenue from underlying Sukuk assets and can be on or off balance sheet. Therefore, the structure of the Salaam Sukuk is firstly the Salaam Sukuk

Holders, or investors, linked to the SPV, which in turn is linked to obligators who are either selling commodities on a Salaam basis or undertaking future sales of commodities for the investors."

Eddie could not help looking at Leila's lovely face as she studied Amir's diagrams. As Amir's familiar voice began to deliver his lecture, though, Eddie was caught up once again in the fascinating subject of Islamic finance.

"I will start with the Definition of Sukuk. Sukuk, which is the plural of Sak, means certificates; Sukuk refers to securities, certificates and papers with the features of liquidity, tradability and cash equivalence. The AAOIFI's definition of Investment Sukuk – Standard 17(2) reads thus: 'Investment Sukuk are certificates of equal value representing undivided shares in ownership of tangible assets, usufruct and services (in the ownership of) the assets of particular projects or special investment activity; however, this is true after receipt of the value of the Sukuk, the closing of subscription and the employment of funds received for the purpose for which the Sukuk were issued.'"

There was slience in the hall and Eddie busied himself taking notes. Amir continued. "Securitization Sukuk is the result of Islamic securitization of assets, and securitization is a form of asset regulated by money supply. Securitization refers to a process of converting assets into cash equivalent in the form of papers that are tradable in the secondary market, the process of packaging financial promises and transforming them into a form which allows them to be freely transferred among multiple investors. Through securitization, a liquid asset is transformed into a tradable security that gives the liquid asset the liquidity feature by the deployment or creation of some market mechanism that allows the borrower to have direct access to the capital market. Lenders or investors are able to liquidate their positions or opt for better investment opportunities, thus creating of secondary market that benefits both borrower and investor."

Eddie saw several of the Middle Eastern delegates nodding in agreement as Amir continued pointing to the slides displayed on the screen when he touched upon their content in his lecture.

"Now for the history of Islamic debt decurities. As far as the Islamic finance industry is concerned, Sukuk are not new. Since the early days of Islamic civilization the concept of Sukuk has been in use – in the first century Hijri, corresponding to the seventh century AD the Umayyad government would pay soldiers and public servants both in cash and in kind. The payment in kind was in the form of Sukuk al-badai, which is commodity coupons or gain permits. The holders of the Sukuk were entitled to present the Sukuk on its maturity date at the treasury and receive a fixed amount of commodity, usually grain. Some of the holders used to sell their Sukuk to others for cash before maturity date and this is considered secondary trading of Sukuk. In the classical period, Islamic Sukuk was similar to the European root cheque inasmuch as it represented any document of a contract or conveyance of rights, obligations or monies done in conformity with the Shari'a. Empirical evidence shows that Sukuk were a product extensively used during medieval Islam for the transferring of financial obligations originating from trade.

In the modern Islamic perspective, the essence of Sukuk lies in the concept of asset monetization that is achieved through the process of issuance of Sukuk. Because Sukuk may be issued on existing as well as specific assets that may become available at a future date, its great potential is in transforming an asset's future cash flow into present cash flow. Sukuk re-emerged in Bahrain in 2001, almost fourteen centuries after they were first recorded, as an Islamic alternative to conventional debt securities. In the domestic market, the State of Bahrain offered Sukuk with an al-ijarah issue. The issue amount was 250 million dollars and had a tenor of five years. The Sukuk al-ijara concept was derived from prevailing practices of 'lease ending with purchase', or ijara muntahia bi-tamlik, known in conventional finance as 'financial lease'. The Sukuk carried six monthly lease rentals that were fixed at the lease inception and paid in arrears during the lease term. The Sukuk offering was highly successful. The Bahrain Sukuk issue was a major milestone in Islamic finance as it marked the birth of an Islamic capital market where Islamic equity and debt-based instruments are issued and traded.

"Another landmark was initiated by Malaysia in 2002 when it issued the first Islamic securities that complied with US Regulation S and Rule 144A formats that are used for conventional global bonds. Prior to that in December 2001 Kumpulan Guthrie Berhad, a Malaysian public listed company involved in the plantation and construction sectors has offered a Sukuk al-ijara issue in the US Regulation S format. The company offered 150 million dollar Sukuk issues with a floating rate return and the tenor was divided into three years – 50 million dollars – and five years 100 million. The Sukuk was listed on the Labuan International Financial Exchange. The first Sukuk to be listed in the Luxembourg Stock Exchange was the Malaysian Sukuk al-ijara and rated by Standard & Poor's and Moody's. The 600 million dollar Sukuk was offered globally to Islamic and conventional investors including 'Qualified Institutional Buyers' in the United States. The issue was highly successful and was oversubscribed twofold. The Malaysian Sukuk was a significant development because it was able successfully to fuse the concept of Sukuk al-ijara with conventional bond practices such as listing, ratings, centralized clearance and dematerialized scripts.

"A number of successful Sukuk issues have followed, including the Islamic Development Bank's offering of 400 million dollar Sukuk in 2003, the State of Qatar's 700 million dollar Sukuk al-ijara issue in 2003 and the Kingdom of Bahrain's 250 million US dollar Sukuk al-ijara issue in 2004. In the Islamic finance markets these successful issues have created much excitement and more issuers looking for a viable and attractive alternative source of funds are considering the Sukuk option."

As Amir paused to sip some water Leila looked at Eddie and smiled. He could see the pain in her eyes, eyes that had no doubt cried many tears over the last month. He wanted more than anything to take her in his arms. His muscles twitched with the effort of restraining himself.

Amir began to speak again and Leila looked away.

"Now to talk about the characteristics of Sukuk. A fundamental requirement of Shari'ah is that the security must reflect or evidence the security holder's share in an underlying asset or enterprise, which must of course be Shari'ah compatible. On the basis that the security reflects the holder's ownership of the underlying assets of the company, contemporary Shari'ah scholars have allowed investment in equity or share in a company. Through the ownership of the company, the shareholders are deemed to indirectly own the company's assets.

"With regard to the link between the ownership of the company and the ownership in the company's assets, Shari'a scholars have allowed 'the buying and selling of these securities on the model not of partnership in the enterprise but of undivided co-ownership of the company's assets.' If the company as a going concern makes a profit by trading in goods, assets or services, the shareholders are entitled to receive a share in the profit, through dividends, from the company.

"However, a conventional bond typically confers on the bondholder a contractual right to receive from the issuer of the bond certain interest payments during the life of the bond and the principal amount at the maturity of the bond. Creditors to the issuer of the bond are the bondholders themselves and are ranked as senior unsecured and unsubordinated creditors of the issuer in priority to the shareholders. The juridical nature of a conventional bond is contrary to Shari'ah. To structure a Shari'ah compatible instrument was the major challenge that embodies ownership characteristic of an equity instrument as well as the priority status and the fixed income characteristics of a bond instrument. The Shari'ah compatible instrument must also be transferable, rated by recognized rating agencies listed on major securities exchanges, cleared through major clearing houses, and documented in terms of legal documents and disclosures to maintain the conventional bond market's existing standards."

Amir paused, looking at the clock. His message was being received very well, but then if it were not received well here ... Eddie thought. Still there were a lot of foreigners in the hall and they all seemed to be hanging on Amir's words.

"So now, ladies and gentlemen, I will close for today and look forward to seeing you all again tomorrow for the next of my lectures on Sukuk."

As the applause died down and the delegates filed out of the hall, Eddie fell into step beside Leila. "Will you join me for dinner tonight?" he asked. "Unless maybe you have arrangements to meet with Amir?"

"I did have but he has to meet with some of the conference organisers about the next couple of days' scheduling. So yes, I would love to meet you, but what about Sheikh Lewa – isn't he your host?"

"He is but he is going back to the tented camp to receive another Sheikh arriving there this evening. He has told me to stay in the suite so that I can work more easily and also so that I can make the calls needed after Mr Mendez's death." Eddie was appalled to realise he had not thought about his colleague at all since Leila had appeared. Was he so shallow? No he was in love, hopelessly and helplessly in love.

"Well that is settled then." Leila said. "I must go to my room now and call the girls. Shall me meet in the foyer at 8 p.m.?"

"Yes, I'll see you then." Eddie said as she got out of the lift before him.

Back in the suite, Eddie kicked off his shoes and rummaged in his bag for his swimming trunks. The sun was low in the sky now but the hot tub on the balcony was inviting. He took the towel extended to him by the butler and stepped out through the doors. As he sat back in the hot tub his mind careered back to another night in another hot tub and he suddenly remembered Byron.

"Damn!" he said out loud. His phone had been off all day. Harry might have been trying to get in touch. Wiping his hand on the towel he reached for his Blackberry, turning it on.

There were three messages. One was from Harry. His voice sounded tense, as though he was close to tears.

"Eddie, you've got to ring me. They can't find Byron. They think he might have been taken out of the country. Hell, buddy, I'm going mad here – ring me, for God's sake!"

Eddie sat for a moment, the bubbles of the hot tub massaging his back and legs. He shut his eyes. He would call Harry later. After all, what could he do from here?

He dressed carefully for the meal that he and Leila would take on the terrace of the hotel overlooking the sea. He felt butterflies in his stomach.

As he passed through the lobby on his way to the terrace, he saw a crowd of people next to the reception desk. As he passed them he could hear snatches of what they were saying.

"Where did he come from?"

"He's obviously not staying in the hotel."

"He's filthy, needs a good wash."

Curious, Eddie tried to see who they were taking about. He could see that they were gathered around a child, an extremely dirty, thin child, maybe a beggar boy who had wandered in off the street, although it seemed unlikely he would be given the time of day. Suddenly catching sight of Eddie, the child bolted, running straight for him, shouting "Uncle Eddie! Uncle Eddie!"

It was Byron.

Chapter Nineteen

The fact that Byron was almost fifteen and behaving as though he was five was not lost on Eddie in the moment that the boy launched himself at him. Admittedly Byron had been through an ordeal and he was undoubtedly small for his age. He looked more like 10 than 15, but all the same Eddie felt physical revulsion for this weakling of a boy who had thrown his arms around him like a toddler. Eddie stood, his arms slightly out to his sides, unable to put them around the sobbing shoulders of his son. From slightly squint eyes Byron looked up at him, bewildered. Behind the boy Eddie could see Leila, her face a mixture of surprise and concern. Selfishly, all Eddie could think about was the implication of the boy turning up and the affect it would have on his evening with Leila.

The manager of the hotel had arrived on the scene now, hovering obsequiously at Eddie's elbow, his face a mixture of concern that such a rough looking specimen had turned up in his foyer and an earnest desire not to do anything to upset the Sheikh's VIP guest who was occupying the 1500 dollar a night penthouse. Seeing the manager, Eddie took Byron by the arm and said, "Could you please send a nanny to the suite to look after this young man?" The manager nodded, relieved to have something practical to do. Looking at Leila Eddie said, "Can you forgive me? I have to sort this out. San we meet in half an hour?"

"Will that be enough time? What has happened to this

poor child? Who is he? How does he know you?"

Recognizing a friendly maternal face, Byron turned his attention to Leila, throwing himself at her. She, despite his ragged and filthy condition, threw her arms around him and held him close to her.

Eddie thought fast. He would not, could not, sacrifice his evening with Leila, but he could also not afford to let her know how he felt about Byron, either.

"Perhaps you can come up with us to the Penthouse? I would appreciate it. Having no children of my own I am not sure how to deal with these things."

Leila's concerned frown relaxed a little.

"Of course!" They set off for the bank of lifts, Byron holding tightly to Leila's hand.

In the suite the butler, alerted to the incoming party, was ready to whisk Byron to the bath, while Eddie and Leila walked through to the large lounge of the suite.

"Who is he? The boy?" Leila asked.

"He's my godson, the son of a friend of mine. He was kidnapped in the States just before I came out here."

"Oh my goodness – his mother must be frantic! Aren't you going to call her?" Leila said, and Eddie realized he had not given Harry and Sandy a thought until that moment.

"Of course!" Eddie took out his Blackberry and dialled Harry's number.

When Harry answered, his voice had a mixture of utter weariness and sorrow with fading hope that this call might have something to do with Byron.

"He's here! Byron's here!" Eddie tried to put the right inflection of excitement that he knew Leila would expect into his voice. Leila stood, looking at him, her eyes sparkling, her hands clasped together, delighted at the fact that Byron's parents would be put out of their misery.

"What? Eddie? What?" Harry did not seem able to take the news in.

Eddie gave him a brief account of how Byron had run to him in the lobby. As he spoke, he realised that Byron had obviously been dropped off at the hotel because whoever had him knew that Eddie was here. Eddie's mouth went dry as the realisation hit him that whoever had taken Byron had taken him because he was his son. What they had not realised was that Eddie really could not care less what happened to the boy. This had been an attempt to hit him where it hurt and to let him know that the secret that he thought was safe was known to at least one other person, a person who meant him no good at all.

"Did you pay a ransom?" Eddie asked.

"No. No one has contacted us at all. But Eddie, how is he? Is he hurt? Can I speak to him?" Eddie heard Harry calling to his wife and tried hard to cover his irritation.

"He's having a bath – he seems fine. He will be able to talk to you in a little while."

"Oh, Eddie; I don't know what to say." Eddie could

hear Sandy snivelling into another phone. Harry spoke to her. "Honey, call the airport, get a flight out there. Eddie, tell him we'll be with him soon. Oh my God I can't believe it. Thank you, thank you." Eddie felt irritation rising in him again like an acrid bile. The last thing he wanted was Harry and Sandy arriving.

"I didn't do anything, Harry. I can get him back to you tomorrow on my private jet."

"No, we're coming out." Harry said. "We will have to get him checked out medically, but you could send the jet for us?" Harry asked, his wheedling tone annoying Eddie even more so that now he had to clench his teeth to stop his face, a face being watched carefully by Leila, from reflecting his true feelings.

"Yes, fine; I'll make the arrangements and let you know what time to go to JFK."

"Oh thanks, Eddie – thanks, buddy." Harry was crying now. "Thanks for everything; you are the best friend a guy could have. Can we talk to Byron now?"

"No – he is still in the bath. I'll get him on to you as soon as I can, OK?" Before Harry could reply Eddie had hung up. Leila was looking at him strangely. He had forgotten she knew him well, probably as well as anyone outside his family did. He had not let people close, except for Leila.

He dropped his head into his hands and sank down on the settee. Leila was beside him in an instant, her hand on his shoulder.

"Poor Eddie. I can see you are overcome. Can I get you anything?"

"Yes please, some Tylenol. I have the worst headache." He smiled weakly and now saw only concern on her lovely face.

Leila called over the butler, who produced Tylenol and a glass of water.

For a while Eddie and Leila sat in silence. This night should have been wonderful, a brief and unforgettable moment in his history with Leila, something for him to cherish and replay in his mind in the long months before he would see her again. Now it was ruined.

"Eddie – how do you feel?" Leila asked.

"Better, thank you" he smiled.

Byron was out of the bath now and hardly able to keep his eyes open. Leila had been to see him in one of the suite's bedrooms. He had spoken to his parents and Eddie had made the arrangements for his private jet to pick them up. It was already in the air.

"I am so sorry, Leila – you must be starving."

"So must you!" she smiled.

"Shall I get dinner sent up here? We could eat out on the balcony?" For a moment she hesitated.

"Yes; that would be nice, Eddie."

Eddie's heart leapt; maybe the night could be saved

after all!

An hour later they sat together on the balcony. Eddie had asked for sparking pear juice to be sent up rather than champagne and they sat sipping it, the cool sweet sharpness making Eddie think that he could easily live without champagne. Maybe it was the cool night air, the breathtaking blanket of stars up above them, or just the chance to sit opposite this wonderful woman with her dark eyes and lovely face, but Eddie felt something shift, deep inside. It was hard to know what is was exactly and he did not want to take any time away from this magical evening with Leila to examine it, but suddenly he felt calmer than he had for a long time. Despite the drama of the evening and the impending invasion of the Jessens and Harry, he felt for the first time that he could peep into his future without despair, that somehow, somewhere, Leila would feature in it, forever.

Leila and he spoke of many things. She spoke tenderly and sadly of her husband but with resignation, a sort of calm acceptance that Eddie envied. It was, he knew, her observance of her religion that gave her strength to cope with his loss, and the absolute belief that because he had been a good Moslem he would be enjoying paradise. When she spoke of this her face lit up as thought she were describing an exciting and wonderful surprise present she had bought to a loved one, her joy as great as theirs when they received it. Eddie envied her faith, and again he thought about how Islam seemed to look after its own, even at this very sad time. Leila was comforted, even thrilled, to think of the reward that her husband would enjoy.

As she spoke, her soft words hanging on the evening air, as he always did in her company, Eddie felt relaxed and at peace. He didn't want the evening to end, the morning would bring Sandy and Harry to his door, he would have to offer them a room in the four-bedroomed suite, and he resented it, bitterly. This was his place, his time to be with Leila to explore the subject of Islam and Islamic finance that was becoming increasingly important to him. It felt like the worst of all intrusions.

After Leila had left, Eddie sat on the balcony for a long time. He had dismissed the butler for the night and was about to reach for a bottle of bourbon when he spotted an opened bottle of pear juice in the ice bucket.

Putting the bourbon back, he opened the pear juice and poured it into the glass that Leila had used. As he sipped it felt as though he was actually touching her lips with his.

Eddie was not awake when Harry and Sandy arrived. The butler apologetically woke him by coughing discreetly at the foot of his bed. As he came to, outside he could hear the uproar of Sandy and Harry and what sounded like Mrs Jessen falling upon Byron, weeping and wailing and thanking God for his deliverance.

Harry, his eyes red from lack of sleep, appeared at the end of Eddie's bed before he could even get out of it. Hesitating for just a moment Harry launched himself at Harry, a lunge almost identical to the one that Byron had made the night before.

"Oh man, I can't thank you enough." Eddie could feel

his friend's hot tears through his pyjama top and patted him awkwardly on the back.

"Let me get up, Harry." Eddie hoped his friend did not notice the irritation in his voice.

The next hour passed in the sort of shambles that Eddie did his best to avoid. Mrs Jessen and Sandy sobbed uncontrollably, alternately clutching Byron to them, their faces developing the same blotches in the same places as they gave vent to their emotions. Harry just kept saying, "Thank you, man" and clapping Eddie on the back as though Eddie had single-handedly wrested the boy from the grips of King Kong. Eddie was very relieved when the butler told him that Sheikh Lewa was on the phone and gratefully shut his bedroom door on the chaotic scene in the suite so that he could take the call.

The Sheikh had heard about the events of the night before, and about the arrival of Byron's parents. He asked if he could be of any assistance and Eddie nearly cried with relief when he said that he was having another suite prepared for the family. He asked if Eddie would be attending the continuation of the lecture and Eddie confirmed he would. They arranged to meet for coffee in the auditorium at 11 a.m.

When Eddie arrived to meet the Sheikh, he found him sitting with Amir and Leila. The three were in animated conversation in Arabic but politely changed to English as he approached.

"I hear that you and his highness are doing business together?" Amir asked.

"Yes, the Islamic finance side of things is what I am here to learn. I know a fair amount already from my college days." Leila smiled at him warmly and Amir followed Eddie's gaze to the lovely young woman.

"That would have been your influence, I have no doubt," Amir said, and Leila nodded.

"Yes," Eddie said. "Leila has given me the grounding to develop a life-long interest in Islamic finance and on this project, which has a mixture of Islamic and Western finance, that has been invaluable."

"I thought that you had more than a passing interest," Sheikh Lewa said. "Others that I have dealt with in the past have had to learn the principles from scratch, but with you it always seemed as though you knew quite a lot."

"I hope to learn more." Eddie smiled at Amir, who looked at his watch.

"Indeed; shall we go? My lecture is due to start in ten minutes."

The auditorium was as full as it had been the day before; in fact Eddie thought there might be more people here and not only delegates from the Arab world – there were many Westerners.

As Amir began to speak, the hall fell silent. "Today I want to start with the principles of Sukuk. While a conventional bond is a promise to repay a loan, Sukuk present partial ownership in—" Amir pointed to his first slide "a debt, Sukuk murabaha; an asset, Sukuk al ijarah; a project, Sukuk al istisna; a business, Sukuk al musharakah;

or an investment, Sukuk al Istithmar. Sukuk structures most commonly replicate the cash flows of conventional bonds, being as they are listed on exchanges and made tradable through the conventional organizations like Euroclear or Clearstream. A key concept to achieve the capital protection without amounting to a loan is a binding promise to repurchase certain assets, which in the case of Sukuk al ijarah is made by the issuer. In the meantime a rent is being paid, which is often tied to an interest rate benchmark like LIBOR. Sukuk al ijarah as debt certificates can be only bought before the finance occurs and then held to maturity from an Islamic perspective, which is critical on debt trading at market value in terms of avoidance of Riba.

"The holders of the Sukuk will be considered under Shari'ah as co-owners of an asset, although held on trust. Each co-owner of an asset is entitled to sell his share in the asset without consent of the other co-owners at whatever price he can command in the market. When the trustee receives the variable rentals from the lessee, the Sukuk holders will receive a proportionate share in the rental proceeds. At the maturity of the lease, which corresponds to the redemption date of the Sukuk, the trustee will sell the trust asset to the lessee for a price equal to the original acquisition cost of the trust asset. On sale, the trustee will redeem the Sukuk and the Sukuk holders will receive their principal investment. The payment profile of the Sukuk is thus comparable to a conventional bond or a floating rate note. As Shari'ah considers money to be a measuring tool for value and not an asset in itself, it requires that one should not be able to receive income from money alone. This generation of money from money is Riba, which is forbidden. This makes impermissible such things as selling of debts, receivables for anything other than par, conventional loans and credit cards.

"In contractual terms, this principle is widely understood to mean uncertainty or the uncertainty in the existence of an underlying asset, and this causes problems for Islamic scholars when considering the application of derivatives. Shari'ah also incorporates the concept of Maslahah or public benefit, so if something is overwhelmingly in the public good, it may still be transacted, which is why hedging or mitigation of avoidable business risks might well fall into this category.

"This brings us on to Types of Sukuk. The following are commonly accepted as types of Sukuk" Amir pointed to his second slide. "Here we deal with Sukuk al ijarah, rental; Sukuk al intifa, operate and use; Sukuk al-musharaksh, subdivided into participation Sukuk, partnership company, Murabaha Sukuk, financing and investment Sukuk Salaam Sukuk, future delivery, Istisna Sukuk, manufacturing, Sukuk al-mudarabah, financing, Sukuk al-muzara'ha, sharecropping, Sukuk al-musaqah, irrigation and Sukuk al-mugharasah, agriculture.

"It is really comprehensive, I had no idea," Eddie whispered to Leila. Dhe nodded.

"And now, ladies and gentleman we are going to do a little exercise to compare bonds to Sukuk." In the hall there was the sound of rustling as people got fresh paper ready. "A bond is evidence of debt issued by the issuer or borrower to an investor or lender, an IOU with a promise to pay the debt or the financial obligation at the end of a specified period. It is also a debt instrument with fixed return, or loan plus interest, the obligation to pay the debt being evidenced by papers certificate called bonds or securities issued by the borrower or issuer; these certificates are tradable on the secondary market. Bonds are evidence of indebtedness only.

"Sukuk provide evidence of financial obligation from the issuer to the Sukuk certificate owner of the underlying asset. It is an asset instrument whereby the issuer pays the value being evidenced by a paper certificate called a Suk, or securities issued by the issuer. This paper certificate is tradable on the secondary market. Sukuk are evidence of assets, not debit; therefore, Sukuk are wider and have higher value than bonds.

"Sukuk investors benefit from better risk profiles, tradable instruments in maturity in the secondary market, and short- and long-term investment. They are priced competitively in line with conventional bond issues."

Amir paused and looked around the room. He had the delegates in the palm of his hand. He felt elated, he had noticed that each time he spoke the audience seemed to be getting bigger.

He loaded his next slides. "Ladies and gentlemen, take a moment to look at these tables, before we continue." There were murmurs around the room as the delegates discussed the information on the slides. "Continuing then," Amir said. "With Sukuk al-ijarah He put up another slide. "Sukuk al-ijarah are subject to risks related to the ability and desirability of the lessee to pay the rental instalments. Moreover, these are also subject to real market risks arising from potential changes in asset pricing and in maintenance and insurance costs. The expected net return on some forms of Sukuk al-Ijarah may not be completely fixed and determined in advance, since there might be some maintenance and insurance expenses that are not perfectly determined in advance. Sukuk al-Ijarah is completely negotiable and can be traded in the secondary markets.Sukuk al-Ijarah will offer a high degree of flexibility from the point of view of their issuance management and marketability. The central government, municipalities, awqaf or any other asset users, private or public can issue these Sukuk. Additionally, they can be issued by financial intermediaries or directly by users of the leased assets. Sukuk al-Ijarah holders, as owners, bear full responsibility for what happens to their property. They are also required to maintain it in such a manner that the lessee may derive as much usufruct from it as possible.

"And the next slide concerns Steps involved in the structure. The obligator sells certain assets to the SPV at an agreed pre-determined purchase price. The SPV raises financing by issuing Sukuk certificates in an amount equal to the purchase price. This is passed on to the obligator as seller. A lease agreement is signed between SPV and the obligator for a fixed period of time, where the obligator leases back the assets as lessee. SPV receives periodic rentals from the obligator and these are distributed among the investors, i.e. the Sukuk holders then, at maturity, or on a dissolution event, the SPV sells the assets back to the seller at a predetermined value. That value should be equal to any amounts still owed under the terms of the Ijarah Sukuk. Now we will look at Sukuk al-ijarah in practice. Look at this heading for a moment: '150 million dollar Serial Islamic Lease Sukuk by First Global Sukuk Inc.'"

There were murmurs around the auditorium. Amir continued.

"The 150 million dollar Islamic Lease Sukuk is part of 395 million dollar Serial Islamic Sukuk issuance that Bank Islam Limited has been mandated to arrange by Kumpulan Guthrie Berhad. In December 2000, Guthrie was granted a 400 million dollar Al-Ijarah Al-Muntahiyah Bit-Tamik by a consortium of banks. The original facility was raised to re-finance Guthrie's acquisition of a palm oil plantation in the Republic of Indonesia. The consortium was then invited to participate as the Sukuk transaction's underwriter/primary subscriber. Now this heading: '250 million dollar Sukuk Trust Certificate by BMA International Sukuk Company'. The Kingdom of Bahrain, acting through the Ministry of Finance and National Economy (in such capacity, the Head Lessor), will lease by way of head lease for a term of 100 years a certain land parcel to the Issuer pursuant to the Al-Ijarah Head Lease Agreement. The Kingdom of Bahrain, acting through the Ministry of Finance and National Economy, (in such capacity, the Sub-Lessee), will lease by way of sub-lease from the Issuer the Land Parcel on the terms set out in the Al-Ijarah Sub-Lease Agreement for a period of 5 years commencing on the Closing Date and terminating on the Periodic Distribution Date falling in June 2009."

Amir paused and sipped some water. "And finally this heading: '350 million dollar Sukuk Trust Certificates by Sarawak Corporate Sukuk Inc. Sarawak Economic Development Corporation raised financing amounting to

350 million dollars through issuance of a series of Sukuk al-Ijarah trust certificates. For the proposed Sukuk, SCSI was incorporated on 23 November 2004 as a special purpose company under the Offshore Companies Act 1990 in Labuan. The certificates were issued with a maturity of five years and under the proposed structure the proceeds will be used by the issuer to purchase certain assets from 1st Silicon SdnBhd. Thereafter, the issuer will lease assets procured from 1st Silicon to SEDC for an agreed rental price for an agreed lease period of five years. The rental payable by SEDC will be supported via a letter of support by the State Government of Sarawak."

As Amir looked around he saw heads bent together as the delegates discussed what they had heard. He looked at his watch, time was pressing on. "Now, ladies and gentlemen—" The auditorium immediately hushed. "Let me draw your attention to Shari'ah Observations on Sukuk al Ijarah. Sukuk al ijarah do not represent debts, they represent undivided proportionate ownership of the leased asset. Thus, Sukuk al ijarah can be bought and sold at whatever price the parties agree to. In this sense the Sukuk al Ijarah are not debt instruments, but participatory certificates similar to equities. Because the Sukuk al ijarah are neither debts nor monetary, the Islamic legal difficulties surrounding the sale of monetary-debts with a discount do not arise. All these factors explain the near universal endorsement of Sukuk al ijarah as Shari'a compliant securities. Sukuk al-mudarabah is next. Mudarabah means an agreement between two parties according to which one of the two provides the capital for the other, the mudarib, to work with on the condition that the profit is to be shared between them according to a pre-agreed ratio. A contract is made between two parties to finance a business venture. The parties are a rabb al mal – an investor who solely provides the capital and a mudharib – an entrepreneur who solely manages the project. If the venture is profitable, the profit will be distributed based on a pre-agreed ratio. The loss shall be borne solely by the provider of the capital in the event of a business loss. Mudarabah Sukuk give their owner the right to receive his capital at the time the Sukuk are surrendered and an annual proportion of the realized profits as agreed. They play a vital role in the process of development financing, because it is related to the project's profitability. mudarabah Sukuk neither earn interest nor entitle owners to make claims for any definite annual interest. This shows that mudarabah Sukuk are like shares with regard to varying returns, which are accrued according to the profits made by the project. Mudarabah Sukuk must represent a common ownership and entitle their holder to shares in a specific project for which the Sukuk have been issued to fund. A Sukuk holder is entitled to all rights, which have been determined by Shari'a upon his ownership of the mudarabah bond in matters of sale, gift, mortgage, succession, etc. On the expiry of the specified time period of the subscription, the Sukuk holders are given the right to transfer the ownership by sale or trade in the securities market at his discretion."

A hand went up and Amir pointed to an English banker. "So how is this structured in regard to the actual project?" Amir nodded.

"The mudarib enters into an agreement with the project owner for construction or commissioning of project. The mudarib collects regular profit payments and final capital proceeds from project activity for onward distribution to investors and to demonstrate Sukuk al-mudarabah in practice I want to tell you about the Shamil Bank of Bahrain BSC which raised a 360 million Saudi riyal investment through the Al Ehsa Special Realty mudarabah, representing an investment participation in a land development transaction with a real estate development company in Saudi Arabia. The objective of the mudarabah was to provide investors with annual returns arising from participation in the funding of a land financing transaction. Profits due to investors are accrued on the basis of returns attained from investing the subscriptions."

There were murmurs around the room and Amir felt himself beginning to tire. He had nearly finished his material.

"I will now touch on mudarabah and muqaradah Sukuk. Mudarabah and muqaradah Sukuk are equity-based and not debt instruments. In the mudarabah Sukuk arrangement, the investors will contribute their capital into a specific project to be managed by the issuer, who will act as the mudarib. The issuer will issue certificates evidencing the capital contribution of the investors and the indicative rate of profit. Profit, if any, will be shared between the investor and issuer at an agreed profit sharing ratio. Losses, if any, will be borne by investors alone to attract market confidence, a third-party guarantee on capital preservation is allowed. The market value of the Sukuk varies with the anticipated or expected profits. Unlike murabaha/ijarah, the financing mode is not set to predetermined amount of profits that are functions of cost but are on real risk on performances. The sale of mudarabah Sukuk to investors in normal circumstances is not a form of sale of debt and discounting is not an issue unless the mudarabah capital is in the form of cash or more than two thirds of it is cash. The need for discounting no longer exists, as the value of the Sukuk will depend on the issuer's company's performance. When an investor wishes to dispose mudarabah Sukuk before maturity, the price depends on the project performance, which implies that mudarabah Sukuk can be sold above or below face value."

"So how does the profit and loss model work with this?" A German banker in the front row asked. "Well, Amir said, profits and losses in mudarabah and Muqaradah Sukuk demand that profits realized from the investment in the mudarabah Sukuk will be distributed between the mudarib and the investors according to the agreement. It is not permissible to guarantee a fixed profit. The mudarib is considered the manager and trustee of the common fund and the project is entrusted to him. The mudarib is not responsible for losses unless due to negligence, mismanagement or dishonesty leading to losses. The mudarabah's risks are on the performances by the mudarib. This could be mitigated by investing in an assured cash flow stream investment such as back-to-back with an ijarah contract."

As Amir concluded there was a slight murmur of disappointment in the hall, as if the delegates wished he would go on. This was followed by rapturous applause perhaps more fitting of a pop stars performance and Amir felt himself blushing. Times were definitely changing.

As they left the hall Leila said to Eddie, "I'm giving a talk at the lecture tomorrow morning. Amir has asked me to talk about women in an Islamic finance context."

"Hey that's great, just like we studied at Harvard!"

"Yes – something like that. Shall we have a meal together tonight, perhaps at the poolside restaurant, and I can sound you out?" Leila paused. "Perhaps your friends and their son would like to come?"

Eddie shuddered at the thought.

"Um, no – they are having such a good family time, I wouldn't want to intrude."

"Of course," Leila said. "Well, just you and me then?"

"Amir?" Eddie said.

"Tied up with conference business – I already checked," Leila said.

"Oh well then. You and me it is," Eddie said, his heart leaping.

As they reached the foyer, Eddie was appalled to see Harry Byron, Sandy and Mrs Jessen steaming towards them. He tried to steer Leila away but it was too late. Byron had seen her and ran over, throwing his arms around her as he had around Eddie the day before.

"Leila!"

"Habibi," she said, using the Arabic term of

endearment. Eddie gritted his teeth. He was terrified that Leila might mention their plans for the evening and ruin everything, but Byron was so full of excitement about the dune buggy riding that the Sheikh had arranged for him with some of his sons that they passed on their way before dinner was mentioned.

Back in his suite, now mercifully empty of Harry and his brood, he called his father. Edward was not in a good mood; Eddie could tell it from the way he spoke in clipped, short sentences. Eddie asked him about Sam Mendez and he told him not to think any more about it. His father's choice of words puzzled Eddie: "Not think any more about it?" Of course he was going to think more about it.

In New York Edward looked at a message that had just been passed to him. The wording sent a chill down his spin.

Chapter Twenty

The poolside restaurant was busy that night as Eddie and Leila arrived for their meal. Many of the conference delegates were taking advantage of the cool and star-filled night to eat a meal beside the lavish pool. Eddie noticed many of the diners they passed casting admiring glances at Leila and envious glances at himself. It was unusual in this culture for a man and woman who were not related to dine together but in a conference setting and in public, Leila explained, she was prepared to compromise.

"Look, Eddie; they have a barbecue. I love barbecue. Don't you?" Her upturned face was so full of life and excitement that Eddie felt a lump in his throat. The smell of the cooking meat wafted over the tables and Eddie suddenly realised that he was ravenous. Usually being in Leila's company made him lose his appetite but they seemed so comfortable together that he found himself looking forward to the meal for its own sake rather than just as an opportunity to be close to Leila.

While they ate, Leila outlined her talk for the morning. She was going to give a talk on human rights to give a breadth of understanding about Islam's guidance in life. It was, along with Islamic finance, a subject that she felt passionately about. Eddie found that he felt nervous for her. It was obvious that she was passionate about her subject but also that she had a healthy amount of nerves.

"It sounds great, Leila. I can't wait to hear you speak

tomorrow," Eddie said.

"Well let's hope that you won't be disappointed," she said.

When they had finished their meal Eddie and Leila strolled around the gardens of the hotel smelling the heady scent of the bougainvillea on the night air. It was possibly the most romantic setting anyone could ever imagine, Eddie thought, and he was forced to walk a respectable distance away from the woman who was fast becoming his world. But he found the experience, although it was new to him, a welcome chance to experience something that his life had brought little of so far – restraint, not getting exactly what he wanted when he wanted it. It made his feelings for Leila somehow even more valid.

It was after midnight before they parted, having had coffee at the coffee shop in the foyer. When he got back to his room Eddie realised that he had left his mobile there. Picking it up he saw that there had been five missed calls from his father. Eddie knew that it had to be something important.

When Edward saw Eddie's name come up on the caller display he snatched his phone up.

"Eddie, son, are you OK?"

"Of course, Dad. I just came up from dinner."

"Oh, right." The urgency in Edward's voice receded slightly.

"When are you due to come home, Eddie?"

"I'm not sure. The conference finishes tomorrow and then I will have a couple of days to go over the project details with Sheikh Lewa."

"The private jet is still out there, isn't it? Are you coming back with Harry and his family?"

Eddie hadn't really thought about it. The idea did not really appeal, but it was the most logical. "I guess," he said.

"OK. I'm sending out my top security man. Don't go near the plane till he has been out and checked it over."

"Right," Eddie said. He had thought that his father was a bit annoyed with the Harry and Byron drama and Eddie's involvement in it but the old man was obviously keen to make sure that Byron was at no further risk.

As he put his phone back down on his desk Edward looked again at the note that had been pushed under the door of the apartment door, although how whoever delivered it had got thorough the building security he did not know.

Daddy bird and baby bird, flying high, two birds with one stone ... dead!

Edward frowned as he looked at the note again. It was obviously a threat against the boy Byron and his father Harry, but why did the writer think he would care? After all, he barely knew them on a personal basis. Obviously the person who had sent the note had been involved with the kidnap, but why should they think it would be that important to Edward? Harry was a friend of Eddie's and not a really close one either from what Edward had observed. He had an uneasy feeling that there was something he did not know. Of one thing he was sure – somehow Sharif was involved in this. It seemed that his life would never be free of the man.

The following morning Leila was first on the podium with her talk on human rights. The auditorium was not as full as it had been for the talks that Amir had given but there were a very respectable number of delegates present.

After introducing herself, Leila began. At first her voice was tentative and soft but as she spoke she gained confidence and the audience settled down to listen to what she had to say.

"In the Prophet Mohammed's (peace be upon him) last sermon during his final pilgrimage, on the Ninth Day of Dhul Hijjah 10 A.H. in the 'Uranah valley of Mount Arafat' in Mecca he said these words. 'I inform you that your lives, properties, and honour must be as sacred to one another as this sacred day of this sacred month, in this sacred town, till you meet your Lord on the Day of Resurrection. One who kills a man under covenant will not even smell the fragrance of Paradise. Hurt no one so that no one may hurt you. You are members of one common brotherhood It is forbidden for any of you to take from his brother save what the latter should willingly give. Do not oppress your people. All Moslems, free or enslaved, have the same rights and responsibilities. No one is higher than another unless he is higher in virtue.' Caliph Umer Ibn Khattab said to Amr ibn al-As, 'Since when did you make slaves of the people, while their mother gave birth to them liberated?'"

Leila paused to allow her words to leave an impression. There was silence in the hall and many of the delegates appeared to be saying silent prayers. Not for the first time, Eddie marvelled at the unifying and profound effect that Islam had on its followers. She continued.

"Human Rights are vital to all beings, a God-given right to his creation, and it conveys prosperity, humanity to all human beings. The birth of Islam and the arrival of Prophet Mohammed gave respect and dignity to the whole world and all humanity of the God-given life. Profit Mohammed gave the first example of human rights when he entered into the first world charter known as 'Medina Charter'. The charter reflects the respect and dignity of the human right of the people regardless of their belief at the time, either Moslem or non-Moslem or Jewish.

"The Moslem caliphs and Islamic scholars have followed the Prophet Mohammed's footsteps and demonstrated human right from Qur'an and Sunnah, they had to go to great lengths to ensure that Moslems are respecting human right for Moslems and non-Moslems. However, all organisations, including the Cairo declaration of Human Rights, Arab Declaration of Human Rights, Universal Declaration of Human Rights and United Nations Declaration of Human Rights have extracted their human rights statement and code of ethics from the Qur'an, Medina Charter, Sunnah, Caliphs and Islamic Scholars who has interpreted to the principal of Islam in Human Right.

"In his paper, Dr Amir Ali, whom you have heard speak in this conference, argues that Islam was the main source of human rights issue and the West are trying to devise man-made human rights issues but the core and the source of their efforts in human rights issues are extracted from the Qur'an, Medina Charter, and Sunnah regardless of their unjustified claims. God has created human being and *He* who is their protector, from abuse, all Prophets of God send the same message: that is to worship God and to protect human rights from abuse. It follows that research and development of new Human Rights declarations and statements by different organisations to refresh and encourage leaders of the world to respect the human rights issues for their people and will encourage individuals to help other people in need."

Leila looked up at the auditorium. She had got into her stride now and her clear sweet voice filled the room. "That, ladies and gentlemen, is the basis of my talk today which I hope you will find interesting, as we cannot hope to arrive at an ethical solution to our financial matters if we do not first look at the foundation of all commerce and endeavour, human rights."

There was a ripple of applause. Leila blushed slightly and continued.

"The modern conception of human rights is vibrant in theory and practice. The Geneva Conventions, international law, the United Nations law on human rights, the Arab League charter on human rights, and the Cairo declaration on human rights all have a parallel source from the Qur'an and Sunnah. Looking at non-Islam based evaluations of Human Rights, the Magna Carta, the French Revolution's Declaration of the Rights of Man, Locke, Hobbes, Montesquieu, Rousseau, Paine and JS Mill or the framing of the US Constitution and Bill of Rights were able to draft or extract human right issues without referencing to the teaching of Islam. Therefore, in as much as the modern principles of human rights can be related, in part, to an accumulation of systematic thinking on the rights of individuals, groups and communities, then Islamic thought does not exhibit the same or similar progression of the set of ideas and principles that underpin modern human rights. However, there is little doubt that Islamic thought and jurisprudence, in the pre-modern era, did deal with many aspects of the rights and duties of various categories of human beings; but in a framework that was conceptually and methodologically different from the western tradition. 'Huqooq al-Insan' in Arabic is the contemporary rendering of 'human rights'. However, they cannot be located as such in pre-modern Islamic literature. But Huqooq itself is a word derived from the root word Haqq – a word that can mean equally truth or right or rights over others, or share. Al-Haqq or the truth is one of Allah's attributes.

"It is in this form that the equivalent principle of human rights and duties in Islam is found in a huge array of original Islamic sources. Such sources can include documents on the principles and maxims of government; sayings of rulers and judges; actions of the muhtassib, a type of ombudsman; treatises on justice, equality, ethics, political and moral philosophy, accountability, toleration, treatment of minorities, property rights, freedom of conscience and expression, and so on.

"Islamic law and practice seems to offer a qualified acceptance to the universals doctrine of human rights principles, as a voice in various world and forums particularly after second World Ware when human dignity was provoked, In particular, diverse injunctions of the commonly acknowledged tenets of the Moslem laws, The Shari'ah appear to restrict, modify, and dilute the significance of the modern notion of human rights."

Leila looked up at the auditorium. Her passion and her obvious love for Islam and its teachings could not fail to move anyone who heard her speak.

"I will leave you with this thought, ladies and gentleman, before I finish for today. In Islam, God grants human hights to the people. The Qur'an states that these are universal and fundamental, and that all individuals are to enjoy and observe them under all circumstances- including war-regardless of whether he is living in the geographical confines of an Islamic state or not: 'O believers, tee you securers of justice, witness for God. Let not sole detestation for a people move you not to be equitable; be equitable-that is nearer to God-fearing.' That is from the Holy Quran 5:8. Human blood is sacred in any case and cannot be spilled without justification. Violating this rule is equivalent to killing all of humanity: 'Who slays a soul not to retaliate for a soul slain, nor for corruption done in the land, should be as if he had slain mankind altogether.' That is from the Holy Quran 5:32."

The auditorium erupted into applause and Leila stepped down from the podium.

Eddie was on his feet. Her words had touched him as they had almost every person in the auditorium. It was not so much the words as the sentiment and the passion that she conveyed.

As they left the auditorium they bumped into Harry and Byron coming back from the pool. Byron looked like a different boy, a slight tan lifting his usual pallor.

"Oh hi, Eddie; how is the conference going?" Harry said, smiling at Leila.

"Fine," Eddie said, wanting to get away as soon as he could. But Byron had taken Leila by the hand and was showing her into the coffee shop in the lobby where ornate chocolate oil-rigs had been fashioned by the hotel's kitchens and even featured little gushers and miniature oil men on the platform.

"Oh aren't those fine?" Leila said. "Shall we all have coffee and one of these little creations?"

"Yes please," Byron said, and despite himself Eddie found himself sitting opposite Harry at one of the tables that overlooked the lush hotel gardens.

They talked about the address that Leila had given and pride shone from Eddie's eyes as he told Harry about the triumph she had pulled off. As he watched his old friend, Harry realised that Eddie was in love. He had never seen his friend in love or even twice with the same woman since their young, wild days. But he could sense that even although his friend was in love with this lovely woman, he was not with her. There was an air of sadness, regret that hung over his friend, a longing and wistfulness in his eyes when he looked at her which spoke a thousand words.

Leila was more difficult to read. He knew from Eddie that her husband had died in the awful plane sabotage at the beginning of the year, but he had never spoken much about her, although it was obvious that the feelings Eddie had for Leila were not new. Harry was puzzled and watched fascinated at the rapport between the two. He felt slightly envious. Whatever closeness he had ever had with Sandy was not a scrap of what this was, although it seemed as though there was not relationship as such. That made it all the more intriguing. Nowadays Harry felt that he was rather surplus to requirements; Sandy had her children and she was happiest when she was left on her own with them. As he watched Eddie he could see the love shining out of Eddie's eyes. That it was a purely platonic love and the fact that Eddie was happy to respect the boundaries of this woman made it seem to Harry as though he did not know his friend, or at least did not know this side of him.

For a while he studied Leila; she was remarkably beautiful and had an endearing habit of tucking a stray tendril of raven's wing hair back into her hijab, which, no matter how tightly she tucked it in, kept coming loose to lie against her flawless skin. Her eyes were dark and framed by long curling lashes and held an innate intelligence and kindness, her mouth a soft cupid's bow with upturned corners that told of a soul ready to smile and laugh. Harry instantly realised what his friend saw in her. She was serene, dignified, beautiful and kind. She smiled at Eddie with a smile that did not hide her affection for him, but it was the same smile with which she graced himself and especially Byron. She had no romantic inclinations towards Eddie, or at least none that she was prepared to own up to, and Harry caught his breath as he realised how painful this unrequited love must be for Eddie.

Sheikh Lewa had arrived at the symposium with his

sons, one older and one younger than Byron. The boys had had a great time playing in the dessert on the dunes the day before and the boys had brought their swimming things with them so that they could all spend the afternoon in the hotel's pool. Sandy had come back from the beauty salon to accompany the boys to the pool while the Sheikh, Eddie and Harry made their way to the symposium lunch, leaving Leila deep in conversation with Amir Ali who had come into the coffee shop.

"I think I might come and listen to the second part of Leila's talk this afternoon," Harry said, and Eddie looked at him in surprise.

"Sure, it will be very interesting. She had the audience eating out of her hand this morning." Harry smiled at the pride in his friend's voice. Eddie caught the look and checked himself. He did not want to give too much away; he felt vulnerable where Leila was concerned and he hated to look that way in front of Harry.

Harry and Eddie took their seats for the afternoon session of the symposium amid a minor flurry as people acknowledged Sheikh Lewa and other dignitaries who were taking their seats in the auditorium. Eddie admired the formal Arab dress for the way the pure white thobe under the outer black gold braided cloak looked both imposing and comfortable and totally right for the climate. With crisp headdresses, a ring of thick coiled braid keeping them in place, the formal garb seemed to be flattering to any figure and to any height.

As all eyes turned to Leila as she made her way to the podium, Eddie felt love well up inside him again. This was something he could not control. With irritation he noticed that Harry was looking at him out of the corner of his eye. He had obviously realised how Eddie felt and Eddie did not want to be the object of his scrutiny. He turned slightly in his seat so that Harry could not watch his facial expressions.

Leila began to speak and it seemed as though the entire auditorium was transfixed by her clear, strong tone as she spoke from the heart.

"I want to talk more about human rights in the Qur'an," she started, and the auditorium quieted. "For Moslems throughout history, the Qur'an has always been the key text upon which Islamic life and civilization has been built, as well as the enumeration and exposition of the rights and duties of human beings to their Creator, to each other and to themselves. The Qur'an covers the dignity and moral perfectibility of human beings; mankind as God's vice-regents on earth; the inherent equality of human beings; elevated status of human beings in the cosmic order; as well as the obligation to consult others in governing; the toleration of non-Moslems and the rejection of compunction in matters of faith and religion. Human beings and haqq are mentioned over 70 and 250 times respectively. However, the pre-modern reading and interpretation of the Qura'nic text was not done with the specific intent of developing a human rights doctrine. This only emerged in the 21st century, mainly in response to the challenge of the modern human rights movement. According to the Qur'an, the dignity of the children of Adam is a divine bestowal, which is to be secured by all means, including the law and the state authorities, and is to be defended by all forces: We have conferred dignity on the children of Adam, and borne them over land and sea, and provided for them sustenance out of the good things of life, and favored them far above most of our Creations. Qur'an 17:70."

Leila paused her voice, reading the sacred words of the Qur'an, even more beautiful as her love for the holy words of her religion shone through. "As a demonstration of this privileged position, God ordered the angels to prostrate themselves before Adam, the first human being. What distinguish humans from other creatures is mainly their intellect and their free will to choose between doing good and doing evil. In the same chapter, the Qur'an states that those who will attain to happiness in the life to come, as it has been mentioned before, are those who don't seek to exalt themselves on earth, nor yet to spread malevolence; for the future belongs to the God-conscious Qur'an 7:157. Justice can be concisely and precisely defined as the maintenance of human rights and equality. 'Behold, God enjoins justice, and going beyond justice to the doing of what is magnanimous and kind, and giving to one's kinsfolk; and He forbids all that is shameful and all that runs counter to reason and morality, as well as transgression; He exhorts you repeatedly so that you might bear all this in mind.' Qur'an 3:195. Any discrimination between men and women in rights or responsibilities is forbidden according to the divine justice- the same as any other discrimination: 'And their Lord does answer them: I shall not lose sight of the work of any of you who works in My way, be it man or woman.' Qur'an 3:195."

On his lap Eddie held a copy of the Qur'an translated

into English and followed Liela's references as she made them. Leila had given him the copy before her first lecture so that he could follow the references.

"Human rights as described by the divine message in Qur'an and Sunna were considered by the Moslem jurists to be the very goal of Shari'ah. The jurists condensed Islamic law, as mentioned before, into the securing and developing human personality in five main areas: life, family, mind, faith, and property. The human rights covered by these five areas include the collective rights of groups and peoples as well as the rights of individuals; political and social rights have their place side by side."

Leila looked up from her podium. As she had in the morning she held her audience in the palm of her hand.

"Now I want to say something about freedom of expression in the Qur'an," she said. "The main goal of God's message to humankind is the attainment of justice in all of its fairness. This justice, the foundation of Islam, cannot be achieved unless human rights are secured for every individual and group in a Moslem state. The member of such a state must be free to choose just rulers, to observe these rules as they practice their authority, and to stand firm against any injustice from them. Primary among human rights are the rights to believe, to express one's beliefs and to assemble to defend one's group's beliefs. In the Medina Charter which was written and promulgated by Prophet Muhammad for the multi-religious ten thousand-strong citizens of the city-state of Medina in 622 CE, is the first and oldest written constitution in operation, it is also modern in the sense that it was circulated for a plural society, giving equal rights to every citizen as well as giving them a say in governmental matters. The Madina Charter is also considered the first written document of Human Rights.

"In considering all these facts, it is amazing that those Moslem leaders and writers who talk and write about the Islamic state seldom refer to this important seminal political document of Islam.

"The Charter consists of 47 clauses. Clauses 1, 2 and 39 deal with the formation of a sovereign nation-state with a common citizenship, consisting of various communities, principally Moslem Arabs from Mecca, the Muhajirin or Immigrants, Moslem Arabs from Yathrib, the Ansar or Helpers, other monotheists form Yathrib, namely the Jews, and others who must be at that time still pagans. These constitute a unified citizenry going under the Arabic term, ummah, having equal rights and responsibilities, as distinct from other peoples.

"The Charter provided a federal structure with a centralized authority, with the various tribes in various districts constituting a unit and enjoying autonomy in certain matters of a social, cultural, and religious character. Provision for this district autonomy is repeated for each district, Clauses 3 through to 11 and 26 through to 35, In fact, many matters were left in the hands of the autonomous units, except state security and national defense, Clauses 17, 36(a) and 47, Provisions for these centralized subjects are made in Clauses 13, 15, 17 and 44. Only in cases of disputes the units could not resolve, recourse for their decisions had to be made to the Prophet, whose decision was final, Clauses 23 and 41.

"It is noteworthy," Leila smiled at her audience, "that the Charter ordained equality to its members and protected them against oppression, Clause 16. The State proclaimed the brotherhood of believers and gave each one a right and support to give protection to any individual, excepting an enemy, Clause 15. It also extended help to its members in debt or in financial difficulties in regard to payment of ransom or blood money, as you will see in clause 12. It prohibited help or for refuge to be given to a murderer, as you will see in Clause 22.

"A very important human right is given in Clause 25 where freedom was guaranteed for each community to practice its own religion. The implication of this clause is that each individual was also free to choose his or her religion, in line with the clear teachings of the Qur'an. 'There shall be no compulsion in religion: the right way is now distinguished from the wrong way.' Qur'an 2:256. This statement of complete religious freedom comes immediately after the grandest statement of God's power to be found in any scripture. It is indeed significant! Another important principle of statecraft is consultation with the people in all matters. This is stated in Clause 37(a). Unlike in modern democratic polity, the voice of the people regardless of whether that voice represents right and truth or not, is given the highest value. This is a basic flaw in Western democracy. Another important principle of just governance is that no quarter is given to an injustice or wrongdoing as you can read in clause 47.

"I think at this point, ladies and gentlemen, I will pause and continue tomorrow. I have placed copies of the charter on the tables outside the entrance for you to read if you are interested."

As they had the day before, the audience got to their feet to applaud Leila and as he had the day before Eddie felt such pride that tears welled up in his eyes. Like a mosquito, Harry was on him immediately.

"Hey man – you really love her, don't you?" Harry tired to put his arm around Eddie's shoulders but he shook it off. He did not want to share this moment with Harry or with anybody. Not for Eddie the comfort of discussing things with friends he had none, except Harry who really was only still connected to him through Byron. As they walked through the auditorium doors into the foyer, crowds of delegates queued for copies of the charter that Leila had left for them.

Eddie took a copy and thought that he would read it that night when he got to bed. He was craning his neck so that he would not miss Leila when she came out of the auditorium surrounded by admiring delegates and an extremely proud looking Amir Ali. As she emerged he was about to make his way to her side when Byron appeared in front of him, his thin gingery hair stuck to his scalp after his swim, his eyes red from the chlorine.

"Uncle Eddie, uncle Eddie!" he said. Eddie felt the familiar annoyance well up in him as well as a sort of panic that Leila would disappear from the lobby before he could speak to her and congratulate her on her talk.

"What is it?" the irritation in Eddie's voice might as well have been the back of his hand for the effect it had on Byron, whose face crumpled as his bottom lip started to tremble like a two-year-old's.

"Hey, steady man!" Harry looked at Eddie, his face confused. "What the hell's the matter with you?"

"Nothing … sorry, Bryon – what was it you wanted?" he said through gritted teeth as he saw the lift doors close behind Leila.

"Nothing," Byron said in a sullen voice.

"Right – I'm going up then," Eddie said, and walked briskly to the lifts before Harry or Byron could say any more.

In the penthouse suite, Eddie called Leila on the phone.

"Sorry I didn't get to congratulate you – you were great!" he said. "Dinner tonight?"

"I can't tonight, Eddie; I've agreed to meet Amir and the conference organisers for dinner with some of the other women speakers."

Eddie was speechless. He felt as though he had been kicked in the stomach.

"But it's the last night of the conference – you go tomorrow evening!"

"Actually, I am going to stay until the next morning, so we can have dinner tomorrow if you like," Leila said shyly.

Eddie's heart leapt again. "Great!" And with that he had to be content.

a tender power

At the airport in the hangar that housed Lancaster's private jet, a man emerged from the shadows. With him was a man in Lancaster uniform. Money changed hands and the man in uniform left the hangar. Alone, the man who had parted with the money began to unload his bag, carefully laying out a kit and deftly connecting wires and crawling underneath the plane to a spot that was just behind where the pilot of the jet would sit. He attached a small box, it's colour identical to that of the fuselage of the aircraft, the tape that held it in place strong enough to hold a man up and also identical in colour to the paint work of the aircraft. The little box, virtually invisible now, blended in so well that it would almost only be detectable by a fingertip examination. Sitting back on his haunches, the man took out a small mobile phone. With a few motions a light came on on the little box which, he quickly cancelled. He crawled back under the plane to be sure of his work once more and then left the little box, silent, its lights off, totally harmless – for now.

Chapter Twenty-one

The last day of the conference brought an even larger number of delegates to the auditorium. Amir was due to speak again to close the symposium and people were eager to hear him speak. But word had also got round about Leila and her talk on human rights and many of the people attending had come specifically to hear her. People who would not normally have come to hear talks on finance had crammed the auditorium so that several dozen were standing at the back and alongside the rows of chairs. Eddie felt pride well up in him again, and he felt for Leila as she saw all faces turn towards her as she walked in with him.

"Oh my goodness," she whispered. "So many people – surely they are not all here to listen to me speak?"

"They are – and they're in for a treat!" Eddie whispered back, giving her a little push in the small of her back to propel her down the aisle towards the lectern. The applause rippled around the auditorium and reached a crecendo as Leila took to the stand. As she began to seat a flustered Harry pushed his way into the row in which Eddie was sitting and took the seat beside him that he had reserved with a jacket.

"Eddie – I need to fly back today," he whispered, and Eddie frowned at him. Leila was about to speak. "There is some problem with Suzi and Sandy wants to go back. Were you planning to leave today?"

"No," Eddie said, thinking of the meal he was planning to share with Leila that evening. Wild horses would not make him miss that. "But you go ahead. I was planning to stay a few more days to meet with Sheikh Lewa, but by all means, take the jet; I can get a flight in a few days' time."

"Thanks, buddy!" Harry clapped Eddie on the back and to Eddie's great relief, gathered up his jacket and left. Leila was beginning her talk.

"Good morning, ladies and gentlemen; I am delighted to be here again today to conclude my talk on human rights and I am very pleased to see so many people interested in this most important aspect of life on earth. I want to start today by talking about Arab Tribalism."

A murmur went around the world. There was no denying that Leila was not afraid to tackle even the most sensitive of subjects and Eddie had no doubt she would carry it off with the grace and eloquence that had been a trade mark of her series of lectures so far. "Arab tribalism can be detected in two clauses where a member together with his family was to be punished because of a crime he committed, Clauses 25 and 36(b). This clearly contradicts another clause, which states that no evildoer is punished except for the crime he commits, as seen in clause 46. The Charter is the first Islamic political-constitutional document, and was given to the people of Medina in the name of Muhammad the Prophet, Clause 1, and also in the name of God as well as Prophet Muhammad – please see clause 47. Why two different ways of phrasing the ultimate source of power? It is to be remembered that during the Western Middle Ages, the Church ruled supreme in the name of God, and God's name was, of course, much misused by hypocrites and opportunists. The modern Western practice of replacing God with the people has, of course, not helped matters very much. In the name of the people, oppression, wars, colonialism, and aggressions have been launched. Thus, even in this modern age of science and technology, mankind cannot ignore a power that is greater than itself. Mankind has an autonomous right to live, and to live happily, but he must do that in a lawfully created universe. It is in this sense that the Charter was given in the name of Muhammad the Prophet, who represented the principle of the good and of right reason, which is higher than the individual man. Likewise, in clause 47 God's name was put first, as God represents the highest Good and the highest principle of right reason. This is necessary to conduct man to higher and ever higher achievements."

The delegates in the hall had been joined by more, standing four deep at the back of the auditorium now, craning to hear Leila's words.

"I would like now to talk about the Cairo Declaration on Human Rights," Leila said, and the delegates opened the leaflets that she had left on each of the chairs in the auditorium before the lecture. "The Cairo Declaration on Human Rights in Islam, which was issued in 1990, is the most authoritative official pronouncement on the issue. The foreign ministers of all the member countries of the Organization of Islamic Conference the OIC approved it after a decade long process of debate, review and consultation, and three summit conferences of the OIC. It was subsequently ratified by a summit of the OIC leaders. It is important to note, however, that the

Cairo Declaration did not try to reconcile or resolve the differences in emphasis and context with the International Bill of Rights, leaving many OIC countries in the uncomfortable position of endorsing two often-conflicting interpretations of human rights. Neither did it result in the establishment of a permanent office or secretariat to monitor human rights in OIC countries. Now we will look at The Arab Charter of Human Rights. This is a separate charter for the Arab world, the Arab Charter of Human Rights, which was issued by the Arab league in 1994, and which soon followed the Cairo Declaration. This charter seemed to defeat its purpose by granting governments the right to suspend the provisions of the charter 'in the interest of national security, economic emergencies and threats to public order.' Partly in response to a heightened awareness internationally of human rights issues, the 1990s and 2000s saw a significant increase in the number of conferences in the Islamic world that examined the issue of human rights in Islam."

Leila paused as one of the conference administrators signalled that it was time that they break for lunch. She concluded and promised more after the lunchtime recess. Eddie smiled as he saw the head waiter of the large restaurant that was hosting the lunch scurrying around trying to ensure that they had enough food for the extra delegates who had turned up to hear Leila speak. Unlike other conferences that Eddie had been to, there was no strict control over the delegates and it appeared that anyone who wanted to come was welcome. The strain this was putting on the staff of the hotel was clear as they brought in food from restaurants to help feed the growing numbers attending.

Sheikh Lewa pulled Eddie to one side before lunch and asked him if he had heard from the police.

Eddie was ashamed to admit to himself that he had not given Sam Mendez a thought since Leila had arrived, and obviously Sheikh Lewa had something to tell him about his colleague's death.

"It appears that Mr Mendez was not the victim of a random violent act. The police are pretty sure that he was targeted because he was connected to the project." Eddie looked at the Sheikh, alarmed.

"But he was not crucial to anything – I don't understand what the point of killing him would be," Eddie said.

Sheikh Lewa shrugged. "A warning, perhaps?"

Eddie felt the icy finger of fear run down his spine again. "About what?"

The Sheikh shrugged again. "We will have to be very careful, Eddie; there is obviously someone who is not keen on our association. I have asked my security operatives to increase surveillance and to double-check my own security – I suggest that you do the same."

Eddie nodded. He had suddenly lost his appetite.

At a point just outside the parameter of the private air strip in Dubai, Sharif sat in a battered pick up truck. As he watched, a car drew up and he trained his binoculars on the occupants as they got out onto the tarmac. He identified Harry, Eddie's friend, the boy, Byron and Harry's wife and his mother-in-law. He swung the binoculars back to the open door of the vehicle waiting to see if anyone else would get out of the limousine. Harry and his family were inside the small jet now, and there was no sign of Eddie. Sharif made a phone call to the hotel.

"Yes, sir, Mr Lancaster is here – shall I connect you to him?"

"No." Sharif snapped his mobile phone shut and swore.

As the jet taxied down the runway, Sharif held his finger over the control for the headlights in his car. Further down the dirt track a man waited in another pick-up truck and waited for a flash of Sharif's headlights. It was the signal to arm the device that would blow the jet, that was now starting to take off, out of the sky. The jet would be at its full speed in a matter of minutes and the device needed to be activated before it was out of range.

Sharif gritted his teeth as his finger hovered over the headlights control. He knew that he had only a few moments left to give the command that would end the lives of Harry and his family as well as the crew of the jet. He felt a hatred for Edward Lancaster and his spoilt son but would it really have much impact on them if he blew Harry out of the sky? He knew that Byron was Eddie's son but he also knew that Eddie cared little for him; in fact, he might be doing him a favour if he were to obliterate the boy. The thought that he might do Eddie a favour was enough to make Sharif drop his hand from the headlight control. In the pick-up truck the man who held the arming device watched unblinking in case he should miss the signal. His eyes ached and sweat stood out on his brow. He glanced at his watch; it would be seconds now before the jet was out of range. No signal. He put the small mobile phone that would have armed the device on the seat beside him. A minute had gone now. The chance was gone. He relaxed as Sharif's pick-up coughed into life and sped off, its wheels throwing plumes of sandy dust into the air.

* * *

Back at the hotel Eddie was only now aware that Harry had gone. He felt relieved that his last evening with Leila would not be threatened by an appearance by any of Harry's family. He knew that Amir Ali was leaving directly after the symposium finished so the evening with Leila was looking promising. He had not had a chance to speak to her over the lunchtime as delegates wanting to know more about her subject, and her, besieged her. Eddie reflected that she had an ethereal presence, an almost hypnotic way of delivering what she had to say, and he was obviously not the only one who thought so. He felt jealous of the time that she spent with others but he would have to be patient until tonight.

He decided to take a walk around the grounds of the hotel while he waited for the conference to start again. Before Leila spoke another speaker was giving a talk on oil revenue and Eddie was not much interested in the subject.

As he walked towards the side of the hotel a battered pick up truck cruised past on the road. The driver seemed to be craning his neck to look at Eddie and Eddie instinctively looked round to see if there was anything else that could be attracting the driver's attention. Suddenly and inexplicably he felt the cold finger of fear pluck at his spine again and almost ran to the side door of the hotel. As he glanced over his shoulder the pick-up sped off, its tyres screeching on the hot tarmac.

Leila's talk was about to start and Eddie took his seat. He still felt rattled; he had had a feeling of impending doom since Shiekh Lewa had told him about Sam's death being connected to the project. He tried to shake the feeling off as Leila took to the podium to rapturous applause. Eddie glanced around the auditorium. If anything there were even more people than there had been in the morning.

Leila began to speak. "In 1996, a conference in Jeddah grouped jurisprudential leaders to develop the Shari'ah-basis of human rights legislation. This was followed in 1997 by a conference held in Amman under the auspices of the Ahl-ul-Bayt Foundation, an official Jordanian institution. The conference was aimed at reconciling differences between Islamically based human rights conventions and prevailing international standards, with a strong emphasis on developing an inter-faith basis for human rights legislation. In 2000, Rome was the venue for a conference organized under the auspices of the World Moslem League, a Saudi-linked institution, which produced the Rome Declaration on Human Rights in Islam. This was followed by a conference in 2001 in Riyadh in which human rights were examined within the historic and legal legacy of Islam. These two conferences were the partly in response to increased agitation regarding the human rights record of Saudi Arabia."

Leila paused and took a sip of water. "And now I want to draw your attention to Children's Human right as set down by the Universal declaration of Human Rights. The United Nations set a common standard on human rights with the adoption of the Universal Declaration of Human Rights in 1948. Human rights are those rights, which are essential to live as human beings, basic standards without which people cannot survive and develop in dignity. They are inherent to the human person, inalienable and universal. With regard to a child's right to an education The Children's Rights consists of two civil rights, two political rights, two social rights, and two economic rights. This article presents country scores on the Children's Rights Index, then examines whether children's rights vary by region and other differences, such as country wealth. It is hoped that the Children's Rights Index will provide evidence on children's rights important to the work of governments and nongovernmental organizations, as well as scholars and others concerned about children's welfare."

Leila looked around the room and said, "It is a matter of personal sorrow to me that so many countries still fail to uphold these basic rights for children." There was a murmur of agreement around the auditorium. "And now we will look at the Cairo declaration on human rights for women. The International Conference of the National Council for Women, the conference entitled 'Women in Leadership Positions as an Achievement of Social Justice'. Believing that women's assumption of leadership positions in the process of development strengthens the concept of social justice, one of the main women human rights, further boosts democracy, The Participants call upon all parties capable of effecting change to the women's right including the Government, Parliamentarians and

Legislative Councils, The Private Sector, Political Parties, Women, Ministries' Equal Opportunities Units and Syndicates' Women's Committees, Civil Society, The National Council for Women, Central Agency for Public Mobilization and Statistics,. Development Partners, and the media."

Leila paused. "And now what I know a lot of you have come to hear to day, The Western Approach to Human Rights." A ripple went around the auditorium. Eddie felt eyes swivel towards him as one of the few Westerners in the audience.

"Human rights and obligations from the early 19th century was the beginning of recognition to the need for human right protection. The impact of the European powers on Islamic institutions and laws was felt especially forcibly in the Ottoman Empire. The demand for a constitution to contain the powers of the Sultan or Caliph introduced the idea of citizenship in place of the millet system. The millet system was based essentially on the recognition of each religious community in the Empire as a separate unit, directly connected to the Sultan or Caliph. Each religious sect set most of its own laws and regulations in light of religious ordinances and customs. The Sultan or Caliph in turn had his power limited to those areas for which the Shari'ah had no ruling. The constitutional movement thus undermined both the principle of Sultan or Subject and the division of autonomous communities according to religious affiliations. Political rights were therefore recast in modern terms of constitutional arrangements, representation, elections, separation of powers, and the institutions and laws that accompanied this profound change.

"The impact of modernity in the 19th century also affected intellectuals, writers, and high officials in the Moslem World in ways that further undermined the familiar concepts and categories of Islamic thought and practice. The principles of the French Revolution, profoundly significant in the early construct of human rights doctrines in the West, seeped into Moslem lands and influenced a whole range of opinion leaders."

There was a commotion suddenly at the back of the auditorium. A man was being retained, bundled away, but before the security could get him through the door, a gunshot rang out and one of the hotel security men fell to the floor, a dark ribbon of blood flowing out from underneath his prone body. Women screamed and two other security guards ran after the gunman, tackling him to the ground on the grass outside the coffee shop.

Eddie felt the now familiar finger of fear, more like a fist now gripping his insides. Somehow he knew that this had something to do with him and as he watched from the front of the crowd that had gathered, the gunman was lifted to his feet and for a moment his eyes met Eddie's and Eddie knew without a doubt that the bullet had been meant for him.

One of the conference oragnisers had taken to the stand and an ambulance had arrived to take the lifeless body of the felled security guard away. The sound of muted sobbing came from various parts of the auditorium and Eddie realised he had not seen Leila. As he rushed to the front of the auditorium he found her sitting on a chair. Her face was white with shock and her hands were trembling. Feeling guilty that he had been concerned about his own safety, he fell on his knees and took her hands in his.

Above, at the lectern, one of the organisers said in a voice that shook, "We will have a break, ladies and gentleman – please help yourself to coffee and tea."

A stiff whiskey would be better, Eddie thought, but he helped Leila up and led her to the dining room and poured her a coffee. As he caught sight of Eddie the Officer, a distinguished looking man in his fifties wearing a silk business suit, walked over to him. Sheikh Lewa was at his side.

"Mr Lancaster, we meet again." The detective extended his hand and Eddie shook it, hoping that the officer would not notice the clammy cold sweat that had made his hand moist.

The officer regarded Eddie for a moment and then said, "Do you think that this shooting was anything to do with your presence at this conference? Or of your connection with the Sheikh?" The officer nodded deferentially in Sheikh Lewa's direction.

Eddie was taken aback by his directness. "I ... I don't know," he said, flustered. But he did know, he knew for certain, that he had been the target of this attack, although he had no idea why. Eddie caught a glimpse of Leila, her eyes wide and tear-filled, her face both fearful and concerned as she heard the detective's question. Eddie longed to put his arm around her and hold her to him to comfort her, but he knew he could not. Amir Ali had arrived and was leading Leila off now. Eddie wanted to go with her, for this whole horrible thing to be over, but he was stuck and followed the detective and Sheikh Lewa to a private room where the detective questioned him and the Sheikh about what possible motivation a killer could have both for killing Sam Mendez and now for attempting to shoot Eddie. Eddie had told the men that he did think he was the target and far from dismissing his account of meeting the eyes of the gunman as hysteria, the detective and the Sheikh listened carefully to his account.

Two hours later the conference organisers announced that the conference would continue. Eddie had found Leila again and was amazed that she was prepared to carry on.

She smiled her shy smile and said. "Isn't that really what my talk is about? The human right to speak freely and to live free of fear? If I let this incident derail me then I am giving into terror and to those who would rob us of our peace of mind and freedom to speak and to lead our lives normally?"

Eddie felt love for her well up inside him. She was showing real courage. A courage that her slight frame and femininity seemed unlikely to posses yet she was determined to carry on, not to be intimidated.

As she took to the podium again, even louder applause greeted this beautiful woman who was prepared to go on despite the terrible events of the day.

"Before I start, ladies and gentlemen, I would like to ask for a minute's silence to remember the brave security office who today gave his life so that we could live in full expectation of enjoying our human rights, not just listening to theories and resolutions, but actually enjoying the freedom that is ours, despite those who would take it from us."

The auditorium fell silent and Eddie felt a cold fear in the pit of his stomach. It could so easily have been him rather than that brave guard lying on a slab in the morgue. He had got the man's name from the police and would make sure that his family was very well provided for. It was the least he could do.

The silence over, Leila began to speak again. "I want now to talk about human rights and Islam after the UN's Universal Declaration of Human Rights. The role of Moslem majority countries in the formulation of the UN's Universal Declaration of Human Rights, UDHR in 1948 was minimal. That is not to say that the Moslem majority did not participate in the negotiations that resulted in the final document, but their concerns, when expressed, were not taken into account. There were few Moslem majority countries in the UN at that point and apart from the interjections of Saudi Arabia, which abstained in the final vote, the other Moslem nations ratified the document without any reservations or comments. Moslem countries all participated in later international conferences in 1966 which set out the civil, political, social, economic and cultural rights, and the collective International Bill of Rights has been ratified in their present form by nearly all Moslem majority countries. The first such attempt to introduce specific provision for human rights in a model Islamic state was the Pan Islamic conference held in

Karachi in 1950, The Karachi conference produced a model constitution for an ideal Islamic state. The provisions of this model constitution became the building block for several similar schemes promoted by Islamist political parties. These schemes culminated in the Al-Azhar University's 1978 proposal for an Islamic constitution, whose significance lies in that it was proposed by the pre-eminent Sunni Moslem religious institution. The idea of a specific Islamic formulation of human rights as a counterpoint to the International Bill of Rights can be traced to these proposals, all of which were triggered by the Universal Declaration of Human Rights and the inadequate response of Moslem governments of the time to the Islamically controversial or problematic provisions of the covenants. In the 1970s Saudi Arabia began to sponsor a series of meetings and conferences with a view to systematising an Islamic bill of human rights as well as propagating the role of religion and religious doctrine in the formulation of international covenants of human rights. These efforts started in 1972 by the Saudi Ministry of Justice, directly and through the offices of the Saudi-financed World Islamic League.

"In 1980, the Islamic Council of Europe, an independent organization that had then a link to the World Islamic League, produced the first specifically Islamic doctrine of human rights, called the Universal Islamic Declaration of Human Rights This was as a result of a conference held in London and attended by over 50 representatives from various Moslem governments. The Universal Declaration of Human Rights acquired a semi-legal status in the Islamic world and was seen as a counterpoint to the Universal Declaration of Human Rights. The Declaration involved the stipulation of twenty-three human rights, all of which were justified explicitly by Qur'anic verses and sayings (hadith) of the Prophet Muhammad. The rights listed did not follow the sequence of the Universal Declaration of Human Rights and included rights that did not feature at all in the Universal Declaration of Human Rights couched as they were in the language of religion.

"The Universal Declaration of Human Rights in time became the main foundational document and support for all subsequent elaborations on human rights by Islamic organizations. The Universal Declaration of Human Rights was unveiled to the world at an elaborate conference at UNESCO attended by a number of former leaders of Moslem countries such Ben Bella of Algeria and Ould Dadah of Mauretania. The Universal Declaration of Human Rights was soon followed by a meeting of Moslem jurists, lawyers and judges in Kuwait in December 1980 that elaborated in detail on the Universal Declaration of Human Rights covenants. A specifically Arab version of human rights emerged out of a conference organized by the Arab League's legal department. The conference, held in Syracuse in Italy in 1986 grouped a large number of Arab legal, academic, religious, and governmental figures. The conference produced a document, The Project for The Declaration of the Rights of Human Beings and Peoples in the Arab Nation. The document detailed the nature of civil rights."

Leila indicated a slide with her pointer as she read the headings. She did so in a voice that was clear but full of emotion, her whole being endorsing the words she knew by heart.

"They are: Recognition of legal rights. A right to life. A right to personal security. Freedom to travel. The economic, and cultural rights. Political rights such as freedom of assembly, freedom to form associations. Nationality right. The right to self-determination, Resistance right from invader.

"Now we will look at an Ethical Perspective of Islam and Human Rights. The ethical perspectives of Islam, broadly understood, can also be explored as a significant new dimension in the on-going debates on Islam and human rights. These would not only be drawn from metaphysics, but also from the realm of tassawuf, Sufism, and 'irfan, metaphysical gnosis.

"Ethics in Islam or the science of akhlaq goes beyond systematic moral philosophy and include the ethics of the Qur'an, the Traditions, philosophical ethics proper, theology and ethics, as well as metaphysical Sufism, primarily the system of ibn 'Arabi, the classical doctrines of Sufism, and hikma or transcendental philosophy. But their legitimacy in Islam must also be related to their spiritual content and their function as pathways into understanding the deeper commands and injunctions of God. These notions will be developed in subsequent lectures on the subject, but in substance they are based on the following considerations: reason and received wisdom are in themselves insufficient to understand the unfolding of the divine commands.

"In conclusion, ladies and gentlemen, the world has not been able to produce more just and more equitable laws than those given 1400 years ago in Islam. The evolution of the principles of human rights in Islam will always be a complex process. On the one hand are claims that Islam should not demand an exceptional status in international conventions and agreements; and that Moslem countries and their citizens are best served if they abide by the international bill of rights. These should be adhered to even if some of their provisions may be problematic from the perspective of traditionally authoritative rulings. On the other hand are the variants of claims that Moslems cannot blithely abandon the bases of their culture and civilization to a system where the idea and ideals of rights might stray even further from commonly agreed norms of Islam. It is incumbent upon them to produce therefore their own version of the principles of human rights and hew to them in defense of their values and faith.

"Of course it is possible that in time, the two systems may co-exist but for this to have any significance in terms of the rights of individuals and peoples, the real abuses that abound in Moslem countries must be reined in. Peoples must see a real improvement in their well being, their rights and freedoms as a result of nations abiding by the stipulations of an Islamic code of human rights, irrespective of its provenance.

"Lastly, the final word on what constitutes Islamic norms has not been given, nor will it ever be definitively determined. In this respect, certain aspects of the Islamic legacy with profoundly humanistic overtones, from which an entirely new perspective on human rights can evolve, can be re-discovered after centuries of neglect and marginalization. This especially relates to the area of ethics in Islam and the field of tassawuf and gnosis from which important insights on the nature of human beings and their duties and rights can be derived. This will be the theme of possible subsequent lectures on the matter – whether a human rights doctrine in Islam can be partly rooted in Islam's gnostic and sufic tradition. It is not permissible to oppress women, children, old people, the sick, or the wounded. Women's honour and chastity are to be respected under all circumstances. The hungry must be fed, the naked clothed, and the wounded or diseased given medical treatment regardless of their pro- or anti-Moslem sentiments and activities.

"The report is Human Rights Watch's nineteenth annual review of human rights practices around the globe. It summarizes key human rights issues in more than 90 countries and territories worldwide, examines the freedom of local human rights defenders to conduct their work, and surveys the response of key international players, such as the United Nations, European Union, Japan, the United States, and various regional and international organizations and institutions.

"The World Report does not addressing important issue such as children's rights, women's rights, arms and military issues, business and human rights, HIV/ AIDS and human rights, international justice, terrorism and counter terrorism, refugees and displaced people, and transgender people's rights, and information about international natural disaster an war area which violate human right.

"This is a brief sketch of those rights which are given by God to all human beings, which was expressed by Prophet Mohammed through the Qur'an and Sunnah, from the birth of Islam fourteen hundred years ago Islam gave to man, to those who were at war with each other, even now in the 21st century, people and nations are still at war with each other. Human rights are vital to all beings; they are God-given rights to his creation, and convey prosperity, humanity to all human beings.

"However, there is little doubt that Islamic thought and jurisprudence, in the pre-modern era, did deal with many aspects of the rights and duties of various categories of human beings but in a framework that was conceptually and methodologically different from the western tradition.

"Islamic law and practice seems to offer a qualified acceptance of the universal doctrine of human rights principles, as a voice in various world forums particularly after second World War when human dignity was provoked. In particular, diverse injunctions of the commonly acknowledged tenets of Moslem laws of the Shari'ah appear to restrict, modify, and dilute the significance of the modern notion of human rights.

"On the other hand it hurts one's feelings that Moslems are in possession of such a splendid and comprehensive system of law and yet they look forward for guidance to those leaders of the West who could not have dreamed of attaining those heights of truth and justice, which was achieved a long time ago. Even more painful than this is the realization that throughout the world the rulers who claim to be Moslems have made disobedience to their God and the Prophet as the basis and foundation of their government. May God have mercy on them and give them the true guidance.

"The evolution of the principles of human rights in

Islam will always be a complex process. On the one hand are claims that Islam should not demand an exceptional status in international conventions and agreements; and that Moslem countries and their citizens are best served if they abide by the international bill of rights. These should be adhered to even if some of their provisions may be problematic from the perspective of traditionally authoritative rulings.

"On the other hand are the variants of claims that Moslems cannot blithely abandon the basis of their culture and civilization to a system where the idea and ideals of rights might stray even further from commonly agreed norms of Islam. It is incumbent upon them to produce therefore their own version of the principles of human rights and hew to them in defense of their values and faith. However, it refreshes and strengthens our faith in Islam when we realize that even in this modern age, which makes such loud claims of progress and enlightenment, the world has not been able to produce just and more equitable laws than those given 1400 years ago.

It is not permissible to oppress women, children, old people, the sick, or the wounded. Women's honor and chastity are to be respected under all circumstances. The hungry must be fed, the naked clothed, and the wounded or diseased given medical treatment regardless of their pro- or anti-Moslem sentiments and activities.

"It is clear from this analysis that the right to respect for private life in Universal charter is of the Convention extends well beyond traditional private law conceptions of privacy. Indeed the all categories of right can be identified from within it - the right to be free from interference with physical and psychological integrity, from unwanted access to and collection of information and from serious environmental pollution, and the right to be free to develop one's identity and to live one's life in the manner of one's choosing."

As Leila finished Eddie hear a catch in her voice, but her parting words to her audience were drowned out by thunderous applause and a standing ovation of those who had listened to her inspiring words and admired her courage in refusing to be deterred by the gunman who had invaded the conference.

As the delegates began to move out into the lobby of the hotel Eddie made his way to the front of the auditorium where Leila was answering questions from women and men who had been inspired by her talk. As he approached the podium Eddie noticed that Leila looked very pale and that tiny beads of perspiration stood out on her brow. Then as he drew level with her and before he could stop her, she slid silently to the floor in a dead faint.

By the evening, Leila had recovered from her faint. She had been seen by Sheikh Lewa's personal physician and pronounced to be well but the dark circles under her eyes told of the strain that she had been under. She had not been widowed long and the pressure of speaking at the symposium and then the horrific events of the final day had taken their toll.

Holding his breath, Eddie asked her if she wanted to cancel the evening meal when he phoned her in her room some hours later. She hesitated for a moment.

"No. I would still like to have dinner with you, Eddie. I have to eat and I would like my last meal here to be with you. I feel a fool for being so dramatic at the Symposium and I have only just persuaded Amir to take his flight instead of waiting here to fuss over me! No the sooner that I get back to normal the better."

Eddie breathed a sigh of relief. "Shall we eat inside the hotel or at the poolside? I'll ring up and book a table if you just say which."

"It feels a lot warmer to me today. Maybe in the Italian restaurant at the top of the hotel?"

"Fine, I'll make the booking. Shall we say 8 p.m.? Are you sure you're up to it?"

"I'm sure, Eddie; I'll see you there at eight."

Chapter Twenty-two

In New York Edward was again sitting in front of his head of security, Dawson. The device planted on the private jet had been found when it landed at JFK and it had fallen to Dawson to come and tell his boss that yet again security had been breached and the bank's jet could potentially have been blown out of the sky.

"What the hell are your boys playing at in Dubai?" Edward's lips were thin and white with rage. Dawson looked down at his hands.

"I can't explain it. All the staff we use are of the highest calibre—"

Edward snorted in derision. "Obviously not!" he said

"The checks we have in place are very thorough. Someone must have got to one of my team." Dawson tailed off.

"Thank you for stating the obvious." There was a long pause.

"Dawson, I now have no confidence in you at all, I'm sorry but you are fired. Leave my office and do not return to yours. I will have your things sent to you."

Dawson stared at Edward, his face ashen, but he could see that it was pointless to argue and got up and left the room, closing the door quietly behind him.

Left alone in his office, Edward pulled out his phone and called Hesham. The Arab man that was now Edwards's last hope answered on the first ring.

"I need to see you," Edward said.

"I will meet you at the Staten Island Ferry at 3 p.m.," he said, and Edward hung up. He felt the old hatred and resentment like a cancer eating away at his insides. Sharif. It was all down to him, Edward knew it and he was helpless to defend himself it seemed. He remembered the note and took it out of a secret draw of his desk ready to show Hesham when they met. The reference to the father and son was obviously to Harry and Byron but why had they not carried out the threat and why Harry and Byron? None of it made sense. For now though one thing was sure – the private jet was not going to be used by anyone. He buzzed his secretary through.

"Mr Lancaster?" she appeared at the door, cool and sophisticated and with a figure hugging shirt that would have had Edward's pulse racing in years gone by. Now though, his preoccupation with Sharif and what he was doing to his family, his bank and his life had taken over every aspect of his thoughts.

"Get someone from procurements up here straight after lunch; I want the jet to be sold."

"Right away, Mr Lancaster"

She was a professional for sure, Edward thought. Tere had been not a flicker of surprise at his instruction.

From his office on Wall Street it was not a long walk

to the Staten Island ferry terminal and Edward found, as he often did, pleasure in the anonymity he could enjoy in mingling with the crowds. A group of Japanese tourists stood outside the historic Wall Street exchange excitedly taking photos of the dealers in their blue jackets who had come out to smoke, the names of their firms on their backs in large letters. Edward smiled to himself as he saw one of the young Lancaster dealers playing up to the crowd and posing for photos, a cigarette in hand. It seemed a long time since he had been that young and he felt the white heat of his rage bubble up in him again as he thought how Sharif had blighted his life. He knew that there must be someone on his staff who was informing the man of movements and vulnerabilities but he had no idea who that could be. Eugene had obviously been involved and was dead for his trouble, and Sam Mendez was dead as well and had had some connection with Sharif although again Edward could not think how or why. If he was in the employ or under the influence of Sharif, why was he killed? He had certainly given no clue to anyone at Lancaster's that he was a "double agent" and no one had suspected a thing, so why had he been targeted? And the explosive on the plane, hard to imagine why anyone would think that the Lancasters would be devastated by the loss of Harry and his family, but the device had not been detonated, maybe because Eddie was not on board. In that case why refer to father and son? Edward closed his eyes as he waited to cross the street; he was losing sleep worrying about all of this, the possibilities going round and round in his head. As he opened his eyes he stepped forward to cross the street, not realizing that the pedestrian light was still red. A wild horn blaring and a screeching of tyres were the next thing he heard as he glanced off the wing of a yellow cab and spun around, landing on the sidewalk. People gathered around him, but Edward was on his feet in an instant. The cab driver, an immigrant, probably from Somalia, Edward thought, looked at him, eyes wide with horror from behind the wheel of his vehicle.

"I'm fine," he said, pushing away hands that seemed to be reaching for him, pawing at him. Panic was rising inside him; the concerned faces around him took on a ghostly menace. As he broke free he heard a siren approaching, an ambulance no doubt called by one of these interfering do-gooders, God, he thought, you hear all the time that guys have dropped dead on the sidewalk in New York and people have just stepped over them. Why don't they leave me alone? He half ran to the entrance of the huge centre built on the site of the Twin Towers, disappearing into the crowds of tourists before anyone could stop him. When he was sure he was out of sight he sunk onto one of the benches in front of a memorial plaque for the firefighters who had been killed helping people on that terrible day. His hands were shaking and he knew it was not just from the fact that he had almost been killed because he was too distracted to watch what he was doing. He felt as though he was losing his mind. Feeling twenty years older and weary beyond imagination, Edward eventually got up from the bench and walked through the centre and down to the walk that ran along the piers to the Staten Island ferry terminal.

As Edward boarded the ferry he looked around half-heartedly for Hesham. The way he felt at the moment he had lost the energy to fight. He felt like lying down and letting Sharif do his worst. Eventually as the ferry set off and the buildings on the quayside got smaller, Hesham found him. In his hand he held a book. Wordlessly he handed it to Edward so that he could read its back cover. Wearily Edward took his glasses from his pocket and began to read:

The year 2008 marked the last of God's warnings to mankind and the beginning in a countdown of the final three and one-half years of man's self-rule that will end by May 27, 2012.

On December 14, 2008, the First Trumpet of the Seventh Seal of the Book of Revelation sounded, which announced the beginning of the collapse of the economy of the United States and great destruction that will follow. The next three trumpets will result in the total collapse of the United States, and once the Fifth Trumpet sounds the world will be thrust into WW III.

The Seven Trumpets of the Seventh Seal, as well as the Seven Thunders of the Book of Revelation (which the apostle John saw but was restricted from recording) are revealed in this book.

Many of the prophecies of the Seven Thunders are being fulfilled and will continue to increase in strength and frequency throughout this final three and one-half years of man's self-rule on earth.

As these events unfold, the world will increasingly become aware of the authenticity of the words in this book and realize that Ronald Weinland has been sent by God as His end-time prophet.

This book is primarily directed to the people of the three major religions of the world (Islam, Judaism and Christianity), whose roots are in the God of Abraham. Ronald Weinland has been sent to all three.

Edward handed the book back, raising his eyebrow.

"Do you find it interesting?" Hesham asked.

"Mildly," Edward replied, "but there are a lot of kooks around, a lot of doom merchants"

"What he says about the American economy – does that resonate with you at all?"

"Yes, I suppose so," Edward sighed. He was not in the mood for guessing games.

"I think I may have discovered what our friend is trying to do," Hesham said. His sleeve slid up and Edward saw again the burnt withered skin of the man's arm.

"Oh?"

"He is trying to bring down the Western financial system. His is not an attack on the West per se, it is on what he sees as the lifeblood, the veins and arteries of the West: the economy."

"But I am only a small part of that, a cog," Edward said.

Hesham shrugged. "He had to start somewhere and your bank is the biggest in the United States. Slightly more than just a cog, I think.

"Even so ..." Edward knew he sounded petulant, like a child who was being told something he did not want to hear.

For a long time they sat in silence. Then Edward remembered that he still had the note in his pocket. He showed it to Hesham, who read it slowly twice before giving it back.

"Who were the father and son? You and Eddie?"

"No – it was one of Eddie's friend, the one whose son was kidnapped. He turned up in Dubai."

"Yes," Hesham said, and not for the first time Edward realized that this man, in the same way as Sharif, seemed to know exactly what was going in his life. Well Edward hoped not in exactly the same way; he hoped Hesham was on his side, but how did he really know that? His growing paranoia made him feel even more weary and he slumped slightly in his seat.

Hesham was not slow to notice. He knew a defeated man when he saw one.

* * *

In Dubai Eddie sat opposite Leila. He never ceased to marvel at her beauty. He had known many beautiful women in his life, many would say much more beautiful women than Leila, but hers was an inner beauty, totally unenhanced by makeup, a sort of inner glow that manifested itself in every part of her face. He really could not find the words to describe her beauty but one thing he did know was that he was utterly in love with her. There was no use in pretending that he would be able to live without her in his life, that he could switch off once he was away from her, this time with her, through all the ups and downs had etched his feelings for her on his soul. How their future would be he did not know; he knew how he would like it to be, and he dared not admit that it might never be, but the fear was always there.

"What are you thinking?" Leila patted her mouth with her napkin. The colour had returned to her cheeks now and she looked at him enquiringly.

Eddie could not possibly tell her what he was thinking, so he said, "I was thinking that you must be dying to get back to your children."

Leila's eyes danced. "Oh yes, I really can't wait to hold them again. But Eddie, I have enjoyed this time together, really I have, and thank you for all your support, through everything, the talk and yesterday..." her voice tailed off and her eyes misted over. "That poor man," she whispered.

"Yes, it really was a very terrible thing," Eddie said.

Eddie's mother Arabella had been trying to call her son. She had left several messages with the Hotel and his mobile phone was switched off. Now she shrieked down the phone.

"I don't care if Mr Lancaster said he did not want to be disturbed – you put me through to him NOW! I am his

MOTHER!"

The desk clerk held the phone away from his ear. Unsure what he should do he contacted the manager who spoke to Arabella in a tone that he hoped would calm her.

"I am so sorry, Mrs Lancaster. Is this an emergency?"

"No, well, yes … look I WANT TO SPEAK TO MY SON!"

"I am very sorry; he did leave us very strict instructions that he was not to be disturbed, unless it is an emergency …"

Arabella was unaccustomed to not getting what she wanted. Her frustration grew as she realized that she was not going to be put through. Her son was probably whoring around with some woman; like father like son, she thought, as she slammed the phone down. For a while she paced up and down her dressing room before picking up a vase and throwing it at her long dressing mirror. The crash brought servants running but by the time they arrived she had thrown herself onto the bed, her rage giving way to long deep sobs.

Arabella had not seen Sharif for months now. She had learned that he always knew where she was and he had popped up to pleasure her in cities as far apart as London and Melbourne. In her fevered mind she thought that somehow he had got caught up in the Middle East, could not leave and could not get a message to her and she was determined to get out there to give him the chance to see her and she him. The fact that she could not get through to Eddie was too much for her. She wanted him to make the arrangements and to meet her. Arabella knew that she could speak to him later but she wanted to go now. The frustration of not seeing Sharif and not knowing where he was was killing her.

In Dubai, Sharif closed his mobile phone. His face darkened. He had just heard that Edward was meeting his old enemy Hesham. He had an idea the two were connected but his agent in New York had just confirmed that the two were on the Staten ferry together. If there was anyone in this world that Sharif feared it was Hesham. He knew the man was as driven as he was himself and that he felt, as did Sharif, that God was on his side. He opened his phone to make another call. As he did so, the phone rang. After listening in silence to the call for a moment he closed his phone again and a faint smile played around his lips. Arabella was coming to Dubai.

As Eddie and Leila ate, their conversation came around to Leila's' talk. "You feel very passionately about human rights and women's rights in Islam, don't you?" Eddie said.

"Yes, of course," Leila said, tucking her trademark stray tendril into her hijab. "Although women are seen as different in Islam to men, there are many messages that are for men and women equally. I will tell you something of the work done by Mary and Anjum Ali whose writing I admire greatly, for instance; they point out that Prophet Mohammed, peace be upon him, sent the clear instruction 'Seeking knowledge is a mandate for every Moslem, whether, male or female.' This includes knowledge of the Qur'an and the Hadith as well as other knowledge. Men and women both have the capacity for learning and understanding. Since it is also their obligation to promote good behaviour and condemn bad behaviour in all aspects of life, Moslem women must acquire the appropriate education to perform this duty in accordance with their own natural talents and interests.

"While maintenance of a home, providing support to her husband, and the bearing, raising and teaching of children are among the first and very highly regarded roles for a woman, if she has the skills to work outside the home for the good of the community, she may do so as long as her family obligations are met. Far from making women somehow inferior to men, Islam recognizes and fosters the natural differences between men and women despite their equality. But the truth is that some types of work are more suitable for men and other types of work are more suitable for women. This in no way diminishes either's effort nor the validity of their contribution. God will reward both sexes equally for the value of their work, though it may not necessarily be the same activity.

"Concerning motherhood, Prophet Mohammed, peace be upon him, said: 'Heaven lies under the feet of mothers.' This implies that the success of a society can be traced to the mothers that raised its citizens. The first and greatest influence on a person comes from the sense of security, affection, and training received from the mother and an absence of this can be seen to produce an equally marked detriment to how an individual develops. Therefore, there is an obvious advantage to a woman with children being educated and conscientious in order to be a skilful parent." Leila paused. "Am I boring you?"

"Of course not. I love to hear you speak and I am

genuinely interested. I remember you mentioned women in politics in your talk and this is an area that many people think that women are not enjoying the same rights as men. Is that true?"

Leila smiled. "God gave the right to vote to Moslems 1400 years ago and on any public matter, a woman may voice her opinion and participate in politics. One example is that Prophet Mohammed, peace be upon him, is told that when believing women came to him to swear their allegiance to Islam, he must accept their oath. This established the right of women to select their leader and to publicly declare their choice and Islam does not forbid a woman from holding important positions in government.

"The Qur'an states: 'By the creation of the male and female; Verily, the ends ye strive for are diverse.'" Leila looked at Eddie. "Don't you think that is beautiful? It is one of my favourite verses."

Eddie smiled; he could listen to her talk all night. And he really was interested. It reminded him of his introduction to Islam and Islamic thinking all those years ago in the Harvard library.

"It is beautiful; go on," he said.

Leila sipped the sparkling grape juice that they were drinking.

"In these verses, God declares that He created men and women to be different, with unique roles, functions and skills. As in society, where there is a division of labor, so too in a family each member has different responsibilities. Generally, Islam upholds that women are entrusted with the nurturing role, and men, with the guardian role. Therefore, women are given the right of financial support.

"The Qur'an states: 'Men are the maintainers of women because Allah has made some of them to excel others and because they spend of their wealth for the support of women.'

"This guardianship and greater financial responsibility is given to men, requires that they provide women with not only monetary support but also physical protection and kind and respectful treatment.

"The Moslem woman has the privilege to earn money, the right to own property, to enter into legal contracts and to manage all of her assets in any way she pleases. She can run her own business and no one has any claim on her earnings including her husband. The Qur'an states: 'And in no wise covet those things in which Allah hath bestowed His gifts more freely on some of you than on others; to men is allotted what they earn, and to women, what they earn; but ask Allah of His bounty, for Allah hath full knowledge of all things.'

"A woman inherits from her relatives. The Qur'an says: 'For men there is a share in what parents and relatives leave, and for women there is a share of what parents and relatives leave, whether it be little or much - an ordained share and among His signs is that He created for you mates from among yourselves that you may live in tranquillity with them, and He has put love and mercy between you; Verily, in that are signs for people who reflect.'

"So you see, marriage is therefore not just a physical

or emotional necessity, but in fact, a sign from God! It is a relationship of mutual rights and obligations based on divine guidance. God created men and women with complimentary natures, and in the Qur'an, He laid out a system of laws to support harmonious interaction between the sexes.

"In the same way that clothing provides physical protection and covers the beauty and faults of the body. Likewise, a spouse is viewed this way. Each protects the other and hides the faults and compliments the characteristics of the spouse.

"To foster the love and security that comes with marriage, Moslem wives have various rights. The first of the wife's rights is to receive mahr, a gift from the husband, which is part of the marriage contract and required for the legality of the marriage.

The second right of a wife is maintenance. Despite any wealth she may have, her husband is obliged to provide her with food, shelter and clothing. He is not forced, however, to spend beyond his capability and his wife is not entitled to make unreasonable demands. The Qur'an states: 'Let the man of means spend according to his means, and the man whose resources are restricted, let him spend according to what Allah has given him. Allah puts no burden on any person beyond what He has given him.' God tells us men are guardians over women and are afforded the leadership in the family. His responsibility for obeying God extends to guiding his family to obey God at all times.

"A wife's rights also extend beyond material needs.

She has the right to kind treatment. The Prophet, peace be upon him, said: 'The most perfect believers are the best in conduct. And the best of you are those who are best to their wives.' God tells us He created mates and put love, mercy, and tranquillity between them.

"Both men and women have a need for companionship and sexual needs, and marriage is designed to fulfil those needs. For one spouse to deny this satisfaction to the other, temptation exists to seek it elsewhere." Leila looked down, embarrassed, and Eddie tried quickly to cover the moment.

"It looks like women are well catered for in marriage in Islam then."

"Yes," Leila said, "but with rights come responsibilities. Therefore, wives have certain obligations to their husbands. The Qur'an states: 'The good women in the absence of their husbands guard their rights as Allah has enjoined upon them to be guarded.' A wife is to keep her husband's secrets and protect their marital privacy. Issues of intimacy or faults of his that would dishonour him, are not to be shared by the wife, just as he is expected to guard her honour.

"A wife must also guard her husband's property. She must safeguard his home and possessions, to the best of her ability, from theft or damage. She should manage the household affairs wisely so as to prevent loss or waste. She should not allow anyone to enter the house whom her husband dislikes nor incur any expenses of which her husband disapproves.

"A Moslem woman must cooperate and coordinate with her husband. There cannot, however, be cooperation with a man who is disobedient to God. She should not fulfill his requests if he wants her to do something unlawful. A husband also should not take advantage of his wife, but be considerate of her needs and happiness."

"It's a pity that more people in the West don't adhere to those tenets," Eddie said.

"Well it's not all perfect in the Islamic world either," Leila said. "There are many things as Moslems that we know that we should or should not do yet we struggle to obey."

"Still I am sure that there are far fewer Christians who know the teachings of their religion as well as you and many others seem to know yours."

"Maybe," Leila smiled. They had just finished their dessert of luscious ripe fruit and Eddie sat back in his chair. The vista of Dubai lay below them and the lights twinkled far into the night up the coastline. The darkness of the sea where there was no light and the land on which a thousand lights burned was magical to see. It was a night when he longed to hold Leila in his arms so that they could look at the stars together. But that, he knew, would not happen.

In the lobby 50 floors below them Sharif was checking in. He knew from his contacts that Arabella would be arriving in the morning. He wanted to be ready for her. He felt that possibly the best way now to achieve his goal was going to be through her. The fact that he had to do what he did with her was becoming more and more repulsive to him but he knew that his prowess was the thing that had captivated her and would keep her a puppet in his hands. He might well need her soon and then he would be rid of her cloying and oppressive presence for good. The thought of her ageing, enhanced body made him shudder. He was going to have to use his imagination and conjure up something a lot more edifying that her plastic body to allow him to perform.

In New York Arabella was packing. Edward had come back from work and was slumped in his study. He seemed very down these days and had hardly commented when Arabella had told him that she was flying out to Dubai to see Eddie. Still at least he had not said he would come too. She had been afraid he might and was ready to put him off by saying that one of her most annoying friends was going with her. But it had not been necessary. If she had cared more she would have asked him what was wrong, but she didn't. All Arabella could think about was seeing Sharif. Her whole body ached for his touch. She had convinced herself that he was in Dubai; he had to be; it was the only explanation. She knew that he enjoyed their meetings as much as she did. She could tell. The fact that they could never be together she had accepted, but not to see him at all was out of the question. It was now the only thing in her life that gave her pleasure.

As Eddie saw Leila to her room that night she tried to say goodbye. "My flight is early tomorrow so I will say goodbye now," she said.

"Oh no you don't. I will drive you out to the airport," Eddie said.

"But Eddie, the hotel have laid on a car; there really is no need."

"I know, but I would like to; let meet for an early breakfast and then I'll drive you."

Leila smiled and shrugged. OK; if you insist! Thank you very much."

And with that, the magical night had ended and Eddie made his way back to the penthouse suite. There were twelve messages on the machine, all from his mother sounding increasingly frantic. It seemed that she was coming out to Dubai. She would see him the next day. The last message told him not to bother to book the room that the first message has asked him to as she had already done it. She sounded distracted and hysterical and Eddie frowned. His mother was known as the "Ice Queen" amongst the servants, a woman who rarely showed emotion. On the phone she sounded close to breaking point.

Not for the first time in recent days, Eddie felt that his life was somehow spinning out of control. He did not like the feeling at all.

Chapter Twenty-three

In Dubai, Eddie was increasingly frustrated with his mother. Arabella had arrived like some sort of banshee being difficult and rude to the hotel staff, and even when she was talking to Eddie, as they sat in the coffee shop of the lobby, her eyes constantly swept the hotel foyer, looking for God knows what or who. She was jumpy and distracted and so far had refused every invitation that Eddie had given to dinner or any other activity outside the hotel. It was as though she was waiting for someone. But that was impossible. She didn't know anyone in Dubai, apart from him. Eddie sighed; luckily he had to be with Sheikh Lewa for the afternoon and he was booked to go back on a flight two days from now. So far his mother had been unresponsive about when she would be returning, and any idea that Eddie had had that she had come out to Dubai to see him had long since been quashed. He had given up trying to work out the machinations of his parents' lives, apart from the fact that they lived more or less separately, and he really did not care much what his mother was doing in Dubai. Even the fact that she had shown no interest in Dubai in all the years that his father and Eddie had been coming here was only mildly interesting to him.

She spent an awful lot of time in her room and when he called her there she often answered with a kind of breathless excitement that he was quite sure was not meant for him. Now that they had finished their coffee, she announced her attention to go up to her room again and Eddie was relieved that he was being dismissed. On the way to the elevator, Arabella checked again with the desk clerk if there were any messages for her, although she had been told that they would either be put in her room or if they were telephone messages they would be on the answer machine of the room phone. Eddie watched as the desk clerk shook his head and his mother turned on her heel and stalked over to the lift. Whatever was going on, Eddie thought, he didn't want to know.

The Sheikh was at his camp in the desert again and Eddie was looking forward to the drive out there. As the busy city roads began to thin out, Eddie looked out at the empty dessert. It was amazing how the city seemed to be all around you one moment and then completely lost in the miles of desert sand. There seemed to be no gradual progression from one to the other, you were just suddenly in the desert. Eddie loved the open and deserted feel of it and the way that the heat shimmered above the dunes like a liquid shield of glass. After driving through the desert they took a long empty road where the only other vehicles were desert safari trucks. It was a strange and awe-inspiring experience because the road was a dual carriageway, but had no barriers. With all the traffic moving in the same direction, it felt to Eddie like a scene from a movie, with the only break to the monotony the occasional overtaking and undertaking and generally fairly risky driving.

Suddenly and unexpectedly the car stopped at a camel farm. The driver got out, smiling, making signs to Eddie that he would not be long. In large paddocks Eddie saw the camels standing under the palm trees that offered shade from the fierce sun. Their tails twitched occasionally to get rid of the flies that buzzed around them and their jaws made rhythmic chewing motions. Two baby camels scampered together in the sun, seemingly oblivious to the heat.

On the road that they had just left, the traffic continued to go past and Eddie could appreciate their speed now that the limousine that he was travelling in was stationary. Now that the engine of the car was off the cool interior of the car was heating up fast and Eddie decided that he would get out and stretch his legs. There was still no sign of the driver, and he wandered over to the palm trees that overhung the fence of the camel's paddock. They eyed him suspiciously but made no move from the shade of the palm tree on their side of the fence. Eddie looked around for the driver. The car was some 100 yards from the farm and even although he was now closer he could see no sign of human life.

Suddenly a car sped off from the far side of the paddock and before Eddie could see what it was the air was full of noise and flying debris and he was thrown over the fence into the paddock. For a moment hooves thundered around him as the camels made for the other side of the paddock, and then he was alone, lying in the sand, the dusty grit in his mouth, ears and nose. Blood trickled down his face and he felt a gash on his forehead. He looked over to the car. It was a smoking wreck, unrecognizable as a car. Rubbing grit out of his eyes, Eddie stared at it. His brain tried to rationalize to say that the car had stood too long in the heat, but he knew that like the shooting, this explosion had been meant to end his life.

A couple of cars had stopped on the road and Arab men in thobes ran towards the car. Eddie got to his feet and walked towards them. Seeing him they changed tack and ran towards him. He recognized one of them as the Sheikh's secretary, Hamid.

An hour later Eddie was in the camp with Sheikh Lewa. He had washed and been given a thobe to replace his dusty clothes. He was not hurt apart from the cut on his head that had only needed a plaster. But he was shaken to the core and was coming to terms with the fact that someone was trying to kill him. Although he had been told that he was the target of the gunman at the symposium he had tried to put it to the back of his mind. He could not, would not, acknowledge the fact. Sheikh Lewa however was more realistic and his next statement hit Eddie like a body blow.

"Obviously ever since flight 602 was brought down without you on it, someone has been targeting you."

"What?" Whether through denial or ignorance this was the first time that Eddie had considered the fact that he and he alone might have been the target on flight 602. The Sheikh, realizing that this seemingly obvious fact had not occurred to Eddie before, tried to soft pedal but it was too late. Eddie felt his nerves jangling and the tension rising in him; he wanted to run, where to he had no idea, but he just wanted to run. The desert that he had so admired in the past seemed now malevolent and ready to swallow him whole. The sound of distant sirens approaching signaled the arrival of the police. Eddie desperately wanted it all to go away, to be home again and safe, but would he ever be safe again? Would he ever be able to stop looking over his shoulder? Was he even safe here? Panic rose in his throat, as out of the corner of his eye he could see men in thobes moving around. They all seemed to be looking at him. Were they waiting for a chance to bury a dagger in his heart? He felt a scream rising inside him and in his attempt to swallow it came out as a sob. The Sheikh quickly cleared the tent and as Eddie collapsed on the cushions he patted his back. He felt sorry for this young man, and he wished he had an answer for him. The police were on their way. Maybe they would know something.

In the hotel, Arabella lay exhausted in the arms of Sharif. He smiled to himself. It had taken some doing but he had managed to rise to the occasion, and the faint blush on Arabella's cheeks and above her breasts showed him that he had done well. He glanced at the phone beside the bed. It would ring in a while, letting her know the bad news. It was only fair that he be there to comfort her. As he looked down at her face, her hair swept back, he saw the tell-tale suture line behind her ears left by her most recent facelift. He struggled to stop himself shuddering; he liked women to be natural – and young. Arabella was very far from what he liked and a million miles from what excited him. It had taken all his imagination and judicious use of the blackout curtains to enable him to perform. He stroked her face, her botox-filled stretched face, and then froze in horror as Arabella's hand snaked greedily across his bare thigh. Jumping out of bed, Sharif quickly wound a towel around himself.

"I have to go, my darling," he whispered; "I dare not stay longer, otherwise I shall never leave. You are too tempting, too sexy."

Arabella smiled at him with perfect white veneered teeth, testament to the art of her very affluent 52nd street dentist. Sharif tried to keep his smile in place.

"Well if you must go, I suppose I will have to content myself with my toys!" She pouted in what would have been a winning way in a 15-year-old but which in a woman on the wrong side of 50 was repulsive. Sharif hurried to the bathroom. He looked at his watch. She should have had the call by now, but he could not wait and would have to go. She was insatiable and there was no way he would be able to summon up an encore.

As he came out of the bathroom, the phone beside the bed rang. As Arabella leaned over to take the call, Sharif saw more stitches behind her shoulder from a recent arm lift.

"Hello? Oh, hello, Eddie." Sharif stopped in his tracks.

"You've had car trouble? Oh yes, that's right; we were supposed to meet. Never mind. I've been a bit tied up." She smiled at Sharif and winked, a gesture that made his stomach turn over.

"Fine. I'll see you later." She hung up and Sharif dodged her embrace as she padded naked from the bed.

"I have to go. See you later, my angel!" He kissed his finger and pressed it on her nose.

Outside in the corridor he leaned against the thick brocade wallpaper, his eyes closed. He flipped open his phone. "What happened?" he said when his call was answered. He listened for a moment and then shut his phone.

As he strode to his room he opened the phone again. "Who have we in London?" He listened or a second then said, "Get him to call me. I have a job for him."

In London Leila was giving a lecture to some female Moslem economics students at King's University. She had been very much in demand since she had given her talk in Dubai and she enjoyed talking about women in Islamic finance.

"In 2008 I attended a seminar at City law firm Norton Rose on 'Women in Islamic Finance'. Many leading Islamic women academics spoke there and Halima Krausen, a Shariah scholar and academic from Germany made a powerful point that resonated with me, this is what she said: 'Women have been actively involved in trade, financial and investment matters throughout Islamic history,' she explained. 'In fact, the Prophet, peace be upon him, worked for a businesswoman Khadija who subsequently became his wife.' London now boasts some six Islamic banks authorized by the Financial Services Authority. But all of them are headed by men. In fact, the dominance of men in top jobs in the City and financial services in general continues unabated. Not surprisingly, Minister Kitty Ussher, Secretary to the treasury, expressed hope that perhaps one day a woman chief executive officer would head one of the UK's Islamic banks.

"While it is true that the involvement of women in senior positions in Islamic finance is increasing in Southeast Asia, the situation elsewhere in the GCC countries, Pakistan, Iran, Turkey and Egypt is really much less encouraging. In the GCC states, for instance, gender segregation policies have put many women aspiring to be bankers at a huge disadvantage. For example, Dr Nahed Taher, the former chief economist of National Commercial Bank, was forced to leave Saudi Arabia to take a post as a CEO in a conventional bank in Bahrain, a position she could never hope to be appointed to in her native country.

"Even in other GCC countries and when we look at wider markets, the involvement of women banking professionals in the sector, are limited. Experienced women bankers, who, I might add, very often outperform their male counterparts, are understandably frustrated that their career chances and choices are governed by socio-cultural norms imposed on them by men. They are not satisfied, and nor should they be, with heading the women-only sections of their banks; or to work in women-only financial institutions. These highly qualified and motivated women want to be acknowledged as leaders in their fields in the mainstream Islamic or conventional financial services sectors, irrespective of their gender. If women are increasingly being required to contribute their part to GDP in GCC and Middle Eastern economies, as the governments seem to suggest they should be, many of them argue that they need to operate on a level playing field with access to equal opportunities so that they have the chance to realize their full potential and to make their own valued contribution.

"Support is growing. Kitty Ussher said 'Islamic finance is one of the most exciting, innovative financial services sectors around at the moment. In the retail sector, the Islamic mortgage market is now worth over 500 million pounds a year, and the UK's Shariah compliant banks now have more than 40,000 customers. Islamic finance products, particularly in the retail market, are also very important for the people who buy them. We do believe that it's right that everyone, regardless of their religion, should be able to participate fully in the financial system – and should have the opportunity to make the most of their money. So, both because of the benefits for customers, and to help make sure that London is at the forefront as the sector continues to develop, we want to do everything we can to encourage the development of Islamic Finance in the UK.'"

Leila looked up at the faces of the girls.

"You young ladies are the future in banking and other financial services. The messages that you take with you as you pursue your careers will be what sails the economic ship of the future. There are many chances for the ship to run aground or be broken up on the rocks, you ladies are the ones who will be charged with the responsibility of sailing your ship to safe harbour. It is a grave responsibility and the way ahead is going to be tough, but this is an exciting time and all of your should feel privileged to be at the birth of a new dawn in finance."

The girls applauded Leila enthusiastically and she stayed behind for a while to answer a few questions and to talk in general with these girls who were just starting out on a career that had brought Leila so much fulfilment. As she spoke, outside on the busy street a car had drawn up on the yellow lines opposite the college. The driver had a mobile phone in his hand and was looking at a picture of a woman standing on a podium. The woman's beautiful face was radiant and despite the fact that she was wearing an hijab the driver of the car knew that he could not mistake that face. The traffic was heavy and he was not worried that he would draw attention to himself on the yellow lines; no one gave him a second glance and the gate in front of which he was parked was firmly locked so he was unlikely to be asked to move. He scanned the faces of the women coming out of the building. Most had hijabs on and for a moment he thought he might not recognise Leila. But when she did emerge, pausing to talk outside the door of the college. He recognised her instantly. Her face was animated and very beautiful as she spoke to one of the other women in a hijab; it seemed almost a shame to extinguish that light, but a job was a job and he raised the gun he had had on his lap and fired. The shot was not even heard above the roar of the traffic and the gunman had made his way back into the stream of cars almost before Leila fell to the ground.

* * *

In Dubai, Eddie heard the news some three hours later. Amir phoned him and told him that Leila was in hospital. At first Eddie assumed that she had had an accident. He was still feeling shocked and deeply afraid after his brush with death, but his feelings for his own predicament immediately gave way to an almost heartbreaking fear for Leila.

"What happened, Amir? Was it a car crash?"

"No, Eddie, it wasn't; she was shot." Eddie could hardly take in what he was hearing and for a moment he dropped the phone. Amir's voice calling his name revived him and he picked up the phone again. As Amir told him what he knew, Eddie could hear anger in his voice, and he knew that that some of that anger was directed to him. It could not be a coincidence that on the day that he had dodged death, Leila had been gunned down in the street.

"Amir, you know that I would not have put Leila at risk for the world. I don't know what to say."

"I think it would be best if you keep away from her," Amir said, but even as he said the words he knew that to keep Eddie away would be impossible.

"I understand how you feel, Amir, but I have to come. How bad is she?" It was the question he had not wanted to ask or have answered, but he had to know.

"Bad," Amir said, his voice shaking. "They don't know if she is going to make it." Eddie felt bile rise in his throat and threw down the phone, running to the bathroom to be sick. This could not be happening. When he came back into the bedroom Amir had hung up. He picked up the phone to ring Sheikh Lewa. In a voice that did not sound like his own he told the Sheikh what had happened.

"I am going to the airport now to get the next flight to London."

"No, Eddie, don't do that. Whoever is behind this will know that is what you will do. You will not be safe on a commercial flight. You can take my private jet."

"Thank you," Eddie said.

* * *

334

In the intensive care unit of King's College Hospital Leila fought for her life. The bullet had hit her in the chest, grazing her heart and was now lodged in her spine. As her doctors pored over X-rays and CT scans they tried to decide whether she would be paralysed or not, and whether if they operated they would seal her fate and make her paraplegic. She had lost a dangerous amount of blood and her heart had stopped three times, but she was a fighter and for now her vital signs were holding their own. Her mother was on the way from Saudi Arabiaand Marwa, Amir's wife, sat, head bowed, in the waiting room.

In the ICU, the quietness of the patients was in direct contrast to the constant beeping of the machines monitoring their every beat and every heartbeat. In the section in which Leila had been put connected to a dozen tubes, the machines that monitored her were in turn being monitored by a nurse, sitting quietly at the end of the bed, her eyes darting from one machine to another. Every now and again she would get up and adjust one or the other, check the bag that was collecting urine and the bags that were delivering saline and blood. There was not a flicker of life from Leila, but she had been put into an induced coma in the hope that her body would recover from its devastating trauma.

Amir had arrived now and told Marwa about his conversation with Eddie. "I told him not to come, but I know that he will." Marwa looked at her husband. "He loves her, habibi, we know that; how could he stay away?"

Amir's jaw tightened. "He could stay away to save any more harm coming to her," He said gravely.

"But he is not with her now and harm has come to her, so would it really make any difference? She has been his friend for many years and whoever wishes to harm him knows that. This is something that could only be avoided by their never having met in the first place, I am afraid that it is too late now to distance themselves from each other." Amir smiled and took his wife's hand. As always she was wise and saw things in perspective. He could find no argument with what she said.

Eddie arrived in the afternoon, just after Leila's parents. Amir and Marwa met him in the waiting room and told him that he could not go in. "Only two visitors are allowed at once and her mother and father are with her now." Eddie slumped down on a chair, his face white and drawn, his pain and sorrow etched deeply into the lines around his mouth and on his forehead.

Leila's parents eventually emerged from the ICU looking shaken and obviously deeply shocked. Seeing Eddie, Maysoon flew at him shouting.

"What are you doing here? Don't you know that my child would not be lying there close to death if it were not for you? Get out of here! Don't ever come here or see her again. You are not welcome and you will be responsible if our daughter dies!"

Eddie fled from the waiting room, Maysoon's words stabbing him like daggers. He stumbled out onto the street and walked for miles, blindly and with no purpose. Finally he arrived at a park where, exhausted, he lay down on a bench. He slept fitfully but by the morning his head had cleared. He checked into a hotel and waited. He let

Amir know where he was and for three weeks he stayed in his hotel room, ordering food from room service and buying a change of clothes and underwear, a toothbrush, toothpaste, a razor and shaving foam from the hotel shop. He let his parents know what had happened and that he would take no calls. The battery on his mobile phone ran out so he sat next the phone beside his bed. He spent his days looking out over Hyde Park from the room of his hotel, He listened to no music and watched no television. All day he stared out of the window, his thoughts completely occupied with Leila.

In his mind he saw her smiling face the day that he had first met her, a shy smile, the smile of a girl, not yet a woman, that stray piece of hair curling gently against her cheek. Eddie was pleased that he could remember his first meeting with her so well because it had not made as much impression on him at that time as it did now in retrospect. No, at that time he was still Eddie the Jock, Eddie the bed hopper, Eddie the shallow self-serving rich kid and Leila was most definitely nowhere near his type. Her hijab and her dress screamed "keep off" and that was definitely not what he wanted in a woman. He luxuriated in his thoughts about her, about the time that they had spent together; it was almost like worshipping at an altar, being able to give his thoughts and his heart entirely to thinking about her. He had cleared his life of everything else. It was just Leila and Leila alone that occupied his every waking moment. He closed his eyes and listened to her voice in his head. The voice of a young passionate woman, a woman who was dedicated to what she believed in, a woman who made him feel depthless and superficial. His mind focused on the project that had brought them together all those years ago. He could remember almost every word and now it played back to him like a movie. In his mind he could see Leila's lovely face, her eyes shining dark and beautiful, full of passion for the subject. He put his hands over his ears, and he could hear her – yes, he could hear her!

"Mudarabah," she had said, and Eddie remembered his attempt to repeat the word. When she was satisfied with his pronunciation she had moved on. "Mudarabah is a partnership where the investment comes from the first partner, 'rabb-ul-mal', and the management and work is the responsibility of the second, 'mudarib'." He remembered how she had looked at him with raised eye brows and he had nodded, signifying that he had understood although her beauty and purity was so overwhelming he had to struggle hard to concentrate. He had repeated her words and she went on.

"We can summarise the points like this." Leila had held up one hand, and bent over one finger. For some reason tears sprung to Eddies eyes as he remembered the gesture. "In musharakah, investment comes from all partners, but in mudarabah, investment is the responsibility of the rabb-ul-mal." Pushing the second finger into her palm she had said. "In musharakah, all partners participate in the management, but in mudarabah, the mudarib alone conducts the management." A third finger. "All partners in musharakah share the loss to the extent of their ratio of investment, but in Mudarabah the loss is suffered by the rabb-ul-mal only as he is the sole investor. However, if the mudarib has been negligent, he will suffer the loss." Eddie had nodded and she pushed down a fourth finger.

He wiped tears from his eyes.

In his head Leila continued, her voice clear and sweet. "The partners' liability in musharakah is unlimited. In mudarabah the liability of the rabb-ul-mal is limited to his investment, unless he has permitted the mudarib to incur debts on his behalf." Eddie remembered taking notes as she had pushed her thumb in to her palm. "In musharakah, the assets, once mixed in a joint pool, become jointly owned by them according to the proportion of investment. In mudarabah all goods purchased by the mudarib are solely owned by the rabb-ul-mal. The mudarib can earn his share in the profit should he sell the goods profitably. He is not entitled to claim his share of the assets."

Eddie recalled how she had paused and looked at him expectantly and how he, stumbling sometimes over the unfamiliar words, repeated the gist of what she had told him. Leila had clapped her hands together softly. "Yes, yes, that is right! I am so pleased that you find it so interesting!" She was achingly beautiful in her happiness and enthusiasm.

Eddie had wanted to say it was her that he found interesting, and it was true he did, but something in the message in the unfamiliar words and in the concept was captivating him and he remembered asking her to go on.

"Restricted mudarabah is when the rabb-ul-mal specifies a particular business for the mudarib to invest the money in. Unrestricted mudarabah is when it is open for the mudarib to undertake whichever business he wishes." Eddie recalled how he had written notes, but he remembered that incredibly he had found that his mind was opening to the message and to the unfamiliar language, and he had felt almost as though he was a blind man suddenly able to see. Eddie cold see the exact moment when Leila had turned her lovely face to him and registered the enthusiasm on his face and they had continued, her voice tinged with excitement, the excitement of imparting a dearly loved message to a willing audience, he with a stirring excitement and hunger for knowledge. Like the showing of a film the rest of the information Leila had shared with him that day played back in his mind as clear and fresh as though it had been yesterday. He remembered how for a while they had talked about what Leila had been saying and how he had been so happy to see her pleasure and surprise as she realised how much Eddie had taken in, and the fact that he even seemed to be getting the hang of the Arabic words. Leila had told him many years later, that the part of her that wanted to be a teacher was exhilarated that her message was being so well received by her pupil and he had hoped that she would mention another reason for her joy, their nearness that might perhaps have made her feel a fraction of what he did. But she did not.

"OK, Eddie," she had said at last, and Eddie smiled, remembering how he loved the way she said his name. They had continued with the project for some time, and then as Leila had paused, Eddie remembered how he had looked at her, his eyebrow raised in expectation and how Leila had laughed and said, "I think that is enough for one day; my throat is dry and I think your brain might explode with any more information!"

Eddie had laughed at her little joke and recalled how

he had got her some water in a little plastic cup from the water cooler. As she sipped it he had watched her, her lovely face flushed from the effort of talking to him for so long and from delivering her message with such passion and conviction. Eddie thought of how he had realised that there was something more to this lovely girl than the usual standards that he used to measure female suitability. There was something precious and fragile that made him want to protect her and keep her safe from everyone and anything that might hurt her. Now as he sat in his hotel window, remembering that long ago afternoon, and he realised that the biggest threat to her had turned out to be him, the feeling of misery and fear that haunted him made him close his eyes tight, as though he was trying to blot the world out.

Chapter Twenty-four

When Leila returned home she was astonished to find the congratulatory notes and messages that had been left for her following her talk at the symposium in Dubai. Two huge bunches of flowers, one from Amir and one from Eddie, scented the hallway of the house and her mother looked at her enquiringly as she read the note from Eddie. Her parents had loved having the time with the twins and the girls had adored having their grandmother and grandfather with them.

"Nice flowers from Uncle Amir," her mother said; "and these other ones?"

"They are from an old friend from Harvard." Leila felt herself blushing under her mother's scrutiny. She scolded herself. What on earth was there to blush about? She had not really examined the events of her time in Dubai yet. Of course she knew that Eddie loved her but was it as a dear friend or something more? She knew that she had a lot of thinking to do, but this was not the time to do it while her mother, who knew her so well, was scrutinizing her every facial expression.

"Were the girls good for you and dad?" Leila asked brightly.

"Very good; they are darlings." her mother said and Leila breathed a sigh of relief. If there was anything that was likely to distract her mother it was talk of her beloved granddaughters. For the time being, at least, she was off the hook. "Remember that Uncle Amir and Auntie Marwa are coming this evening. You seem so distracted; I thought perhaps you had forgotten. I have started to prepare the food. Perhaps you would like to help me while the girls are out at school?"

Leila ignored the comment from her mother, a blatant attempt to dig further into her relationship with Eddie, and followed her to the kitchen, rolling up her sleeves. "I thought tomorrow we could go for a day out. It wouldn't hurt to take the children out of school for the day, would it? After all, your father and I leave next week and we want to spend as much time with the girls, and you, as we can."

Leila hesitated. Nasser had been very strict about letting the girls miss school. Even at this early age he had believed that discipline was essential, but on the other hand it was true that she had not seen much of her parents and that a day out together with the girls would be wonderful. Maybe if they chose an educational attraction?

"What did you have in mind?" Leila asked.

"Well you are the one that lives in London. What do you suggest?"

"How about the zoo? The girls love animals and it would be educational for them."

"That sounds great. I can't wait to tell them today when they come back from school and see their little faces light up!"

Amir and Marwa arrived for dinner at eight. It had

been some time since the four had been together and conversation turned to the events of the symposium in Dubai. Leila had not told her parents about the shooting of the security guard at the hotel during her talk and Amir was immediately apologetic about bringing it up.

"Why didn't you tell us?" Leila's mother had gone white.

"Because there was nothing you could do and it's over now," Leila said.

"But what was the motive?" Leila's father asked.

"Well apparently the target was one of the delegates, one of Leila's' friends, Eddie Lancaster from the huge US bank Lancaster's," Amir said.

Maysoon looked at Leila sharply, remembering the flowers.

"Well in that case I am very glad that you are home and away from him. How could you put yourself in danger like that? Haven't your twins been through enough?" There was an awkward silence.

"I'm sorry, Maysoon," Amir said. "I really did not intend for this to upset you or to spoil our evening together. I thought you knew about it."

"Well we didn't." Maysoon excused herself from the table and Marwa went after her, closely followed by Leila herself.

Left alone, Anwar and Amir began to talk about the world's current financial predicament.

"Did you see the piece written for the Arab news by Mushtak Parker?" Anwar asked his friend. He was not keen on emotional situations and was very happy to leave his wife and daughter and Marwa to sort things out.

"I did, and I agree with a lot of what he says. In fact I have it here." Amir took a copy of the paper from his briefcase. "It is very true that as Sarah McCarthy-Fry, the MP and exchequer secretary to Treasury, said at the 'New Year, New Opportunities in Islamic Finance' seminar in London recently." He read from the paper: "'Islamic finance is, and will continue to be, an important part of the UK government's overall commitment to ensuring a competitive financial services sector in the UK.' It is interesting," Amir said, " that this statement of intent coincides with two notable developments relevant to the European Islamic finance sector in the last two weeks or so. Firstly, the UK Treasury and the Financial Services Authority have been working to remove barriers and uncertainty in the regulation of sukuk alternative finance investment bonds. Following consultation with the industry, the statutory instrument, the Financial Services and Markets Act 2000 was sent to the House of Commons in mid-January, and the government is confident that the new regulations will come into effect by the end of February. These measures should reduce compliance and legal costs for these instruments, and facilitate the issuance of corporate sukuk in the UK."

"I heard that there had been some movement in Luxembourg too," Anwar said.

"That's right," Amir said, and read out another passage: "'The Luxembourg Tax Authorities, also in mid-January, published the tax treatment for sukuk and a range of Islamic financial products with the aim of facilitating tax neutrality for such products compared to equivalent conventional ones. The wider aim is to develop Luxembourg as another European hub for Islamic finance, especially sukuk origination and listings and registration domicile for Islamic funds and trusts. Luxembourg in fact is emerging as the fastest growing Islamic finance hub in Europe with key developments in the process of being implemented with counterparts in Saudi Arabia and Malaysia over the next few months. In this respect Luxembourg is emerging as a serious alternative hub for Islamic finance to London and Paris, although officials and market players on all sides stress that there is room for all given the nascent state of the industry in the European Union. The Norton Rose seminar that I attended, also saw the first public statement made on behalf of the opposition Conservative Party regarding Islamic finance. Mark Hoban MP, shadow (Conservative) financial secretary to the Treasury, confirmed that the Conservative Party has supported the steps taken by the government to create a level playing field for Islamic finance and that it would continue the same approach. He recognized the concerns raised by the audience in respect of a need for clearer criteria to enable the industry to address any government concerns in relation to a UK government sukuk.

'The cross-party support including support by the opposition Liberal Democrat Party for UK government's Islamic finance initiative has been welcomed by the industry. Farmida Bi, London banking partner, Norton Rose, emphasized'." Amir continued reading from the paper. "'It is extremely good news for the City of London that there is cross party support for the promotion of Islamic finance and that the helpful legislative changes that have been made will be continued irrespective of which party is in power.'"

"It is all very interesting," Anwar said, and due in no small part to your efforts, Amir, old friend.

"I don't know about that!" Amir said, "but you are righ. It is encouraging. The situation has been on a knife-edge ever since in December 2008. The government announced that it was postponing any decision regarding the issuance of a sovereign sukuk for the time being. Minister McCarthy-Fry reiterated at the Norton Rose seminar that the Treasury currently has no intention to launch a UK government sukuk. The minister highlighted the current market conditions and the government's concern that a UK government sukuk would not offer value for money for both the Treasury and investors. It is true that the financial crisis and global downturn at the end of the last decade precipitated exceptional change in financial services, both in the UK and around the world. McCarthy-Fry did warn that the world must continue to learn and implement the lessons that will help strengthen the financial services industry so that it is better able to serve the global and individual economies in future."

Amir took up the paper again. "We will continue to pursue a regulatory framework that is an international benchmark. And we will continue to pursue a consistent, politically neutral legal system that is widely used and understood globally. Together, these will help reinforce confidence in doing business with the UK and in investing in the UK.

""""And these goals will help the UK to continue as a leading financial center, one able to take advantage of growth areas in financial services, including the area I am here to talk about today – Islamic finance,'" she said, according to Parker's piece in the Arab News. The Treasury acknowledges that capitalizing on growth areas such as Islamic finance and supporting their expansion will be hugely beneficial for the health of the sector in the future. Indeed, this support for growth areas relates to one of the lessons from the crisis – the need for a more diverse financial services sector.

"'Islamic finance,' says the UK Treasury, 'is an area that has been helped by the openness to new influences and ideas that we have here in the UK, especially in London. With our depth of skill, experience and connections all around the world, we have ensured that the UK has long been the leading Western center for Islamic finance.'"

"So how many banks are there in the UK that do offer Islamic financing?" Anwar asked.

Amir nodded vigorously; there was nothing that made him more enthusiastic than discussing Islamic finance. "There are at present twenty-two banks offering Islamic financial products in the UK, including five that are fully Shariah-compliant, which means that there are more banks in the UK offering Islamic finance than in the whole of the rest of Western Europe. The UK also has a Takaful provider, an Islamic hedge fund and nine Islamic fund managers."

"So the adoption of Islamic financial practices are growing, taking hold around the non-Islamic financial world?" Anwar said.

"Yes, despite the impact of the global financial crisis, Islamic finance remains a growth sector around the world. It is under conditions like the ones faced by international financial markets during the crisis and in its aftermath that new opportunities for growth and development become increasingly important. This woman McCarthy-Fry is very interesting, in fact." Amir read out another statement: "The issue of corporate sukuk by GE Capital in November, showed the continued appetite around the world for Shariah-compliant finance. This was first listed on the London Stock Exchange, and brought the total number of sukuk listed in London to 20, with total funds raised of over $11 billion. Worldwide, only the Dubai NASDAQ exceeds these figures. The Islamic finance market presents huge long-term opportunities for London and the UK. And it is a market that this government would like to continue to nourish.

"It seems that the UK government's dual objectives for Islamic finance are for business, to maintain London's position as a European leader for international Islamic finance and for individuals, to ensure that everybody, irrespective of the religious or ethical beliefs, has access to competitively priced financial products.

"To facilitate the above, the UK government over the past five years has made a series of reforms to establish a level playing field – in tax and regulation – between conventional and Islamic finance. These include products such as Shariah-compliant mortgages, individual savings accounts and child trust funds.

"In the 2009 pre-budget report, the Chancellor of the Exchequer announced further measures, especially the government's intention to provide relief from tax on capital gains for alternative property refinance, subject to satisfactory safeguards. The proposed change would allow those who own property that has appreciated in value to obtain additional bank finance in a Shariah-compliant way, using the property as collateral. Such refinancing currently faces prohibitive tax barriers where principal private residence relief does not apply.

"The government is also committed to creating, as far as possible, a level playing field on VAT for retail consumers of Islamic finance products. This includes VAT guidance on corporate sukuk.

"On the UK government's position on issuing a sovereign sukuk, McCarthy-Fry dismissed recent speculation that the Treasury may be going down this route.

"'Contrary to recent speculation, our position on this matter has not changed, and remains that a UK government wholesale sterling sukuk would not at present offer value for money. But I would like to reiterate that this decision was taken after a lengthy consultation and after extensive consideration of a wide range of factors. We will keep this judgment under review and revisit should factors change in such a way that sovereign sukuk issuance becomes more viable,' she advised.

"Minister McCarthy-Fry has urged the Islamic finance industry to seize the opportunities that the new financial landscape offers. With the whole of the financial services industry taking stock of its actions and looking to rebuild trust, there are some key principles underpinning Islamic finance that could help shape this new landscape.

"The rejection of certain speculative activities and the encouragement of an ethical approach to finance, to name a couple, could contribute significantly to the wider debate on the future of the financial markets, she added. In this respect, she would also like to see the sector grow in size and in influence since a more diverse financial sector will be better placed to provide businesses with the services they need for sustainable growth." Amir paused.

"The conference I have just attended in Dubai has been discussing these matters in detail. I think we can really see, for the first time, a promising trend."

Before Anwar could reply, the women came back to the table.

"I am sorry," Maysoon said, taking her seat.

"It's fine; don't worry." Anwar smiled.

The rest of the evening went well and Maysoon settled down after the shock of hearing about the events at the symposium in Dubai. When Anwar and Marwa left, Leila make her excuses and went up to bed before her mother could ask any more about the events in Dubai, or Eddie.

The next morning Leila, her parents and the girls who were beside themselves with excitement set off for London Zoo in Regent's Park. From their home in Wembley they took the Underground, which dropped them off a 15-minute walk from London Zoo at Camden Town Tube

Station.

As they walked through Regent's Park from Camden Town the girls ran excitedly ahead. Leila and her parents enjoyed the warm sun that was shining form a blue sky and Leila felt at peace with the people she loved most in the world around her.

"How long has the zoo been here?" her father asked as he linked arms with Leila.

"Actually London Zoo is the world's oldest scientific zoo, run by the Zoological Society of London. It is a charity run for the worldwide conservation of animals. It was originally set up by Sir Stamford Raffles in 1826. He planned the building of the zoo but sadly died later that same year. The zoo was first opened in April 1828 but was not opened to the public until 1847."

"Oh why was that?" her mother asked.

"Well", Leila said, "originally the zoo was intended to be a private collection for scientific study. There are over 750 species of animals here and many of these represents 'firsts' in their field, such as the first reptile house which opened in 1849 which houses a vast array of reptiles. It houses many venomous species such as black mambas, and vipers as well as venomous lizards. Almost every other reptile you could want to see and more is housed there from the smallest bright blue tree frog through to alligators. The girls love it!"

Leila's mother and father laughed. Leila knew that her mother was not a big fan of reptiles but the girls loved anything slimy or scaly.

"I have read something about the aquarium," her father said.

"Ah yes, that was another first, the first public aquarium which was opened in 1853 and again it houses a vast range of sea fish and tropical corals. Actually some of the coral here has been donated after it was confiscated by customs officials. It is illegal to bring coral into the country and it is nice to think that where coral has been brought in illegally at least it ends up somewhere like this. Oh yes, also there is a big fish tank which houses a variety of big fish, all of which have been rescued by the zoo because they have grown too big for their owners' facilities. Another section of the aquarium houses fresh water Amazonian fish, including the piranha, another favourite with the girls!"

"My goodness," Maysoon said, "for such dainty little things they certainly do have gruesome tastes. Mind you, you were exactly the same at their age!"

"Another of our big favorites is the monkey walkthrough where you can wander through a 150-metre enclosure and where the monkeys run around beside you. On our last visit the monkeys were being very illusive which was a little disappointing, so hopefully they will not be so shy today!"

"There is a big bird enclosure here, isn't there?" her father said.

"Yes; actually the bird walkthrough is very similar to the monkey one, with birds flying about you and a real chance to see them close up, with their many different colours in as natural an environment as you're ever going to find outside the wild. A lot of the birds seem quite tame and are really inquisitive about the visitors walking through their enclosure. I absolutely love the humming birds."

"I can't wait to see that," Leila's father said.

"Oh yes, and another brilliant walk-through section is the butterfly tent. The girls love it, running and walking amongst the wide variety of colourful butterflies. Some of the moths are as big as your hand. Last time we came they were absolutely fascinated by the caterpillars in cocoons preparing to emerge as butterflies."

"That's a bit more like it!" Leila's mother said. "Much more suitable for young ladies, rather than those horrible scaly creepy crawlies!"

Leila and her father laughed at her. They had arrived at the gates of the zoo now and the girls were jumping up and down in excitement.

They paid for their tickets and began their walk around the zoo. It was warm and Leila loved the feel of the sun on her face, and the sight of her children running excitedly from one display to another.

They strolled around taking in the exhibits of gorillas, tigers, giraffes and wild dogs, penguins, meerkats and hippos.

At the bird-walk, Leila and her mother at on a bench outside as the girls and their grandfather spent time inside as he identified the birds to the girls.

"The girls do you proud, Leila, and their father. It must be hard for you without him."

"It is," Leila said. It was still difficult to talk about Nasser without crying and she did not want to spoil the day by getting upset. Her mother sensed Leila's sorrow and put her arm around her lovingly.

As the hours slipped by and the sun began to sink in the sky, they made their way to the exit.

"We'd better try to distract the girls as we go past the gift shop," Leila said. "Most of what is in there is overpriced and the girls go mad for those lovely stuffed animals. But as you have seen their closets are already bulging at the seams!"

The girls fell asleep on the tube journey home and Leila smiled as her father carried them one in each arm gently to their front door. For a moment Leila felt a lump in her throat. It was exactly the way that Nasser had carried his girls. She did miss him.

In the event it was not until her parents had flown back to Saudi Arabia a week later that Leila found herself able to think about the time she had spent with Eddie in Dubai. She missed having her mother and father around but she had had to dive for cover twice during their visit to take calls from Eddie and she did not like being secretive. Now lying in the bath, the scented steamy air relaxing her, she wondered if the fact that her mother sensed something about her friendship with Eddie and that she herself felt the need to hide from them to take his calls should tell her something.

a tender power

As she lay with her eyes closed she saw Eddie's face in her mind's eye, his kind blue eyes smiling down at her, or watching her face intently as she spoke to him. She thought about the support that he had given her at the conference, the real fear she had seen in his eyes when she had fainted, the comfortable silences they had enjoyed together in the scented nights as they looked out over the quiet gardens of the hotel towards the warm sea lapping at the shore. Leila had noticed other women casting admiring glances towards Eddie and his tall and athletic figure and handsome face always seemed to attract a lot of attention. She thought about those moments, about what had she felt. Being brutally honest with herself she had to admit that she had a sort of smug pride that she was with Eddie, the object of so many other people's admiration. She was not proud of the fact that she had those feelings about Eddie. He was a friend, nothing more, and the feelings of pride she felt in being with him were totally misplaced and should make her feel ashamed. And yet she did not. She knew that Eddie cared deeply for her as she did for him. Had his feelings not been the very reason that she had left Harvard to come to Oxford to study? But surely after all these years, her marriage and children, he could not still have those romantic feelings for her. And yet she knew that he did. She did not often allow herself to admit it but in the interest of complete honesty in her introspection, Leila had to lay bare all the elements of her relationship and her feelings for Eddie. So was it cruel to allow him to hope? Did he hope? Leila did not know but she guessed that he did.

He had never married, never even come close. Surely he could not have been waiting for her, or spoiled for other relationships because of his feelings for her? Leila felt dismayed at this possibility. She wanted the best for Eddie, wanted him to know the happiness and fulfillment she had had with Nasser, the joy that her children had brought her. She did not want to think that her existence had robbed another human being of his chance to experience what she had. But she had to admit it. It seemed obvious that her worst fears were true, and Eddie did not or could not consider a relationship with another woman because of the way he felt about her. What should she do about it? It was obviously not pressing as they lived on different continents, but did that really matter? If she knew how he felt, if she had admitted to herself the effect she was having on this man, should she not do something about it? What though? What could she do about it? She could not cut off all contact with him, that would be cruel and without having a full discussion with him about his feelings she could not think of any excuse that would be acceptable or even credible. Maybe she should confront him with what she thought. No, that would be awful because at the moment, not acknowledging his feelings to her was probably the only thing that kept Eddie sane. Having to confront the situation would force them into action that neither of them might be happy with.

Leila sighed. She knew that she loved Eddie dearly as a friend, but was that all? Of course it was all! Nasser had been her true love and she missed him so much. She felt guilty about examining the feelings that another man might have for her or she for him, even if she had no intention of pursuing. It was too confusing, too perplexing and Leila plunged under the warm water of the bath. As she held her breath she would hear her heart beating in her ears, its regular rhythm reminding her that she was mortal, that it could stop and she would be no more, but it could also love and bring her great happiness and contentment. The contentment that she felt being with her children, her lovely daughters. But was that going to be enough for her, forever? She was still young; would she never want another man in her heart or her bed? Under the water she felt her face suffuse with blood as she blushed at the thought of a physical relationship with another man. A tiny thought tried to surface at the back of her brain, a tiny forbidden thought, a curiosity of what her life would be like married to Eddie. But she beat it back and extinguished it as her face broke through the surface of the water and she gulped in a breath. It was never going to be.

On the other side of London, Amir sat in his study. He had another big symposium coming up in New York in a few weeks' time and he was wondering whether to ask Leila to come along with him and Marwa. But something about the night that he had had dinner with Leila and her family was bothering him. Maysoon had reacted very badly to the idea that Leila had put herself in danger by being in Eddie's company. But it was more than that, because he knew that Maysoon would know that the attack was not something that Eddie had been expecting, and in fact had been a complete surprise to him. Amir had noticed the bouquet that Eddie had sent to Leila, displayed next to his own in the hall of the house. He knew how close Leila and Maysoon were and he wondered if something of the concern that had always niggled at him about Leila and Eddie had also touched Maysoon. Amir respected Eddie and knew that he would never do Leila any harm but she was very vulnerable now, having lost Nasser, and Amir wondered if Maysoon's reaction had been something to do with a mother's intuition about her daughter. And yet Amir was confident that Eddie, even with his playboy reputation, would never cross the line with Leila. Something in the man's eyes when he looked at her told Amir that. Eddie obviously loved Leila deeply, anyone could see that, but there was something deeper, a respect, almost an awe of her that was apparent at any time one observed Eddie in an unguarded moment, looking at Leila. Maysoon had obviously sensed something of this, but as she had never met Eddie her instincts and reactions had to have come only from the vibe she got from her daughter. This was something new to Amir. He had never really thought that Leila might reciprocate Eddie's feelings. Of course the thought never entered his head while Nasser was alive; they had been such an ideally suited couple and so happy.

Amir shook his head. He still felt a deep helplessness and anger about the events that had robbed Nasser and so many others of their lives. Suddenly Amir sat bolt upright in his chair. He had just remembered that Eddie was supposed to be on the flight that had been blown out of the sky on that dark winter night. And at the symposium it was Eddie who had apparently been the target of the attack by the gunman. Could it have been Eddie who was the target of whoever blew up flight 602? Of course it could. Amir felt a coldness engulf him and his teeth began to chatter. He felt shocked to the core; his realisation and the undoubted truth of it sent cold shivers up and down his spine. Maysoon had been right; Eddie was a target and her daughter being connected to him in any capacity was putting her at great risk. But did Leila know that? Amir guessed she didn't. He sighed. He would have to talk it over with Marwa. Her quiet wisdom had rescued him from many a quandary. He had communicated to her his fears for Leila before and as both he and Marwa regarded her as another daughter, she had been worried as well. But this was something else, a whole new level of risk. As he sat thinking, another thought hit Amir like a hammer blow. The boy Byron, Eddie's best friend's son: had his kidnap been something to do with Eddie? Of course it had! Obviously whoever was after Eddie was not above trying to get at him by whatever means, even a child.

Amir thought about the conference he was to attend in New York in a few weeks. If he mentioned it to Leila she would probably want to attend. But what he realized now was that she could not come with him, must not see Eddie, or be seen to be associated with him. She was at great risk, Amir knew it, and somehow Maysoon had realised it too. What neither of them knew however, was how close to danger Leila really was.

Chapter Twenty-five

In Dubai, Eddie was increasingly frustrated with his mother. Arabella had arrived like some sort of banshee being difficult and rude to the hotel staff, and even when she was talking to Eddie, as they sat in the coffee shop of the lobby, her eyes constantly swept the hotel foyer, looking for God knows what, or who? She was jumpy and distracted and so far had refused every invitation that Eddie had given to dinner or any other activity outside the hotel. It was as though she was waiting for someone. But that was impossible. She didn't know anyone in Dubai, apart from him. Eddie sighed, luckily he had to be with Sheikh Lewa for the afternoon and he was booked to go back on a flight two days from now, so far his mother had been unresponsive about when she would be returning, and any idea that Eddie had had that she had come out to Dubai to see him had long since been quashed. He had given up trying to work out the machinations of his parents lives, apart from the fact that they lived more or less separately, and he really did not care much what his mother was doing in Dubai, even the fact that she had shown no interest in Dubai in all the years that his father and Eddie had been coming here was only mildly interesting to him. She spent an awful lot of time in her room and when he called her there she often answered with a kind of breathless excitement, that he was quite sure was not meant for him. Now that they had finished their coffee, she announced her attention to go up to her room again and Eddie was relieved that he was being dismissed. On the way to the elevator, Arabella checked again with the desk clerk if there were any messages for her, although she had been told that they would either be put in her room or if they were telephone messages they would be on the answer machine of the room phone. Eddie watched as the desk clerk shook his head and his mother turned on her heel and stalked over to the lift. Whatever was going on, Eddie thought, he didn't want to know.

The Sheikh was at his camp in the desert again and Eddie was looking forward to the drive out there. As the busy city roads began to thin out, Eddie looked out at the empty dessert. It was amazing how the city seemed to be all around you one moment and then completely lost in the miles of desert sand. There seemed to be no gradual progression from one to the other, you were just suddenly in the desert. Eddie loved the open and deserted feel of it and the way that the heat shimmered above the dunes like a liquid shield of glass. After driving through the desert they took a long empty road where the only other vehicles were dessert safari trucks. It was a strange and awe-inspiring experience, because the road was a dual carriageway, but had no barriers. With all the traffic moving in the same direction, it felt to Eddie like a scene from a movie, with the only break to the monotony the occasional overtaking and undertaking and generally fairly risky driving.

Suddenly and unexpectedly the car stopped at a camel farm. The driver got out, smiling and making signs that he would not be long to Eddie. In large paddocks Eddie saw the camels, standing under the palm trees that offered shade from the fierce sun. Their tails twitched occasionally to get rid of the flies that buzzed around them and their jaws made rhythmic chewing motions. Two baby camels scampered together in the sun seemingly oblivious to the heat.

On the road that they had just left, the traffic continued to go past and Eddie could appreciate their speed now that the limousine that he was traveling in was stationery. Now that the engine of the car was off the cool interior of the car was heating up fast and Eddie decided that he would get out and stretch his legs. There was still no sign of the driver, and he wandered over to the palm trees that overhung the fence of the camel's paddock. They eyed him suspiciously but made no move from the shade of the palm tree on their side of the fence. Eddie looked around for the driver. The car was some 100 yards from the farm and even although he was now closer he could see no sign of human life. Suddenly a car sped off from the far side of the paddock and before Eddie could see what it was the air was suddenly full of noise and flying debris and he was thrown over the fence into the paddock. For a moment hooves thundered around him as the camels made for the other side of the paddock, and then he was alone, lying in the sand, the dusty grit in his mouth, his ears and his nose. Blood trickled down his face and he felt a gash on his forehead. He looked over to the car. It was a smoking wreck, un-recognizable as a car. Rubbing grit out of his eyes, Eddie stared at it. His brain tried to rationalize to say that the car had stood too long in the heat, but he knew, that like the shooting, this explosion had been meant to end his life.

A couple of cars had stopped on the road and Arab men in thobes ran towards the car. Eddie got to his feet and walked towards them. Seeing him they changed tack and ran towards him. He recognized one of them as the Sheikhs. Secretary, Hamid.

An hour later Eddie was in the camp with Sheikh Lewa. He had washed and been given a thobe to replace his dusty clothes. He was not hurt apart from the cut on his head that had only needed a plaster. But he was shaken to the core and was coming to terms with the fact that someone was trying to kill him. Although he had been told that he was the target of the gunman at the symposium he had tried to put it to the back of his mind. He could not, would not acknowledge the fact. Sheikh Lewa however, was more realistic and his next statement hit Eddie like a body blow.

"Obviously ever since flight 602 was brought down without you on it, someone has been targeting you."

"What?" Whether through denial or ignorance this was the first time that Eddie had considered the fact that he and he alone might have been the target on flight 602. The Sheikh realizing that this seemingly obvious fact had not occurred to Eddie before tried to soft pedal but it was too late. Eddie felt his nerves jangling and the tension rising in him; he wanted to run, where to he had no idea, but he just wanted to run. The desert that he had so admired in the past seemed now malevolent and ready to swallow him whole. The sound of distant sirens approaching signaled the arrival of the police. Eddie desperately wanted it all to go away, to be home again and safe, but would he ever be safe again, would he ever be able to stop looking over his shoulder? Was he even safe here? Panic rose in his throat, as out of the corner of his eye he could see men in thobes moving around, they all seemed to be looking at him. Were they waiting for a chance to bury a dagger in his heart? He felt a scream rising inside him and in his attempt to swallow it came out as a sob. The Sheikh quickly cleared the tent and as Eddie collapsed on the cushions he patted his back. He felt sorry for this young man, and he wished he had an answer for him. The police were on their way maybe they would know something.

In the hotel, Arabella lay exhausted in the arms of Sharif. He smiled to himself. It had taken some doing but he had managed to rise to the occasion, and the faint blush on Arabella's cheeks and above her breasts showed him that he had done well. He glanced at the phone beside the bed. It would ring in a while, letting her know the bad news, it was only fair that he be there for comfort her. As he looked down at her face hr hair swept back, he saw the tell tale suture line behind her ears left by her most recent face-lift. He struggled to stop himself shuddering; he liked women to be natural – and young. Arabella was very far from what he liked and a million miles from what excited him. It had taken all his imagination and judicious use of the blackout curtains to enable him to perform. He stroked her face; her botox filled stretched face and then froze in horror as Arabella's hand snaked greedily across his bare thigh. Jumping out of bed, Sharif quickly wound a towel around himself.

"I have to go my darling" he whispered, "I dare not stay longer, otherwise I shall never leave. You are too tempting, too sexy."

Arabella smiled at him with perfect white veneered teeth, testament to the art of her very affluent 52nd street dentist, Sharif tried to keep his smile in place.

"Well if you must go, I suppose I will have to content myself with my toys!" She pouted in what would have been a winning way in a 15 year old but which in a woman on the wrong side of 50 was repulsive. Sharif hurried to the bathroom. He looked at his watch, she should have had the call by now, but he could not wait and would have to go, she was insatiable and there was no way he would be able to summon up an encore.

As he came out of the bathroom, the phone beside the bed rang. As Arabella leaned over to take the call Sharif saw more stitches behind her shoulder from a recent arm lift.

"Hello? Oh hello Eddie." Sharif stopped in his tracks.

"You've had car trouble? Oh yes, that's right we were supposed to meet, never mind, I've been a bit tied up." She smiled at Sharif and winked, a gesture that made his stomach turn over.

"Fine I'll see you later." She hung up and Sharif dodged her embrace as she padded naked from the bed.

"I have to go, see you later my angel!" He kissed his finger and pressed it on her nose.

Outside in the corridor he leaned against the thick brocade wallpaper, his eyes closed.

He flipped open his phone. "What happened?" he said when his call was answered. He listened for a moment and then shut his phone.

As he strode to his room he opened the phone again. "Who have we in London?" He listened or a second then said. "Get him to call me; I have a job for him."

In London Leila was giving a lecture to some female Moslem economics students at Kings University. She had been very much in demand since she had given her talk in Dubai and she enjoyed talking about women in Islamic finance.

In 2008 I attended a seminar at City law firm Norton Rose on "Women in Islamic Finance". Many leading Islamic women academics spoke there and Halima Krausen, a Shariah scholar and academic from Germany made a powerful point that resonated with me, this is what she said: "Women have been actively involved in trade, financial and investment matters throughout Islamic history, explained In fact, the Prophet, peace be upon him, worked for a businesswoman Khadija who subsequently became his wife. London now boasts some six Islamic banks authorized by the Financial Services Authority. But all of them are headed by men. In fact, the dominance of men in top jobs in the City and financial services in general continues unabated. Not surprisingly, Minister Kitty Ussher Secretary to the treasury expressed hope that perhaps one day a woman chief executive officer would head one of the UK Islamic banks.

"While it is true that the involvement of women in senior positions in Islamic finance is increasing in Southeast Asia, the situation elsewhere in the GCC countries, Pakistan, Iran, Turkey and Egypt is really much less encouraging. In the GCC states, for instance, gender segregation policies have put many women aspiring to be bankers at a huge disadvantage. For example, Dr Nahed Taher, the former chief economist of National Commercial Bank, was forced to leave Saudi Arabia to take a post as a CEO in a conventional bank in Bahrain, a position she could never hope to be appointed to in her native country.

"Even in other GCC countries and when we look at wider markets, the involvement of women banking professionals in the sector, are limited. Experienced women bankers, who, I might add, very often outperform their male counterparts, are understandably frustrated that their career chances and choices are governed by socio-cultural norms imposed on them by men. They are not satisfied, and nor should they be, with heading the women-only sections of their banks; or to work in women-only financial institutions. These highly qualified and motivated women want to be acknowledged as leaders in their fields in the mainstream Islamic or conventional financial services sectors, irrespective of their gender. If women are increasingly being required to contribute their part to GDP in GCC and Middle Eastern economies, as the governments seem to suggest they should be, many of them argue that they need to operate on a level playing field with access to equal opportunities so that they have the chance to realize their full potential and to make their own valued contribution.

"Support is growing and Kitty said, 'Islamic finance is one of the most exciting, innovative financial services sectors around at the moment. In the retail sector, the Islamic mortgage market is now worth over 500 million pounds a year, and the UK's Shariah compliant banks now have more than 40,000 customers. Islamic finance products, particularly in the retail market, are also very important for the people who buy them. We do believe that it's right that everyone, regardless of their religion, should be able to participate fully in the financial system - and should have the opportunity to make the most of their money. So, both because of the benefits for customers, and to help make sure that London is at the forefront as the sector continues to develop, we want to do everything we can to encourage the development of Islamic Finance in the UK.'

Leila looked up at the faces of the girls.

"You young ladies are the future in banking and other financial services. The messages that you take with you as you pursue your careers will be what sails the economic ship of the future. There are many chances for the ship to run aground or be broken up on the rocks, you ladies are the ones who will be charged with the responsibility of sailing your ship to safe harbour. It is a grave responsibility and the way ahead is going to be tough, but this is an exciting time and all of your should feel privileged to be at the birth of a new dawn in finance."

The girls applauded Leila enthusiastically and she stayed behind for a while to answer a few questions and to talk in general with these girls who were just starting out on a career that had brought Leila so much fulfilment. As she spoke, Outside on the busy street a car had drawn up on the yellow lines opposite the college. The driver had a mobile phone in his hand and was looking at a picture of a woman standing on a podium. The woman's beautiful face was radiant and despite the fact that she was wearing an hijab the driver of the car knew that he could not mistake that face. The traffic was heavy and he was not worried that he would draw attention to himself on the yellow lines, no one gave him a second glance and the gate in front of which he was parked was firmly locked so he was unlikely to be asked to move. He scanned the faces of the women coming out of the building, most had hijabs on and for a moment he thought he might not recognise Leila. But when she did emerge, pausing to talk outside the door of the college, he recognised her instantly. Her face was animated and very beautiful as she spoke to one of the other women in a hijab, it seemed almost a shame to extinguish that light, but a job was a job and he raised the gun he had had on his lap and fired. The shot was not even heard above the roar of the traffic and the gunman had made his way back into the stream of cars almost before Leila fell to the ground.

In Dubai, Eddie heard the news some three hours later. Amir phoned him and told him that Leila was in hospital. At first Eddie assumed that she had had an accident. He was still feeling shocked and deeply afraid after his brush with death, but his feelings for his own predicament immediately gave way to an almost heartbreaking fear for Leila.

"What happened, Amir? Was it a car crash?"

"No, Eddie, it wasn't; she was shot." Eddie could hardly take in what he was hearing and for a moment dropped the phone. Amir's voice calling his name revived him and he picked up the phone again. As Amir told him what he knew, Eddie could hear anger in his voice, and he knew that that some of that anger was directed at him. It could not be a coincidence that on the day that he had dodged death, Leila had been gunned down in the street.

"Amir, you know that I would not have put Leila at risk for the world; I don't know what to say."

"I think it would be best if you keep away from her," Amir said; but even as he said the words he knew that to keep Eddie away would be impossible.

"I understand how you feel, Amir, but I have to come. How bad is she?" It was the question he had not wanted to ask or have answered, but he had to know.

"Bad," Amir said, his voice shaking. "They don't know if she is going to make it." Eddie felt bile rise in his throat and threw down the phone, running to the bathroom to be sick. This could not be happening. When he came back into the bedroom Amir had hung up. He picked up the phone to ring Sheikh Lewa. In a voice that did not sound like his own he told the Sheikh what had happened.

"I am going to the airport now to get the next flight to London."

"No, Eddie, don't do that. Whoever is behind this will know that is what you will do; you will not be safe on a commercial flight. Take my private jet."

"Thank you," Eddie said.

In the ICU of King's College Hospital Leila fought for her life. The bullet had hit her in the chest, grazing her heart and was now lodged in her spine. As her doctors pored over x-rays and CT scans they tried to decide whether she would be paralysed or not, and whether if they operated they would seal her fate and make her paraplegic. She had lost a dangerous amount of blood and her heart had stopped three times, but she was a fighter and for now her vital signs were holding their own. Her mother was on the way from Saudi Arabia and Marwa, Amir's wife sat, head bowed, in the waiting room.

In the ICU, the quietness of the patients was in direct contrast to the constant beeping of the machines monitoring their every beat and every heartbeat. In the section in which Leila had been put connected to a dozen tubes, the machines that monitored her were in turn being monitored by a nurse, sitting quietly at the end of the bed, her eyes darting from one machine to another. Every now and again she would get up and adjust one or the other, check the bag that was collecting urine and the bags that were delivering saline and blood. There was not a flicker of life from Leila, but she had been put into an induced coma in the hope that her body would recover from its devastating trauma.

Amir had arrived now and told Marwa about his conversation with Eddie. "I told him not to come, but I know that he will." Marwa looked at her husband. "He loves her, habibi, we know that. How could he stay away?"

Amir's jaw tightened. "He could stay away to save any more harm coming to her," he said gravely.

"But he is not with her now and harm has come to her, so would it really make any difference? She has been his friend for many years and whoever wishes to harm him knows that. This is something that could only be avoided by their never having met in the first place, and I am afraid that it is too late now to distance themselves from each other." Amir smiled and took his wife's hand. As always she was wise and saw things in perspective. He could find no argument with what she said.

Eddie arrived in the afternoon, just after Leila's parents. Amir and Marwa met him in the waiting room and told him that he could not go in. "Only two visitors are allowed at once and her mother and father are with her now." Eddie slumped down on a chair, his face white and drawn, his pain and sorrow etched deeply into the lines around his mouth and on his forehead.

Leila's parents eventually emerged from the ICU looking shaken and obviously deeply shocked. Seeing Eddie, Maysoon flew at him, shouting, "What are you doing here? Don't you know that my child would not be lying there close to death if it were not for you? Get out of here! Don't ever come here or see her again! You are not welcome and you will be responsible if our daughter dies!"

Eddie fled from the waiting room, Maysoon's words stabbing him like daggers. He stumbled out onto the street and walked for miles, blindly and with no purpose. Finally he arrived at a park where, exhausted, he lay down on a bench. He slept fitfully but by the morning his head had cleared. He checked into a hotel and waited. He let Amir know where he was and for three weeks he stayed in his hotel room, ordering food from room service and buying a change of clothes and underwear, a toothbrush, toothpaste, a razor and shaving foam from the hotel shop. He let his parents know what had happened and that he would take no calls. The battery on his mobile phone ran out so he sat next the phone beside his bed. He spent his days looking out over Hyde Park from the room of his hotel. He listened to no music and watched no television. All day he stared out of the window, his thoughts completely occupied by Leila.

In his mind he saw her smiling face, the day that he had first met her, a shy smile, the smile of a girl, not yet a woman, that stray piece of hair curling gently against her cheek. Eddie was pleased that he could remember his first meeting with her so well because it had not made as much impression on him at that time as it did now in retrospect. No, at that time he was still Eddie the Jock, Eddie the bed hopper, Eddie the shallow self-serving rich kid and Leila was most definitely nowhere near his type. Her hijab and her dress screamed "keep off" and that was definitely not what he was wanted in a woman. He luxuriated in his thoughts about her, about the time that they had spent together, it was almost like worshipping at an altar, being able to give his thoughts and his heart entirely to thinking about her. He had cleared his life of everything else; it was just Leila and Leila alone that occupied his every waking moment. He closed his eyes and listened to her voice in his head – the voice of a young passionate woman, a woman who was dedicated to what she believed in, a woman who made him feel depthless and superficial. His mind focused on the project that had brought them together all those years ago; he could remember almost every word and now it played back to him like a movie. In his mind he could see Leila's lovely face, her eyes shining dark and beautiful full of passion for the subject. He put his hands over his ears, and he could hear her, yes he could hear her!

"Mudarabah," she had said, and Eddie remembered

his attempt to repeat the word. When she was satisfied with his pronunciation she had moved on. "Mudarabah is a partnership where the investment comes from the first partner, "rabb-ul-mal", and the management and work is the responsibility of the second, "mudarib". He remembered how she had looked at him with raised eyebrows and he had nodded signifying that he had understood although her beauty and purity was so overwhelming he had to struggle hard to concentrate. He had repeated her words and she went on.

"We can summarise the points like this," Leila had held up one hand, and bent over one finger. For some reason tears sprung to Eddies eyes, as he remembered the gesture. "In musharakah, investment comes from all partners, but in Mudarabah, investment is the responsibility of the rabb-ul-mal." Pushing the second finger into her palm she had said. "In musharakah, all partners participate in the management, but in Mudarabah, the mudarib alone conducts the management." A third finger. "All partners in musharakah share the loss to the extent of their ratio of investment, but in Mudarabah the loss is suffered by the rabb-ul-mal only as he is the sole investor. However, if the mudarib has been negligent, he will suffer the loss." Eddie had nodded and she pushed down a fourth finger, he wiped tears from his eyes.

In his head Leila continued, her voice clear and sweet "The partners' liability in musharakah is unlimited. In Mudarabah the liability of the rabb-ul-mal is limited to his investment, unless he has permitted the mudarib to incur debts on his behalf." Eddie remembered taking notes as she had pushed her thumb in to her palm "In musharakah, the assets, once mixed in a joint pool, become jointly owned by them according to the proportion of investment. In Mudarabah all goods purchased by the mudarib are solely owned by the rabb-ul-mal. The mudarib can earn his share in the profit should he sell the goods profitably. He is not entitled to claim his share of the assets."

Eddie recalled how she had paused and looked at him expectantly and how he, stumbling sometimes over the unfamiliar words, repeated the gist of what she had told him. Leila had clapped her hands together softly. "Yes, yes, that is right! I am so pleased that you find it so interesting!" She was achingly beautiful in her happiness and enthusiasm.

Eddie had wanted to say it was her that he found interesting, and it was true he did, but something in the message in the unfamiliar words and in the concept was captivating him and he remembered asking her to go on.

"Restricted Mudarabah is when the rabb-ul-mal specifies a particular business for the mudarib to invest the money in. Unrestricted Mudarabah is when it is open for the mudarib to undertake whichever business he wishes."

Eddie recalled how he had written notes, but he remembered that incredibly he had found that his mind was opening to the message and to the unfamiliar language, and he had felt almost as though he was a blind man suddenly able to see. Eddie cold see the exact moment when Leila had turned her lovely face to him and registered the enthusiasm on his face and they had continued, her voice tinged with excitement, the excitement of imparting a dearly loved message to a willing audience, he with a stirring excitement and hunger for knowledge. Like the showing of a film the rest of the information Leila had shared with him that day played back in his mind as clear and fresh as though it had been yesterday. He remembered how for a while they had talked about what Leila had been saying and how he had been so happy to see her pleasure and surprise as she realised how much Eddie had taken in, and the fact that he even seemed to be getting the hang of the Arabic words. Leila had told him many years later that the part of her that wanted to be a teacher was exhilarated that her message was being so well received by her pupil and secondly. He had hoped that she would mention another reason for her joy, their nearness that might perhaps had made her fell a fraction of what he did. But she did not.

"OK, Eddie" she had said at last, and Eddie smiled, remembering how he loved the way she said his name. They had continued with the project for some time, and then as Leila had paused, Eddie remembered how he had looked at her, his eyebrow raised in expectation and how Leila had laughed and said, "I think that is enough for one day; my throat is dry and I think your brain might explode with any more information!" Eddie had laughed at her little joke and recalled how he had got her some water in a little plastic cup from the water cooler. As she sipped it he had watched her, her lovely face was flushed from the effort of talking to him for so long and from delivering her message with such passion and conviction. Eddie thought of how he had realized that there was something more to this lovely girl than the usual standards that he used to measure female suitability. There was something precious and fragile that made him want to protect her and keep her safe from everyone and anything that might hurt her. Now as he sat in his hotel window, remembering that long ago afternoon, and he realised that the biggest threat to her had turned out to be him. The feeling of misery and fear that haunted him made him close his eyes tight, as though he was trying to blot the world out.

Chapter Twenty-six

It had been ten days since Eddie had arrived in London. The man who sat at the window of his room in the hotel that looked over Hyde Park was thinner with a coarse beard, his clothes unchanged and his hair uncombed. Lost in his thoughts Eddie no longer bothered to shave or to wash. He barely bothered to eat, just enough to keep him alive; peanuts that were replenished daily in his mini-bar by an increasingly bemused chamber maid who had learned that after she knocked she was to enter despite no bidding to do so, and should on no account speak to the man sitting the chair staring out of the window. He never turned around or even moved and more than once the chambermaid wondered if he was still alive. But the three bags of peanuts that she left in the mini-bar every day were gone the next day, the empty packets placed neatly on top of the little fridge. The bed was rarely slept in, and the bath towels remained undisturbed. All the windows of the room were closed and the air conditioning off, and the smell of unwashed body was becoming quite unpleasant. But it was one room that she had to do very little in each day, Eddie had forbidden any vacuuming or cleaning and for that she was grateful and willing to put up with the smell.

Hours ticked by unmarked by this barely human being and long periods went by when Eddie did not even blink. Eddie's hunger made him lapse into a kind of hallucination at times, his childhood playing out like an old ciné film in his head. He saw himself seven or eight years old at the lodge that his parents had on the banks of Lake Clear. He saw himself sitting by the jetty holding on to one of the jetty's wooden props with one hand while the two-man kayak that he went out in with his father bobbed up and down on the water. His father had gone back in to take a phone call just as he had been about to climb into the kayak behind Eddie. The young Eddie had felt his heart sink. His father had said he would be two minutes but Eddie knew he wouldn't be. Eventually Eddie's hand went numb where it was holding on tight to the jetty, and he got out of the kayak sadly, and walked back to the lodge, shaking the pins and needles out of his fingers.

They had gone out later that day but Eddie had never forgotten the times of disappointment, and there were many, when a trip had to be postponed or cancelled because of "the bank". Young Eddie had sworn to himself that he would never have anything to do with the bank, the entity that was responsible for all the misery of his childhood. His mother was not the apron and cookies type either and Eddie could remember being pushed away more than once because of recently applied nail varnish or clothing that was too delicate to withstand a hug from a boy. When they were not thrown together in the supreme awkwardness that was their annual holidays and weekends, his parents rarely spoke to each other or to him and as he sat at the grimy window overlooking Hyde Park, a tear ran down his unwashed face, a tear for the boy who had spent a childhood more or less alone and unloved, surrounded by the best toys that money could buy and who hid his unhappiness in jockish behaviour and as he grew older, bedded as many girls as he could, looking for what? Love? No, or at least not what the girls thought of as love. At the first hint of an attachment he was off. That was, until he met Leila.

He smiled a crusty smile over unbrushed teeth as he thought of Leila, how she had literally bought sunshine to the darkness of his life. He had thought he was happy, doing the things that boys like him did, playing and running with the pack but until he met her until the days that they spent together in the library, he had not known what happiness was. Her goodness, her purity and her warmth shone from her and made his life and its living seem all the more shallow in her radiant glow.

If she died, what would he do? It was the first time he had asked himself the question but now that days had gone by and no word of her death had reached him he had convinced himself that the danger was over, that the woman he loved would recover. She had to recover – he could not, would not, live without her. He realised now how deep his feelings for her were. The fact that their relationship was platonic made no difference; he was devoted to her. He wanted her to live, he needed her to live. There was just no point to his life without her.

As he thought of her Eddie saw her face on the inside of his closed eyelids. He knew every single inch of her face; it was permanently etched on his brain. He smiled and leaned back a fraction in his chair, getting more comfortable to remember her. This time they were returning to Harvard after the break and Eddie could still feel the cold churning feeling in his stomach that he had felt after he had called her during the holiday. He remembered agonising over why he had called her. All his instincts and everything he understood about her had told him that he should not be in touch, but he had still gone ahead and made the call. And that had led to them being forced to acknowledge what was going on between them. He remembered how he thought he might even have frightened Leila off for good. He felt sick as he threw things into the drawers in his room, barely passing the time of day with his roommates. He could now, with hindsight, clearly pinpoint this as the time when his friends had begun to tire of him, but then as now, he was powerless to stop them drifting away. He recalled how he had noticed that over the holidays that he had been invited out less, called seldom and approached for conversation almost never when he was in social gatherings. The part of him that could still think straight at that time knew that he was making a big mistake. What was it he and his buddies had always vowed? He forced his brain to remember the long forgotten chant of the young and arrogant alpha male: "Never let a piece of tail see a brother's friendship fail."

It was a stupid piece of nonsense made up by one of the group who fancied himself as a poet. They had laughed at him and the ditty at the time, but it had stuck and never was it more appropriate than that time of change after the holidays, all those years ago, Eddie thought. He had hated himself for blanking his friends but he could not help it. He recalled how he had felt at once miserable and elated, euphoric and depressed, He had told himself with a rueful smile that being in love did not suit him at all.

If he closed his eyes tight he could see the dorm again, hear the voices of his friends, smell the mixture of liniment and sweaty socks that always seemed to hang in the air.

Eddie thought about Harry Masters, wondered how his friend was doing. That was another link in his past that was broken. He knew that they could never get the closeness back that had been obvious in Dubai. He thought about his son Byron and frowned. He did not want to think about Harry or his son, or the stupid frat brothers of his dorm. He wanted to think about Leila, only Leila.

Eddie remembered now writing a note and pinning it to her dorm door asking her to meet him at the library at their customary spot at 6 p.m. He had been already there when Leila arrived looking flushed, her eyes bright, and Eddie had jumped to his feet, his face breaking into the widest smile, a ghost of which now appeared again on his face in the loneliness of his hotel room. He remembered that Leila had offered him her hand. But he had been unable to help himself and had gathered her into his arms for a momentary hug. He let her go as quickly as he had grabbed her to him but for a fleeting moment Eddie had felt her body arch towards his. He could see her now, lovely and breathless, sitting opposite him in the library as he held the tips of her fingers on his for a moment. Although they had been alone in their corner Eddie had kept his voice to a whisper.

"I missed you, Leila, and I am sorry that I called you; did it make things difficult for you?"

"No, my parents are loving and fair, and they trust me."

He had pressed gently and found out that there had indeed been an inquest at home following Eddie's call and Eddie remembered Leila's downcast eyes and long lashes that brushed her cheeks as she related what had happened to him. "My parents are good people; they were very gentle, asking about you and why you were calling me from so far away. I reassured them that nothing improper was going on and they could tell that what I said was true. Not that they ever really doubted me. They have raised me well and they know that I would never do anything to dishonour myself or my family." She had blushed at the implication of what that dishonour might entail and her eyelids had fluttered on her cheeks. Eddie had had again to fight the urge to crush her to him, to hold her in his arms and never let her go. He remembered every syllable that she uttered and the soft intonation of her voice, a voice that was to him like the most beautiful of music, something that he could never imagine another woman could replicate; it was the essence of her, Leila's most intimate gift to him: her voice and the words that it uttered words for only him to hear. It was like a precious gift and he treasured it.

Eddie smiled at the memory as tears ran from his eyes. Would he ever hear that voice again? The fact that he knew nothing recent about her condition was killing and comforting him in equal measures. Amir would call occasionally to report that she was making a slow recovery but did not go into any detail. His calls were hurried and surreptitious as though he felt that he was being disloyal to his friends by even letting Eddie know that their daughter was still alive.

So with this, Eddie had to be content and following Amir's calls he would immediately lapse back into his reverie, his memories crowding in on him.

"I'm so glad it was not a major problem, and I am

sorry, Leila, for putting you in that position. Other than that, how have you been?"

"I've been very well, Eddie, and you?" she had replied.

"To hell with it Leila, what are we doing? What are we talking like this for?" Eddie remembered the passion of his young self, the aching to hold this girl who had come to mean so much to him. He had continued, unable to stop himself, "I told you that I loved you, and I know that you feel the same. We have to make plans, we have to talk the future, we have to—" Leila had put her finger to her lips and he had stopped talking.

Then the words that were burned into his heart with a searing pain that would never heal. "Eddie, I'm sorry, there will be no future; there can't be. I do love you but I will not marry a man who is not a Moslem. And before you offer to convert think about your future, Lancaster bank; it just could not happen." He recalled her looking down at her hands.

"This will be my last term at Harvard. Next semester I'm going to a different university."

Eddie had never felt such raw pain. In that instant his heart broke, his dreams shattered and his life lay like a discarded rag at his feet. Leila went on speaking softly, urgently trying to make him understand. Her parents had not pressured her; quite the contrary, in fact - they had said they would support their daughter whatever her decision. But the sad thing was, Leila had said, she really had no choice. She knew what she had to do. Making the decision to move college had been a natural progression.

a tender power

Leila had had an offer from Oxford University in England as well as Harvard when she had initially applied and a few calls from her uncle Amir had smoothed the way for her to start the next semester 7,000 miles away. She told Eddie that she had wanted to start sooner, never to return to Harvard but she knew that she had to see him, to have the courage of her convictions and to speak to him face to face.

Eddie remembered the surprised look on her face as he got up, then quietly and without anger left the library. He knew that this was not what she had expected; she had expected him to plead, to beg, to promise, but not this silent exit. Back in his room Eddie recalled feeling the bile rising to his throat and remembered that he had vomited for what seemed like hours. He remembered the fear he felt; he never would have believed that love could make you physically sick. He had felt out of control, had felt as though he was desperately ill. He had thought of every permutation, including giving up his inheritance. It meant nothing to him compared to this girl, but even as he formed the thoughts he had known that she would not let him. He thought about how he had read more about Islamic finance over those holidays; it made him feel closer to Leila, who had now broken his heart just as surely as if she had stabbed him. And despite all the thoughts and possibilities that he grasped at in desperation he had known that what had happened was irreversible, that there was no point in trying to persuade Leila. Part of the reason he loved Leila was for her strength, her unwavering obedience and love for her faith and he knew that she would not change her mind, could not change her mind, and in the meantime he had been going out of his.

He thought with a wry smile of his pathetic attempts to avoid Leila, trying to forget her, to throw himself into his work, into sport, back into the crowd he used to hang with. But this morose, gaunt and haunted guy was not someone his old crowd felt comfortable with. For three weeks he had kept his distance until their excellent grades on their project sent from Amir Ali brought them together briefly to receive their tutor's accolade on the success of their project. Eddie remembered noticing that Leila had lost weight. As their tutor left the room Leila had said, "Would you like to review any more Islamic finance before I go?"

To anyone looking in, Eddie thought, it would have been laughable, pathetic, even ridiculous, but Islamic finance was what had brought them together, their mutual interest, hers greater than his admittedly but he had discovered that he had found in the subject something that really did strike a chord with him.

"That would be good," Eddie remembered saying, and he found to his huge surprise that he had missed the subject as well as Leila.

The next day they met and once again Eddie listened to her gentle voice, full of enthusiasm for her subject, her eyes bright with intelligence and with passion for the last session they would have together in their spot in the library.

Eddie could feel the same fresh grief in his heart as he had the day that she had left Harvard. He had watched her go, her beauty and her grace, her girlish ways, that stray tendril of hair and her simple goodness, lost to him. He had thought he would never recover, and in some ways he never did. But life had gone on. His childhood was over and he felt no sorrow for it, rather a relief that the stark and glaring shortcomings of his parents and their selfishness and hostility to each other could not hurt him any more. He was a different man now, a man who had some depth. When he looked at the friends he had around him he could see the shallow level that they operated on, how many baskets they could shoot, how many women they could bed, how big a car they could get out of their old man. Eddie was glad that he was not like them any more. His was the loneliest path, the way of the few rather than the many, but he loved the inner peace that his maturity gave him, the certainty in his decisions and in his course in life and the embracing of his responsibilities. He supposed that these things came in time to most people but for him it had almost been a lightning bolt, a lightning bolt called Leila!

He knew with absolute certainty that she was the catalyst to making him a man rather than a spoilt boy, the steadying influence and the connection with reality that had been lacking in his life. He supposed that his father and mother being so distant and unavailable to him as a child had made him precocious and attention seeking, rebelling against the unhappy loveless prison that had been his childhood. Leila had taught him humility, to cherish and accept people for who they are, despite or even because of their limitations and that had brought him a peace, even a love for his parents that he never thought he could have. Eddie sighed, a weak sounding expiration that crackled with the rust that had formed on his unused vocal cords, as he thought about what Leila had brought to his life. He had thought about it before, of course, but never in so much detail; it was like deconstructing his life and putting it back together piece by piece.

Even in the years when they had had no contact it had felt as though they did. She was always in his thoughts and gradually even the one-night stands and occasional two- or three-night stand girls that came and went in his life lost their charm as he found himself longing for something more meaningful.

Eddie had thought about going to the hospital and seeing Leila when she was alone. But he had now way of knowing when that would be. Besides that, he knew that the hospital had strict security. He had done enough damage; he was powerless to do anything other than wait. He could not face another run-in with her mother. The thought of the hatred and fear on her face haunted him. But Eddie did not blame Maysoon for her reaction.

He had brought this on Leila, he knew that, and the fact that he would have offered himself up one thousand times over to die a most painful and slow death rather than have a hair of her head harmed did not help now. He had put her in harm's way and harm had come to her. Her mother probably saw him as an irresponsible and shallow western man. He had the faint hope that Amir would speak up for him but the truth was Eddie did not even feel that he could summon up the heart to speak up for himself, so why would Amir? Amir would have the welfare of Leila and her parents as his first concern, so most likely Eddie's name would not be mentioned.

And so he survived the day in a sort of half- waking, half-sleeping state. At one point the chambermaid, convinced that he had died because he was so still, with the peanuts in the fridge undisturbed, decided to put a packet on the end of the bed within reach of the man in the chair who always had his back to her. Later she looked in to change the pristine towels, and the packet had been eaten, the smoothed-out empty wrapper on the end of bed where she had left it. From that day each day she put the three packets next to him, leaving the mini-bar sealed. Hell, she thought, he might as well have some freebies, poor man. He always ate them and anything else that she brought. They began a relationship that had no communication beyond the placing of peanuts and the occasional piece of fruit or a chocolate bar on the bed with the peanuts and the eating of some, all or none of them, depending on the day.

Nothing what went on outside the window registered with Eddie at all. Inside his head, in contrast to the stillness of his body, ferocious activity abounded as he forced his brain cells to dredge up the tiniest memory of Leila from some forgotten corner of his mind. His childhood played next to the memories of her, at the conference in Oxford, in Dubai, on every phone call they had, while the little boy that would become the man so devoted to Leila grew up, changed and metamorphasized into the man he was today. The hurt and the tears of his childhood, the neglect and the overcompensation, the trips, the bikes, the computers the cars all looked like what they were as he sat hour upon hour without moving, buy-offs, things to keep him quiet, keep him from realising how life should be, how gentle how pure and how joyous life could be. He had not known that, any of it, until he had met Leila. And now it was in danger of being taken away, and if it was, he knew that he would go after her, as he always had.

Chapter Twenty-seven

Finally, one day three weeks later, Amir called and said the words Eddie had longed to hear.

"Eddie, Leila is asking to see you." Eddie did not reply. He replaced the phone on the hook and walked to his bathroom. His toothbrush, razor and shaving cream were ready and the small hotel soap out of its packet placed beside a bottle of aftershave and shampoo that stood ready by the shower. Eddie cleaned himself as though it were a ritual, scrubbing off the dirt and grime of the time that he had been waiting for Leila to come back to him, the invisible shield guaranteed to keep everyone else away from him. After his shower he went to the wardrobe where he had had his clothes on one hanger in readiness and where they had remained, since the day he had entered the hotel room. As he pulled on his trousers and put on his shirt he noticed that he had lost a lot of weight. He pulled his belt tight and was astonished at how little strength he had in his wasted arm muscles. He felt dizzy and weak with the effort of just moving but his focus was now on seeing Leila and twenty minutes later he was at Leila's bedside. He passed her parents sitting outside the room that he had arranged for Leila to be moved to for her recovery in a private clinic in Harley Street. Her mother had seemed about to say something, but her husband had put his hand on her arm and she had looked away.

Inside the room Leila was sitting up in bed. She did

not have her hijab on and she looked pale and thinner, but still every bit as beautiful. As he sat down at her bedside Eddie lowered his head onto the sheets and began to cry long loud sobs that shook his whole body. Leila put her arm around his shoulders and patted him gently, tears standing out in her own eyes. Her mother came to the door and looked around it, concerned, but Leila shook her head and her mother went back outside. Leila understood Eddie's pain and that it was pointless to tell him not to cry. He needed to and she let him.

Finally he looked up at her serene face and whispered, "I am so sorry."

"Please do not say that, Eddie, life is to blame, not you, and if I had to choose never to have met you, I would not, even although this has happened."

Eddie took her hand and held it as tightly as his weakened hands would allow him. His voice croaked with lack of use and his eyes watered as he tried not to blink, so desperate was he to drink in every detail of her. "How are you, Leila? What have the doctors said?"

"Well I was lucky and I will be fine. The operation to remove the bullet from my spine was a success, I can walk and as soon as I regain my strength I can go home."

"What about your heart. Your lungs?"

"They say there will be no lasting effect." She smiled at him gently. "Poor Eddie, you look as though you have suffered as much as I have. You look pale and thin and old."

"Well you know how to make a man feel good about himself." Eddie smiled, a strange lopsided affair that taxed the muscles of his face, inactive for so long. Then suddenly they were laughing together, although the sound that Eddie made was more a snort than a laugh, his vocal cords doing their best to keep up with the demands being made on them after so long a period of inactivity. But despite his weakness, his strange sound and his tears, for the first time in a month Eddie felt alive.

Her twins arrived and he left, his steps lighter and only a day to wait before he saw Leila again. Over the next few days, Leila and he talked for hours, while her parents looked after the twins.

Eddie had started reading the newspapers again and had made tentative contact with his father, who had ordered him to come home immediately. Eddie had put the phone down. He got into the habit of reading the newspapers to Leila. On a warm summer morning he found her with a bulletin that Amir had brought in to her, from CNS news by their International editor Patrick Goodenough.

Leila was still weak and found it difficult to concentrate, so she asked Eddie to read it to her.

He scanned it quickly and frowned. He did not want to upset Leila and he was sure that this piece of writing would do that.

"Come on, Eddie, I'm not a child; please - I have to know everything about my subject or how can I counter arguments or criticisms?"

Eddie nodded and began to read.

"Critics Protest Promotion of 'Seditious' Islamic Finance. The shari'a-complaint banking sector has been growing rapidly in recent years. Charging that principles of Islamic law are being introduced in the United States by stealth, critics on Thursday will protest outside a U.S. Treasury Department seminar on shari'a-complaint finance. Although this is not the department's first 'Islamic Finance 101' seminar, it comes amid a new push by Moslem figures in recent weeks to promote Islamic finance as a response to the debt-fuelled global financial crisis. Controversial Sunni scholar Sheikh Yusuf al-Qaradawi, a leading advocate of shari'a-complaint finance (SCF), told a conference in Qatar last month that Moslems should take the opportunity provided by the crisis to replace capitalism with an Islamic financial system.

"'The collapse of the capitalist system, which is based on usury and securities rather than commodities in markets, shows us that it is undergoing a crisis and that our integrated Islamic philosophy – if properly understood and applied – can replace the Western capitalism,' he said.

"At a subsequent economic forum in Saudi Arabia, the head of the Islamic Development Bank – an affiliate of the Organization of the Islamic Conference (OIC) – reiterated that the crisis offered an opportunity Islamic finance should seize.

"'Global investment banks should be set up that realize the Islamic economy and offer the world a new vision and different way to manage assets, invest wealth and create products,' Islamic Development Bank President Ahmad

Ali told the forum.

"Saleh Kamel, head of the General Council of Islamic Banks, said Islam could be a 'third way,' given what he called the failures of communism and capitalism.

"On a visit to Saudi Arabia coinciding with the forum, Deputy Treasury Secretary Robert Kimmitt was quoted as saying the U.S. government was examining features of Islamic banking to see the extent to which it may be useful in tackling the crisis.

"Islamic financial products are those that comply with shari'a, the Islamic legal code associated with notorious punishments including the death penalty for apostasy, and stoning and amputations for other offences.

"In essence, SCF bans usury – the collection and payment of interest – and discourages heavy borrowing.

"In a recent article touting SCF as an alternative that should be considered seriously, Saudi-based banker Imran Iqbal described it as a system "that is not based on debt or encourages people to live beyond their means.

"Money is not regarded as a commodity but rather 'only a medium of exchange and a measure of value,' he wrote in the Dubai-based Khaleej Times.

"While still a small part of the global financial system, Islamic finance has been growing fast. The value of assets of Islamic financial institutions worldwide in 2004 were in the $200-$300 billion range. Today they are estimated at between $700 billion and $1 trillion, according to the Malaysia-based Islamic Financial Services Board."

Eddie read the heading: "Demystifying Islamic banking", watching Leila's reaction carefully; he did not want to upset her but she wanted to know, he knew that. He continued: "The Treasury Department held its first seminar on Islamic finance in April 2002, when then undersecretary for international affairs John Taylor told the meeting, "we have had a growing interest in Islamic finance because of its rapid growth and significant presence in many partners of the United States such as Bahrain, Egypt, Indonesia, Kuwait, Malaysia and Pakistan.

"Speaking seven months after 9/11, Taylor also said it was crucial to ensure that legitimate Islamic banks, services and charities were not exploited by terrorists."

Eddie paused and glanced at Leila again, she was lying back on her pillow, with her eyes closed listening to him. As he mentioned 9/11 she frowned slightly and he knew that she felt the pain of this dark day in history keenly.

"The 2002 seminar took place after then-Treasury Secretary Paul O'Neill attended a meeting in Bahrain where participants described the philosophy behind Islamic finance. Taylor said the American officials had left that meeting 'with a sense of what Islamic finance really is' and decided to host the seminar in the U.S. 'to 'demystify' Islamic banking for our colleagues in Washington.

"Later that year, O'Neill's successor, Secretary John Snow, and Taylor attended an International Islamic Finance Conference in Dubai.

"Two years later, Taylor in a speech at an Islamic finance forum at Harvard that the topic was 'very important to us in the Bush Administration.' He also announced a new Islamic finance scholar-in-residence program, naming Mahmoud El-Gamal of Rice University to the position.

"El-Gamal is one of the scheduled speakers at the half-day Treasury Department seminar planned for Thursday and run in conjunction with the Harvard University Law School's Islamic Finance Project which is currently sponsored by four Islamic financial institutions in the Gulf.

"It will be hosted by Assistant Secretary Neel Kashkari, recently named as head of the Office of Financial Stability and the official who will oversee the government's $700 billion financial bailout fund.

"Washington's interest in SCF has drawn a strong response from critics concerned about what they call 'the stealthy insinuation' of shari'a into the U.S.

"A new coalition of public policy organizations, human rights activists and religious groups plans a press conference Thursday to call on the Treasury to cancel the seminar, which it is calling 'an indoctrination session'.

"Saying it 'speaks for peoples of all faiths and political affiliations who do not want to submit to the jihadist doctrine' of shari'a, the Coalition to Stop Shariah said it wants the application of SCF to U.S. financial institutions and products to be banned.

"In a statement, it noted that the advertised agenda for Thursday includes 'no discussion of the seditious nature' of shari'a.

"'The coalition is particularly concerned about the possibility that the Treasury Department will use the vast powers it has been given to cope with the subprime financial crisis as a means of promoting [SCF],' it said, adding that Kashkari's involvement heightened that fear.

"The Treasury Department did not respond this week to queries about the seminar."

Eddie read another heading: "Threat to America's security".

"Asked why concern was being voiced especially now, six years after the Treasury first held a seminar on Islamic finance, Coalition to Stop Shariah spokesman Christopher Holton said this week that much had been learned since then.

"Since 2002 it had become clear that 'Islamic finance' was in fact 'shari'a-compliant finance,' which had the purpose of promoting 'the barbaric doctrine of shari'a,' he said.

"'Shari'a is a threat to American security because it is inherently seditious, since it is mission-driven to supersede all other forms of governing, including our constitution,' he said.

"Holton also noted that Islamic financial institutions had in the past been used to fund terrorist groups through 'zakat,' an Islamic tithing concept.

"One such institution, Bank Al Taqwa, was designated a terrorist financier by the Treasury Department on November 7, 2001. The department said it was set up by the Moslem Brotherhood and provided banking services to al-Qaeda and Hamas before it was shut down by sanctions. Qaradawi, a senior Moslem Brotherhood figure, held shares in the bank.

"The Koran requires Moslems to give alms to charity, distinguishing between voluntary charitable giving and obligatory giving, known as zakat.

"'Zakat is the most important source of financial support for the al-Qaeda network, essentially because it is the most usual and unregulated way to raise donations in Saudi Arabia,' stated a report on terrorism financing, prepared for the U.N. Security Council in 2002.

"'Unfortunately, terrorist organizations exploit this admirable Islamic practice to support their mission of violence,' the Treasury Department said in a document on money laundering and terrorist financing the following year.

"In an October 2007 paper on SCF, Alex Alexiev, vice president of research at the Washington-based Center for Security Policy said Islamists were exploiting Islamic finance for their own purposes, chiefly the objective of making Islamic law acceptable in the West.

"'The ability to have shari'a recognized as legitimate Islamic law by Western governments and publics will be a huge step towards making it acceptable and gradually implementing it in Moslem communities in the West, in family law for instance,' he wrote.

"'This, of course, is a long-standing objective of the Islamists ... who aim to create parallel Moslem societies ruled by shari'a and progressively decoupled from the secular and democratic mainstream Western society.'"

As he finished reading Leila sighed deeply. "I am afraid that it seems impossible for anyone to think about Islamic finance and not connect it to terrorism. I will have to speak to Amir about this; he will have to make some reply. The talk that I gave to the young women students of King's University the day I was shot ..." she lowered her eyes "... was about trying to recruit more women to the system. It seems that we are always going to be haunted by terrorism; it is going to make it so difficult to have our message taken seriously."

Eddie put his hand over hers for a moment. The room smelt of the dozens of roses he had had sent to her and he wanted her to relax and enjoy it, to get better and not to worry. He wanted to take all her worries on his shoulders, he wanted that so much, but he knew that this particular battle was hers to fight, with Amir. Eddie thought about the time that he would be back in New York at Lancaster's. He had come to love the Islamic finance message over the years of his exposure to it by Leila and Amir and he had the greatest respect for it. But he was a realist; he knew that to Joe Public Islam meant terrorism. The challenge was going to be to clear that image so that people could see what was behind it, the real benefits that the world might enjoy from Islamic finance.

Leila still tired easily and as he left the room quietly, Eddie ran into her parents. Maysoon looked at him through eyes that could have been Leila's beautiful dark eyes had there not been comprehensive loathing in them. Her husband looked less forbidding and extended his hand to Eddie.

"We have heard a lot about you from Leila. Thank you for being such a good friend to her." Eddie smiled at him gratefully.

"I wanted to speak to you both," Eddie said.

Maysoon spoke for the first time, her hostile words short and clipped. "If it is about the room, we will be happy to repay you the cost." Her husband put his hand on her arm but Eddie knew that this was a confrontation that had to happen. He could not be in the life of a woman whose parents, or at least mother, hated him.

"Mrs Al Mansour," he started.

"You may call me Maysoon." Eddie was surprised, then he remembered that Moslem women did not take their husbands' names so her name would not be Mansour. Still it was a small concession and he was pleased to take it.

"Thank you, Maysoon," he said softly. "I know that you have worried about my association with Leila, not least because you feel that she might be in danger, I know that you are aware of what has gone on in my life, and I can tell you that if I could take your daughter's place in that bed I would."

His sincerity shone from him and a small glimmer of doubt appeared in Maysoon's eyes. But it was momentary and she countered: "But it is not you in that bed, is it?" Anwar put his hand on her arm again but she shook it off. "My daughter has two children, and she has already lost her husband on a flight that I believe that you were supposed to be on." Eddie bowed his head. "Don't you think that you have done enough damage? We are grateful for your interest and your friendship but maybe this is a friendship that my daughter cannot afford."

Eddie's head shot up. "I cannot change what has gone before, but I can promise you that I will do everything in my power to keep her safe."

"Anything?" Maysoon's tone was challenging.

"Yes, anything."

"Then stay away from her!" And with that she opened the door of Leila's room and went inside.

Anwar could see the distress that Maysoon had caused Eddie, a man who looked weak and ill and not at all the way he had imagined, in fact nothing like the way he had looked on that fateful day when Maysoon had sent him away from the hospital nearly a month ago. Had worry for his daughter caused such a deterioration? Anwar thought Eddie was an enigma. He knew about Western men and Eddie should have been a prime example of a spoilt American used to getting anything and everything he wanted. And yet he could suffer so much for a woman that he was not even intimate with. Of that Anwar was sure; he knew his daughter. It was most unusual for a Western man, in Anwar's experience, to waste time on a woman whom he could not take to his bed, but that was exactly what seemed to be the case with Eddie. Leila had told them how, over the years, she had shared her love of Islamic finance with Eddie and he knew from Amir Ali that this was a very important young man in terms of world baking's future and that he was well schooled in Islamic finance. Amir would not go so far as to say that he was using Eddie, but Anwar could see that he could be an important weapon in his friend's arsenal.

Anwar took Eddie by the arm and led him to the day room. It was empty and Anwar shut the door softly behind them. Eddie had tears in his eyes and looked vulnerable and Anwar felt sorry for this young man who had lost his heart to his daughter.

"I really did not mean anything bad to happen to Leila. If I had thought, for a second ..." Eddie tailed off, if he had thought for a second then what? Would he have distanced himself from her? He would not, he knew that.

"Listen, Eddie. My wife is very emotional at this time; you must forgive her. I know Leila and I know that she would not be so fond of you if you were not a very worthwhile person. She talks about you a lot, much to her mother's annoyance." A smile played around Anwar's lips for a moment. "But I can tell how much she respects you and how much she loves you, as a friend." Eddie drank up Anwar's words like a parched man at an oasis in the desert. "Please give Maysoon time to come round. But Eddie, you have been very kind, paying for the private room, I must insist that I pay you back and continue the payments myself."

"No, I can well afford it as you know and I feel at least that this is something I can do," Eddie protested.

"That and the roses!" Anwar smiled, and Eddie smiled back.

"Leave Maysoon to me; just keep a low profile for a while," Anwar said. Eddie extended his hand and Anwar noticed again how weak and bony he seemed. And so began the conspiracy. Eddie had given Anwar his mobile number and Anwar would give a couple of rings as he and Maysoon set off for the hospital each day. That way Eddie managed to leave Leila's bedside before her parents arrived. She was getting stronger now and they had long talks about all sorts of things. Eddie always came early and although visiting did not strictly start until later the staff turned a blind eye. Eddie spent a great deal of time reading to Leila and they talked about the items that he read out from the newspaper. As ever she had a thirst for knowledge and Eddie loved studying the expressions on her face when she thought he was not looking. Generally she lay back on her pillow, her eyes closed, and Eddie loved the way that her long dark lashes rested on her cheeks, the odd little frown or smile playing on her face as he read her the news of the day. Occasionally when she heard something that startled or surprised her, her eyes would fly open and she would fix him with a stare that demanded that he elaborate. Eddie was happy to do that; he loved every moment that he spent with Leila and she in her own way tended to his own recovery from his self imposed starvation by ordering food that they would share together, so that she could be sure that he was eating.

When they had finished the papers they often went on to the magazines that the nurses would let Leila have when they had finished reading them. They were trashy and full of celebrity gossip but some of the antics that people got up to made them laugh. In one particular magazine Leila always liked Eddie to read out the problem page, mostly about spots and unfaithful boyfriends and best friends who had turned out not to be.

On a particularly warm day, with the curtains fluttering listlessly in a tepid breeze Eddie had started to read some headlines from a magazine newly delivered by the ward clerk. After laughing together about the latest TV soap story lines, Leila said, "Come on then; what is the problem today? Let's see if we can get the answer right."

It was a little game they played, and Eddie flipped through the magazine to the problem page. As he read the headline he hesitated. Leila opened her eyes. "Go on then," she said, and Eddie began to read.

"Dear Jenny

"Can a Christian-Moslem Marriage work?

"My boyfriend and I have been dating for a year now and we are buying our first house together. And yes I have heard it all before ... it won't work out if we buy a house together etc etc etc... But we love each other and have agreed to set up a contract between us should we break up and still have the house.

"We have obviously spoken about getting married and having children and I cannot wait to do so. I have given some thought on changing to Islam ... as I know that a Christian/Moslem marriage could get complicated especially once there are children. As he already informed me that if I wish to stay Christian we can get married that way ... but the kids will have to be Moslem.

"I don't have a problem with that at all. I want to have a family and he has treated me like gold since the beginning and I have seen his bad sides and he has seen mine and despite that we still want to be together.

"I just need to know if I should change to Moslem or stay Christian and get married that way? Saffy"

Eddie looked over at Leila but her eyes were tight shut, although a small smile played at the corner of her mouth. He continued to read.

"Hello Saffy

I know from a lot of experience in this exact situation that a Christian/Moslem relationship can work very well but it can also go horribly wrong and to a large extent what happens will depend on the type of people you two are. Perhaps you should look at it in the same light as any other obstacle that two people face when they are getting married.

"I know of a lot of people in the same situation. If he accepts you for who you are that's all that matters. Will problems arise with his family friends or community? Possibly, but be tactful and understanding. At the end of the day it will help a lot if you can never be accused of being difficult or unreasonable. Whatever happens, if problems arise, stay untied.

"On the matter of converting to Islam, I don't

know how much you know about the religion but no Imam will allow you to convert just because you want to get married to someone. You need to know about the religion and study it and see if you are serious about making that commitment. What if it doesn't work with you two? Would you go back to being a Christian? So, my advice is, be yourself, and if living with him over the years and learning about his religion makes you want to convert, go ahead. Also, be open. Don't judge his culture or religion if it is different from your own, be open-minded and allow him to practice freely. I don't know where he is from but I know many Moslems feel that it is hard enough being Moslem in any non-Islamic country, so he definitely doesn't want to feel he has to justify himself at home as well. Good luck and I hope you are very happy together.

Jenny

As he finished reading the reply, Leila's eyes flickered open and she looked at him. Something in her eyes warned him not to speak of the piece, that it would be too difficult, too painful, so he did not. But the fact that she had been affected by it gave him hope. Perverse as it seemed, her very unwillingness to speak of the Moslem-Christian marriage that had been talked about in the piece made his heart sing!

Leila changed the subject. "You know, Eddie, God has saved me for some purpose; I truly believe that and it is my duty to make sure that I make a difference, a real difference. I have been looking into charitable work. I want to see what I can do for others. There is a charity in South Africa that provides help for children with AIDS. One of the nurses here has been doing voluntary work with those children and told me about it.

"You're not thinking of going out there?" Eddie asked with alarm.

"No, not in person, initially, but I want to set up a charity for it, help raise funds, that sort of thing. Perhaps you could do it with me? Or make a donation?"

"I'll make a donation by all means, Leila, but with the time I have been out of the office I think I will be pretty tied up once I get back to New York. Let me know if you need anything though, won't you?"

"I will." Leila smiled.

Privately Eddie hoped that by the time that she was well enough to leave the hospital she would have forgotten the idea, but he knew that she wouldn't, not his Leila! Always thinking of others.

That evening, Anwar did not give his normal ring and Eddie was still at Leila's bedside when her parents arrived. As he jumped to his feet Maysoon put her hand out, indicating that he should sit down. She sat on another chair, Anwar beside her on the other side of Leila's bed.

"I will say this in front of my daughter. I am sorry for the anger I displayed towards you. You have been very kind to my daughter and you obviously care for her deeply." Eddie dropped his eyes and looked at his hands. When he looked up he glanced at Leila. She was looking at her mother, love in her eyes and relief in her expression. "We saw the doctor in the corridor and he says that it will only be a few days before Leila can come home. I would like to thank you for all your care and ask you to join us for a meal when Leila gets home."

Eddie felt a huge weight lift off his shoulders and glanced at Anwar, who gave him a small, almost imperceptible, wink.

"Thank you," Eddie said.

The meal with Leila and her family was the night before his flight out of the UK. Eddie felt relaxed and happy amongst the loving family and felt that he could at last return home with peace in his heart. Leila was out of hospital, her family had accepted him and she was back with her beloved twins again. On his last night in London Eddie slept better than he had done in months and dreamt of Leila. He woke up with a smile on his face and a feeling of calm that he had not felt in years.

* * *

As Eddie was waking up in London, in Dubai Sharif was sitting in a hotel café. He had heard from his sources that Leila was almost recovered and in a way he was not sorry. He had lashed out, in a fit of pique and frustration because his plans to kill his enemy's son had failed. But the woman that Eddie loved so much was a good Moslem woman and did not really deserve to die and apart from being frustrated at the ineptitude of those around him Shairf did not really want her to die. In fact he had a feeling that to Eddie, his own death would be preferable to that of

Leila. It would no doubt have destroyed him, but he was still alive and so was she. It was getting more and more difficult for Sharif to operate as law enforcement agencies in the USA, the UK and in the UAE were on the lookout for him. For the time being he was going to have to lie low. Once the immediate furore had died down he could think about it again. It seemed to Sharif that Eddie was Teflon-coated, or had the luck of the devil. Sharif smiled to himself. That was it, the luck of the devil, the protection and the characteristics of the devil. That was how this loathsome family survived.

As the heat of full summer descended on Dubai, locals left for cooler climes and hopeful tourists started to arrive only to be driven in from the sea and the pool by the merciless sun. As Sharif watched one family burnt lobster-red waddle in from the pool he wondered how people could be so stupid; coming to Dubai in October or November would offer far better conditions. The roads shimmered in the heat and the desert looked as though it had a molten sheet of glass caressing its sand dunes.

Sharif sighed. He had been here long enough. He felt safe, less conspicuous. He had friends here but he could not stay. He would have to go to America, to New York. He needed to see Edward. He had come to the conclusion from what she said that Arabella had neither the ear nor the heart of her husband and if that was true he had no further use for her. The fact that he would not have to see her again or service her insatiable hunger for him was a great relief; his last encounter with her had almost ended in disaster when his distaste for her surgically enhanced body and suffocating presence had almost rendered him impotent. Luckily he had brought tablets with him and had had to keep her happy with almost half an hour of foreplay before he could get it over with. Not for the first time, he shuddered. Still, there was no further need for her. In fact he thought if he did kidnap Arabella, Edward would probably thank him rather than pay a ransom or give in to his demands.

In the early hours of an August morning Sharif and Eddie touched down at JFK airport at almost the same time into a stifling New York heat wave.

Chapter Twenty-eight

Eddie's welcome back from his father was muted to say the least. He had been away a long time and had kept his contact to the bare minimum needed to reassure his parents that he was still alive. He had answered no emails concerning the bank or the Lewa Project and had even ignored Sheikh Lewa's calls. The Sheikh had been understandably insulted as he had done so much for Eddie, and while he understood that Eddie was concerned about Leila, he also understood, as Amir Ali did, that there could be nothing between the two, such was his implicit understanding of Leila's commitment to her faith. Sheikh Lewa found it inexplicable that a man should let his business go to hell for any reason at all, let alone that of unrequited love for a woman who could never be his.

Edward was furious with Eddie. He thought his son self-indulgent and weak, and he wasted no time in telling him. Eddie, because he was so relieved that Leila was going to be okay barely felt the barbs that his father directed at him. He met with Harry and some of his old college friends but he was distracted and distant and none of them bothered to call him for a repeat outing. Eddie knew that he was getting more and more isolated but he couldn't help it. He struggled to get up in the mornings and was only half concentrating at work each day. He made his peace with Sheikh Lewa, just about, and although the Sheikh was not entirely happy with the situation he gave Eddie the chance to get the project back on track. That would mean another trip to the UAE and Eddie didn't fancy it in August as the heat would be stifling and the Shiekh would no doubt want him to join him in his desert camp. He just could not, no matter how hard he tried, get up any enthusiasm for any aspect of his life. He missed Leila so much that it hurt and spent all his waking hours with her on his mind.

The intern program had lapsed since he had been away and his father had arranged for him to lecture the interns that week on the history of Wall Street. Normally it would have been a task that Eddie undertook happily but as he stood in front of the fresh-faced eager youngsters he felt old, jaded and unhappy. He felt that his life was passing him by without delivering him any true happiness.

He sighed and took a breath.

"Once upon a time, before New York City was a city, there really was a wall. It was built in 1644, on the lower end of Manhattan Island by the Dutch to protect them against attacks by the British. Many years later, the wall was long gone, but the road alongside was still there and was, of course, called Wall Street. Nowadays we tend to think of Wall Street as the financial centre of the world, but this wasn't always the case.

"Early in our country's history, Boston was the financial centre of America. Bonds for projects such as roads, canals and bridges, and contracts for commodities such as hides and molasses, were bought and sold mostly by Boston dealers. However, there was not yet an official place to conduct such business.

"Other countries had had such 'exchanges' for many years. Belgium established the world's first in 1531. Amsterdam soon followed, with brokers conducting their activity on a street called Warmoesstraat. In 1602, under the Amstel bridge, shares of the East India Company were bought and sold. Money was raised here to finance the Pilgrim's trip to America.

"At this time, Paris conducted their financial business on Rue de Quincampoix. In the early 1600s, Berlin's traders and merchants conducted their business at the Grotte in Schlossgarten.

"London's stock exchange began as an outdoor market cantered on Exchange Alley. By 1725, many London brokers began doing business at Jonathon's Coffee House which was renamed 'The Stock Exchange' in 1773. An advertisement of the time by a broker named John Taylor proclaimed 'Buyeth and selleth new lottery tickets, Navy victualling bills, East India bonds, and other publick securities'."

Some of the interns sniggered at Eddie's attempt at Olde English and he felt more depressed than ever. It was a talk he had given many times before and he usually enjoyed a laugh with the interns as they made fun of him, but he had no enthusiasm and energy for it now.

"It was just a matter of time before our new country, The United States of America, would organize formal stock and bond trading. 1792 was the year. In 1792, New York City's population was about 34,000, not including Brooklyn and Queens which were still separate towns. Much of Manhattan had just been rebuilt with brick buildings after the devastating Great Fire of 1776.

"Wall Street was New York's centre of commerce. Just a few blocks long, from Broadway on the west to the East River at the other end, Wall Street was not yet paved or even lined with cobblestones. There were warehouses for furs, coffee and tea, and other goods from all over the world. To the south, streets were crowded with slaughterhouses and tanneries.

"Wealthy businessmen, along with their ordinary trade, would sell lottery tickets, bonds, and shares of stocks in new banks that were forming. The hottest trading and speculating, was in treasury bonds issued by the new Bank of the United States.

"Until 1792, a person wishing to buy or sell an investment would either advertise, or spread the word among associates and friends. Some of the first merchants to keep a supply of stock shares on hand were Leonard Bleeker at 16 Wall Street and Sutton & Harry at 20 Wall. On one day in 1791, 100 shares actually changed hands. Imagine that!

"The first organized stock exchange was created in 1792, when under a buttonwood tree in Castle Garden, now called Battery Park, John Sutton, Benjamin Jay, and 22 other financial leaders signed an agreement of rules, regulations and fees.

"Then in a building at 22 Wall Street, securities were auctioned every day beginning at noon, sold to the highest bidder. The seller paid the exchange a commission on each stock or bond sold.

"They originally called this organization The Stock Exchange Office. This was a very exclusive organization, allowing only the elite of New York's financial community to join. And certainly no women were allowed! In just recent years, Muriel Siebert became the first female member of the New York Stock Exchange.

"In 1817, the name was changed to the New York Stock and Exchange Board. In 1850 the stock exchange was located at Wall and Hanover, its fifth address. At that time, the Board's total yearly costs including rent and salaries, was less than $5,000.

"In 1863, the Board changed its name to the New York Stock Exchange, and moved into the majestic building at the corner of Wall and Broad Streets, where 140 years later, the big exchange still does business today.

"The NYSE had competition from smaller exchanges both in New York and other cities. One of the largest New York organizations to compete with them was a group of securities dealers who conducted their business outside, rain or shine. They were known as the Curbstone Brokers.

"The Curbstone Brokers were willing to deal with stocks of smaller companies that couldn't meet the requirements to be listed on the Big Board, as the NYSE began to be called.

"Relying on prices set earlier in the day at the Board's auction, they would gather in the evenings where they would auction as little as a single share at a time. The big exchange set a minimum of 100.

"In 1880, William Worthington Fowler described

these after-hour brokers as 'they are all eyes and ears, scud and scamper, their fingers quivering like aspen leaves, their mouths pouring out a stream of bids and offers. Disencumbered of all the spare syllables, while they telegraph signals with the ten digits and with nods and winks'.

"After over 100 years, the Curbstone Brokers decided it was time to move inside. In 1919, they purchased a lot at 86 Trinity Place at the west end of Wall Street, and erected a tall modern building. In 1928, they renamed themselves the New York Curb Exchange and moved into their new home. It wasn't until 1953 that the Curb changed its name to the American Stock Exchange."

From the back of the room a hand went up.

"How many companies were traded on the early exchanges?" A spotty young man with an Adam's apple that bobbed violently up and down in his thin neck asked.

Eddie nodded. "The first was the Bank of New York, being established in 1784. In 1800 there were only 295 corporations, of which about 20 traded publicly. In 1835, the listings on the NYSE swelled to 121, many of them railroads. The first American investment bubble occurred at this time and burst in what came to be called The Panic of 1836. In 1869, there were 145 companies listed, including insurance, steel, farm equipment, tobacco, and other manufacturers.

"In 1900, the biggest stock was U.S. Steel. Other companies on the New York Stock Exchange were AT&T, Westinghouse, Eastman Kodak, Procter and Gamble,

Pillsbury, Sears, Kellogg, and Nabisco Crackers.

"At this time, the market was roaring. The prevailing wages around the country were quite low, with 10 cents or less per hour considered a fair wage. Women and children, working in sweatshops in the garment district, were paid as little as 25 cents for a 12-hour workday. But a good Wall Street runner delivering paperwork and stock certificates between brokerages could make the amazing sum of $8 a day, and some successful traders, of course, were making millions.

"Although Wall Street has always been an exciting place to work, it has had its danger too. We are all too familiar with the bombing of the World Trade Center in 1993 and its horrific destruction on September 11, 2001.

"Even before then, though, New York's financial district is no stranger to terrorist assaults. On September 16, 1920, at about noon, a horse-drawn carriage stopped in front of the JP Morgan Building on Wall Street. A powerful bomb exploded, killing 35 people and injured hundreds. No arrests were made. This building still bears the scars of this senseless attack. And of course the latest terrorist attack on the twin towers took place very close by when the shock waves were felt and windows were shattered."

The young interns looked down at their hands and looked solemn. Some of them had, Eddie guessed, lost family and friends in the attacks. As they filed out Eddie slumped down in a chair. He was tired, despondent and he just wanted to go home. His father passed the door and looked in.

"How did it go, son?"

Eddie shrugged. "It went."

Edward came into the lecture room and closed the door.

"Look, Eddie, you've got to pull yourself together. I don't know what it is but whatever it is I'm getting sick of it. I am supposed to be laving you in charge of all this soon and as it stands I can't see that I could leave you in charge of a children's tea party."

Eddie made no reply.

"What the hell is the matter with you? Are you sick? Why don't you let Dr Latimer give you the once over?" Edward's tone softened. Maybe that was it; it would explain a lot. Maybe Eddie was ill.

Eddie shrugged again. "Okay," he said.

Dr Latimer gave Eddie a clean bill of health, as he knew that he would, but advised that he seemed run down and could do with a break. Edward was not impressed. As far as he was concerned Eddie had had a good break already and another one was certainly not going to help the bank at all. In the end they compromised on a long weekend before Eddie flew out to Dubai.

On a whim Eddie hired a 1960s Ford Mustang for his trip to Lake Clear. As he took Route 87 out through Albany he thought about the lake that he had not see for so long. The family had a lodge by the water there and as a boy Eddie had often taken school friends, usually Harry, there in the summer holidays, to kayak and to enjoy the water. The air was fresh and clear after the smog of New York and Eddie was looking forward to getting out on the water again.

As he drove Eddie remembered the blurb that he and Harry had read about the resort that they sometimes visited along the lakeside. They had thought it was corny at the time but now, Eddie felt his soul crying out for the cool calm that he remembered. He could imagine that it was the 1800s in the Adirondack where he found himself in a fireside chatin an Adirondack historical lodge espousing Adirondack history, where the writer Robert Louis Stevenson was cured from tuberculosis in Saranac Lake just minutes away where Albert Einstein stayed on the very shores of Lake Clear. Eddie remembered those summers filled with mountain climbing, canoeing or skiing and with the idle chatter of boyish conversations he had not had in years. The deep breathes of cool, clear mountain air with the Northern Lights of the Adirondack Wilderness, "the Great Woods", living green, relaxed and stimulated senses in a way that Eddie hoped would reawaken his soul for something new, cleansing and calming. For too long he had felt unhappy, tense and on edge. He remembered the smells of wild game, fresh vegetables and Adirondack herbs and spices from the garden simmering in the crackling fire they had had at the Lodge. He and Harry would sometimes imagine these delicacies prepared by an Old World immigrant family who brought with them centuries of old world traditions dating back to medieval Europe of sautés, stews and original smoked biers, hefeweissens, mulled wines and blackberry brandy lindsor tortes of German food and a host of unfamiliar foods that Eddie had grown to love as they reminded him of his boyhood holidays. In fact his mother had bought many of the dishes they enjoyed from the resort's restaurant, but it all added to the romantic vision the boys had built up about the place as they ate the unfamiliar food ravenously after days spent on the lake and enjoying the outdoors.

Eddie could picture himself able to stand again in the absolute stillness of a mountain morning where he could smell the freshness of the air and the call of the Lake Clear loon family and the glimpses he would have of other Adirondack wildlife.

Eddie was looking forward to getting lost in the 25-acre Adirondack estate in Lake Clear where as boys their father had told them that Einstein had come and relaxed in the midst of the St Regis Wilderness area of lakes, streams, rivers and ponds and where Thoreau and Oliver Wendell Holmes created the Philosophers' Camp. This information was lost on the boys who were more interested in exploring than history but now Eddie thought that it was kind of cool that he was walking in the footsteps of such great men.

Eddie was also looking forward to the sunsets over the lake shore and St Regis mountain when it looked for all the world as though the sun was a lantern warming a mountaintop silhouette that appeared to be the outline of a human figure in repose. He and Harry had frightened themselves by calling him the Mountain man and at night told ever more vivid and far-fetched stories of what he would do if he caught you. Eddie smiled to himself, despite everything he was looking forward to his break.

His perspective of the sunset would be different, he knew, seen through adult eyes, and he felt that if anything would tug at the heart strings that were firmly joined across the ocean to Leila, the magical sight of the sun diffusing into reds and oranges on the horizon would do it but he knew that he had to pull himself together, had to get control of his life back. But nearly losing Leila had brought things into focus. Eddie supposed that he had always thought that somehow, things would turn out okay for them both, and that they had all the time in the world left to them to get it right. Leila's brush with death had brought sharply into focus the fragile hold that anybody had on life. It could all be over in an instant.

Lost in his thoughts, Eddie arrived at the cabin in record time, or so it seemed to him. His mother had called ahead and got Mrs Juno to clean the old place that had not been opened up for many years. Mrs Juno was in her 70s now and was waiting for him as he drew up on the dry sun-baked earth drive.

She threw her arms around him as though he was her long-lost grandson and fussed around him as he brought his things in from the car. The cabin looked smaller from his adult perspective but as clean as a new pin with fragrant flowers from the woods in vases in the lounge and beside his bed. The place smelt of summer and the open air and the remembered familiar heady scent of pine. Eddie felt a lump in his throat. His mind and heart were back in the days when he had been young and carefree when his biggest concern was whether he would catch the biggest fish or jump the furthest into the lake off the jetty from the rope swing that hung from the branch of an enormous willow beside the water.

As he stood the kayak up against the old garage that was filled with the old playthings of his youth Eddie waved Mrs Juno off. He took out his mobile. Somehow he wanted to call Harry, maybe recapture the times they had had as youngsters. He hesitated and then flipped the phone shut. It would be too complicated. Harry was a family man, and he had responsibilities, people to ask if he could take off for the weekend. Not for the first time Eddie felt keenly the fact that he had no one who would want him to stay home, no one waiting for him on his return. He had no one and he wanted no one except Leila.

His first night at the lodge was all he had thought it would be. He sat for a long time watching the sunset and thinking his thoughts.

He was about to go in when a kayak skimmed silently over the glassy surface of the lake towards him. He got up hastily, wanting to get away before he was spoken to. But the person in the kayak called out to him.

"Excuse me!" Reluctantly Eddie turned around.

The young man was the first of three heavily laden kayaks, a group obviously touring the lake and the surrounding rivers and rapids.

"I'm looking for the camp site; do you know where it is?"

"Yes," Eddie said as the kayakers drew level with the jetty. "Further down about half a mile."

"Thanks." the man smiled at him and Eddie was about to turn and go back into the lodge when he stopped. When he looked at the group again there was something about them that reminded him of years gone by, of his own youth, and suddenly he wanted their company.

"I'm Bill," the man said, and these are Jim and Anton.

"Eddie," Eddie replied.

Bill held up a line of fish the kayakers had caught in the lake. "I could cook them for you if you let us camp on your lawn?" he asked with a cheeky grin. Despite himself Eddie smiled.

"Okay then!" Suddenly he realised how long it had been since he had wanted to be with anyone, but surprisingly the thought of spending the evening with these young men who had appeared out of the mists of the lake seemed like something he needed to do. He had almost lost the art of conversation; he had been such a loner. He helped the kayakers out on to the jetty and they began to take their tent packs off their kayaks.

"Hey, I've got a spare room; three, in fact. You can bunk down in them if you like."

"Thanks, Eddie."

Now that they were ashore Eddie could see that the young men were probably college students in their early twenties, their arms smooth and brown from paddling under the hot summer sun on the lake. They reminded him of the summers he had spent with Harry.

"Hey, that's great, man; I can't tell you how long it's been since we had a bed to sleep in!" Jim said, clapping Eddie on the shoulder as he showed him into one of the downstairs bedrooms.

Once the boys had dumped their belongings, they sat outside underneath the willow by the jetty on the old wooden swinging chair and garden benches, their original cushions now frayed and musty smelling.

As the fish cooked over the barbecue pit Eddie asked Anton, "Where have you been kayaking?"

"Well today we started from Union Falls Pond - do you know it? It's a great kayak route but it drops rapidly with class one to two rapids in the first four miles then a class five drop at Teft Pond Falls. There is a bit of a carry then, and then the next five miles has a complex series of class two to three ledges, drops and hydraulics. It's pretty tough going there; you have to know what you're doing and there has to be a lot of water. It's pretty rocky and there is a wide fluctuation in the water level due to dam releases, but yesterday it was pretty cool." Eddie was impressed, he knew the stretch of water and it was definitely not for beginners. "Tomorrow we're going for the Silver Staircase. It's pretty much continuous white-water and it needs a bit of know-how to manoeuvre through the rapids. Some of them are rated up to class four. Scouting is not always possible but I'm hoping we will be able to check it out before we commit tomorrow." Jim paused for a moment then said, "Do you fancy it? I saw the kayak by the garage."

Eddie was taken aback. He had once been able to navigate such demanding kayak routes but that had been a long time ago. But wasn't that what he had come here for? After a pause in which he was conscious of all three men looking at him, he finally said, "Yes, why not."

As the fish cooked, Eddie brought out salad, fresh tomatoes and the crusty bread that Mrs Juno had left for him.

They ate amid lively chat between the boys and Eddie. They spoke about the lake and kayaking and what the boys had been up to at college and on vacation. That suited Eddie just fine. He did not want to talk about his life, his depressing life that was so unfulfilling. They completed their meal with a watermelon, the deep red flesh dripping crimson rivulets down their chins. By the time that they had finished, the stars were out and the moon shone down in silver ribbons across the still lake. Eddie lay down on the cool grass, a cushion from the swinging chair behind his head.

"So what do you do, Eddie?" Jim asked, and Eddie sighed.

"I'm in banking," he said.

"Hey that's a coincidence. We're doing economics and banking degrees at Yale!"

"Is that right?" Eddie said. "I was a Harvard man myself."

"Well we won't hold it against you!" Jim laughed.

"Are you enjoying the course?" Eddie asked.

"Yeah, it's kinda tough at times and next semester

we are doing a whole module on Islamic finance. Some dude called Amir Ali is coming to lecture us and the deans are making a huge deal of it. I don't really see the point myself."

Eddie sat up. "Amir Ali, you say?"

"Yep; you know him?"

Eddie smiled and said softly, "Yes I know him. And give it a chance, guys; it's really interesting. I've done a lot on it myself."

"Yeah, well how about giving us a taster so we can get a jump on the others for next term?" Jim said with a smile.

"Well okay, Eddie said; what do you know already?" The three young men shrugged.

"Really nothing" Bill said, "apart from something about not charging interest?"

"That's right," Eddie said. As he paused Leila's face came into his mind and he remembered the first lesson he had had with her in the library. It was as good a place to start as any.

"Before you start, dude," Anton interrupted, "can I set up the video camera over here? We're kinda making a video record of our trip and this is a highlight so far!"

Eddie was surprised but said, "Sure; why not?"

He began to talk cautiously at first, checking that he was not boring the boys, but they looked interested and asked him questions. Eddie was surprised at how easy it was for him to answer their queries; he knew more about Islamic finance than he realised.

"Look," Eddie said, "one in five people in the world is Moslem. There are anywhere between twenty and fifty Moslem countries depending on the definition you use. Clearly Moslems represent a significant demographic in the global economy and many Moslems use their wealth to serve the common good."

Eddie saw the glances pass between the young men but continued.

"Islam does not see wealth as inherently evil or inherently good. The status of wealth in Islam is inherently neutral. A hadith, a saying of the Prophet Muhammad, tells us that while envy is usually a sin, it is permissible to envy a man who has wealth and strives to spend it on good causes. However, another hadith said, 'Avoid cruelty and injustice ... and guard yourselves against miserliness, for this has ruined nations who lived before you.' From this text, you can see three injunctions connected to the use of wealth. Moslems are told they should not use their money to promote cruelty. Also, they should not use their wealth to promote injustice. In addition, they should not be misers that hoard their wealth like the infamous Dickens character Scrooge.

"The language of the Qur'an is Arabic so a lot of important terms in Islamic finance are in Arabic. Don't be put off; it will come naturally to you in the end."

Again, the glances.

"You mentioned Riba, which is the Arabic term

for interest, especially usury, an exorbitant amount of interest that makes it difficult for a debtor to get out of debt. Moslems try their best to avoid paying or receiving interest. Some situations make it very difficult to avoid, such as if you need to take out a mortgage for instance. However, by saving wisely, Islam suggests that you can pay the mortgage off quickly and minimize the interest that has to be paid.

"The ban on interest has led to different responses. Some Moslems have argued that Islamic law only prohibits excessive interest and that the interest used in the modern global economy is permissible. Others have resorted to complex legal devices to avoid interest. Neither of these options have appealed to devout Moslems who think it disingenuous to argue that interest is not really interest and dishonest to try to exploit legal loopholes in Islamic law."

The boys glanced at each other again but this time Eddie detected a look of interest, of enquiry.

"Many Moslems have even gone so far as to avoid using banks and formal financial institutions. This has proved dangerous both for both the individuals concerned and indeed for the nations that carry out this practice. It puts the assets of individuals at risk of major loss. Also, the distrust of institutions can prevent Moslem nations from accumulating capital.

"When a Moslem loans money to a friend, he or she should only ask for the principal in return. Asking for interest on top of the principal is not allowed in most cases."

"How does that work?" Anton asked. "Is that always the rule?"

Eddie nodded; he was enjoying passing on the knowledge that Leila had given him.

"If the loan has not been repaid for a long time or the local economy is in such a mess that significant inflation has occurred, some scholars say that the lender has the right to ask for additional money to offset the loss due to inflation.

"In the past thirty-five years, Islamic banks have emerged around the world. Islamic banks act much like mutual funds in that there are shared risks and shared returns for individuals and institutions. Individuals put their money in these that then use the money to invest in a variety of enterprises that adhere to Islamic law. When the enterprises make profits, the institutions pass the profits on to the investors. When the enterprises lose money, the investors lose money."

The boys raised their eyebrows but their expressions told Eddie that they were interested in what he had to say.

"Another interesting thing to talk about is Zakat. This is the portion of a Moslem's wealth that he or she is obligated to give to the needy."

"Really?" Bill asked.

"Yes, the typical value for zakat is 2.5 per cent of one's annual income. The value varies slightly in relation to different kinds of property such as real estate and to some precious metals. Zakat is seen as a means of purifying wealth. By setting aside a small portion of their assets for the sake of Allah, a person protects his or her wealth."

"What is the money used for?" Jim asked.

"It can be used to feed the hungry, clothe the poor, provide shelter for travellers, heal the sick, and for many other worthy causes. Zakat is more than a tax; it is a fundamental aspect of Islam. It is as important as daily prayer and fasting in the month of Ramadan to those of the Islamic faith."

"Does every Moslem pay zakat?" Anton asked.

"Not every Moslem, no. Some Moslems are not obliged to pay zakat because they do not meet nisab. Nisab is a threshold of wealth owned by an individual, any excess over which is subject to zakat. The American tax code has a similar threshold so that anyone who earns income exceeding that value must pay taxes. Not surprisingly, pre-pubescent children and the mentally insane are also free from the obligation of zakat.

"Sdaqah ..." Eddie said the unfamiliar word carefully "... is a non-obligatory charitable contribution that serves the communal good. According to Hadith ..."

Eddie paused and Jim said, "A saying of the prophet?"

"That's right." Eddie smiled at him. "Wealth does not decrease because of charity." This means that when a person spends money in charity, Moslems believe that God responds by either blessing his or her remaining wealth or by increasing his or her wealth.

"Among the causes that Moslems see as especially noble are supporting orphans and building places of Islamic worship. One reason why Moslems are devoted to orphans is because their Prophet Muhammad was an orphan from the age of six. His father died before he was born and his mother died later. Also, in most societies orphans are particularly vulnerable to poverty and abuse as they lack parents to protect them. Mosques have importance both as places where God is worshipped five times a day and as cultural centres.

"Islamic economic philosophy is based on the absolute sovereignty of God, brotherhood or sisterhood, and social justice. Moslems believe that God will hold them responsible for their duties to Him, their duties to other Moslems, their duties to other humans, and their duties to every living organism.

"In another Hadith that I always think is a great way of looking at things, the Prophet Mohammed apparently said: "No human will move from his station of accounting until he is asked about four things: his lifetime, how did he consume it, his body, how did he wear it out, his knowledge, how did he use it, and his wealth, how did he earn it and how did he spend it."

The young men smiled, and Eddie could tell that this had made an impression on them as it had on him when he had first heard it all those years ago in the library in Harvard.

"Moslems believe that God will hold them responsible for every resource that He gave them. This includes one's life, one's body, one's knowledge and one's wealth. Even spending money on something as trivial as shoes has a religious dimension to it since God is the ultimate source of wealth so one should be neither extravagant nor stingy in spending. It may seem odd to us to think of God as the source of personal wealth but if you believe that we are created by God, sustained by God, taught by God, and healed by God, it makes sense to believe that whatever wealth we have, is due to the benevolence of God.

"I think that in some ways, Moslems face a unique set of financial challenges. They have to avoid interest. They are not allowed to support injustice, nor can they be miserly. They keep away from businesses that deal in things that Islam forbids. Some investment opportunities that would be perfectly acceptable and normal to non-Moslems are totally abhorred by Moslems. For instance, many people would have no qualms about investing in Anheuser Busch, the manufacturer of Budweiser. Moslems would find this to be morally repugnant since Islam prohibits the consumption of alcohol.

"In other ways, Moslems face the same financial issues as non-Moslems. They have assets, which they want to grow. They take financial risks and reap financial rewards. Their motives in transactions can range from selfish to altruistic. It is a very interesting subject."

Eddie looked around at his audience; all three young men were looking thoughtful.

"Hey; we'll sure have the jump on the class when Mr Ali comes to lecture next term!" Jim said and the others laughed.

"Tell him Eddie Lancaster said hello," Eddie said quietly, and the boys stopped laughing and stared at him.

"Eddie Lancaster?" Bill said. "*The* Eddie Lancaster?"

Eddie nodded. "Yes, but tonight I'm off duty!"

They spoke of Islamic finance long into the night and made plans for their trip to the Silver Staircase. Eddie felt butterflies in his stomach; he knew that he should not have accepted the boy's invitation but he wanted to do it, he needed to do it, to drive his demons out, the demons that the evening beside the lake with these three uncomplicated young men had started to exorcise. He needed the demons to be gone, and he felt that he might do that on the wild waters of the silver staircase.

Chapter Twenty-nine

The next morning was warm and sultry and the paddle to the rapids took about an hour along the Saranac River. Bill scouted down the banks of the river before he got back into his kayak and led the way downstream to the white water. Once the rapids were ahead of them, Bill held himself steady on a rock while Eddie held on to the side of his kayak.

"Are you ready? It looks pretty fierce today. Are you sure you are up to it?"

Eddie nodded. He was not at all sure he was up to it, but he had come too far now to turn back. It was not that he wanted to keep up with them, there was no macho competitive challenge, and he knew that they would not mock him if he pulled out, but he wanted to do this.

Anton went first, his kayak bobbing in and out of sight through the raging rapids. As he disappeared around the corner, Bill pushed off then Jim. Finally Eddie pushed off. The fast current immediately took his kayak and he was tossed into the middle of the foaming swell of rushing water. His kayak hit a rock and he lost his paddle. Helpless to guide the kayak without a paddle he held on to the sides of the craft as he was tossed against rock after rock, his craft disintegrating around him. Suddenly a huge rock loomed ahead of him and he was thrown out on to it, his helmet-less head hitting it with a sickening crack before he slid unconscious down into the water to be tossed like a cork through the rocks and channels of the turgid river.

Bill found his lifeless body at the bottom of the rapids, his life jacket snagged on a branch, his head dangling over the water.

Jim and Anton were there almost immediately and at first they thought he was dead. His leg was badly broken the bone sticking through a jagged tear in the skin of his shin and blood gushed from a huge gash on his head. Blood trickled from his mouth and ear and he seemed not to be breathing.

Jim expertly felt his neck for a pulse. It was there; very faint, but there. Anton had already called the emergency rescue team from the mobile he kept in a waterproof pouch around his neck and they could hear the blades of the helicopter in the distance. They waited beside Eddie, letting off a flare when they were sure the helicopter was close enough to see it.

The rescue from the time of Anton's phone call to Eddie being airlifted to the hospital in Albany took exactly three quarters of an hour. The lads got back in their kayaks, watching the helicopter take off and then paddled away. Eddie's family were not informed of his accident until the next day. The boys had told the emergency crew where he was staying and they told the local police who eventually retrieved his details from his wallet there. Mrs Juno let them in and offered to call Arabella.

Two days later Eddie was transferred to hospital in New York and news of his accident had hit the world's press. Leila read about it in the newspaper

Banking Heir in Serious Accident.

Edward Lancaster III Close to Death.

Leila immediately called Amir.

"I have to go to Eddie," she said, close to tears. "He was so good, so patient when I was shot; they say he is very badly hurt."

"I believe so," Amir said. When would this nightmare end, he thought. Leila should be keeping away from Eddie, not running to his side, but he knew it was pointless to argue with her.

"Dear Uncle, I hate to ask you, I know you are so busy, but would you and auntie Marwa please come with me? Just until my parents can get there from Saudi Arabia. I can't go on my own. I will speak to Harry and his wife; you remember, they were in Dubai, and they have said I am always welcome to stay with them, with the girls, I know it is a lot to ask, but I could ask them if you could stay too?"

"Slow down; it's all right, Leila, we were due to go out to New York soon anyway, and we have an open invitation from one of Marwa's sisters who lives there. Let me know what flight you book on and we will book on the same one."

Twenty-four hours later, Leila arrived at the door of Eddie's private room. Eddie's condition had been stabilized but he remained in a coma. His leg and several ribs had been broken and there was a fracture to his vertebrae. There were question marks over whether he would be completely paralyzed from the neck down, but this was all academic speculation when compared to his skull fracture and the possibility that he may have sustained brain damage that would render him a vegetable if he ever came out of his coma.

Edward and Arabella, unused to any meaningful contact with each other, struggled to comfort each other and eventually retreated into their own private worlds. They sat either together or separately at their son's bedside, making sure that he was never alone in case he woke. Now they were being told that a friend of his had come from the UK to see him and Arabella who was in the room at the time that Leila arrived followed the nurse outside into the corridor, curious to see who this young woman could be. She must be someone significant if she had flown all the way from the UK. Perhaps someone that Eddie was involved with? Arabella dismissed this idea as soon as she saw Leila dressed in a demure black dress with her black hijab tied around her hair, the stray tendril of hair that always escaped visible over her left eye. This girl was very beautiful but hardly Eddie's type. As she looked Leila up and down she realized that she did not really know what Eddie's "type" was any more. She had been so wrapped up with her own life she could not recall the last time that she had seen him with a girl.

"Good morning, Mrs Lancaster." Leila extended her hand to Arabella, who took it briefly.

"I am a friend of Eddie's. We used to be at Harvard together and he was very kind to me recently when I was in hospital in the UK."

Arabella looked at the girl again. Surely this could

not be the girl that had kept Eddie from is work and his home for so long, the girl whose pull on Eddie had wound Edward up so much, and could ultimately have cost the bank the Lewa Project? It was not possible. But apparently it was, and here was the young woman, living proof that the stories that they had began to doubt about his being with a friend were true.

"May I see Eddie, please?" Leila said to end the awkward silence and the open visual examination that Arabella was subjecting her to.

"Yes; go ahead." Arabella, still stunned, stood aside to let Leila enter the room.

In the bed Eddie did not look like the man that had left her in London. His face was pale and the side of his mouth was crusted. Electrodes were attached to his battered head, one side shaved where a jagged scar had been stitched shut over his fracture. Drips and other machines were attached to him and monitors recorded his heartbeat and various other values. Leila tried to think that this is how she must have looked after she had been shot but she could not stop the shock rising in her and a deep sadness coming over her. She reached out to his hand and touched it gently. There was no response. She said his name and still no response.

Arabella was at her elbow and Leila asked, "How did this happen?"

"He was canoeing, or kayaking, with a group at a Lake in New York State." Arabella looked at Leila, searching for a reaction. Leila looked surprised but not shocked, and nodded, but asked no more.

Shortly afterwards Edward arrived. He was surprised to see Leila and tried to understand what it was about this woman that Eddie found irresistible. He could not; she was so far from the kind of woman that he liked and thought that his son liked too.

Leila felt intimidated and shy with Eddie's parents and they both realized that. Despite her unease, however she was polite and gentle and drew from both of them, for the time being, a grudging respect.

Edward said in a low voice, "Dr Jessop is coming to see us in a moment. He wants to talk to us about Eddie's condition." Something in the way he looked made Arabella go cold. "He wants to talk to us about ..." Edward hesitated, "... about turning the machines off."

"No," Arabella shrieked, and Leila put her hand to her face. Dr Jessop arrived a moment later.

"Is it all right if I stay? Or would you like me to leave?" Leila asked.

"Stay if you want," Edward said.

Dr Jessop was a man of Edward's age, and he had Eddie's chart with him.

He had a kind face and he spoke softly. " I want you to understand that we are not thinking of turning off the life support for Eddie now, or at any time until you are ready but I do need you to understand a little about the persistent vegetative condition. The outcome for coma and vegetative state depends on the cause and on the location, severity, and extent of neurological damage, and as we have said outcomes range from recovery to death. People may emerge from a coma with a combination of physical, intellectual and psychological difficulties that need special attention. Recovery usually occurs gradually, with patients acquiring more and more ability to respond. Some patients never progress beyond very basic responses, but many recover full awareness. Patients recovering from coma require close medical supervision. A coma rarely lasts more than two to four weeks. Some patients may regain a degree of awareness after vegetative state. Others may remain in a vegetative state for years or even decades. The most common cause of death for a person in a vegetative state is infection such as pneumonia and we are of course doing all we can to make sure that Eddie gets the best treatment. It is too soon to say with any certainty what his long-term prognosis will be. The swelling in his brain has not completely resolved yet. We are watching him carefully, but I did want you to be aware of the whole picture. With God's grace it will not come to a choice for you to make, but you need to be aware that it might."

Edward, Arabella and Leila stood in shocked silence. Leila looked across at the bed. Eddie was sleeping like a child. If it were not for the tubes and wires he would look peaceful and untroubled. The thought that his life might be ended was unthinkable. Leila thought that probably that was how Eddie had felt seeing her in her hospital bed, although she had been conscious once she had got out of ICU. Brain injuries were always what she was most afraid of. The brain was so complex that the slightest thing could throw it into imbalance. She could not bear to think of

Eddie as anything less than the vital, intelligent, funny and compassionate man who had been her friend for so many years.

Edward stared at the doctor. He could not believe that with all his money and influence he could do nothing for his son. He felt helpless, impotent and not for the first time in the past few years, he felt his life was unraveling.

Arabella held a handkerchief to her mouth and sobbed quietly. She did not want to deal with this, did not want to feel Edward's hand on her shoulder in an awkward touch, almost that of a stranger, which, she thought, in reality was probably what he had become over the long empty years of their marriage. She felt old and unloved and although she hated herself for it, she thought about Sharif, as she did for most of her waking hours. She had not heard from him for the longest time and she had now accepted that she never would. Why should she? Despite her plastic surgeon's best efforts, she was almost an old lady, and with a world of women to choose from why would he choose her? He wouldn't; that was clear. She looked at her son lying in the bed, at the mercy of the medical team who were looking after him. How could she think about Sharif at a time like this? She hated herself, and hated her life.

Eddie's parents left after a while and Leila remained sitting quietly at Eddie's bedside. She did not want to be where she was not wanted or overstay her welcome but she could not bear to think that Eddie would be left lying alone in his bed. So she sat for hours silently examining every feature of his sleeping face, remembering the times that they had had together, and praying.

At his sister-in-law's apartment in Manhatten, Amir was putting the final touches to a document for publication the next day in the *Financial Times*. He was frustrated beyond belief. Just when they seemed to be getting somewhere with the Islamic finance message an attack had come form the American Bankers' Association, accusing Islamic finance of being unaccountable. It was a difficult one for Amir. He agreed with them to a certain extent but he did not want the impetus to be lost, the awareness of Islamic finance to be sullied, or its credibility dismissed. He would have to word his article carefully. He read through the final draft:

Shariah banking has been trying to market itself to investors, businesses and the general public as a credible alternative to conventional western banking. At first glance, exponents of Islamic finance certainly have a bulletproof argument - which the reckless risk-taking and bad decisions that tipped global banking into meltdown and will do again, could not happen under the wise leadership of the Shariah sector.

If only it were that simple. While international finance suffered humiliating government bailouts, there is little evidence that Islamic banking has stepped in to fill the void. But Shariah baking's secular cousin, the ethical banking sector, has clearly benefited.

Are the men at the top of the Islamic finance tree engaging in self-criticism and calls for rejuvenation? Is there even much call from outside this elite group for a revolution that could bring success?

There are 1.7 billion Moslems. The rate of education in the Moslem world stands at 40 per cent - that is, 680 million with a basic education. Of this number, 0.01 per cent - 680,000 - are highly educated. There are 1500 BA graduates from Shariah and fiqh colleges per year, and 300 Masters and 30 PhDs in Al-Azhar University in Egypt alone. There are around 16 Islamic teaching universities in Islamic countries plus several universities in the Western counties that confer PhDs. Put simply, the number of candidates capable and competent of serving as Shari'ah board members exceeds 6800 candidates, the fact is that there are many more fully qualified candidates who would be suitable for Shariah board membership than would be required!

When Islamic finance was taking shape in the West, it needed help from scholars able to advise on the principles and prohibitions under Shariah. These consultants provided advice and helped to set up a working practice, although they did not understand how the Western economic system was regulated, governed and run. In most cases they made a positive attempt to create a working Islamic system by Islamising the existing conventional system. It has worked fairly well but not enough to create a truly alternative financial system.

To make themselves valuable and for personal gain, Shariah scholars have managed to create a mysterious screen, one that has made the financial industry believe that, without them, our sector can't be Islamic. The origin of trading and dealings in Islam emphasizes permissibility - prohibition is the exception. The scholars have reversed the principle and made the exceptional - which needs their advice and stamp - supersede the basic fact of Islam of the middleness between far right and far left. This is similar to the Catholic Church, which puts its priests as mediators between God and people, "the issue of confession".

Huge increases in oil prices have led Western financial institutions to look at investing surplus cash into Islamic Shariah-compliant investments to satisfy their clients. Western financial institutions are not that concerned about which investment, but by having Shariah board members create a "glass barrier"—of that permissible and that not permissible—they will distance themselves from the whole Islamic system, and the global economy misses out on a fair and just economic system.

Graduates of the Islamic Studies may attain the qualifications necessary to sit on Shariah boards, but they have found it difficult to open the door because the Old Guard is protecting their own personal interests under the umbrella of experience and qualifications. But it is they who need the experience of the world economy; the new blood is the only hope for Islamic financial to become an alternative to the conventional system.

a tender power

With Shariah boards so insulated from accountability and scrutiny, they can go on in defiance—or in ignorance, if we're being charitable - of the real world. We must not forget that this young system is still run by some of the very people who pioneered it, along with their loyal acolytes. Criticism and accountability, they would say, is not part of the model because the backbone of Shariah banking is the Holy Quran itself. Who can argue with that?

Shariah scholars are allowed to sit on numerous boards and gain a kind of celebrity status in financial circles, acting as rubber stamps for new products - of which there are shockingly few. Imagine the media reaction if it were discovered that the chairman of Shell or Barclays was a member of 76 other boards, possibly with competing interests, was remunerated handsomely and was rarely if ever seen around the table. Surely there would be a shareholders' revolt, or possibly at least the threat of a government inquiry.

If we're hoping for a consistent approach to be imposed by the IFSB, we might have some time to wait. After much deliberation and consultation, the board issued two important drafts: Guiding principles on the Shariah governance system and IFSB exposure draft on conduct of business". Accountability is given supreme importance, but nowhere in the pages of these highly detailed documents does the issue of accountability or transparency get an airing. Competence, independence, confidentiality and consistency are certainly given the IFSB treatment, but the elephant must have been led into another room, if and when the subject of accountability came up.

The AAOIF produced a complementary document whose four aims are to:

Complement other prudential standards issued by the IFSB by highlighting in more detail, to the supervisory authorities in particular and the industry's other stakeholders in general, the components of a sound Shariah governance system, especially with regard to the competence, independence, confidentiality and consistency of Shariah boards;

Facilitate a better understanding of Shariah governance issues and outline how stakeholders should satisfy themselves once an appropriate and effective Shariah governance system is in place.

Provide an enhanced degree of transparency in terms of issuance, and the audit/review process for compliance with Shariah rulings; and

Provide greater harmonization of the Shariah governance structures and procedures across jurisdictions, especially since there are increasing numbers of IFIs with cross-border operations.

It would appear that they also see no need for an urgent review of corporate governance or accountability.

So where are the calls for accountability from outside the inner circles? They are surprisingly numerous, but uncoordinated and dispersed enough to be described as being from individual cranks, bitter dissenters or heretics.

Perhaps the case for reform and accountability has not been put strongly enough. In my experience, even some relatively astute members of the Shariah banking community express surprise at the mere existence of an opposing view from the status quo. Opening minds to the inertia and nepotism at the top of the sector is the first step on the path to reform. But for the sake of Islamic finance it is vital that Shariah board members become more accountable.

The most important reason is credibility. Investors - be they fund managers or families— need to feel that the people looking after their money are trustworthy. As things stand, they have to take a guess or a leap of faith, and the post-recession figures breathtakingly suggest that the discredited mainstream sector is still a more attractive option to many Moslems.

Next up is confidence. The markets are confidence. Fortunes are made and lost on good and bad feeling, and strong businesses are better able to reinvest and become stronger still. Investors simply don't know enough about the running and decision-making of Islamic banks to place their money confidently in them.

If a transparent model can be successfully adopted in combination with the inherently risk-averse and conscientious of Shariah banking, the sector could act as an example to conventional banking. Shariah financial experts' opinions would be sought and valued, and the kudos of this model would blossom. Perhaps, then, Western banking would take notice and avoid another catastrophe.

The credibility that comes with board membership counts only if the board served on is itself credible, just as a footballer's credibility is enhanced when he plays for a top club. It is in board members' interests to improve credibility, but this ostensibly only the members themselves can resolve chicken-and-egg situation.

The Islamic financial system can be viewed as oil to the global system's water – that is, the two simply don't mix. If the doors are opened, people will see that the two systems have more similarities than differences, and that the two are compatible.

The tools that form the basis of Islamic finance - its risk management mechanisms - is pretty solid, perhaps more so in theory than in their currently applied practice. But they would, if more widely understood, be of great value to world banking.

a tender power

All religions and philosophies have an alien feel to them outside their heartlands, and Islam is no exception. By introducing a modern and successful Shariah banking sector, the principles of ethics, fairness and honesty that underpin Islam would be better understood globally.

Not all Moslems are experts on the Shariah, which is why we haves scholars and jurists. Managers and shareholders will get better quality advice under an open door, transparency-based system.

Sometimes it feels like the same old products are being tinkered with and peddled without regard to the goings on in the rest of the financial world. A new, credible system of board administration will allow research into and development of brand new products designed from scratch that will be open to examination and approval the world over.

First, fatwas issued with the full consideration of transparent boards will be granted more respect globally. Second, the open demonstration of the strict auditing standards that have helped to keep Islamic finance on an even keel throughout the crisis would serve as a demonstration of all that is stable about Shariah finance. Third, corporate governance of Islamic financial institutions - always a matter for concern for those on the outside (and many inside) - would be strengthened immeasurably if all dealings and decisions were transparent.

With the existing and potential advances Islamic finance has made in recent years, it is worth reminding ourselves that it is adherence to Islam that lies at the heart of all we do. By promoting the benefits of transparent governance and the resulting success of the Islamic banking sector, the ethical principles underpinning Shariah banking will be preserved.

If Islamic principles are followed, there would be no fraud or abuse in banking. Openness would simply guarantee this. The money-laundering and capital adequacy issues of Basel II and Pillar II would be upheld.

At present, anyone on a board can hide behind the layers of secrecy to perform illicit transactions. The solution is not as difficult as it seems - consistency with our religious principles must ultimately prevail if Islamic finance is to succeed.

Amir hesitated for just a moment before he hit the send button that would take his work to the editor of the Financial Times. What he was saying would win him enemies and would be pounced upon by Western bankers wishing to discredit the Islamic banking system. But Amir knew that it was a necessary step; he had to acknowledge the criticism, take ownership of the problem; if he did not it would be too easy for his opponents to use them against him. He knew that the time was coming when Islamic finance would be important in the world. He could almost see the Western banking system slipping ever nearer to the abyss, and he and the others who believed in the system had to be ready, to have faced all comers and to have acknowledged their weaknesses and imperfections. As he got up from the computer, he thought that he had better go to the hospital and see Leila and Eddie, although from what Leila had said the poor man was in a coma it was thought that he might never come out of. Amir sighed and shook his head. Lancaster's bank was one of the banks that he could see was close to the edge; their stock had been falling steadily due in part to the collapse of the Lewa project that had been abandoned in the financial crisis in Dubai and only last week had been reported as having gone bust. He felt sorry for Eddie's father, Edward Lancaster; things were certainly tough in his life, and although he had always been one of Amir's harshest critics, Amir had always thought that Eddie would be more open-minded, and maybe offered the only hope for Lancaster's Bank. Now that was looking unlikely.

Arabella had returned to the hospital to find Leila still there. She was bemused; surely there had been nothing between Eddie and this frumpy looking woman? She felt a bit irritated, guilty maybe that this woman had sat by her son while she had not.

"So kind of you to visit my son, but I would really rather you did not come for a while. There are many others who want to visit and we will call you if anything changes," Arabella said in her clipped English accent.

Leila reeled at the hostility seeping out of Arabella and almost ran out of the room. In the corridor she bumped into Amir and Marwa. She had not seen them since she had arrived and she hugged them, tears in her eyes.

"Oh, Uncle, he is so sick; I just can't believe it. They came and talked to his parents about turning off his life support machines! And his mother has asked me not to visit." Leila sobbed on Amir's shoulder and he noticed how fragile she was under her clothes, as he patted her on the back. She was skin and bone; there was nothing to her. He felt concern for her wash over him as Marwa led her to a chair.

Chapter Thirty

In another part of the hospital, in the cafeteria, Sharif sat reading a newspaper, a bulletin on Eddie's health giving a grave warning about how badly injured he was. Sharif smiled to himself. It was ironic, after all the effort he had put into getting rid of that particular thorn in his side, it seemed that Eddie's own attempt to impress some kids had almost killed him. Sharif laughed out loud. A few heads turned towards him. One in particular, recognizing his laugh, spun round from the counter where she was buying water. Arabella had to fight hard not to fall to the floor. She could not believe it; Sharif was there in the hospital. Leaving the counter without the water she walked unsteadily over to him, banging into several chairs as she walked, kicking one woman's purse clear across the room as she stumbled towards Sharif. Too late. Sharif spotted her, and before he could get out of his chair, she was in the chair opposite him, her face florid, her eyes hungry and desperate in a way that turned his stomach. In the harsh strip lighting of the canteen she looked as though she was made of wax, a cold sweat standing out on her upper lip and on her brow and Sharif felt his stomach lurch uncomfortably. He hated to be trapped, to be out of control in any situation, and that was how he was feeling now as several more heads had swivelled to watch Arabella's unsteady progress towards him.

"Sharif, my love, you dear man, coming here because you have heard about my son." Arabella indicated the paper he had open on the table in front of him.

Sharif did not know what to say. His dark eyes darted around the canteen, looking for a way out, watching the nosy onlookers, waiting for their attention to be diverted elsewhere so that he could make his getaway. He cursed himself for coming to the hospital. Why had he done it? He was getting sloppy.

"How is he?" he asked Arabella.

"Oh, much the same," she said, then brushing concern for Eddie aside she lowered her voice and leaned towards him, the skin of her cleavage crepey and loose. More work to be done, he thought, feeling the Danish he had had with his coffee threatening to make a reappearance.

"When can we meet?" The predatory look in her eye reminded Sharif of a cat playing with a mouse before devouring it and he felt bile rise in his throat.

"I am sorry,;I am not feeling well," he said, pushing his seat back so violently that it fell back. And with that he made a very ungraceful dash for the men's room.

As he fled from the restaurant, Sharif did not notice the man staring at him from the news-stand that was at the entrance to the canteen. Edward Lancaster would have been powerless to speak to him any way. He stood frozen to the spot. He had watched his wife pounce on his old enemy in a way that sent chills down his spine. It was obvious the pair knew each other and more than that, by his wife's body language, in which she had all but stripped her bony old body naked, and laid it out on the table in front of the man, that they had obviously been intimate. The idea made him physically retch. How could she? She, who had shown no interest in him, ever, apart from the necessary contact to produce Eddie, was giving herself to this dirty … A cold fist closed around his stomach as he thought about all the times over the years that he had puzzled over how Sharif had known about his family's movements so precisely. Now he knew. His mind swung to Hesham. Did he know? It seemed impossible to imagine that the man he had employed to help him overcome Sharif and who seemed to know everything about everyone, especially Sharif, did not know that he was sleeping with Arabella? He felt his breath coming shorter as he tried to unravel the tangle of thoughts in his head. Did Hesham know? If he did, why hadn't he told him? If he didn't, why didn't he? Edward steadied himself on the counter of the newsstand, vaguely aware of the assistant asking him for the money for the newspaper he had put on the counter, and he looked towards her.

"Sir? Are you alright?" The alarm on the woman's face told Edward that he looked as bad as he felt. "Shall I call someone?" Edward waved his hand, dismissing her offer and, leaving his paper on the counter, he stumbled to the lift shaft.

As the lift doors closed, Arabella came out to the foyer where she waited outside the men's room for half an hour. Then, looking at her watch she realised that Edward would be here by now so she would have to go or explain her long absence. By the time that she got up to Eddie's room Edward had composed himself, but he felt hatred tighten his chest as he looked at her.

Edward had brought some CDs that Eddie had had in

456

his car and his apartment. The doctors had told them that sometimes something familiar could jolt a coma patient into consciousness. As Arabella sat at her son's bedside she hated herself for being so distracted, so preoccupied with Sharif, but she couldn't help it; she was furious that she had had to leave before she could arrange a meeting with him but at least now he knew that she wanted to see him. And he would be in touch. Surely he would, wouldn't he?

Edward played the music to Eddie, but there was no response at all. Finally he turned it off and began to speak to his son. He told him of what had been going on at that bank, although he did not mention the Lewa project or how dire the situation was. He told Eddie how friends were and how Harry had asked to come and see him and of the many others had phoned with their good wishes. Nothing, no response at all.

The nurse had given them a video that had been dropped off. On it someone had written "To Eddie, get better soon, man! Your kayaking friends." Slotting it into the machine of the entertainment unit on the wall, Edward watched as the home-made video flickered onto the plasma screen. In it his son sat with three young men. He seemed to be talking to them about something. Edward turned the sound up. For a moment or two he could not grasp what they were talking about but then the words Islamic finance gave him the context he was searching for. He and Arabella sat transfixed as their son's animated face filled the screen, his passion for the subject he was talking about obvious. Edward felt tears streaming down his face as he realised he might just as well have been looking at a stranger. How could this have happened that the son that he loved so much was so unknown to him? Hell, they worked together, how could he know so little about this passionate and eloquent man that was his son? And now it might be too late. Arabella was staring at him as he made no attempt to hide his emotion. He thought he saw tears in his wife's eyes. Perhaps she was feeling the same regret for the fact that they had let their son drift so far away from them. Edward put his hand out for hers, and she extended hers briefly, giving his a sort of awkward little shake before replacing it in her lap.

Edward felt a wave of despair wash over him. He had made a mess of his marriage and his relationship with his son. As Eddie's voice filled the room he looked over at his son's still form in the bed and wept openly.

Eventually, as his sobs subsided, the film finished.

"You speak to him." Edward prompted his wife, his voice still raw with tears.

Lost in her own thoughts, Arabella was taken by surprise and started to repeat the messages of well wishes that Edward had already spoken of.

"I've said that, Arabella; weren't you listening? Say something different. Doesn't this mean anything to you?"

"Of course it does." Arabella cleared her throat

"Your friend Leila is here from the UK," Arabella said, spitting the name out as though it was poison. Almost imperceptibly, Eddie's eyelids flickered momentarily and Edward clasped his hand.

"Son, did you hear your mother? Squeeze my hand if you can hear me. Leila is outside. Do you want her to come in?"

For a long moment there was nothing and then the slightest, weakest of pressure from Eddie's hand in his father's.

"Again, Eddie, squeeze my hand again."

Again Edward felt the faintest of pressure on his hand from Eddie's. It could almost have been an involuntary spasm of the muscles but Edward knew it was not. Even Arabella was sitting on the edge of her seat.

"*Leila.*" Edward repeated the name slowly. "Do you want to see Leila?" Again there was a faint movement of Eddie's eyelids and the faint pressure on his father's hand.

"He wants to see the girl from the UK!" Edward said. She might be the answer! She might be able to get through!"

"I sent her away," Arabella said quietly.

"You did what? Why?" Edward asked.

"Oh, I don't know! She was getting me down, hanging round like a bad smell!" Arabella said viciously. Edward stared at his wife, his jaw clenched. He could not be bothered to wonder at her motives, he could not be bothered to think about her at all. In fact he hated her, he realized. She was selfish and seemed not to be that interested in their son's condition. In fact she might even have been the source of all the attempts made on his life, through her association with Sharif. Edward had never hated anyone as much as he hated his wife in this moment.

"Maybe she is still here. I thought I saw her outside." Edward strode out of the room. If this girl was the only person that her son would respond to, then she had to be there. As he searched the corridor he thought about the last conversation he had had with Eddie, how he had all but accused him of being weak and pathetic, and what about his mother's last conversation with her son? God knew, Edward thought, it was likely that she could not even remember the last time she had spoken to Eddie apart from to respond to his request to have the Lake House opened up. They had been miserable parents to their son, Edward admitted to himself. He had wanted for nothing material, but the love and support of two parents who cared about each other and him? Edward thought he spotted Leila talking to a couple at the waiting area next to the nurse's station. As he walked up to them, he saw that Leila was crying. The result of Arabella's cruelty no doubt.

He smiled at her.

"I am so sorry about my wife; she is under a lot of pressure," he lied. "I just want you to know that you can visit Eddie any time. In fact, when I mentioned your name just now there was a flicker of response, so perhaps , if you have the time, you could sit with him?" Edward held his breath. But he need not have worried. Leila was on her feet and almost running along the corridor back to Eddie's room.

Arabella was there when they arrived. She got up and made to leave the room but Edward caught her arm in his hand, holding it so tight that it hurt his fingers, leaving white imprints on her sallow skin. He would have liked to snap her scrawny arm in two, his hatred had such a grip of him, and he could see beads of perspiration standing out on Arabella's lip as she clenched her teeth against the pain, looking at him wild-eyed, genuinely afraid of this new side of him.

"My wife would like to apologize to you, Leila," he said, ignoring Arabella's struggle to free herself. "Wouldn't you?" He squeezed tighter.

"Yes," she said through gritted teeth. "I'm sorry."

"And she would like you to come as often as you can, to see Eddie, isn't that right?"

"Yes, please, as often as you can." Edward released her arm and stumbling slightly she backed hastily out of the room.

But Leila was not listening. She only had eyes for Eddie and before the door had even closed behind Arabella she was sitting beside his bed.

She fell to her knees beside Eddie, clasping his hand with both of hers. "Eddie," she whispered softly, "I'm here, Eddie; you can wake up now." For a moment there was nothing and then slowly his eyelids opened a fraction. Leila kissed the tips of her fingers and pressed them to first one eyelid and then the other, and Eddie's eyes opened a fraction more.

Behind her Edward had come back into the room and held his breath as his son's eyes began to open. He wanted to rush to his bedside, to kneel beside Leila, but he knew instinctively that this was a moment that Eddie and Leila needed to have together. As he stood in the quiet room Edward thought that he could feel a physical wave of love emanating from this quiet, dignified young woman who had obviously stolen his son's heart. Edward felt ashamed of himself for thinking of her in physical terms, for wondering if she and Eddie had a physical relationship. It seemed unlikely but he could not comprehend a love that could exist without the very Western expectation and almost routine sharing of bodies, often without much other common ground. But looking at Leila, being in her presence, he could see that it was more than that, much more than that. She had touched his son's very soul. For a moment he felt jealous, jealous that his son should know a love he had never experienced.

"Eddie." Leila was continuing to talk softly to Eddie and as she opened her hands so that his hand lay flat on hers Edward saw Eddie's fingers moving, as though he was trying to curl them around Leila's.

"That's right, habibi, hold my hand, I'm here to help you; you are going to get better!"

Eddie's eyes were moving behind his half-closed lids now and Edward sat down, unable to trust his legs to hold him. He sat on the other side of the bed and as he did, Leila looked up at him. The love and the tenderness that shone from her eyes took his breath away momentarily.

She continued to speak to Eddie, talking about times they had shared and Edward felt almost like a voyeur as he learned about a life that his son had led that he had known nothing about. He thought about the way he had treated Eddie when he came back from Leila's bedside in London. He felt deeply ashamed.

The nurse on duty had called Eddie's doctor, Dr Jessop, and he stood quietly at the end of the bed as Eddie continued to move his eyes, making real grasping movements with the hand that lay in Leila's.

"Are you going to examine him?" Edward asked.

Dr Jessop waved his hand in a motion that said he was not.

"Some things are more powerful than our feeble scientific attempts to intervene." Edward looked at the man and felt the hairs on the back of his neck rise.

It was true; the change that was coming over Eddie, gathering momentum as every minute passed, could not be explained as anything short of a miracle. As this remarkable woman's voice surrounded him, softly coaxing him to understand and to come back to her, Eddie was easing his way back into the conscious world. The door to the room opened and more medical staff came in. Edward found himself hoping that Arabella would not come back. Spitefully, as a parent, he wanted this moment to be his alone; he wanted to deny her this miracle, hoped with all his heart that she would miss it.

On the bed, sounds were beginning to come from deep in Eddie's throat. Hoarse and unintelligible at first but then more distinct, the same name over and over again. "Leila, Leila."

Edward looked at Leila, tears were streaming down her cheeks, her hand now clasped tightly around Eddie's, willing him to open his eyes, to look at her.

And then he did. Through half-closed eyelids, he focused on her and the moment his eyes met hers, his mouth twitched in an unmistakable smile. Leila was crying now, her tears flowing unchecked down her face, her shoulders shaking and through her tears she smiled down at Eddie as a small frown creased his brow.

"Why ... crying?" Even from where he was sitting, the words were clear to Edward and they were words that came from a brain able to reason, able to enquire, a brain that would recover! He found himself crying too.

As Eddie opened his eyes fully, he smiled up at Leila then looked beyond her to the medical team standing three deep in the room. Edward followed his son's gaze and was surprised to see at least a dozen doctors and other professionals in the room. Dr Jessop had Eddie's file open in his hands and was studying it, shaking his head slightly. Behind the bed the monitors that had faithfully recorded every brain wave and heartbeat since Eddie was admitted were alive with frantic activity.

"Excuse me a moment," Dr Jessop said to Leila, trying to get to the machines behind the bed, but as she rose from her chair to leave, Eddie's hand suddenly clasped hers in a vice-like grip and she sat down again, surprised.

Dr Jessop smiled as Eddie said, "No! Don't go."

"I'm not, habibi; the doctor needs to see you now. I'll be right there."

Eddie loosened his grip but followed her with his eyes as she walked over to the other side of the bed. Dr Jessop pressed a button and a long ribbon of paper spewed from the machine measuring Eddie's brain function. He looked across at Edward and indicated that he should follow him into the corridor.

In the corridor more medical and nursing staff were queuing to get into the room. Edward realised what an unusual medical outcome that this must be presenting. As Dr Jessop led Edward along to the day room he was still studying Eddie's chart and the machine's findings.

"I can tell you frankly' Edward, I'm baffled; everything I am seeing here tells me that Eddie should be still in a coma, and that we should be having another conversation about switching off his life support."

Edward swallowed hard. He could barely take it all in. "Thank you, Frank," he managed through a voice thick with emotion.

"Don't thank me, Edward, I've done nothing. I really can't explain it. I do remember, when I had only newly qualified, there was a man who went into a coma after a serious car crash during his late teens and woke nearly two decades later as a middle-aged man with an adult daughter."

"Really?" Edward said. Frank Jessop nodded.

"He was 19 and newly married with a baby daughter when his truck plunged through a guardrail and he was left paralysed and in a coma. He remained outwardly unresponsive for years, and his recovery was all the more remarkable because he was never given specialist care. His father was too poor to afford a neurological examination and state medical insurance was reluctant to pay for a man not expected to return to the work force. But, according to the popular legend the family never gave up hope. His parents and wife continued to hold one-sided conversations at his bedside, and brought him home from hospital on alternate weekends. At the time I remember that the conclusion was drawn that this stimulation kept his mind functioning. A few years before he regained consciousness, he began responding to questions by blinking his eyes. Then suddenly, out of nowhere, he spoke for the first time, calling out for his mother.

"His powers of speech slowly returned, and he was able to tell his family that he remembered snatches of the conversation from around his bedside. His speech remained laboured, and he was left with short-term memory problems, but none the less it was the most amazing thing I had ever seen, until today."

"Will Eddie make a full recovery?"

Frank Jessop shrugged his broad shoulders. "Hey, Edward, I wouldn't have given you any odds an hour ago that he would even survive this. By the way, who is that woman? I am sure it's just coincidence that he has come round at this time, but all the same she seems to have played a part in coaxing him along."

Edward slumped down on one of the chairs in the day room. He suddenly felt exhausted. "Frank, it is everything to do with her; I could almost feel the energy in the room, something like a force field." Edward struggled for the right words. "Something went on in that room, something beyond any understanding, and the only word I can think of to describe it is love, pure and simple."

"Eddie and that woman?" Frank Jessop sat down next to his old friend.

"Leila; her name is Leila."

"Eddie and Leila?" Frank looked at his friend.

"Yes, but not in the way you think. They met at Harvard and have kept in touch." Edward realised how totally inadequately his words described the bond between his son and this amazing woman. In his mind what he had just witnessed was nothing short of a miracle. "Is there any chance he might, you know, slip back?" he asked

Again Frank Jessop shrugged. "I shouldn't think so but look, what has happened here so far today has defied science, so I really don't have anything I can say for definite."

The door to the day room opened and a nurse came in. "Mr Lancaster, your son is asking for you!" her face was flushed with excitement, and Edward recognised her as one of the nurses who had been in regular attendance at Eddie's bedside.

Edward was out of his seat and out of the door before she could finish the sentence. In the room, the crowd of medics had dissipated somewhat and Leila sat quietly beside Eddie, his hand in hers. Her face was serene and lovely and Edward thought again that something about her almost defied worldly description.

"Hi, dad," Eddie croaked, and Leila applied a little cream to his dry lips.

"Eddie, son." Edward felt tears in his throat choking off the words he wanted to say.

"Damned Silver Staircase!" he said with a weak smile and all of a sudden they were laughing together, remembering the times they had fought about Eddie going down the unforgiving water of the Silver Staircase when he was younger.

"You'll put me in an early grave, son!" Edward said.

"That's the idea; all that money!" Eddie joked and Edward picked up his son's other hand from where it lay on the white sheets of his bed. He realised that he had not held his son's hand since he was a little boy crossing a busy New York street. It felt so good to feel his warm flesh, responsive in his.

"Shall I leave you for a while?" Leila asked.

"No!" Edward noticed a slight grimace on Leila's face as Eddie tightened his grip on her hand to prevent her leaving. It was almost as though he was afraid that if she left he would relapse.

"Eddie, Leila may need to go to the powder room or something," Edward chided.

"Oh sure, sorry Leila." It was very much the old Eddie who smiled up at Leila as she left, casting a grateful glance in Edward's direction. "Where's mom?" Eddie asked.

Edward's jaw tightened and he said, "She had to go

home; no one really expected that you would ... that it would be so soon ... that you would be up to speaking to people today."

Eddie laughed hoarsely. "You mean you all thought I was a gonner! Well you don't get rid of me that easy!" Edward put a hand out and touched his son's face. "Aw, come on, dad; don't go all soppy on me!"

Edward swallowed his tears. It felt like a second chance to him, a second chance to know and to love his son.

As the days passed Leila more or less camped in Eddie's room. Leaving discretely when Arabella came in, she stayed when Edward did, and she noticed that they never came together.

Leila felt sorry for Arabella. The woman was hard, brittle and obviously very unhappy. Where most other mothers would be overjoyed in her situation she seemed distracted and unhappy, preoccupied and restless and she only ever stayed for as long as would seem a suitable amount of time.

Amir and Marwa came in often, visited briefly with Eddie and then sat in the day room, offering Leila support and news from the outside world. Her twins were having a ball staying with Harry and his family, swimming in the pool and going on all sorts of interesting outings. Leila was so grateful to them but in truth having the two girls to stay had lifted the strained atmosphere of Harry's house and their laughter and hijinks were welcome.

Then one day, three young men, tall and brown from a summer spent in the sun, arrived at Eddie's door. One of them held a bunch of flowers, one a box of chocolates and the third some kayaking magazines.

As they were shown in, Eddie looked up. "What's this then, the three wise men?"

"Hey Eddie man, are we glad to see you!" Jim said.

"Hi guys, really good to see you all!" Eddie said.

"Here buddy; got you some magazines to show you how it should be done!" Anton laughed, putting the magazines down on Eddie's bedside cabinet.

"Yeah, thanks!" Eddie laughed back.

The young men looked out of place the hospital setting, their vigorous health and brown sun-kissed skin making them look out of step with the white sterile surroundings and the thinner paler patient in the bed.

Eddie introduced the boys to Leila and she smiled at them, the warm shy smile that always made Eddie's heart melt.

"Are you the lady who taught Eddie about Islamic finance?" Bill said.

"Well I can't take all the credit!" Leila said, "how did you know that?"

"When we spent the night at Eddie's lodge on the lakeside the day before his, um ..." Bill glanced at Eddie "... his accident, he spent the evening telling us a bit about it."

"Hey that's a point, Leila, is Amir here today?" Eddie asked.

"Not yet, but he should be in about half an hour or so."

"Then stick around boys and you will be in for a treat!" Eddie said.

"Amir Ali, here?" Anton looked confused.

"Yes, he has grown to know Eddie well over the years, we have all been very worried about him." Leila looked over at Eddie, her eyes soft with concern and relief that he was recovering.

"It's a kind of a cultural thing, too." Eddie said. "It would not be acceptable for Leila to spend all this time with me without a chaperone of some sort and Amir and his wife have been here a lot. I am very grateful to them, hey, and to you guys too! Without your help I guess I wouldn't be here now."

The three muttered, embarrassed. Anton broke the silence. "It's not long now till we start our next semester, Amir Ali is due to speak pretty soon after we get back. Do you think that he would see us here, give us a bit of a head start?"

"Hey, Anton, be cool man; he's not working. Just wait for term. He must have better things to think about at the moment," Bill said.

"Actually I am quite sure that he will be delighted to speak to you," Leila said. And when he arrived, Amir was indeed very pleased to meet the young men who would be his audience so soon.

Eddie was still tiring quite easily and while he napped, Amir and the boys took a stroll in the grounds of the hospital while Marwa and Leila met Sandy Masters and the twins to do some shopping.

"You know, Dr Ali, we were pretty surprised to find a dude like Eddie so stoked with Islamic finance. What with him being Lancaster bank and all that."

Amir smiled. "Well, there is an old saying: 'The truth can be found in many different places.' Maybe that is what your friend discovered. Eddie is a very deep thinker; it has taken him many years to appreciate the whole of what Islamic finance can offer, but I think he does now."

"He sure does. You should have heard him talk to us at the lodge."

"What interested you most about what he said?" Amir asked.

"I think it was the whole concept," Bill said.

Amir nodded. "It is quite difficult to grasp at first, because the conventional concept of financing is that the banks and institutions deal in money only. But the thing is that Islam except in some particular cases, does not recognize money as the subject of trade. Financing in Islam is always based on liquid assets, which creates real assets and inventories. Financing based on musharakah, mudarabah, salam and istisna' creates real assets"

"That was it!" Anton said, stumbling over the

unfamiliar word 'mudarabah'." Amir smiled.

"Well as you can imagine these means of financing are criticized as having the same result as interest-based borrowing. However, they are backed with assets and can be distinguished from interest-based borrowing on the following grounds: In conventional financing the financier has no concern about how the money is used by the client in an interest-bearing loan. In murabahah, the financier purchases the commodity the client needs, producing asset-backed financing."

Amir smiled again as he saw the interest in the boy's faces; Eddie had obviously done a good job, they were eager to hear more.

"In murabahah, the purpose of the loan must be under Shari'ah. Do you understand the term 'Shari'ah'?"

"Yes. According to Islamic law?" Jim said.

"That's right; so a loan has to conform to Shari'ah while in conventional financing there is no such ruling. So in murabahah the financier who purchases the commodity takes the risk, and the profit is the end reward for this risk and this risk is not assumed in an interest-based loan."

"So in a loan that we would understand, the repayable amount increases, but not in murabahah?" It was Jim's turn to struggle with the unfamiliar word.

"Exactly!" Amir was pleased; they had open minds, open to new concepts. "In an interest-bearing loan, the amount to be repaid increases with time, but in murabahah the price is fixed, agreed from the outset. As the risk of a lease is placed on the financier, it follows that it is the financier who will suffer the loss if it is damaged. Assets always back Islamic financial transactions; there is no gap between the supply of money and the production of real assets, which is the case in conventional economies that suffer inflation."

"But Dr Ali, until recently I can't even say that I had heard of Islamic banks. Are there really that many?" Bill asked.

"Islamic banks have been growing, and have had to contend with constraints in the non-Islamic countries in which they have been established such as lack of support from governments and legal systems making it difficult to abide with the full requirements of Shari'ah. This has been allowed for in Shari'ah, which says that in abnormal conditions some flexibility can exist. This comes from the premise that it is preferable to save those attempting to spread the word from being punished for disobedience in favour of the bigger goal of establishing a total Islamic order."

The boys looked at each other. This was difficult territory. Any talk of world domination brought with it memories of the twin towers and other terrorist atrocities. Amir, sensing their discomfort, said, "Relax, boys, I am not a terrorist, far from it, but does your religion not teach you to spread the word? That is all I am saying: we are bound by our religion to bring its message to as many people as we can. Maybe I chose my words badly. It may look an aggressive stance to you, but there is no religion that asks its followers to be secretive, not to spread the word, and Islam is no different. And my part of that is the financial side of things. I am convinced that Islamic finance is the answer to the world's economic ills and I will do all I can to get the chance to prove it."

"Well it sure as hell couldn't do any worse," Anton sighed. Have you seen the market openings this morning?"

Amir had. "Precisely. At the moment the Western banking systems are lurching from one crisis to another, and I fear the worst is still to come, the day of reckoning is about to be upon us! Look at this." Ali opened his paper and read out loud: "'Continuing with the stock market chaos of last Thursday, it appears that hedge funds have escaped suffering little losses. The Dow Jones Industrial Average shot down about 1,000 points and then bounced back before close, and few hedge funds were among the big losers that day, according to prime brokers and hedge fund investors. Two investors with client money in dozens of hedge funds told The Wall Street Journal that they expected one-day losses of no worse than 5 per cent. Prime brokers told the newspapers that smaller hedge funds could have lost as much as 20 per cent on the day, but losses of that magnitude were few and far between. Major US exchanges decided to cancel any trades made between 2:40 p.m. and 3 p.m. on Thursday at 60 per cent above or below a stock's price at 2:40 p.m. Meanwhile, regulators continue to try to figure out why the market took its unprecedented dive. The Securities and Exchange Commission and Commodity Futures Trading Commission are gathering data from exchanges, and have taken anecdotal reports from hedge funds and other market participants. The failure of electronic exchanges to slow down in tandem with the New York Stock Exchange is currently considered the leading possible culprit. The NYSE imposes a controlled slowdown in such situation to boost stability on the markets.' How long do you think this kind of yo-yo swing is viable?"

The boys nodded. Ali was enjoying talking to them; he missed giving his lectures to universities during the summer holidays and he thought that all three had the open-minded approach that had first made him admire Eddie.

"Hey, perhaps we should be getting back up to the room, see how the old man is doing!" Bill jumped up from the grass.

By the time the boys left in the afternoon, Eddie felt stronger than he had in days. He had enjoyed the teasing and the banter and the way that the three cast admiring glances at Leila. He knew that he was not the only one who could see how special she was.

Leila was his almost constant companion. They had joked about him getting his own back for all the time he had spent at her bedside and she was so kind and gentle that part of him never wanted to get well, wanted always to be in this bed being looked after by her. The only uncomfortable moments they had were when his mother came in to visit. Leila would always leave the room discreetly with his mother's eyes boring into her back as she went. Eddie could not help feeling a dislike for his mother who had neither Leila's gentle touch nor, it seemed, any desire to be beside his bedside. She would stay for as long as would seem decent during which time they would speak rarely and would flick distractedly through magazines. In some ways Eddie felt sorry for her. If any woman was the exact opposite of the serene, contended and fulfilled Leila, his mother was it. She was restless and looked haunted, as though she had not slept for a week. She looked old and worried, her shoulders tense and her thin, painted lips set in an uncompromising tight line.

The truth was that Arabella was tortured with her almost animal need to see Sharif. He had kept his silence since their chance meeting in the hospital and she was beginning to think that he did not want to see her. But that could not be possible; he had always said how he lived for their meetings, how beautiful she was.

In another part of New York Sharif had not given Arabella a second thought since he had bumped into her at the hospital. He had bigger fish to fry. The money that he had been siphoning off from Lancaster Bank over the years was about to be put to good use. When he and his lieutenants had finished, the West would be brought to its knees. He was feeling particularly pleased with himself this morning as he had got word that a particularly irritating mosquito that had buzzed around him for years had finally been swatted.

In his office, Edward studied the trading figures for Lancaster's and felt the blood drain from his face. Lancaster shares were being sold in thousands and Lancaster stock was plummeting on the exchange. He flicked the TV on, trying to find a financial commentary. As he flicked he halted at a news channel as a familiar face stared out at him. It was Hesham. He pressed the volume button.

"This morning police found the badly mutilated body

of this man in the harbour side area of the city. They say that they have rarely seen such barbaric injuries on a victim who apparently was already badly scarred and partially disabled. Police are appealing for anyone who has information about him to come forward."

Edward dropped the remote and sat down on the settee in front of the window that looked out over the city. He felt numb, but as feeling began to return he felt panic well up inside him. He was alone now, any doubt he had had about Hesham removed. Sharif was behind this, he knew that, and he knew that he was coming for him. Sharif had started with the bank; he had to be behind the share sell-off somehow. Edward knew he had neither the strength nor the courage to try and find out how and why he was doing what he was doing. And now without Hesham the last barrier had been removed. He thought about Eddie in the hospital and made a call to double security.

In the hospital Eddie and Leila, unaware of the drama being played out outside their safe cocoon, continued to enjoy each other, sometimes talking, sometimes just sitting in silence, content to be in each other's company. Neither of them knew it but it was the last peace that either of them would enjoy for a very long time.

Chapter Thirty-one

As Eddie got stronger, and summer days turned to autumn, he began to notice something in his father that he had never seen before. Suddenly his father looked old. His grey hair seemed to recede almost by the day and the lines on his face seemed deeper etched into his sallow skin. He looked pale and haggard and although Eddie knew that his accident had taken a lot out of his father he instinctively knew that there was more to his decline than that. He knew that his father had tried to keep the newspapers away from him but Eddie had seen them all and was having work sent to him from the office. The extent of the problem was profound and the cause of it baffling. He could not work out why so many Lancaster's shares were hitting the market, wave after wave of them. He could not discuss it with his father who had barred anyone in the office talking to him about work, but Harry Masters had smuggled stuff into him. Harry was worried and from what he said it seemed as though the staff of Lancaster's were pinning all their hopes on Eddie.

In truth Eddie felt well enough to return to work. His broken bones had mended and he now felt better than he had in years. The rest and even the coma Dr Jessop had said might have been a chance for him to recharge and Eddie certainly felt as though he had. He felt sharper than he had in years, and the time he had spent with Leila had soothed his soul. Even the kayak boys' visits were fun and they lapped up any information that they got from Eddie,

Leila or Amir. It was not unusual to find them all crowded into Eddie's room having an impromptu talk on one or another aspect of Islamic finance.

Today the whole group were out enjoying the warm sunshine of early autumn in the grounds. The boys sat on the grass while Eddie, Leila and Amir sat on one of the benches. Eddie walked unaided now apart from a stick; he was likely to be discharged within days.

Today the lads wanted to know about women in Islamic finance. Eddie smiled to himself as he noticed that Bill had a book on Islamic finance with him, it was one of the books that he and Leila had studied in the library all those years ago. Amir gave a mock bow in Leila's direction and said, "Leila is your woman for this; she has talked extensively all over the world on the subject. What she does not know is not worth knowing!"

The boys smiled at Leila admiringly. Leila blushed slightly and Eddie felt his heart melt; he loved her so much.

"What is it you are curious about, boys?" she asked.

"Well," Anton said shyly, obviously trying to phrase his question in a way that would cuase no offence. "We always thought that women were, well, sort of, second-class citizens, no, maybe that's not right, I mean sort of under the control of men, no, that's not right either ..." he tailed off, embarrassed, and the others laughed at him.

"It's okay, Anton; I now what you mean." Leila smiled at the awkward young man. "It is an opinion that is often expressed by those outside the world of Islam who think that Moslem women are treated as second-class citizens, with few options or opportunities in life. Like most prejudices, this opinion is not based on much of a solid foundation. Whilst the equality gap certainly could - and should - be narrower, it would be wrong to assume that the problem is significantly worse than in Western society."

The boys looked at each other. This was news to them.

"Let me try and explain contemporary roles of women, as laid down by the Qur'an, particularly as it applies to Islamic finance, and tell you about a notable woman who has made a contribution that simply would not have been possible, were the imagined restrictions on women by Islam, based on truth."

Eddie smiled as he heard Leila say the words, so familiar to him, taking him back to that library in Harvard. He looked at the rapt faces of Leila's audience as the young men listened to her speak.

"To evaluate the effect of Islam on the status of women, we must discuss the status of women in pre-Islamic Arabia. And there is some evidence to show that women before Islam were more liberated, particularly in relation to marriage and worship, although it is true that the status of women was generally poor because they had been deprived, by their men-folk, of their inheritance. Pre-Islam women were more or less, as you had thought, the property of men, like any other world religions notably Hinduism, Christianity and Judaism," Leila said pointedly. "Islam changed the structure of Arab society and to a large degree unified the people, reforming and standardizing gender roles throughout the region; Islam improved the status of women by instituting rights of property ownership, inheritance, education and divorce. In terms of women's rights, women generally had fewer legal restrictions under Islamic law than they did under certain Western legal systems until the 20th century. For example, you might be surprised to know that a restriction on the legal capacity of married women under French law was not removed until 1965." Bill gave a low whistle and Leila laughed. "Yes, it is easy to forget these things," she said.

"So how has the situation for Islamic women changed since those early days?" Jim asked.

Leila nodded. "Early women's rights reforms under Islam in the 7th century affected marriage, divorce and inheritance. Women were not given similar legal status in other cultures, including the West, until centuries later. Under Islamic law, marriage was no longer viewed as a 'status' but rather as a 'contract', in which the woman's consent was imperative. Women were given inheritance rights in a patriarchal society that had previously restricted inheritance to male relatives, and where they were supposed to be the property of the man, so that if a man died everything went to his sons.

"Muhammad, however, by instituting rights of property ownership, inheritance, education and divorce, gave women certain basic safeguards. Prophet Muhammad granted women rights and privileges in the sphere of family life, marriage, education and economic endeavours, rights that help improve women's status in society."

"But I can't recall ever having read anything about Moslem women in trade or any other area of finance," Anton said.

"It is true that history of women in Islamic trade and finance has not adequately been written about. At a cursory look, Moslem women's stories and any interest in them always seemed to focus on family matters like marriage, divorce and children. But let me give you an example. Khadija is often proudly pointed to as the first Moslem and one of the Prophet's greatest spiritual, emotional and material supporters. She is known as a businesswoman who employed young Muhammad and then married him. Details after that are scarce, and a lot of questions remain unanswered like how did she become the rich businesswoman at a time when newborn girls were sometimes buried alive? Or what were her arrangements with Muhammad regarding the work he did for her and on what basis she continue with her business after their marriage?"

"Do you think it could be a sort of made up thing, some sort of propaganda?" Jim asked.

Leila looked at him sharply. Whatever else she might make allowances for, doubting the teachings of the Qur'an was not something she could accept. "No, I don't think that, Anton, and some of the answers can be found by drawing conclusions from various traditions. Khadija inherited her import-export business from two previous marriages; but as women in those days did not normally inherit, she was probably a trustee on behalf of her children. The agreement with Muhammad, we do know, was apparently based on profit sharing, with her investing capital and administration and he making his contribution in the work he did.

"We hear how impressed she was with his reliability, but would that be enough to be the basis for marriage, even considering that, in principle, a marriage contract is not too far away from a business contract? Perhaps this was a key point. But there was another thing they had in common. Both of them were committed to helping the poor: Except for the fact that the business continued to be successful, we have no other information about their business agreements, but considering their personalities and later Islamic property rules, they cannot have been far away from a partnership that lasted though years of persecution and boycott after Muhammad started teaching in public until the time of Khadija's death."

Eddie looked at the young men sitting on the grass mesmerised, as he had been, by Leila's words.

"So now, bringing things up to date," Leila said, "the average spectator from Western countries, might think, like you did ..." She smiled at Anton who looked at his hands, embarrassed, "... that women in the Moslem world are introverted and restricted to their homes by their male partners. In fact real life is different, particularly so over the last few decades. Women in Islamic countries are now in charge of large corporations, are ministers and prime ministers, have reached top jobs and are imposing success on their own terms. As Queen Rania Al Abdullah of Jordan said on the subject, 'The landscape is starting to change'.

"Women are now business owners in Jordan, Bahrain, Lebanon, Tunisia and the UAE. They are finding their own place in the business and community and creating opportunities for themselves and their participation in business is on an upward trend. Making a significant contribution in the booming economies, women's business networks have grow rapidly across the region. And not just business - the advancement of Arab women in all occupations, particularly in this millennium, has certainly been impressive."

"What percentage of the work force in the Middle East are women, then?" Bill asked.

"Recent statistics show that women in the Gulf region represent 35 per cent of the total Arab workforce. The UAE alone is home to more than 11,000 women entrepreneurs managing investments worth more than 4 billion dollars. Women are increasingly becoming very proactive investors; women investors in the UAE now manage investment worth more than 38 billion dollars; and these numbers are growing at an extraordinary rate. Women have been involved in medicine, education, engineering, research, academics, sports, business, law or media; they are now judges and are involved with Moslem jurisprudence. Women's rights in the region have been progressively enhanced."

"I am really surprised!" Jim said, "I seriously had no idea!"

Leila smiled. "I know it is a common misconception. I hope you will spread the word that we are not all at home, what is that expression? Bare foot and pregnant?" The men laughed. Eddie laughed too, it was not something he would have expected Leila to say, it gave him further insight into this fascinating woman.

Leila continued. "Over 40 per cent of the workforce of the UAE, Bahrain, Kuwait, Egypt, Jordan, Morocco, Tunisia and Algeria is composed of women. Women hold 30 per cent of management positions in finance, 32 per cent of the transactions of the financial and banking sectors are undertaken by women, 20 per cent of management jobs in financial institutions are held by women.

"What about the actual number of women who have the top jobs in business?" Bill asked.

"The number of women heading businesses in the Middle East has grown significantly; there are a growing number of highly skilled Arab women in the Middle East region who are putting to good use their education, intelligence and creativity. Arab countries have invested significantly in human resource development and in providing equal opportunities for both men and women to have access to education and other opportunities. That has helped in providing women with a proper education and skills. With more open-minded leaders of Moslem countries, there are increasing opportunities for women to do extremely well in the workplace if they have the qualifications and drive. The majority of the women surveyed in Bahrain and Tunisia were sole owners of their firms, at 59 and 55 per cent, respectively. This compares with 48 per cent sole owners in Jordan and the UAE, and 41 per cent in Lebanon. Most survey participants own established businesses and many have extensive years of experience.

"On average, women in Lebanon have owned their

businesses for 10.6 years, in Bahrain for 10.2, in Tunisia for 8.6, in Jordan for 6.1 and in the UAE for 5.9. Female-owned firms in the MENA region are as large, successful and tech-savvy as male-owned firms. Apart from being successful businesswomen, a number of Arab women have also excelled in the public sector. Even on a much smaller scale, micro-finance initiatives have helped scores of women across the region to gain access to financial services and enabled them to start up business ventures."

"So now women have complete equality with men?" Anton asked.

Leila shook her head. "Although women still do not have equal access to economic opportunity, they are in control of their own wealth according to Islamic principles. As a businesswoman or an entrepreneur, women in the Middle East have an amazing opportunity to step into their destiny and live out their full potential. However, in order to become more diversified and globally competitive, more needs to be done to empower women and address issues that inhibit female entrepreneurship."

Eddie's nurse came towards them over the grass. "Come on, Mr Lancaster," she scolded. "You were supposed to be back in your room half an hour ago! Dr Jessop wants to see you. He has signed you off to go home tomorrow!"

Leila clapped her hands in delight. She was so pleased for Eddie. Eddie himself had mixed feelings and as the young kayakers clapped him on the back he thought how empty his days would be without Leila, and without the company of these young men, and Amir and Marwa.

In fact Leila had been worrying about the girls being due back at school. Now she would be able to take them back to the UK safe in the knowledge that Eddie was out of hospital and on the mend. She had seen some of the work that he had had smuggled in to him and they had discussed the sudden rush on Lancaster's shares. He had a lot of work to do and it was obvious that Edward was not up to it. Like Eddie Leila had noticed his decline, and was worried about him. They had become close, Edward admiring Leila's quiet calming presence, her inner beauty and serenity, while she felt his pain for the years he had missed with his son, and the obvious effort he was making now to become closer to him. Arabella was still very much a cold fish as far as Leila was concerned. She wondered what was torturing this woman so much that it had robbed her of her joy and her peace. Even her son's recovery did not seem to have penetrated her brittle shell. She barely spoke to Leila as they passed each other in Eddie's room and gave off almost tangible waves of hostility and bitterness. Leila knew that Eddie did not look forward to her visits, although he never spoke about her to Leila and she admired him for his loyalty in the face of almost breathtaking indifference from his mother.

Harry Masters was sitting outside Eddie's room when he got back. Inside Dr Jessop smiled as he signed Eddie off for discharge in the morning.

"I am not ashamed to say that in this case, although we did our bit, I am convinced that your recovery has been largely due to this young lady here." Dr Jessop put his hand gently on Leila's shoulder. Leila blushed but Eddie knew it was true.

After giving his instructions, Dr Jessop left and Harry came in. His face was the picture of gloom. "What's up, buddy?" Eddie asked him.

"It's bad, Eddie, really bad, I think this might be a hostile takeover, or that's what I've heard; I'm not really into that side of things. What does it mean?"

Eddie sighed, looking at the latest figures that Harry had brought him. "It seems inconceivable, but there are are several reasons why a company might want or need a hostile takeover. They might think Lancaster's will generate more profit in the future than the selling price. If a company can make 100 million dollars in profits each year, then buying the company for 200 million dollars makes sense. That's why so many corporations have subsidiaries that don't have anything in common - they were bought purely for financial reasons. In fact purchase factors are the same for friendly acquisitions as well as hostile ones. But as a target of this hostile take over, if that's what it is, we don't want to be acquired. In some cases, purchasers use a hostile takeover because they can do it quickly, and they can make the acquisition with better terms than if they had to negotiate a deal with the target's shareholders and board of directors. The two primary methods of conducting a hostile takeover are the tender offer or a proxy fight, and the odd thing is we have heard nothing from anywhere, no proposals, offers, nothing."

Leila and Harry looked at him intently. He was obviously trying to work out what was going on.

"A tender offer is a public bid for a large chunk of the stock at a fixed price, usually higher than the current market value of the stock. The purchaser uses a premium price to encourage the shareholders to sell their shares. The offer has a time limit, and it may have other provisions that the target company must abide by if shareholders accept the offer." Eddie looked at Harry, "Thing is, Harry, that we don't know who is selling, not the shareholders we know anyway. This is like lots of little idividual shareholders who are somehow connected. I've seen this before. Sometimes a purchaser or group of purchasers will gradually buy up enough stock to gain a controlling interest that is known as a creeping tender offer, without making a public tender offer. And this is what I think is going on here. It is risky because now that the strategy is obvious we can take steps to prevent it."

"What steps, Eddie?" Harry said. "If we don't know who is selling how can we counter?"

"I don't know, Harry, I don't know." Eddie frowned. The sooner he got out of hospital and back behind his desk the better.

The three friends sat in silence. Leila felt a deep sense of worry for Eddie. She felt rather than knew that some evil forces were at work and she had a horrible feeling that rogue members of her own religion may be behind what was going on at Lancaster's bank. She had chatted with Amir earlier and he had said that he was watching the situation carefully. Other banks were beginning to get jittery on both sides of the Atlantic and some were even being subject to the strange and relentless flooding of the market with their shares as Lancaster's were. Amir himself had come under fire in his capacity as the figurehead of the only other financial system in place in a world lurching towards financial disaster. He knew that he had been investigated, every stone unturned in an attempt to discredit him or at least find him is some way culpable for what was going on in the world of Western finance. Amir also knew that nothing would be found. He was a straightforward man, a man who believed in fairness, transparency and adhering totally to the laws both of the land and of his religion. It did not stop people taking pot shots at him in the press however.

Marwa had been in tears earlier in the week after one attack. He had shown it to Leila who had frowned as she read it. It was by a well-known commentator. The article started strongly:

"I am sick and tired of Amir Ali peddling his idea for a 'brave new world' to be achieved via the medium of miraculous Islamic finance. There are lots of reasons why his way will not work in the world economy today and these are some of them: the foremost requirement for an Islamic economy is one of overall vision, understanding and distinctiveness - the unity concept or tawhid. Yet neoclassical economics has no genuine sense of overall relatedness. It separates the economy from society and denies the need for morality in economics. At the same time, it hypocritically claims that all its outcomes are just and believes that, in a very fundamental way, it has no need to change because it is the perfection of the development of history.

"Secondly, Islam requires free markets yet, although the labor markets today are relatively free, the markets for productive capital are not free. They are unfree so that, throughout the world, productive capital is narrowly owned generally by around 5 per cent of the population. As things stand, it will remain narrowly owned and 'free market' finance capitalism is better described as unfree market finance capitalism.

The third Islamic requirement - for widespread ownership of productive capital - is intimately connected with free markets but, because of the lack of freedom in present capital markets, private property in productive capital is not widely spread, which is a big mistake. Apart from the obvious political and societal virtues of wide capital ownership, there is the economic benefit coming from spreading what, increasingly, is the major contributor to wealth creation - productive capital. With wide ownership comes the spreading not only of productive power but also of the associated consuming power thus ensuring a proper balancing of supply and demand as required by Say's Theorem.

"The fourth Islamic requirement - economic efficiency - is connected to both free markets and private property. It is fundamental to market theory that who or what creates the wealth should get the resulting income. But this does not happen at present. Moreover, it is fundamental to market theory that there cannot be a genuine balancing of supply and demand unless productive capacity is spread so that those with reasonable consuming needs can fulfil them. This also does not happen at present. In summary, there cannot be genuine market efficiency unless there is the spreading of productive, and hence consuming, capacity which results from widespread capital ownership.

"The fifth Islamic requirement - for social and economic justice - is connected to the requirements for free markets, private property, widespread ownership of productive capital with economic efficiency, and also to the requirement for an interest-free money supply. Such supply is essential if productive capacity, both public and private, is to be created at half the present cost.

"Generally, conventional neoclassical economics believes that social and economic justice cannot be furthered without decreasing economic efficiency - i.e., conventional economics thinks efficiency and justice are incompatible. In thinking this, it is wrong. With a proper use of an interest-free money supply, social and economic justice on the one hand and efficiency on the other are compatible. Indeed, they are related so that the one reinforces the other. In the true Islamic economy justice creates the efficiency and the efficiency creates the justice.

"Islam is opposed to inflation. It desires a stable level of prices and even counter-inflation - an increase both in wealth and money's purchasing power. Yet, today, all economies have inflation. Over decades, the amount of money in an economy always increases. This is primarily due to the banking system which creates money out of nothing and then adds interest. In many countries well over 90 per cent of the money supply is created in this way. The overall increase in the amount of money is due to the money for the principal being created (and, when repaid, cancelled) but not created for the interest. Therefore, if there is to be enough money in the economy, there is a continual need for more and more money to be created. But since this money is also interest-bearing, the need for more money creation increases even further. The inevitable result is not only inflation but also individuals, corporations, towns, cities and nations being put into rocketing and often un-repayable, debt. On a world scale, the situation is now serious and could result in a collapse of the whole global economic system.

"Inflation and debt are structural parts of the present system. Inflation will never be moderated, let alone eliminated, unless the interest-bearing nature of the present money supply is understood and an alternative interest-free money supply instituted.

"Riba, or interest, is viewed by Islam as wrong yet the present system and its main money supply is based on interest-bearing debt. Moreover, present Islamic Banking (whether it likes admitting it or not) is a part of that system. Islamic Banking bravely endeavours to avoid the appearance of interest by using various legal devices, yet the underlying reality is that at the heart of the present system - of which Islamic Banking is now a part - is the creation of interest-bearing money by the banks. Islamic Banking should not be condemned for this - it is doing its best in a difficult, if not impossible, situation.

"As for the Islamic requirement for a direct connection between the money supply and the real economy, the present banking system does several things including administering various sorts of financial arrangements. But, where investment is concerned, its prime claim is that it directs resources towards the real economy. Yet, despite the claim, it does not do so. Today, most of the new money supply goes into consumer credit, derivatives, a huge rise in existing asset prices, particularly houses, and to putting individuals, corporations, towns, cities and whole societies into ever-increasing debt. Debt debilitates, and interest-bearing debt destroys. Therefore the conventional fundamental justification for the present banking system Ñü that it allocates resources efficiently - is an untruth.

"Lastly, Islam requires an ethical ethos. It says there can be no economics without morality. There are many aspects to this - they range from a desire for an overall sense of relatedness to a simple concept of justice, ethical investment or better accounting practice. But conventional economics eschews morality because it thinks that all the outcomes of the un-free market are just. It thinks that the present economy and society are the same thing or rather that society does not exist. Thus the work of a carer who sometimes has to work for 24 hours at a time and is often unpaid is ignored as not being part of 'the economy'.

"In sum, because of the acute discrepancy between the realities and rhetoric of un-free market finance capitalism on the one hand, and the fundamental requirements of Islam on the other, un-free market finance capitalism without modification is unacceptable."

As Leila finished reading she put the paper down. "I am surprised, Uncle, that with the state of Western finance at the moment, attacking the only viable alternative is becoming so prevalent."

Amir sighed. "I am afraid it is a bit like a rat being tapped in a trap. It will try anything to avoid death, even chewing off its own leg!"

* * *

Half way around the world Sharif was reading the

same editorial. He smiled. "That fool Ali, he is fighting a losing battle." He looked at his computer screen. He frowned slightly. Leashman shares were dropping. He had expected they would drop slightly along with other banks' shares; hell, he had instigated it, but Leashmans were an investment bank dealing in big and complex deals and investments not one of the high street banks that were in the firing line.

Sharif felt a thrill of excitement; the end of a long journey was near. He had thought long and hard about where he wanted to be when the oil ran out, or to be more accurate, was shut down by him and he had decided that Dubai was the best place, it was never so cold you needed heating, and heating was going to be a thing of the past for a lot of the Western world soon. He smiled to himself. The orphans of the Gulf War fund had finally delivered and the 'orphans', young men recruited at school and trained as divers in the oil industry, were now in position around the world to complete Sharif's plan. The shadowy wings of Sharif's organisation were now all working towards the same end. The one thousand five hundred men were ready to go, he had his finances in place and as soon as he released the funds, all would be placed in major oil drilling companies across Siberia and the Middle East. These were not the only drilling sites in the world but between them they provided 94 per cent of the world's oil. Without them life, as it was enjoyed in the 21st century, would cease to exist. Without oil to fuel their machines of war the fight against the West would be taken down to street level. And on the street, Sharif and his many thousands of followers were ready for them. They had held them at bay for decades in Afghanistan, the mountains and the very terrain their main weapon, and they would do it again now. Sharif and his people had had decades to prepare for this day and they had done so well.

As he began to make plans to release his investment from Leashman's bank, Sharif thought about his old adversary Edward Lancaster, a man he had brought to his knees, and he laughed out loud. It would not be long now before Lancaster bank was on its knees too, the final bullet in its head a relief to end its suffering. And where it was going, many, many others would follow.

Chapter Thirty-two

Eddie was discharged on a bright autumn morning. He was staying in his parents' flat in the same room he had occupied as he was growing up and a nurse had been employed to care for him. He was frustrated that his recovery was not quicker. He would wake in the morning feeling fine but by mid-morning he would be exhausted. Frank Jessop had warned him about doing too much but, as usual, it was Leila who made the biggest impression on him.

"I am leaving the day after tomorrow to get the girls back to school, Eddie. Please don't make me worry that you are doing too much and will end up back in hospital; promise me that you will take it easy, in small steps. Do what the doctor says?" Eddie felt a wave of guilt wash over him. Leila had spent the whole of the summer at his bedside, and he owed her this.

"I promise," he said, taking her hands in his. "And you promise to come back soon to see me?"

"Of course," Leila said. "The girls are now quite at home at Harry and Sandy Masters, they will be wanting to come back as soon as we arrive in London, it has been a great summer for them, much better than what we would have had if we had stayed at home!"

Eddie knew that she was trying to make him feel that it had been no sacrifice to come and be with him all summer and he loved her all the more for that. He really did believe that it was Leila who had saved him. He had a memory of her voice coaxing him out of his coma, and to Eddie it sounded like angels calling him back from the darkness. Looking over Leila's shoulder, Eddie saw his mother hovering at the door to his room. He had felt keenly the lack of privacy he had with Leila now that he was in his parents' apartment. His mother always seemed to be within earshot, as though she were trying to catch him out. She never spoke to Leila and rarely even spoke to him, but her presence was always there like a spectre at the feast. Eddie was not proud of it, but he really did feel that he thoroughly disliked his own mother.

After Leila had gone back to Harry Masters he picked up a paper to read a piece by a favourite journalist of his, Suzy Jagger. The headline was stark:

> *Sub-prime and banking crisis: Who caused this nightmare? The blame spreads.*

> *Guns don't shoot people, people do. So goes the defence of America's arms lobby.*

> *In the same way, sub-prime mortgages and the bonds secured by them have not caused the financial and banking crisis that America faces today: it is individuals who bought and sold them who emerge as the real culprits. So whom can we blame for Wall Street's mortgage and banking crisis - the nightmare that has seen around $2 trillion wiped off the value of American homes in the past two years? Who can the one family in every 30 in Stockton, California, blame for losing*

their home? And to whom should Bear Stearns's shareholders direct their anger after Wall Street's fifth-biggest bank almost went bankrupt on Thursday afternoon?

The culpable are spread across the whole gamut of America's political, economic and banking infrastructure. They trickle down from Capitol Hill with the policies devised at Washington's Federal Reserve Bank and head up the coast to Manhattan's Wall Street chief executives. Downstairs from the chairman's office lie more culprits populating investment bank trading floors, and the maths graduates in front of their Excel spreadsheets, designing ever more complex structured debt products. The blameworthy also sit in the credit rating agencies who endorsed the debt and extend wide across America to the network of thousands of mortgage brokers and lenders who sold bad mortgages over the past decade. Sitting at the top of the blame tree, many look to Alan Greenspan, the former Chairman of the Federal Reserve, America's central bank.

Under Mr Greenspan's leadership, the Fed continued to cut interest rates during the 1990s - the cheap cost of borrowing helped inflate the housing market, with some states such as Florida and California experiencing doubling house prices over a five-year period. Cheap money and surging house prices also created fertile ground for mortgage brokers to push home loans that borrowers could ill-afford, in the hope that property values would continue to rise and homeowners could simply re-mortgage.

Pushing the dream of universal home ownership was former President Bill Clinton, whose policies helped encourage individuals whose low incomes and poor credit ratings should have prevented them from taking on mortgages at all. Chris Whalen, founder of the Wall Street consultancy Institutional Risk Analytics, also blames Washington for the design of America's mortgage industry. He said: "The real father of sub-prime is Congress for setting up Fannie Mae and Freddie Mac. Their existence effectively meant that the Government had the monopoly on mortgages. The banks had to scrabble around with what was left - and what was left were jumbo loans [big mortgages] and bad credit quality debt."

Because of the way the market was structured, the likes of Lancaster Bank, the Bank of America and JP Morgan between 2004 and 2005 were so hungry for mortgage assets, they took market share from Fannie Mae and Freddie Mac."

Countrywide and Bank of America, among the US's biggest mortgage lenders, stand accused of predatory mortgage lending, and of being complicit with mortgage brokers, who sold home loans aggressively to boost their commissions. In order to manage the higher risk associated with either very big or very shaky mortgages;

investment banks needed a means of trading the debt on. They devised a means of pooling the loans, paying a credit rating agency to rate them, and the pools - from which they could sell bonds - became liquid and tradable.

In the 1990s Bear Stearns was the best - now they are perceived as being the worst - at designing these complex pools of mortgages to sell on. Bear Stearns, under the leadership of James Cayne, who resigned as chief executive earlier this year over the toxic securities, was the King of Sub Prime.

Unlike its Wall Street rivals, Bear Stearns had a cradle to grave model - they sold their own sub-prime mortgages, through their own retail-lending arm. Bear Stearns was the market leader in creating new and ever more complex structured debt and selling it on through its extensive fixed income sales teams.

Joseph Mason, associate professor of finance at Drexel University, argues: "Bear Stearns was the most innovative, and by innovative I mean 'worst', at creating these complex instruments. They had a cradle to grave mortgage structure. They originated it, pooled it and sold it on."

Professor Mason also explained that it was the likes of Bear Stearns, Leashman Brothers and Citigroup who, in 2001, tried to find ways of splitting out the worst bits of the mortgage pools and securitising them separately. In turn, they split out the worst of the secondary pools into a higher risk set, then repeated the process into a third pool. "Bear, Leashman, Citi - they are big in this space. It means that they created a way to sell on high-risk debt, which is crucial to be able to securitise further. They feed the bubble."

Most of the structured debt products - known as collateralised debt obligations - were typically designed by less than five mathematics experts in their twenties at each bank, armed with a spreadsheet, as part of the fixed income teams.

Professor Mason argues that not only did the likes of James Cayne not understand either the debt products themselves or the risks they posed, but neither did the banks' heads of fixed income. "The heads of fixed income were more interested in whether they could sell the bonds, rather than how risky they were or whether they would actually perform "

Eddie closed his eyes and put his head back on the pillow. His head was thumping. He knew he was doing too much but he could see that the world was on the brink of financial disaster and something in him knew that he had to be there for it. He was aware that someone had come into the room. He opened his eyes.

"Dad," he called to his father's retreating back.

"Sorry, son; did I wake you?" Edward came back into the room.

"No, just shut my eyes for a moment after reading a Suzy Jagger piece."

"I read it." Edward lowered himself into chair beside Eddie's bed. God. he looks old. Eddie thought.

"Not very encouraging reading, was it?" Eddie said. His father shook his head. He looked as though he was about to say something but instead he put his head in his hands.

"Eddie, it's really tough going at the moment; the market is all over the place, I really don't know where it is all going to end."

"What's our position?" Eddie asked.

Edward sighed and shrugged his shoulders. "Pretty bad, son, pretty bad." Eddie put his hand on his father's and his father grabbed it like a drowning man. "Eddie, I hoped things would improve before you came out of hospital. I am so sorry."

"Sorry for what? It's not like it's your fault - everyone is going through the same shit; thank God we've got that holding in Leashman's, so far the investment banks seem not to be affected as much." Edward looked as though he was going to speak again, but he didn't. He held tight to Eddie's hand and father and son sat like that in comfortable silence until Eddie fell asleep. When he was asleep Edward spent another hour at his son's bedside, just watching him, every twitch of his face in sleep, every breath in and out. It was almost as though he was trying to memorise Eddie.

As Leila prepared to return to England with her girls, the news of financial collapse was worsening. She was with Amir and Marwa for a farewell meal with Marwa's sister. All the talk on the television that played in the corner of the brownstone flat in the Bronx was of the crisis. Amir turned up the volume as one earnest commentator started to speak.

"It's official. Mark your calendars. The crash of the U.S. economy has begun. It was announced the morning of Wednesday, June 13, 2007, by economic writers Steven Pearlstein and Robert Samuelson in the pages of the Washington Post, one of the foremost house organs of the U.S. monetary elite." The financial commentator picked up a newspaper from his desk and started to read.

"Pearlstein's column is titled, 'The Takeover Boom, About to Go Bust' and concerns the extraordinary amount of debt vs. operating profits of companies currently subject to leveraged buyouts.

"In language remarkably alarmist for the usually ultra-bland pages of the Post, Pearlstein writes, 'It is impossible to predict when the magic moment will be reached and everyone finally realizes that the prices being paid for these companies, and the debt taken on to support the acquisitions, are unsustainable. When that happens, it won't be pretty. Across the board, stock prices and company valuations will fall. Banks will announce painful write-offs, some hedge funds will close their doors, and private-equity funds will report disappointing returns. Some companies will be forced into bankruptcy or restructuring.'

"Further, 'Falling stock prices will cause companies to reduce their hiring and capital spending while governments will be forced to raise taxes or reduce services, as revenue from capital gains taxes declines. And the combination of reduced wealth and higher interest rates will finally cause consumers to pull back on their debt-financed consumption. It happened after the junk-bond and savings-and-loan collapses of the late 1980s. It happened after the tech and telecom bust of the late '90s. And it will happen this time.'"

The commentator stopped and took a sip of water. Amir thought he could see the man's hand trembling. Leila looked at him.

"This is getting worse, Uncle." Amir nodded as the commentator started again.

"Samuelson's column, 'The End of Cheap Credit,' left the door slightly ajar in case the collapse is not quite so severe. He wrote of rising interest rates, 'As the price of money increases, borrowing and the economy might weaken. The deep slump in housing could worsen. We could also discover that the long period of cheap credit has left a nasty residue.'

"Other writers with less prestigious platforms than the Post have been talking about an approaching financial bust for a couple of years. Among them has been economist Michael Hudson, author of an article on the housing bubble titled, 'The New Road to Serfdom' in the May 2006 issue of Harper's. Hudson has been speaking in interviews of a 'break in the chain' of debt payments leading to a 'long, slow economic crash', with 'asset deflation', 'mass defaults on mortgages', and a 'huge asset grab' by the rich who are able to protect their cash through money laundering and hedging with foreign currency bonds.

"'Among those poised to profit from the crash is the Carlyle Group, the equity fund that includes the Bush family and other high-profile investors with insider government connections. A January 2007 memorandum to company managers from founding partner William E. Conway, Jr., recently appeared which stated that, when the current "liquidity environment" - i.e., cheap credit - ends, "the buying opportunity will be a once in a lifetime chance."'

"The fact that the Post is now announcing the crash shows that it is a done deal. The Bilderbergers, or whomever it is that the Post reports to, have decided. It lets everyone know loud and clear that it's time to batten down the hatches, run for cover, lay in two years of canned food, shield your assets, whatever.

"Those left holding the bag will be the ordinary people whose assets are loaded with debt, such as tens of millions of mortgagees, millions of young people with student loans that can never be written off due to the 'reformed' 2005 bankruptcy law, or vast numbers of workers with 401ks or other pension plans that are locked into the stock market.

"In other words, it sounds eerily like 2000-2002 except maybe on a much larger scale. Then it was "only" the tenth worse bear market in history, but over a trillion dollars in wealth simply vanished. What makes today's instance seem particularly unfair is that the preceding recovery that is now ending - the "jobless" one - was so anaemic.

"Neither Perlstein nor Samuelson gets to the bottom of the crisis, though they, like Conway of the Carlyle Group, point to the end of cheap credit. But people who run central banks and financial institutions set interest rates. 'The market may influence them' but people with money who want to maximize their profits control the market.

"Key to what is going on is that the Federal Reserve is refusing to follow the pattern set during the long reign of Fed Chairman Alan Greenspan in responding to shaky economic trends with lengthy infusions of credit as he did during the dot.com bubble of the 1990s and the housing bubble of 2001-2005.

"This time around, Greenspan's successor, Ben Bernanke, is sitting tight. With the economy teetering on the brink, the Fed is allowing rates to remain steady. The Fed claims their policy is due to the danger of rising "core inflation." But this cannot be true. The biggest consumer item, houses and real estate, is tanking. Officially, unemployment is low, but mainly due to low-paying service jobs. Commodities have edged up, including food and gasoline, but that's no reason to allow the entire national economy to be submerged.

"So what is really happening? Actually, it's simple. The difference today is that China and other large investors from abroad, including Middle Eastern oil magnates, are telling the U.S. that if interest rates come down, thereby devaluing their already-sliding dollar portfolios further, they will no longer support with their investments the bloated U.S. trade and fiscal deficits.

"Of course we got ourselves into this quandary by shipping our manufacturing to China and other cheap-labour markets over the last generation. 'Dollar hegemony' is backfiring. In fact China is using its American dollars to replace the International Monetary Fund as a lender to developing nations in Africa and elsewhere. As an additional insult, China now may be dictating a new generation of economic decline for the American people who are forced to buy their products at Wal-Mart by maxing out what is left of our available credit card debt.

"About a year ago, a former Reagan Treasury official, now a well-known cable TV commentator, said that China had become 'America's bank' and commented approvingly that 'it's cheaper to print money than make cars anymore.' Ha ha.

"It is truly staggering that none of the 'mainstream' political candidates from either party has attacked this subject on the campaign trail. All are heavily funded by the financier elite who will profit no matter how bad the U.S. economy suffers. Every candidate except Ron Paul and Dennis Kucinich treats the Federal Reserve like the fifth graven image on Mount Rushmore. And even the so-called progressives are silent. The weekend before the Perlstein/ Samuelson articles came out, there was a huge progressive conference in Washington, D.C., called 'Taming the Corporate Giant.' Not a single session was devoted to financial issues.

"So what is likely to happen? There are four possible scenarios the author suggests: One, Acceptance by the U.S.

population of diminished prosperity and a declining role in the world. Grin and bear it. Live with your parents into your 40s instead of your 30s. Work two or three part-time jobs on the side, if you can find them. Die young if you lose your health care. Declare bankruptcy if you can, or just walk away from your debts until they bring back debtor's prison like they've done in Dubai. Meanwhile, China buys more and more U.S. properties, homes, and businesses, as economists close to the Federal Reserve have suggested. If you're an enterprising illegal immigrant, have fun continuing to jack up the underground economy, avoid business licenses and taxes, and rent out group houses to your friends.

"Two, Times of economic crisis produce international tension and politicians tend to go to war rather than face the economic music. The classic example is the worldwide depression of the 1930s leading to World War II. Conditions in the coming years could be as bad as they were then. We could have a really big war if the U.S. decides once and for all to haul off and let China, or whomever, have it in the chops. If they don't want our dollars or our debt any more, how about a few nukes?

"Three, Maybe we'll finally have a revolution either from the right or the centre involving martial law, suspension of the Bill of Rights, etc., combined with some kind of military or forced-labour dictators

"Four, We're halfway there anyway. Forget about a revolution from the left. They wouldn't want to make anyone mad at them for being too radical. Could there ever be a real try at reform, maybe even an attempt just to get back to the New Deal? Since the causes of the crisis are monetary, so would be the solutions. The first step would be for the Federal Reserve System to be abolished as a bank of issue and a transformation of the nation's credit system into a genuine public utility by the federal government. This way we could rebuild our manufacturing and public infrastructure and develop an income assurance policy that would benefit everyone.

"The latter is the only sensible solution. There are monetary reformers who know how to do it if anyone gave them half a chance."

Leila and Amir looked at each other. In some ways they were sorry to be going home. Although he crisis was apparent in the UK, the heart of Western finance always felt like it was in New York. They set out for Edward's apartment to say their goodbyes. Arriving they found Bill, Jim and Anton already there, saying their farewells before they went back to Yale for the fall semester.

Leila looked around Eddie's bedroom fondly. She would miss the company of these young men, the young men who were going to be the future of world finance. They were watching the video that Anton had made of Eddie at the lake again and laughing but as Leila watched Eddie's expressive face as he imparted knowledge to his eager audience, she felt proud of his obvious passion for the subject that she had introduced him to.

When the film was over the mood in the room turned more serious as they talked over the events of the week.

"So, Amir, is Islamic finance taking the same kind of hit in this crisis?" Jim asked.

Amir smiled at him. There are now more than 200 Islamic financial institutions spread across the Middle East, with more in the Far East, controlling assets of around 200 billion dollars and growing at around 15 per cent a year. It's a whole other economy that doesn't charge interest when it lends money, but takes an equity stake instead. The difference is that money invested in an Islamic bank keeps working in the 'real' economy. And if you invest in a business that doesn't make money, then neither do you. You are familiar with this concept by now?" Amir said and the boys nodded.

"It's true that when it comes to getting a bank loan for a car, the difference between equity and interest can be pretty wafer-thin. But in the details, Islamic finance means that money grows by growing things or making things. It doesn't grow all by itself, making money out of money. It also flies in the face of conventional economics by putting religion at the heart of financial decisions. But," Amir said, "just because someone is using an Islamic bank it doesn't mean that he is guaranteed to be moral, even good Moslems can be tempted by the devil. Like other kinds of ethical investment, Islamic finance is based on a different kind of world view from the simple bottom line. Islamic economics emerged in the 1940s - no more than an idea until the oil boom of the 1970s and the problem of investing that new Arab wealth. The first Islamic development bank opened in the Gulf in 1973. Now it's big business. Even HSBC and Citibank have opened Islamic operations in the Gulf - and HSBC offers Islamic mortgages in New York. There's a Dow Jones Islamic index. Malaysian banks have even started issuing Islamic bonds, much to the horror of some Islamic scholars. In the UK, where I live, things are moving more slowly. Only the United Bank of Kuwait offers Islamic banking products, and the half a million Moslem households there have to wait for the resolution of the remaining regulatory issues to be sorted. They are finally talking to the Bank of England about it, after a bizarre meeting about community banking that brought Sir Eddie George and Moslem community leaders face to face at the Whitechapel Art Gallery in 1998. And if the multiplication of money with interest threatens the sustainability of the planet, as it is doing now, then it follows that interest-free money is more sustainable. The corporate responsibility movement haven't taken the problem of interest on board yet - but there are signs that they might."

"But could Islamic finance really take over if things got worse?" Bill asked.

Amir nodded. "It could, but whether it would be allowed to or not is another matter. Maybe some kind of symbiotic relationship would be more realistic, but whatever happens after this crisis has been played out, it will have to be something more sustainable than the system we have at the moment."

All too soon it was time for goodbyes. Leila felt tears prick her eyes as she kissed Eddie on the cheek, holding his hand tight.

"Look after yourself," she whispered to him and he nodded, unable to trust his tear-heavy voice.

The boys promised to come back at mid-term break and Amir and Marwa wished him and Edward well. Edward had listened to what Amir had been saying about

Islamic finance without comment, his head bowed. He could not help admiring this confident and quiet man. His knowledge and passion for Islamic finance was obvious. It was foreign to everything he had ever learned from the cradle to this point in his life but his son was obviously an admirer, and so Edward wanted to know more.

* * *

In Dubai, Sharif had awoken to find 25 messages on his mobile phone. After reading the first two he flicked on the TV, searched for CNN and sat, his mouth dry and his heart racing as he listened to the news report.

"In breaking news this hour, Wall Street bank Leashman Brothers has filed for chapter 11 bankruptcy protection, rival Merrill Lynch has sought refuge by selling itself to Bank of America, and insurance giant AIG needs emergency funding.

"The collapse of Leashman has triggered turmoil in global financial markets, but the repercussions go much wider. Nobody has a Leashman Brothers chequebook or current account. The company is an investment bank that specialises in big and complex deals and investments. Despite this, Leashman's collapse and the troubles of other financial institutions will probably be felt by millions of people around the world - at least indirectly. Most of our banks and pension funds have dealings with Leashman, or with firms like hedge funds that traded extensively with Leashman.

"Unwinding Leashman's complex deals will take months if not years. During that time the global financial system will be snarled up. Many banks won't know for sure how much they are exposed to Leashman, and will have difficulty freeing up the money in those deals.

"This in turn is likely to intensify the credit crunch, with potentially dire consequences for businesses and consumers. And the dramatic collapse of Leashman Brothers has also shaken the financial markets, with share prices slumping around the world. You will feel the impact even if you are not a banker or shareholder. Your pension fund may have a wobble. Your employer may find it more difficult to do business. And you yourself may have more difficulty getting a personal loan or mortgage."

Sharif had stopped listening. There was a sort of rushing noise in his ears, a ringing that cancelled out the voice of the newsreader. He felt sick and cold and his teeth started chattering. He knew the signs, he was in shock. He knew that the banking crisis would hit at the heart of the West, of course he did, it was what he wanted, but Leashmans was supposed to be above it all, a few jitters maybe, but a collapse? Never. Yet here it was in glorious Technicolor. Everything he had put together so carefully over the three decades, wiped out in one news bulletin. Others would be going through the process, he knew, of getting something back in the dollar, but he couldn't even do that. He could not open up his organisation to scrutiny by the authorities, so that was it, all he had worked so hard for, all his plans, gone, in one throw of the dice.

Edward heard the bulletin at the same time as Sharif. Edward had known it was coming and that was the only difference to the shattering effect it had had on the two men. Edward let out a long sigh. He didn't have the energy to go on any more. He couldn't be here for the interrogations, investigations, and post mortems on the collapse of the system that he had fuelled all his working life, that his family had fuelled all of theirs.

He called the airline and booked tickets for himself and Arabella to fly to Miami. Eddie would not go, he knew that, he was not far off getting up and at 'em again. Somehow the current crisis seemed to be speeding up his recovery, as though he needed to be in the thick of it, to defend the bank and his family name. Edward smiled to himself. He cold remember the days when he was like that. Hesham's murder had hit him hard too; he felt unprotected, had even had to defend himself to the cops who thought he might have something to do with the murder. He had wanted to tell them about Sharif, longed to tell them, but looking at their homegrown New York faces, he knew it was beyond them. It was beyond him.

He had no idea how to deal with Sharif, did not know where he was or even if he was still alive. In the end he had told them that he was having Arabella followed. He caught the glance between the policemen, who had been shown into his study by Arabella. The glance clearly said that he was wasting his time - no need to follow that one! Well, Edward thought, neither he nor Arabella were oil paintings any more these days, and although he had much less plastic content than his wife, who seemed to give off a waxy glow in certain lights, he felt every bit as tired looking. He still had no idea what her connection with Sharif was, but he could guess. The thought of her lily white skin pinned under the swarthy bulk of Sharif still made him retch. He did not trust Arabella, that was for sure, so he was taking her with him to Miami. He knew what it looked like - like he was running away, running scared - and that was exactly how it was. He was old and tired and he could fight no more.

Chapter Thirty-three

Even as Leila, her girls and Amir and Marwa flew into Heathrow airport the situation had worsened from when they had left New York just eight hours previously. Several more banks had declared bankruptcy. Lancaster Bank was being investigated as being seen, in some, so far unexplained way, to have started the downward spiral. The collapse of Leashman's had kicked the last leg out from underneath the ailing bank and it too was now about to collapse.

An emergency summit for the world's financial leaders was being hastily planned and as Amir let himself back into his house, his phone was ringing, the message light flashing and the counter reading 17 messages. As they had passed through the streets of London they had seen rioting and sporadic fires as all five of the major high street banks in the country had declared bankruptcy. People unable to get any money to buy food were looting and holding angry riots. Leila's twins whimpered in fear at what they saw and she hurried them into the front door of their home, slamming it behind her. She stood leaning against it for a moment, fear gripping her stomach and making her mouth dry.

What on earth had happened? Things had been bad when they left New York but not this bad. How could so few hours have made such a difference?

She flicked on the news while her mother and father

who had flown in from Saudi Arabia to see them ushered the girls to the kitchen to make them something to eat to take their mind off the horrors outside.

"To anyone not in denial, the industrialized nations have entered the greatest calamity the world has ever known," an earnest reporter for CNN announced. "35 Million Americans on Food Stamps: 12 Percent of U.S. Population on Food Stamps Highest Since Records Kept in 1969, and that's before the Obama administration announced a planned three-year budget freeze on government discretionary spending. Count them, there are 18 million empty houses in the United States and 39 million Americans who are no longer working or even looking for work, and now our banks have finally sunk without trace. People cannot cash pay checks, get any cash at all, they can't buy food.

Add these to the now well over 150 million Americans who feel stress over these things on a consistent basis. Over 60 percent of Americans were living paycheck to pay check and now have nothing at all.

"In an effort to explain our escalating financial crisis this reporter suggests that our American 'capitalism' and our consumer economy never made economic, environmental or common sense - unless the goal was ecocide. Capitalism and a not-so-free market economy based on consumer products, that is, products we are manipulated to want, not need, was never sustainable. Consumers consume ... the resources of the planet but whom can we look to, who is responsible for this mess? Again the 'experts' are under the impression this is the natural order of things. Have they looked out of their windows? We are a heartbeat away from civil unrest. It has already started in London and it will start here, you mark my words."

Leila picked the phone up. It was Eddie. He had seen the news from London.

"Leila, are you and the girls OK?"

"We are. Don't worry, Eddie."

"Did you see any sign of the rioting?" Leila hesitated. She didn't want to alarm Eddie, but she could not lie either.

"Some," she said, "but we are safe at home now."

"Have you spoken to Amir?"

"Not since I left him at the airport - why?"

"There is going to be a world summit, all world financial and political leaders, in Washington, it will start the day after tomorrow. I am sure that Amir will come. Will you come too?" Leila hesitated again. She knew that her parents would be dead against it and she felt that she owed it to them and to the girls to keep safe in these difficult times.

"I don't think so, Eddie. I would be an observer anyway, whereas Amir, well, he might be able to get his message across, don't you think so?"

Eddie sounded disappointed. "Yes, I suppose you are right, and yes I think he might, things are worse than I thought; my father has taken off for Miami. I'm really worried about him. All this has hit him really hard."

Leila was surprised, and worried. "Well you won't do too much, will you?"

"I don't really have a choice, but really I feel a lot better now, ready to take it on."

"I understand, Eddie, but please, try to take care of yourself."

"I will; I'll call you later." Eddie hung up.

The bank was like a battlefield. Senate investigators swarmed over the place swooping on files, gathering up computers and interviewing staff. It was beginning to feel as though they were close to something. The mood of the officers had revved up a gear; they were like dogs on the scent of a fox. The officer assigned to talk to Eddie in the absence of his father had an annoying air of knowing something that Eddie didn't and as Eddie answered his questions he would nod with a knowing look on his face, as though he already knew the answers to the questions he was asking.

Harry was coming up trumps. He had been Eddie's eyes and ears while he was away from the bank and now he stood beside his old friend as the situation worsened. Eddie felt humbled. He knew that he did not deserve Harry's friendship - he had been hard on his friend, or just ignored him - and now Harry was prepared to stand beside him when even his own father could not. As they sat watching the television with more reports of rioting in London, Harry said. "We're very worried about Leila. Things look pretty bad in London - have you spoken to her?"

"Yes. I tried to get her to come back for the summit, but really because I would feel better if she was where I could make sure she was safe."

Harry put his hand on his friend's shoulder. "I know, man, but then you're going to be up against it here, by the looks of things; I am sure she will come when it's all over."

"When it's all over?" Eddie said bitterly. "Who knows when that will be, and who knows what that will mean?"

Harry nodded sadly.

* * *

Sharif was still in shock. He could not take in the fact that all he had worked towards for nearly four decades had been wiped out. But it was wiped out. He had nothing, his organisation had nothing, the men that he had so carefully nurtured and had trained to work on the rigs were being laid off, not because, as he had planned, the rigs had been blown to pieces, but because world economies had collapsed and no one had the money to pay for the oil. With the world's banks in meltdown there was no way of transferring funds, and the funds themselves had all but dried up.

* * *

In Miami Edward was feeling freer than he had in decades. His decision made, he could relax. The police in New York had been on the phone to him, disturbed, apparently that he had left the city while they were still investigating Hesham's death. He smiled to himself. This would, just a few short days ago, have filled him with despair and anxiety, robbing him of even the little sleep that he managed these days. Even Arabella was not annoying him. She seemed to sense that he wanted to be left alone and had actually put up very little resistance to coming to Miami with him. She spent a lot of her time down on the beach under her umbrellas, displaying her enhanced and half plastic body in one after another of her expensive swimming suits. Edward supposed that from a distance she might look quite attractive. She was still slim thanks to hours of liposculpture, whatever that was. But close to, that was another matter. She had been a beautiful if slightly pale and ethereal looking girl when Edward had first met her and he had liked her haughty British reserve. But that reserve had become a brick wall over the years, at least as far as he was concerned. She was spoilt and self-obsessed, and Edward knew that he was partly to blame. He should have demanded his rights, been more of man in the bedroom and out, maybe that way she would have been different. After all, she had proved that she had a sexual appetite - it just wasn't for him. Now when he looked at her, she didn't bear any resemblance to the girl with the English rose complexion he had known all those years ago. She was testament to her plastic surgeon's skill, her face fixed in an expression that was neither happy nor sad, just ... fixed.

For a moment or two Edward felt pity for his wife. After all, the failure of their marriage cannot have been all her fault. These things never were just one person's fault. Had her life been as empty as his? Yes, he had had his affairs, and she had obviously had hers, so what was the point of living the sterile existence that they had, in each other's company but as far away from each other as it was possible for two people to be?

He thought of Eddie and Leila. He still could not really fathom out what it was that made their bond so close, but it was, and not accompanied by anything even remotely hinting of an intimate relationship. Yet their relationship was more intimate than any he could think of, certainly despite the many women he had had over the years, and his marriage to Arabella, he had never had anything even a fraction as satisfying and sustaining as Edward obviously found in his relationship with Leila. And the girl herself, she was so serene so feminine and gentle yet so strong and determined. Her beauty shone from her and he could barely imagine how she had had the strength to sit hour by hour beside his son's bed, not drinking, not sleeping or eating, her eyes fixed on his face, speaking her soft words of encouragement, that had eventually brought Eddie back to them. As Edward thought of his son, tears rolled down his cheeks. It was unutterably sad that he and Eddie were at last getting close, and now that would end. He wondered how what he was planning to do would affect Eddie. If anything could have swayed him from his course, it would be his son, but he knew that it was too late for that. He did not have the energy to go on any more to put up with the scorn and hatred that he knew would be visited on him soon, when the senate committee found what they were looking for. And it was only a matter of time now.

In London Leila was speaking to Eddie. She was worried, very worried, but she tried to keep her tone light so that Eddie would not worry. She had been watching the news and knew that Lancaster's bank was the centre of the investigation into the current banking crisis. She knew he hardly had time to eat or sleep, let alone worry about her and the girls.

Marwa had come round to tell her that Amir had flown back to New York. Leila was not surprised and was very grateful that he had gone without contacting her, so that she would not have to make the decision as to whether to stay or go, again.

The situation was getting worse in London. Leila was glad that Marwa had come round. She didn't want her to be alone with Amir gone. As they sat watching the evening news, Leila hurried her girls out of the room. This was not for their eyes.

A reporter on London bridge stood in front of a scene of chaos.

"Protests here in central central London turned violent today ahead of the forthcoming world financial summit to be held in the United States. A band of demonstrators are now close to the Bank of England and have stormed several other high street banks. You can see behind me baton-wielding police charging a sit-down protest being held actually on Tower Bridge.

"This protesting started with an estimated 6,000 people in the financial centre of the capital, and was initially peaceful, but more and more bloody skirmishes are breaking out as police try to keep thousands of people in containment pens that have been erected around the

Bank of England on Threadneedle Street.

"The demonstrators now seem determined to cause damage, seeking confrontation as they surge towards police lines. As I am speaking to you this evening, much of the City remains cordoned off.

"Since about 8 p.m., running battles between riot police and demonstrators have been taking place across London Bridge. Bottles, sticks, bricks and other missiles are being thrown.

"Nearer the heart of the City, the police have moved in to break up a sit-down protest with baton-wielding officers said to be pushing through with a at least five armoured police vehicles backing them up.

"The trouble broke out as news of the upcoming global financial summit was announced to address the world's fast deteriorating financial situation. This rioting in London is unprecedented as the summit is to be held in Washington. But such is the fear on the streets here that earlier today protesters were targeting the Bank of England and were met by lines of police whose tactics were to try to contain these demonstrators inside multiple cordons of officers. But chanting 'We will pass!' the demonstrators surged forward.

"Just now, riot officers and police dogs and horses have removed some twenty protesters who had spent a quarter of an hour ransacking a London branch of Lancaster's bank. Lancaster's bank is seen as somehow being involved in the beginning of this world crisis. The protestors have torn out computers and telephones. To loud cheers and shouts, the bank's windows, were smashed with the crowd chanting 'burn a banker' and 'American scum'. Police in riot gear inside the bank have tackled protesters trying to climb in through the smashed windows.

"Subsequently, at least sixty protesters had taken up a position with placards which read 'You got us into this. Who's going to get us out?' and 'Bankers, scum of the earth!' in a street close to the Bank of England, protestors have been left with bloody head wounds after being charged by officers with batons drawn. One woman, said to be a young mother, has been carried off unconscious.

"Tonight the Metropolitan police are saying that more than 300 people have been arrested and dozens more injured, some even feared dead. The offences the police are delaing with range from threatening behaviour and criminal damage to violent disorder; two protestors were arrested for aggravated burglary on the Lancaster Bank building and one was arrested for attempted arson on the branch. And this is not isolated rioting; reports are coming in from all major cities in the UK of rioting as people find they cannot use their bank cards or withdraw money from cash machines. St Paul's in Bristol has been particularly badly affected with a reported twenty or more people dead. Disturbances are being reported in major towns and cities all over the UK."

As the night wore on the situation worsened. Leila and Marwa and her parents watched in silence as report after report came in telling of blackouts due to vandalising of electricity substations and communications being cut off as telegraph poles were felled by rioting mobs. The police were completely overwhelmed as the rioting spread over the country. Police had initially been deployed to London from the surrounding counties and now found themselves not able to leave, as protestor numbers grew.

In New York rioting was starting too, as the city's bankers made their way the short distance to Washington for the financial summit. Police in New York and the National Guard were an overwhelming presence around JFK airport that was closed until all the world leaders had arrived. Fleets of cars with armed outriders stood ready to take them to Washington and with a minimum of protocol newly arrived leaders were bundled into cars together, three or four at a time to make the journey.

Eddie had arrived at the summit with the first vanguard from the city. He had never seen such a desperate group. Bankers with years of experience and who had been responsible from millions of dollars and some of the biggest deals the world had ever seen were standing around looking like naughty school boys. Many were from banks already declared bankrupt and their haunted faces were testament to the sleepless nights they had endured. Everyone had one thing in common though: they were all looking for answers.

Many seemed surprised to see Eddie and almost all asked where Edward Lancaster, the big daddy of them all, was. The truth was that his father had run away. Eddie knew that but he did not feel any resentment. He had seen his father literally age before his eyes over the previous months. He knew that even although nothing had been said, the baton had been passed to him. He had had a very uneasy feeling since the Senate committee had started their investigation of the bank. He knew that his father had done the odd dodgy deal, hell, he had done a few with him, but something was not right. He was also desperately worried about Leila. Things were looking very bad in London and he wished he had forced her to stay. If anything happened to her ...

Sharif was watching the delegates arrive for the summit in Washington on a television in his hotel room. Rioting on a limited scale had started in Dubai, mostly among low-paid expatriate workers who could not be paid at all because their employers could not access any money. As he watched leader after leader arrive he felt impotent, helpless. All those juicy targets in one place and he was powerless to do anything about it. He had to think of a way to recoup and regroup. His mission could not end here.

In London the mob had breached the woefully inadequate police lines and surged into the Houses of Parliament. Ancient buildings that had stood as the symbol of power in England since 1870 were torched, their magnificent halls engulfed in a massive inferno. In Leila's house her mother and Marwa were crying quietly. Leila started to pray.

It took Amir three hours to find Eddie at the summit. The hordes of delegates from all corners of the world had been summoned so hastily that there was not enough accommodation to house them, or any catering laid on. Local people had brought food and Prime Ministers and Presidents sat crossed legged on the floor sharing home-baked cookies, while other leaders slept on the carpet, their briefcases serving as pillows.

The summit was being held in the Paul H Nitze School of Advanced International Studies, a division of Johns Hopkins University, one of the world's leading and most prestigious graduate schools devoted, approriately in this instance, to the study of international affairs, economics, diplomacy and policy research in education.

The SAIS main campus, located on Massachusetts Avenue's Embassy Row, was woefully inadequate for the numbers who now beseiged it and by the time that Amir had found Eddie he had counted hundreds of delegates in every square inch of the place.

Eddie was pleased to see Amir. He seemed somehow like an oasis in the middle of the desert of their ruin.

"How's Leila?" he asked, and Amir smiled.

"Fine when I left; her parents had flown into London and Marwa is with them now, at Leila's home."

The relief on Eddie's face was obvious. He felt much better knowing that she was not alone, that her parents and Marwa were with her. He had been trying to find a moment to call her but it had been hopeless. The press were following him around like a pack of hungry dogs, their mobile phones primed for the news that was supposed to break from the Senate Committee at any time. Colleagues too tried to pick his brains, convinced that he had to know something. The truth was he did not. He knew that there was something wrong, very wrong at the bank and he knew that he should have asked his father what it was - he nearly had on several occasions. His father knew for sure. Eddie was certain that his decline had to do with what he knew was about to be revealed. But it was testament to the new closeness between them that Eddie did not hound his father for answers. He let him go to Miami and protected him fiercely to everyone, and asked him nothing. After all, what was done was done now; there was nothing that either he or his father could do to change that. So Eddie let his father go; he was ready to stand as the head of Lancaster's and to take the flak that was coming, whatever it was.

As it turned out he would not have to wait long. A bearded boffin with thick glasses who had been set the task of excavating years of complicated and well-hidden transactions at Lancaster's Bank had hit the jackpot. As he pieced together the trail that led back of 40 years and took in such landmarks as the Lockerbie disaster, 9/11 and the London Bombings, the colour drained from his face.

The conference was under way. Amongst the furore, Eddie had taken to the podium. In front of him were the microphones of dozens of news agencies and journalists jostling for space beside the most eminent of world leaders. Suddenly a reporter pushed to the front. "Mr Lancaster." The reporter looked wild eyed and something in his expression stopped all other activity as the cameras that had been trained on Eddie swung round to take in this short, balding man, sweat standing out on his brow, his face almost spasming as he tried to speak. He cleared his throat and started again. "Mr Lancaster, I wonder if you would comment on a discovery made just moments ago by the Senate Committee?" His tone was conversational, as though he had just asked Eddie how the weather was, but his skin was a blotchy red and his Adam's apple bobbing precariously in his scrawny neck betrayed his seemingly calm voice. The cameras were back on Eddie now, as the media smelt blood.

In Miami, Edward winced as he saw the confusion and fear on his son's face. In Dubai Sharif sat holding his breath and in London Leila put her head in her hands. She could not bear to watch this slaughter.

His voice shaking, the reporter read out a statement.

"The Senate Committee have discovered that Lancaster's Bank, has, for the past 40 years, had direct links to a terrorist organisation. Through funds supplied directly from the bank through a bogus charity, funding has been made available for such atrocities as the bombing of the Pan Am flight over Scotland, the 9/11 attacks on the twin towers and the London bombings. There have been many other terrorist activities that have been funded directly by Lancaster Bank and the apparent suicide of one of its long-term employees is being examined in relation to this information."

For a moment there was silence, and Leila watched in terror as Eddie stood exposed on the podium as a roar began in the hall and people surged forward. As the world watched, another man jumped up onto the podium – it was Amir. Marwa shouted his name involuntarily and Maysoon put her arm around her.

Grabbing the microphone from Eddie's paralysed hand, he pushed him down on the seat behind the podium and began to speak.

"This man knew nothing of this." Then louder. "THIS

MAN KNEW NOTHING OF THIS!"

"Who are you? One of his terrorist friends?" a reporter asked.

"No I am Amir Ali, an expert in Islamic finance. I have known this man for many years and he has had no part in this. I can prove it to you. I have a letter." He waved a white sealed envelope. The crowd quieted slightly. Amir tore open the envelope, glancing at the letter within it. "This letter was given to me by a father who was sitting at the bedside of his son, a son who was not expected to live, let alone recover enough to be with you today. That son was Eddie Lancaster and this letter is from his father, Edward." Silence had now fallen in the auditorium as Amir began to read.

"I know that today you will hear unimaginable details about the bank that my family have served for many years. I alone am responsible for the horrible facts that you have learned today. I was a young man when this started and I was a weak man when, having realised my mistake, I did not put it right. I was afraid of what would happen to me and to my bank and my family, if I cut off funds from what was a constant shadowy and menacing presence in my life. And so the leaching of funds from the bank has gone on year on year in ever-increasing sums, and although I have never known what it has been used for I can imagine that it was nothing good. Please believe me that the precise nature of how this money has been spent will be as much of a revelation to me as it is to all of you.

"My son has no knowledge of this. He has, on occasion, asked questions that might have led him to discover the facts, but I have been careful to hide them from him and from everyone. Again Eddie has no knowledge of this. I am sorry that this news will hurt him as much as it will all of you, and for that reason I will not be with you by the time that you read this letter. I am sorry, more sorry than you could ever imagine. I know that I cannot ask for forgiveness, but I do ask that you believe that Eddie is innocent in all of this. Trust him. As I have come to find out over the last few months, he is a man of great worth, as is the man who is delivering this message to you. Trust them both."

There was complete silence in the auditorium as the implications of Edward Lancaster's letter hit home. This and the revelations of the Senate report had silenced the crowd.

Amir stood holding the letter in the silence, the full impact of it sinking in. Behind him Eddie sat, his face chalk white. As Amir looked down he looked right into the face of the President to the United States, surrounded by bodyguards, jostled in with the rest of the men and women crammed into the conference hall.

"Please, sir?" Amir indicated that the President should take the stage. The phalanx of bodyguards manoeuvred their leader up onto the stage and the crowd responded by clapping.

"Ladies and gentlemen. What we have heard here today has been devastating both on an individual level ..." the President looked at Eddie, "... and to us as a country and to the world at large. Better people than I will investigate properly what has happened and we have to look forward to the fact that the information being uncovered today will help us bring our enemies to justice, but for now I think that we have to turn our attention back to the crisis we find ourselves in."

There was a murmur of agreement.

"There have been other crises and other solutions and yet we keep finding ourselves back at the brink of disaster. It had been my intention to ask you all to think outside of the parameters that we have traditionally worked within, to embrace other ideas. Professor Amir Ali who has just spoken to you all has interesting information for you on Islamic finance." There were groans around the room. The President put his hand up. "Please; we have to look at everything. It may already be too late for our system, and I have no idea whether this is a good idea or not, but we owe it to ourselves to look at everything, don't we? Or has anyone got a better idea?" His voice was raised now and silence fell over the auditorium. He sat down beside Eddie as Amir took to the podium.

There were loud jeers and boos at first but Amir carried on talking over it all and in the same calm voice that he always used. He spoke from his heart and he spoke from a wealth of learning and knowledge and love for the world that they all lived in, Christian, Moslem, Buddhist, Hindu, it made no difference - they all shared the same air, the same ground and the same responsibility for their planet.

And as that world teetered on the brink of disaster, he spoke, his voice echoing through the auditorium, to the good and the evil through their televisions and radios. Leila heard him and wept for the truth that he spoke. Sharif heard him and wondered where he would find a hiding place. In the auditorium Eddie heard him and found the fractures in his heart were beginning to mend. The terror he had felt was subsiding now. In Miami Arabella heard him and stirred from her sun-bed as sirens drew nearer to their block on the beach, congregating at the bottom of the tower. Arabella thought she could hear the Bentley's alarm going off, but the sound of the breakers on the beach muffled it. She lay back down and listened to Amir. The man had a haunting voice.

All around the world people heard Amir, and the others who spoke that day, but it was Amir they would remember. They remembered him and that momentous day because it was the beginning of a new era, the beginning of a new page in the history of our planet.

The End